THE LAST BLUE PLATE SPECIAL

NOVELS BY ABIGAIL PADGETT

Child of Silence
Strawgirl
Turtle Baby
Moonbird Boy
The Dollmaker's Daughters
Blue
The Last Blue Plate Special

ABIGAIL PADGETT

THE LAST BLUE PLATE SPECIAL

Published by Warner Books

A Time Warner Company

Mysterious Press books are published by Warner Books, Inc., 1271 Avenue of the Americas, New York, NY 10020.

Visit our Web site at www.twbookmark.com

A Time Warner Company

The Mysterious Press name and logo are registered trademarks of Warner Books, Inc.

Printed in the United States of America

First Printing: March 2001

10 9 8 7 6 5 4 3 2 1

Library of Congress Cataloging-in-Publication Data
Padgett, Abigail.
    The last blue plate special / by Abigail Padgett.
        p. cm.
    ISBN 0-89296-731-5
    1. Women psychologists—Fiction. 2. Social
psychologists—Fiction. 3. Lesbians—Fiction. 4. San Diego (Calif.)—
Fiction. I. Title.
PS3566.A3197 L37 2001
813'.54—dc21   00-060096

For Iris Rochelle Greer

THE LAST BLUE PLATE SPECIAL

1

"Greave"

At 7:05 P.M. on Friday, October 22, California State Assembly-woman Dixie Ross drove through a red light at the corner of Tenth Street and University Avenue in San Diego's Uptown District. The medical examiner's office would later release a report stating that when Dixie Ross ran that light, she was already dead.

Ross had left a dinner rally half an hour earlier and was five blocks from her destination, a political fundraiser at an art gallery called Aphid. The *San Diego Union-Tribune* would describe her in its Sunday edition as "a trailblazer for women in politics and a clear-eyed liberal who wasn't afraid of the boys in the back room," whatever that means. The local political scene, the paper would conclude, was already in sad disarray after the death of State Senator Mary Harriet Grossinger, sixty-three, of a massive stroke only two weeks earlier.

The paper did not point out that the statistical likelihood of two politicians from the same congressional district dying of natural causes within fourteen days of each other was not great. Almost nonexistent, really. But then most people, even journalists, don't run around incessantly thinking about statistics like I do.

At 7:05 when a dead body ran a light, I was grazing the Aphid Gallery's appetizer table wearing a trendy little black and tan suit and a name tag that merely read BLUE McCARRON. I hate those name tags that read HELLO, MY NAME IS . . . In real life, anyone approaching you with that phrase has something to sell. Usually a diet program involving all-natural vitamins at hugely inflated prices.

I also hate that trendy little suit. The skirt's too short and makes me look bow-legged even though, at a gangly five-six and 133 pounds, I'm not. And the jacket, with its black and tan triangles each ending in a gold button, reminds me of court jesters. Wearing it, I feel a need to juggle oranges while asking riddles of kings. But I've been trying to shed my desert rat image and I was supposed to look like a political staffer for the fundraiser, so I wore my jester outfit. Also big ugly earrings and a pair of bizarre shoes I would later bury in the desert, where I live.

Burying uncomfortable clothing in the desert is one of my hobbies, but then so is the investigation of murder, lately. The San Diego County Sheriff's Department had just officially closed the Muffin Crandall case, in which I came close to getting myself killed, when I took this job designing political polls for a San Diego City Council candidate named Kate Van Der Elst. The job had seemed safe enough, but my track record for picking safe jobs hasn't been great lately.

I'm fairly sure I was scooping domestic caviar onto tiny slices of bread with a spoon designed to fit the hands of mice when the corpse of Dixie Ross ran that light. I later learned that her dark green sports utility vehicle hit the left rear bumper of a water delivery truck at the intersection of Tenth and University. Then it spun to rest after shattering the side-window glass of a white Honda Accord parked at the curb. Dixie Ross was fifty-three, had been in good health, and was wearing a seat belt during these collisions, in which her vehicle's airbags also inflated. She sustained no injuries. Nonetheless, when a teenage skateboarder reached into her car to feel for a pulse, he knew that Dixie Ross was dead.

What was clear at the Aphid Gallery was merely that Dixie was unaccountably late. Invitations to the cocktail party fundraiser, printed on paper made from jade plant cuttings, had read 6:00–8:00 P.M. Kate Van Der Elst, the political candidate for whom funds were being raised, knew she couldn't wait much longer. A speech was expected. Checks would be written. Then everybody could leave with just enough time to make their eight o'clock dinner reservations.

"Blue," Kate whispered as I watched the mayor of a wealthy suburban community neatly capture the last sturgeon egg from a blue willow plate with his little finger, "I can't start without Dixie. She's the shill!"

It was a moment only a social psychologist could love. Since I am a social psychologist, I loved it. Kate Van Der Elst had been a successful commercial real estate broker prior to her marriage sixteen years ago to Pieter Van Der Elst, the Dutch pharmaceutical baron. Before that a blonde and savvy younger Kate had gone to Sarah Lawrence and then played tennis with old money all over Western Europe. Kate does not run in circles where people say "shill" even when they mean a shill. In Kate's world the generic term "consultant" would be used, accompanied by slightly raised eyebrows suggesting a dollop of perfectly legal foul play.

At political fundraisers like this one, the shill dramatically writes the first check while standing beside the richest guy in the room, who of course has to follow suit, starting a trend. I found the cultural slip amusing. Kate Van Der Elst, smoothing well-styled hair from her aristocratic face with both hands, didn't.

"Stop smiling like that," she said. "This is serious. Where *is* Dixie?"

"Way down south in the land of cotton?" a deep voice suggested, causing both Kate and me to groan.

It was Bernard Berryman, better known as BB, a gay ex-con hired by me to design the event. BB had hand-made the jade-plant invitation paper and sewed green tablecloths from awnings he got dirt cheap at a mortician's bankruptcy auction. BB had also taught Kate Van Der Elst about shills. Everybody else in the room knew already.

"Don't know who donated that plate of liver paste and fish eggs, but they gone now," BB noted, shooting the cuffs of a blue-and-white pinstriped Egyptian cotton shirt. "Wasn't no note when they was delivered. Had a bunch of canned figs on the plate, too, but I threw 'em away. Looked like little blind wet mummy-eyes piled on some lettuce. Not somethin' anybody'd eat."

The shirt flashed attractively beneath yellow suspenders every time he walked under any of the gallery's hundred and fifteen high-density track lights. His dark dreadlocks were conservatively fastened at the back of his neck with an antique brass napkin ring, and his brown skin gleamed like an ad for a Hershey's product in the uneven light. At the bar across the main gallery I could see a prominent radical clergyman in aviator frames and a tie-dyed gray clerical shirt observing our conversation. BB responded by sliding his hands into the pockets of knife-pleated brown gabardines and doing an F. Scott Fitzgerald stroll toward the clergyman, who quickly ordered another drink.

"I'm going to wait three minutes and then begin," Kate said. "Do you think somebody else could begin the check-writing ritual in the event that Dixie just doesn't make it?"

Kate had a bit of an accent, the result of living in the Netherlands for fifteen years. I made a mental note to locate a speaking coach. Southern California voters prefer a John Wayne drawl to accents hinting of the Continent. In fact, many Southern California voters secretly believe there is only one continent, and it is North America, and it ends at the Mexican border. I knew that even before I started running polls for Kate Van Der Elst.

"Sure," I answered. "Any prominent wealthy person will do."

"But I don't know any of these people," Kate said, dismay coloring her alabaster cheeks a peach daiquiri color.

We were even. I didn't know any of them, either.

"Just begin your speech," I said with fake gusto. "BB and I will arrange something if Dixie doesn't show within ten minutes. She's probably just stuck in traffic."

So Kate launched into her speech about saving San Diego from urban sprawl while protecting endangered things like wild button celery and spadefoot toads from imminent extinction. Somebody was taking flash photographs of her, and periodically the room froze in light. I staggered in my atrocious shoes toward one of several pocket galleries off the rear of the main room. It looked like a good place to think about what to do next.

Of course, it wasn't. It was dim and small with pinlights illuminating a strange collection of grainy, overdeveloped black-and-white photos that might have been taken by a child with a simple box camera. Some were of mountain shacks, some of dilapidated houses on concrete blocks. Others featured abandoned cars and trucks half buried in tumbleweeds or disintegrating in gullies. Some were photos of unidentifiable structures taken from odd angles, like toys left on a carpet and seen from the perspective of a passing insect. Something about the photos made me forget Kate Van Der Elst and the spadefoot toads even though I could hear her voice in the room behind me. Something about one photo in particular.

It was one of the unidentifiable structures. Just a crumbling adobe building beside a road, half its length obscured by an immense shadow. The terrain had a California high desert look, with scrubby vegetation and lots of rocks. That desert sense of things known but never revealed. I guessed that the shadow had been cast by a hill or mountain ridge behind the photographer, to the west. Lights were visible through two windows in the shadowed half of the structure, and blurry figures. The other side, illuminated by a setting sun, seemed blasted by light. Bombed. As if the photographer had captured the precise moment of some deadly explosion. In the lower right corner of the photo was a signature in spidery black ink. "Greave," it said.

The name meant nothing to me, but my reaction to the photo did. My reaction was visceral and made me shaky. Fascination.

And fear. Something frightening in that scene, something terrible and close. It didn't make any sense, but these creepy little recognitions never do. Which is why I rarely talk about them. They aren't rational, and irrationality scares people. What's the point? You either understand how these things happen or you don't.

Yeah, what? I mouthed toward the ceiling and my concept of the universe beyond it. A universe which in my mind is a curved grid on which everything moves at intense speeds. The past, the future, everything in between, and more. Sometimes it crosses the little band of reality in which we live and there's a buzzing sound, a scent of ozone, and some completely irrelevant thing is suddenly fraught with relevance. Usually these events are meaningless to us. I was sure this one with the photo had achieved new heights in that regard. It was pointless. But I couldn't stop staring at that photograph until the cell phone in my purse began to ring.

I should probably explain that I am not one of those people who talk on cell phones in grocery checkout lines in order to impress total strangers with my importance. I didn't even own a cell phone at that point. The one in my purse was Kate Van Der Elst's, handed to me just in case somebody called during her speech. I was also carrying a Ziploc bag holding Kate's snack—half an apple, a stick of low-fat string cheese, and two macadamia nuts. She was on one of the fad diets that regularly sweep the country, so I had to dig the phone out from under a bag of food which was making my purse smell like an apple. The voice answering when I whispered, "This is Blue McCarron," was that of Pieter Van Der Elst, Kate's husband. He was calling from her storefront campaign headquarters a few blocks away. And his voice was strained.

"Something terrible has happened," he said, his Dutch accent turning "something" into "somezing." "Dixie Ross is dead."

"What?" I replied too loudly. "What happened?"

"I don't know. We just got the call. There was an automobile accident, but they're saying she was already . . . gone . . . by the time of the accident. She'd been at some picnic rally in north county—an organic bean growers' cooperative—and died while driving. She was on her way to Kate at the gallery. Her death was sudden. I don't know. Tell Kate I'm on my way over there."

Some of the well-dressed crowd in the main room were watching me, curious about the phone call and its potential for political intrigue. There is nothing more boring than a cocktail-hour political fundraiser, and I didn't fault them for hoping this oaf in a designer suit might provide some relief. Sadly, I was about to.

After penning the news of Dixie's death on a one-hundred-percent recycled paper napkin, I waited five minutes or so for a lag in Kate's speech and then clomped toward her in my shoes-from-hell. BB noticed the look on my face and moved, pantherlike, to the precise point along a wall where I would withdraw after handing Kate the note.

What's going on? his eyes asked as I realized for the hundredth time the sort of social awareness learned in prisons. After three years behind bars for a youthful drug offense, BB misses nothing.

"Oh, my God!" Kate breathed into the microphone after I handed her the napkin, neatly capturing the full attention of all seventy-five people present. "Dixie Ross has . . . has died."

In the ensuing seconds there was an outburst of dismay, a few strangled sobs, and finally the voice of the radical clergyman at the bar intoning, "Kate, what happened?"

"It isn't clear," Kate began as Pieter Van Der Elst burst through the door and hurried to stand at his wife's side. "Dixie was in an accident on her way here, but she wasn't injured. It seems that . . ."

"The call just came in to our campaign office," Pieter continued breathlessly, his pale blue eyes somber beneath a prematurely white brush-cut that always makes him look like a Renaissance monk. "There are no details as yet, but it is believed Assemblywoman Ross suffered some fatal event prior to losing control of her car. There will be an autopsy, of course. One scarcely knows what to say. We lost Mary Harriet Grossinger only two weeks ago. Now Dixie. I'm afraid I just don't know what to say."

BB had approached the clergyman during this exchange, and the man quickly slipped a white plastic tab into the collar of his shirt. Then he moved gracefully to stand before Kate's microphone. If he'd been slightly drunk two minutes earlier, he wasn't now.

"Dear Lord," he began softly as every head in the room bowed and the photographer ducked out the front door, "you have taken another of our friends and we are saddened . . ."

At the end of the prayer he urged continued dedication to everything Dixie had stood for. Racial justice. Funding for schools. The protection of our precious environment.

I was sorry that he left out the spadefoot toads.

Kate Van Der Elst was sobbing against her husband's madras plaid shirt when the first check was written. After that there were many, many more.

"Shee-it, who this dude?" BB said quietly, his mouth close to one of my grotesque earrings. "Sucker work a crowd like putty in his hands!"

I had never seen sheer respect in BB's face before, and it took a few seconds for me to identify the emotion.

"He's a preacher, BB," I said. "They're expected to work crowds."

"World fulla preachers, Blue," he answered. "Half of 'em in prison. I seen preachers could talk a man down from hangin' hisself and I seen preachers could talk yo' grandma outta her walker long enough to give him a little head, but this dude solid gold!"

"The crowd's in shock, BB. And you don't understand what's happened. Two major political leaders dead within two weeks. It's very upsetting."

"And they both ladies," he replied before easing away to begin cleaning up.

I hadn't thought of that. Another variable in a statistical setup that continued to nag. Liberal politicians are a minority on the Southern California political scene. And liberal *women* politicians are a very small minority of a minority. I wondered exactly how odd was the coincidence of two of them dying within weeks of each other. And of course it had to be coincidence, didn't it?

I stayed to help BB clean up after the crowd's somber exodus. Then we locked up, dropped the gallery keys through the mail slot, retrieved my Doberman, Brontë, from my truck, and walked her through the residential streets behind University Avenue. When Brontë was sufficiently exercised we headed over to Auntie Buck's Country and Western Bistro to meet Roxie, my significant other, who has no interest in politics. Not that I do, either. What I have interest in is making money, and Kate Van Der Elst was paying me well to design polls for her. Meanwhile, Dr. Roxanne Bouchie, forensic psychiatrist and line-dance coach at Auntie's, had followed through on her earlier suggestion that we work together.

"McCarron and Bouchie," our business cards read. "Consulting." I was already consulting with mall designers about how women shop, and Rox just added a new dimension. Jury selection. In the month or so since we set up business we'd gotten three jobs profiling juries for private attorneys in criminal cases. Good money and the work was interesting. Then Van Der Elst needed somebody to design polls and I took the job. After the election, I thought, I'd go back to malls and juries. After the election maybe Roxie and I would find a way to spend more time together. My life, I thought, was approaching perfect. The word itself is a warning, but I didn't notice.

"Who died?" Roxie asked when BB and I joined her at a table. "You two look like *Tales from the Crypt*."

"Two ladies," BB answered succinctly before abandoning us for the dance floor and a wrenching ballad about trains.

"Dixie Ross died this evening, in her car on the way to Kate's fundraiser," I told the gorgeous black woman at whose touch my heart races, every time. Roxie has big ears and a spill of freckles across her face and wears her hair in a mop of beaded braids. The sound of those beads clacking together has become music to me. My own private symphony. Sometimes I think if

Roxie knew how much I love her she'd leave town. I'll never tell her, though, because not only are we of different races, but we imagine ourselves to be mature and deeply sophisticated lesbians who are acutely aware that our "lifestyle" is full of pitfalls we're determined to avoid.

Of course, a psychiatrist and a social psychologist understand perfectly the female proclivity toward instant bonding, nesting, and total enmeshment. So quaint. We, of course, would avoid that ickiness by maintaining our separate lives, not moving in together, keeping boundaries. The result is astronomical phone bills and a lot of driving between my place out in the desert an hour and a half from San Diego if you drive like a bat out of hell, and Roxie's uptown urban condo. Still, we feel confident that we've skirted the embarrassment of typicality, at least. Meanwhile, I hoard in my heart the fact that, really, total enmeshment doesn't look all that bad to me. I have never told Roxie that sometimes I look at expensive flatware in department stores, although I have told Brontë. Hey, we all have secrets.

"Girl?" Rox asked, meaning I was supposed to tell her who Dixie Ross was and what her death might mean.

"State assemblywoman, Democrat, big on environmental issues, education, all the good stuff," I began. "She wasn't very old, fifty-three, I think. Had a chance at major office later, people say. Governor, maybe. She talked Kate Van Der Elst into running for city council after Kate and her husband moved back here from the Netherlands when he retired two years ago. Dixie had been at another political thing, a bean growers' rally or something, and was on her way to Kate's fundraiser when it happened. She just dropped dead. But what bothers me—"

"Wait a minute," said Roxie the doctor. "People don't 'just drop dead.' You need a disease, organ failure, trauma, something like that."

"There will be an autopsy, Rox. We'll know then. Meanwhile, she's the second woman politician from San Diego to die in two weeks. It's weird."

Roxie swung her head, stretching her neck and setting off a

soft rattle of beads. I had to lean over and kiss her cheek, which made her smile.

"Why weird?" she asked, looking at me in a way that suggested every politician from here to Cleveland could perish from gout without attracting her attention. Which was elsewhere.

"Weird statistically," I answered. "Wanna dance?"

"Not here," she said softly, as if I might not be feeling the same way.

Right.

So we managed to get to her condo before falling into each other with that unnerving hunger for which the word "love" seems less than adequate. Later I would bring up the deaths of Dixie Ross and Mary Harriet Grossinger again.

"Grossinger died of a stroke," I said into Roxie's ear.

"Yeah?"

"What if Ross had a stroke, too?"

"What if she did?"

"Well, she's dead," I noted. "Both of them are dead. That's really all we know. It's only nine-thirty, Rox. I'm going to call Kate at home, see if she and Pieter have heard anything more."

Roxie merely sighed and then began pulling on clothes.

"Why are you getting dressed?" I asked.

"Because we're going to your place, of course. Blue, I know you, and I can see the handwriting on the wall. You'll turn into a pumpkin if you can't get to that computer of yours tonight and crank out three hundred charts showing why these two dead women shouldn't be dead."

She was right.

"I'll bring you breakfast in bed tomorrow," I offered. "Waffles, sunnysides, I'll make strawberry syrup from scratch."

"Deal," she answered, grinning despite the fact that she isn't exactly crazy about the desert. "It's my turn to sleep at your place, anyway. Now where did I put the *Guide to Western Poisonous Snakes*?"

"It's under your scorpion coloring book," I answered as I dialed the Van Der Elst home number.

"I don't think the autopsy will be performed until Monday,"

Pieter told me, "but a preliminary assessment suggests that Dixie died of a lethal stroke. We're just devastated, Blue. She and Kate had known each other all their lives."

"Um, did Kate mention any medical problems Dixie had?" I asked. "Anything that might point to this?"

"That's what's so strange." He sighed. "Kate and Dixie played tennis almost daily, told each other everything. Dixie was so careful about her health, she had a physical before each campaign. Her last exam was six months ago. She told Kate the doctor said her heart was that of a thirty-year-old. Kate had been urging her to go on this diet Kate's on, but Dixie said the medical exam proved she didn't need it. This thing just doesn't make any sense."

"No," I told Pieter Van Der Elst, "it doesn't."

Slightly more than ninety minutes later I unlocked the gate to my desert Shangri-la, an abandoned motel I was able to get for a song because it has no piped-in water. Rox was yawning in the front seat beside me, humming the final bars along with Mary Chapin Carpenter on the tape deck.

"I'm dead," she noted, heading straight for the queen-size bed in one of only two rooms actually furnished, the others unfinished and empty. It's hard for one person to fill twelve motel rooms. The bedroom is off the area which would have been the motel office, now my office. I switched on the computer even before saying good night. Then I ran Brontë in the moonlight for a few minutes and buried those god-awful shoes in a shallow grave between two cholla cactuses before going back inside to check out stroke Web sites. The last thing I thought before leaving the starry outdoor silence was of a grainy black-and-white photo of an adobe building both blasted by light and hidden in shadow. The image left a taste of ozone on the back of my tongue.

2

Women Who Die Too Much

After draping my jester costume on its padded hanger I dropped the ugly earrings in my kitchen trash compactor. They would be smashed, along with a few soup cans, plastic bottles, and old newspapers, into a tidy rectangle I would eventually drive into Borrego Springs and toss in the dumpster behind a supermarket. Since I live two miles off a road that ultimately just stops at an unused horse camp in the middle of nowhere, there's no trash collection here. In fact, there's not much of anything here, which is why I like it. Just desert. Ocotillo and smoke trees, heat and silence, rocks.

Time expands in the desert, stretches and carries you along. Nothing much matters, which is why it's easier to see it when something does. What was mattering to me was a mathematical problem. Two dead women politicians. Not one, which in any circumstance might be attributable to chance, but two. The odds had more than doubled. No longer chance. Something else.

From a bookcase I pulled the college text most likely to cause migraine headaches. Blalock's *Social Statistics,* now in its umpteenth printing and impenetrable as ever. As a graduate student I studied Blalock, and later taught it. Nonetheless, the mere sight of it makes me clench my teeth.

Thus clenched, I turned to the chapter entitled "Probability" and forced my brain to ask the right question in the right way. Not, "What is the probability of two women politicians in the same town dying within weeks of each other?" Rather, "In an infinite progression of female politician-deaths, what proportion of them could be expected to occur within two weeks in the same town?" The difference between these two questions underlies all successful marketing projections, political polls, jury selections, strategies for disease control, urban planning, you name it. Still, it's a difference not easily grasped. Especially by Americans, who traditionally despise generalizations and so never really understand what is meant by probability.

Americans believe in the concept of the individual and are therefore easy prey to schemes based on statistical estimations. Ask yourself why thousands of homes featuring grossly inadequate diets, parasite-infested children, and not a single book will nonetheless have cupboards full of chemically flavored petroleum by-products, ninety-channel cable TV, and a useless plastic contraption that was supposed to promote weight loss, except it broke. That's what I mean. Fortunes are made every day by people who know how to calculate the *proportion* of an infinite series of, say, eighteen-year-old white males who will buy purple-sole athletic shoes at two hundred and fifty dollars a pair. The infinite series thing is the key.

And problematic for my purposes that night. There is no infinite series of dead women politicians, no database. In fact, the existence of women politicians is so recent a social artifact that even if there were a database it would be too small to be useful. I would have to spread my net more broadly. Plain "dead women," then. Dead white women between forty-five and sixty-five, U.S. No problem.

On the Web I logged on to the Monthly Vital Statistics Report and learned that for every hundred thousand women in that age group, a little over five hundred tend to die every year, close to half of those from cancer. Of the remaining causes of death, only about twenty-two per hundred thousand may be expected to die of cerebrovascular events, of which "stroke" is only one. The odds in favor of Dixie Ross and Mary Harriet Grossinger both dying of strokes had just dropped drastically, as I suspected.

Next I went to the *San Diego Union-Tribune* archives and read a ton of articles on both women. Neither smoked, although Grossinger had until she quit in 1987. Grossinger was the mother of three children, Ross childless. Both were committed to fitness, as is de rigeur in Southern California, Grossinger having been a jogger and Ross a tennis player. Grossinger had at one time admitted to being vegetarian but was later photographed eating fried chicken after a flare-up from the California Poultrymen's Association. I suspected that the photo was staged for political reasons and included "vegetarian" in Grossinger's health variables column. Ross had no food preferences known to the media. Grossinger's sixty-eight-year-old brother was still alive and working full-time as the dean of a small private law school. Ross's three siblings, two older and one younger, were also alive and apparently free of health problems. Grossinger's official obituary named "cerebral hemorrhage" as the cause of death, citing her death certificate.

The American Heart Association's Web site explained that of all four types of stroke, the type characterized by cerebral hemorrhage accounts for only ten percent. Another drop in the odds. For the purposes of my research, I decided to assume that Dixie Ross had also succumbed to a cerebral hemorrhage even though Ross's cause of death wouldn't be available until after the autopsy.

Brontë, asleep on the indoor-outdoor Berber carpet at my feet, growled amiably at some dog-dream phantom. Her paws paddled at the carpet and a dog-smile twitched beneath her whiskers. Chasing something, I thought. She was chasing something in her mind. And so was I.

"It's called a single dubious assumption," I whispered to my dog. "My hypothesis. Which is that there's something peculiar about these deaths."

Hours later I'd keyed everything I had into a program I use to analyze factors presumed to be statistically independent of each other. Like two dead women. The deaths either were independent of each other, with no causal connection or common variable, or they weren't. In minutes I had results. The probability of a healthy sixty-three-year-old white woman and a healthy fifty-three-year-old white woman, both Americans with good medical care and no prior history of cardiovascular disease, succumbing to cerebral hemorrhages within two weeks of each other in the same town was not statistically significant at .001. One-tenth of one percent, odds of a thousand to one. That's a significance level so tight it's only used in life-and-death situations, like FDA approval of new pharmaceuticals, things like that. In other words, at that level of significance it's safe to say the thing you're looking at is so unlikely that it just really could not happen.

"But it did happen," I said to the numbers on my computer screen. "Which means there's a common variable we don't know about. Something Dixie Ross and Mary Harriet Grossinger had in common. Something that, for all practical purposes, killed them."

It was after two when I crawled into bed with Roxie.

"Don't tell me," she said, not really awake.

"It couldn't have happened," I answered. "That's all."

She sighed. "I told you not to tell me."

In the morning we swam in the motel pool, I made waffles, and we swam some more. Rox had never learned to swim growing up in Gary, Indiana, despite the town's proximity to Lake Michigan.

"Blue," she'd explained two months earlier, "there are certain cultural differences between us. I'm black; you're white."

"What's that got to do with swimming?" I'd asked in full idiot-jacket.

"I've never thought about it, but it probably has something to do with cars."

"Cars?"

"Yeah. As in transportation. Not many folks in my neighborhood had cars, and you had to drive to get to the lake. On really hot days sometimes the fire department would send a guy around to open a hydrant so we color-challenged kids could cool off in the water. Not much chance to learn the backstroke."

Actually, Roxie didn't feel her life was a total waste in the absence of swimming. She'd done just fine, she pointed out, managing college, medical school, a psychiatric residency, and forensic board certifications in two states without swimming to them. She had a secure job at Donovan State Prison, a lucrative private practice, and now our little consulting business, which was pulling in impressive fees. From time to time she got job offers from hospitals and universities all over the country, but so far none had appealed to her.

I was so mortified at my own lack of social awareness, however, that I felt compelled to right the wrong. I would teach Roxie to swim or die trying. In the first few lessons I thought I really *might* die trying, until I bought a book on swimming instruction. It suggested starting with a kickboard, and that did the trick. Lacking supervision, Rox could still probably drown in a wading pool, but she loves that kickboard. Brontë does, too. The two of them were splashing up and down the pool, Brontë on the board in her teal-blue life jacket with Rox hanging on and kicking, when I first mentioned what I thought should be done next.

"Probably ought to call the FBI, don't you think?" I said casually.

"Why FBI?" Rox answered from churning blue water, not looking at me.

"Well, two elected officials dead under statistically impossible circumstances. The FBI should be informed, shouldn't it?"

"Why?"

"Doesn't the FBI investigate suspicious deaths of elected officials?"

"No," Roxie answered, clearly hoping her firm, businesslike tone would end the discussion.

I sat on the edge of the pool and remembered my mother

trying the same ploy. No dice then, no dice now. At thirty-five, I realized, I still have characteristics of a second-grader.

"What do you mean, 'no'?" I asked.

"Tell me the part you don't understand," she said, giving up and paddling dog and board to my side of the pool.

Brontë climbed out and I took off her life jacket so she could shake the water from her fur. Rox stayed in the pool, every one of her beaded braids sparkling in sunlight. I hated to be tedious about this, but I had to know.

"The part about the FBI *not* investigating suspicious deaths of elected officials," I said.

"What does the *F* in FBI stand for, Blue?" Rox the professor.

"Federal."

"Meaning?"

"Meaning the national government. What's your point?"

Roxie rested her chin on the pool edge and spoke into the splash gutter. "The FBI would only investigate the suspicious death of a *federal* official, Blue," she explained. "Also espionage, terrorism, bank robbery, kidnapping, bribery, crimes which cross state lines, and those especially mandated by law. Police brutality, for example. That's a relatively new one. But not deaths of state or local elected officials unless local law enforcement authorities request FBI help."

"Oh," I thought out loud as I stood to pull on a baggy T-shirt and shorts I'd thrown on a chaise. "Then I should call the San Diego Police Department, right?"

"Wrong. You shouldn't call anybody because you don't really know anything. Your numbers are based on guesses. Dixie Ross hasn't even been autopsied yet. Wait until Monday, and then if the autopsy finds cerebral hemorrhage as the cause of death you might offer your statistical analysis to the local police as a courtesy, nothing more. They won't read it anyway."

Rox kicked off to the steps at the shallow end of the pool and climbed out to sit in the shade and read. I went into my office/living room to get a book for myself and stared at the phone. It seemed a shame to let all that research wait.

"San Diego Police Department, Desk Sergeant John Garcia," a young male voice answered seconds later.

"Um, I'd like to report a statistical analysis," I began. Dumb as a mud fence, as everyone used to say back in Waterloo, Illinois, where I grew up.

"A what?"

"It's about the deaths of Mary Harriet Grossinger and Dixie Ross. I'm a social psychologist," I said, and then gave my name, address, phone number, and credentials. "These deaths are a statistical anomaly. What I mean is, if Dixie Ross also died of a cerebral hemorrhage, then the police should be aware that the likelihood of both these deaths occurring naturally is pretty much zero."

"You are aware that this call is being tape-recorded," Garcia said over the every-ten-second beeping of a legal taping device.

"Yes."

"I'll make sure the information gets to the right department, Dr. McCarron. Thank you for calling."

The response wasn't exactly a tribute to my skill with unusual data, but I felt that surge of self-righteousness you get when you've done the Right Thing. It's a heartland concept, the dubious birthright of people born in a thousand little towns with a church at one end of Main Street and a grain depot at the other. Unfortunately, the Right Thing is almost always a gross oversimplification which will later reveal itself to have been the Wrong Thing. But its immediate, gooey glow is at times irresistible. I picked up the novel I was reading about incest within a religious cult in Nova Scotia and went outside to join Rox.

"Were you a victim of incest?" I asked the woman about whom after a relationship of only two months I still knew not nearly enough.

"Nah, my grandma wasn't into kinky stuff," she answered from beneath a bright blue beach umbrella. "You called the police department, didn't you?"

"Yeah. Why do you think there's so much attention to themes of incest in contemporary fiction?"

"Everything's economics, Blue. Incest may be a metaphor for

fears about not participating in the global marketplace, the ills inherent in keeping the money at home. Also, it gives you a feeble dodge from my question about calling the police. I can't believe you did that. What did they say?"

"That the information would be given to the right department."

"I take it they were deeply impressed, then?"

"Rox, it was just a desk clerk. Want to drive up to Julian for the afternoon?"

Roxie is easily distracted by desserts, and the little mining town just up a mountain from my place in Borrego Springs has become an apple-growing mecca. Julian offers the best apple pies in California. Besides, it's always twenty degrees cooler up there.

So we loaded Brontë into my truck cab and spent the afternoon gorging on apple pie à la mode and perusing Julian's shops. I bought a quilted red bandanna for Brontë and Rox got a pretty inlaid wood kaleidoscope for her office at the prison. She said it might help some of her clients grasp the concept that there are different ways of looking at things. We were having such a good time I didn't point out the fact that her clients were more likely to steal it than ponder its message.

On the way back we stopped at a grocery and got ground turkey and veggies to grill outside by the pool. We'd listen to Rossini and Garth Brooks on my outside speakers, full blast, we decided. Then Sousa marches and Strauss waltzes and when it got dark, old Charles Aznavour songs, in French. It occurred to neither of us that the best-laid plans of mice and even women frequently run afoul of reality. And also the law.

There was an unmarked car which nonetheless bore not-so-subtle marks of cop parked beside the locked gate to my property when we got home. Why don't they ever get it that band radios, mikes, riot gun racks on the doors, and perforated metal plates separating front and back seats are dead giveaways? A fortyish guy with a sandy, graying crew cut, sunglasses, and a blue nylon windbreaker with SDPD across the chest unfolded his skinny six feet from the car and scowled at the sunset, then at us.

Brontë growled from her seat on Roxie's lap, clearly wishing she didn't look so lapdoggy.

"Looking for Dr. Emily McCarron. Police business. You her?"

"She," I countered. "It's a nominative of address. Are you she. And yes, I am."

"Emily" is legally my name, but I never use it except on tax forms and other official paperwork. It sounded like an alias.

"I hate it when this happens," Roxie grumbled. "Next he's going to show a badge, and there goes dinner."

"We have a package of ground turkey in this vehicle," she addressed the cop, who I was certain was going to turn out to be a detective. "Excessive delays between here and the refrigerator could be life-threatening. Salmonella, E. coli, botulism, anthrax. Surely I don't need to go on."

"Detective Rathbone." He identified himself as if his surname had been a lifelong burden. Then he held up a badge in a leather wallet and lit a cigarette. Unfiltered. "Dr. McCarron, did you phone police headquarters earlier today with some information about the deaths of Senator Mary Harriet Grossinger and Assemblywoman Dixie Ross?"

"Yes. I said these deaths could not have happened by chance. You drove all the way out here to confirm a statement you have on tape? And my calculations, as I said to your desk clerk, are based on the assumption that Ross also died of cerebral hemorrhage. We won't know whether that's true or not until Monday, after the autopsy."

"Oh, we know it's true. The autopsy was performed this morning." He pushed his Ray•Bans to rest across the top of his bristly hair, then pulled them to rest on his nose again. I suspected the gesture meant something coplike, maybe even threatening, but since I wasn't sure, it seemed merely indecisive.

"What we'd like to know," he went on, trying for a knowledgeable sneer, "is how *you* knew it was true before anybody else did." Here his tanned brow grew furrows as he gazed at the cigarette between his fingers. "I'm afraid I'll have to ask you to come down into San Diego, to headquarters, answer a few questions. We've already got your ex-con friend, Berryman. Says he doesn't know anything. They never do."

"You've got BB?" Rox and I said in unison.

"Yup." Bad John Wayne imitation.

"He was at a fundraiser where Ross was expected yesterday evening, except she died before she got there. Apparently he got some kind of job at this fundraiser through some guy who calls himself a psychiatrist. Somebody named Bushy he met in prison. And you were at this fundraiser, McCarron. Since you seem to know more than anyone about what happened to Dixie Ross, we'd like to talk to you. Another detective is out looking for this so-called Dr. Bushy. We need to get to the bottom of this, fast. So why don't you just turn around and head down to San Diego. I'll meet you at—"

"Wait a minute, Rathbone," I began. "There's more to this than an autopsy. You guys wouldn't be running around harassing innocent citizens on a Saturday if—"

"And I'm Dr. Roxanne Bouchie," Rox snarled from beneath Brontë, who also was snarling, showing teeth. "That's Boo-she, not Bushy. It sounds as though you're detaining Mr. Berryman illegally, and you have no business detaining Dr. McCarron or me. You're out of your jurisdiction here and you know it, so stop grandstanding. This is San Diego County Sheriff's Department's turf, not the city police department's. What's going on?"

"You're this bogus shrink Berryman met in prison?" Rathbone said, nodding over what was trying to be a snide grin. "Sure. Except Berryman was at Donovan. No women prisoners out there last time I checked."

Rox was grinding her teeth. I could see jaw muscles working in the left side of her face.

"I'm the staff psychiatrist at Donovan Prison," she said in a tone I don't ever want directed at me. A tone that could turn ordinary cottage cheese to a tub of cinders. "What, exactly, do you want of Dr. McCarron and me?"

To his credit the detective scuffed a black leather shoe against the bleached-out ground before answering. I had a sense that his tough-guy act was a skin he's shed some time ago and now barely remembered.

"I'm sorry," he said finally, taking off his shades to look straight at Roxie. "Can you confirm your identity and vouch for Berryman and McCarron here?"

Rox sighed, a long sigh full of history. Then she took her wallet from her purse and showed Rathbone a lot of identification proving, among other things, that she outranked him and made a lot more money, too.

"Mr. Berryman was employed to organize the political fundraiser for Kate Van Der Elst, who was a friend of the deceased, Dixie Ross," she said in the petrified cottage cheese voice. "He is an ex-con and also African-American, but that doesn't mean he had anything to do with whatever it is you're investigating. I'll vouch for him. Dr. McCarron scarcely needs my endorsement. You may not have noticed, but she's white."

The detective appeared to be making a difficult decision as he stared at a clump of dried-out locoweed growing beside the road. A tea decocted from the leaves and stems of this plant, not to mention its particularly nasty flowers, affects the central nervous system and brain. Locoweed can cause madness, even death, in large mammals such as sheep, horses, and SDPD detectives.

"Eat that plant!" I whispered, glaring at Rathbone, who didn't hear me.

"Look," he said, reaching into his car and retrieving a manila folder, "I'm going to show you what's going on. Then I'd really appreciate it if both of you would tell me what you think. We got this three weeks ago in the mail. Nobody took it seriously at the time. Now everybody does. I'm afraid we've got a situation on our hands."

Rox took the envelope, propped it on Brontë's back, and opened it. Inside was a photocopy of a typed letter. Around two sentences of text its author had glued about fifty article headlines clipped from newspapers. All were about Dixie Ross or Mary Harriet Grossinger.

"Ross Opposes Landfill Project" or "Grossinger Calls for Further Discussion on Term Limits." Typical political headers.

The message read simply, "These woman trying to be men and have to dye. There not the only one."

It was signed with the typed words, "The Sword of Heaven."

"Uh-oh," Roxie said softly. "There goes dinner."

As Rathbone followed us in his car to my motel, I couldn't help wondering about the presumed relationship between women in nontraditional lines of work and hair coloring. It was clear to me that, if nothing else, the letter's author was a lousy speller.

3

A Habitation of Dragons

The 'Sword of Heaven' reference is probably from the Bible,"
Roxie said as Rathbone stood around in my bare dirt driveway
trying to decide whether to help carry groceries in or remain
coplike. Roxie handed him the two heaviest bags. "Of course
anyone could assume that," she went on. "What is it you want
us to do with this letter, analyze it? And did I mention we charge
a fee?"

"Fee?"

"Consulting. You want to know something about whoever
wrote this, right?"

Rathbone nodded, his clean-shaven jaw hidden behind the
edge of a brown grocery bag that looked yellow in the late afternoon glare.

"Well, we can probably tell you a few things, but we'd prefer to do so professionally."

"The department uses consultants all the time," he said, standing to the side of the door so that Roxie and I could enter first.
One of those moments. With both arms full of groceries, he
couldn't hold the new screen door I'd installed after ramming

my truck through the old motel office door only months ago.
Roxie had to go back outside to hold it open for him, after
which they headed for the kitchen while I closed the bottom
half of the custom steel-core Dutch interior door but left the
top half open against the interior wall. I love Dutch doors. And
when both halves are closed, this one can stop just about anything shot from a conventional weapon. You can't be too careful.

"But can the San Diego Police Department afford us?" Rox
asked after mentioning an hourly fee nearly twice what we
charge for polls and jury selections and interrogation protocols.

"I guess so," Rathbone answered, looking around. "You two
live in a motel? Can't imagine you get much business out here.
Just a dirt road in the middle of nowhere. Suppose you could
book conferences for hermits or something, right? Pa-hahm."

His laugh reminded me of the sound potatoes make in the
microwave when you forget to punch holes in them with a fork
and the steam inside bursts through the skin. That muffled popping. I didn't want to explain my unusual choice of living arrangements to a detective right then. But his failure to go into shock
at Roxie's proposed fee for our services was alluring. We'd make
a bundle if Rathbone recommended us as consultants to the
SDPD. Besides, I was curious about the deaths of two women
I'd already demonstrated couldn't have died naturally when and
where and for the reasons they presumably did.

"This is my place," I told him. "My dog and I live here alone.
Dr. Bouchie lives in San Diego."

"You live out here by yourself? Some kind of hermit," he answered, nodding thoughtfully at my kitchen floor. "This Pergo?"

The reference was to my floor covering, a laminate manu-
factured in Sweden. He'd captured my attention.

"Yeah. Travertine Stone. I thought it picked up the mood of
the place, the way it sort of repeats that creamy yellow band
in the sandstone boulders outside the kitchen window."

Rathbone considered the view and then the floor again. His
hands hanging at his sides were cluttered with freckles and veins
that stood out in tree limb patterns.

"My wife, Annie, she's got a bug about getting this flooring for the kitchen and the hallway, keeps showing me samples. I kind of like Rustic Oak. Did you see that one?"

"Too dark for here," I answered. "But I liked it."

"Annie's pushing for a lighter one, too. Planked Natural Pine."

"I *almost* went with that one, but then the stone look just seemed—"

"I don't believe this," Roxie muttered to a cluster of cherry tomatoes she was rinsing in the sink. "This isn't happening. Two complete strangers are not standing around in a desert bonding over a vinyl floor."

"It's not vinyl," Rathbone and I said in unison, bonding over a laminate floor. It was clear that we were probably going to get along. An interest in floor covering can do that.

"You might as well stay for dinner," Roxie told the detective, smiling and shaking her head. Rox's braids were done in turquoise that week, and Rathbone cocked his head at their pleasant rattling.

"My sister-in-law, Annie's younger sister, keeps trying to do her hair like that," Rathbone said with interest. "I don't think it works if you're not black. She's a lawyer up in the Bay Area. International law. Travels a lot. And sure, that'd be fine. I need to call Annie and tell her I won't be home. Mind if I use your phone?"

"Only if you call and make sure they're not holding our friend BB," I told him. "Can you do that first?"

"You mean Berryman? Sure."

I showed Rathbone to the phone in my office/living room and flipped on the TV to muffle his conversation. We Midwesterners are nothing if not sensitive to the privacy of others.

Back in the kitchen I fed Brontë and skewered turkey meatballs with the cherry tomatoes, mushrooms, and bits of red onion and pineapple until Rathbone yelled, "Berryman's free, but look at this!"

Rox and I rounded the wall separating my miniature kitchen from where he was and followed his rapt gaze to the TV. A woman announcer in a red silk Bijou jacket was wrapping up a story about the cancellation of a religious revival apparently scheduled for the next day, Sunday. On the right side of the split screen was a photo of what looked like a Christmas tree angel wearing too much makeup. On second glance it appeared to be a woman with sparkling blonde curls in a pale green choir robe. The photo had been shot through a heavy scrim and looked fuzzy.

"A spokesman for the Reverend Ruby Emerald urges her followers to organize prayer gardens for the charismatic revivalist. Ticketholders for tomorrow's sold-out event are assured that refunds will be available at the box office as well as all Ticketstore locations in the event of a cancellation tomorrow. Now here's Martin McGuire with a look at the weather...."

"What?" Roxie asked. "Look at what?"

Rathbone was scowling and jabbing a freckled finger at the TV.

"Just a feeling," he muttered. "This revival preacher has a sold-out show for close to fifteen thousand at forty bucks a person and she winds up in a hospital the night before? We're talking some big money in the toilet if the thing is canceled. I've just got a feeling about this. Mind if I use the phone again? Wanna check something out."

Rox and I listened as he talked to another detective at San Diego's police headquarters.

"She was taken from her home to the hospital in an ambulance? Good. See if you can talk up the paramedics, find out what was wrong with her. I think there's something fishy here. Call me back."

We were sitting by the pool watching Rathbone, who told us his first name was Wesley but that he preferred being called Wes, finish his fifth turkey kabob when the phone rang. Abandoning all pretense of courtesy, we all jumped up and dashed inside at once, Rathbone only at the last second deferring to my right to answer my own phone.

"Just a moment, he's right here," I said, and handed him the cordless.

"Paramedics said headache," he repeated. "She had a killer headache, a lot of pain, sweating like a pig, shaking all over."

"What about blood pressure?" Roxie asked, her brown eyes interested, professional now. I realized I was watching a cop and a doctor at work in my living room, only there was no crime, no patient. It seemed strange, as if we were characters in a play that made no sense and nobody was watching it, anyway.

"Um, high," Rathbone repeated after asking. "One-ninety-something over one-twenty-something. Mean anything?"

"Could mean she'd just run for twenty minutes up a steep incline while drinking strong coffee and smoking," Rox answered. "Or any of a thousand other things. Drugs, allergic reactions, anything. The levels are dangerous, though. Very dangerous."

"Did the ambulance guys think she was druggy?" Rathbone said into my phone, the light from a floor lamp painting one side of his face in pale yellow glare and leaving the other in shadow. I thought about the photo I'd seen at the Aphid Gallery the night before, one side of a simple rectangular building exploding in light while the other side was buried in darkness.

"She denied any drug use," he said moments later. "Paramedics said it was probably a stress headache, said they'd seen it before in rock stars and people like that, performers. They get jumpy before a big show, get these headaches. At the hospital they'll just give her some tranquilizers, calm her down. The paramedics said she'll probably be okay by tomorrow."

"Hmm," Roxie mumbled when he hung up the phone.

After Rathbone consumed half the angel food cake iced in chocolate sorbet I'd thrown together for dessert, he left, promising to contact Roxie's answering service on Monday with an almost-certain confirmation of our employment as consultants to the San Diego Police Department. When he was gone Rox and I looked at each other in the moonlight spilling through my open Dutch door.

"So whaddaya think?" I asked.

"I dunno. Looks like somebody called the Sword of Heaven

informed police three weeks ago that Mary Harriet Grossinger and Dixie Ross were going to die, and they're dead."

"A number of people have noticed that, Rox," I said, more to the sky outside than to her. "And the data don't lie. There *has* to be a missing piece, some common variable linking these two deaths. I'm not saying Sword has to be that missing piece; the letter could just be an odd coincidence and the missing variable could be something else entirely. But for the sake of argument, what if Sword *is* the missing piece? What if somebody out there found a way to kill a state senator and an assemblywoman?"

Roxie pursed her lips and paced thoughtfully around my office/living room.

"Well, there isn't much to go on," she said, shrugging. "If it's what it looks like, then what we've got is a serial cerebral hemorrhage killer." She grinned at my computer monitor and then went on. "It's not possible, Blue. It's ridiculous. There's no way . . . well there's no *easy* way to manipulate blood pressure like that, jack it up enough to blow a vessel in the brain. It could be done, of course, but only by someone with medical training. An injection, most likely. The wrong stuff and death would occur within seconds. But Dixie was alone in her car, wasn't she?"

"Yeah."

"So what you're suggesting is that somebody was with her in the car, that she allowed this person to inject her with something as she was driving, and then she politely dropped the person off at a corner a few seconds before her brain exploded?"

"What about a pill of some kind?" I was pacing behind Rox now, following her. "What about something in her food, something that would force her blood pressure through the roof but not until it was digested and in her bloodstream? Could somebody do that?"

"It's possible, but not likely, Blue. And it would have turned up in the autopsy. They always check stomach contents. Rathbone didn't say anything about any lethal chemicals turning up in her stomach."

"But just for the sake of argument," I pushed on, "what if somebody *did* slip something into Dixie Ross's food? Then what've we got?"

"They *didn't,* Blue, or the substance would have showed up. And what we'd have would be a poisoner."

"And who kills with poison?" I concluded.

"Almost always women," Rox acknowledged, walking into the kitchen and gesturing at the remains of a meal we'd prepared and shared with a stranger. The room smelled like poultry seasoning and tropical fruit. Homey.

"Breast identity," I filled in, sighing. "Women constantly nurturing, feeding everybody, keeping life going. But when that instinct gets turned inside out, when it goes bad, women using the same method to kill. Why does the damned hormonal chemistry have to be such a trap?"

"It just is," she murmured. "That's why nobody ever talks about it. It's not politically correct to acknowledge how much of what we are is controlled by wiring and chemistry we don't even know is there."

Something happened then, as evening shadows fell heavily across the room. A boundary crossed. A moment of truth, of dead-certain understanding. The deepest bonds are made of these moments, I think, not of passion. Rox and I understood each other, were *alike* in that moment, and it felt like doors and windows all opening at once. A rush of air and a sense of being drawn somewhere. Just two women in a kitchen, saying things no one wants to face. Like that, when pushed too far, the girl next door can become absolutely deadly.

After a while Roxie looked me in the eyes. "So should we work on this case, track down what may well turn out to be a woman?"

"Dixie Ross and Mary Harriet Grossinger were women," I said, looking straight back. "Whatever we find out may not be easy to take, but it can't be as bad as what's already been done, right?"

Roxie merely nodded and turned to brace her hands on the edge of my stainless steel sink. Her gaze roamed the desert landscape beyond the window as if she were searching for something lost. I could see her brown knuckles turning beige as she gripped the edge of the sink hard. Too hard.

"Oh, Rox!" I whispered as I remembered something she'd told me. "Your mother. You're afraid we might be going after somebody . . . somebody like that, aren't you? We don't have to do this. Let's forget it. The cops will . . . We don't have to be involved, Roxie. I don't want . . ."

She'd told me about her mother when I asked, with a characteristic absence of subtlety, why on earth she'd wanted to be a psychiatrist. Med school, then specializing, the diplomates and certifications. These things were all difficult and prohibitively expensive for a young woman raised in poverty by a grandmother whose only source of income was a welfare check and whatever she could earn on the side cleaning houses or cooking. But Rox and her grandma hadn't let anything get in the way of their dream, that one day Roxie could help people like the one they *couldn't* help. Roxie's mother. Stricken by schizophrenia as a young woman, terrifying to a little daughter who hid in a closet when her mother came ragged and incoherent from the streets, begging for food. Dead in a psychiatric hospital fifteen years in the past, when Roxie was twenty.

"No, Blue," Roxie said softly. "I can guarantee that if, in fact, anybody's behind these deaths, it isn't somebody with schizophrenia. That's a stupid Hollywood myth and you know it. Somebody with untreated paranoid schizophrenia *might,* in a crisis, harm somebody. It rarely happens and the person is usually easily apprehended. These crimes we're looking at aren't the result of delusion-driven impulse but are carefully planned and executed. Nobody with active schizophrenia could even *begin* to organize crimes of this complexity, involving, apparently, mysterious drugs, prominent people, no immediate suspects or motive. That's not what—"

"Then what's wrong? You're about to make a modernist sculpture out of my sink."

She tossed her head in the general direction of where we'd just been standing in my kitchen. The gesture managed to create us again as we were in that moment, ghosts from seconds past hovering inches away, almost visible.

"That," she answered.

"That?"

"Blue, this thing keeps happening between us, like a minute ago."

"I know," I said without my usual attitude. "It's like walls dissolving. We say something and it makes us closer to each other because we understand what's said. I don't think it happens very often between people, do you?"

The turquoise beads in her hair were eerily silent as she turned to look out the kitchen window again. "No, it doesn't. But we can't get too close, Blue," she said.

"What do you mean?"

She inspected the cuff of the turquoise-blue cotton cargo shirt I'd ordered for her from one of the twenty or thirty catalogues I get every week. The shirt has lots of pockets and zippered compartments, and she loves it.

"It scares me."

"Feeling close to me scares you?"

"When it's like that," she said, nodding again at our ghosts, "when we understand each other like that, it's so comfortable I want to stay there; I forget what I need to do with my life. It's so seductive I forget about my work. And I can't do that, Blue. I can't ever do that."

Her voice was serious.

"And you won't," I chirped, stuffing my hands in the pockets of my shorts in an attempt to appear lighthearted. "We're not about mirror-sickness and terminal enmeshment. We're women, but we're not like that. It can't happen."

"Can't it?" she answered somberly.

"No. We won't let it."

"Okay, Blue," she said, grinning, "let's catch us a killer, then."

4

The Haunt of Jackals

The Bible is not short on references to swords. Rox, raised as a Baptist, was sure the letter's signature, "The Sword of Heaven," was biblical, but I wanted to look it up before calling my father, Father Jake, to get insider information on the phrase. An Episcopal priest, dad would sew his tongue to his lower lip before spouting scripture at anyone. Episcopalians traditionally refrain from spouting scripture. But when not shooting skeet with his collection of rifles, my father does savor the odd bit of biblical research. I'd looked up five of the thirty-four references to "sword" in the concordance to my old King James Bible when I gave up and called him in St. Louis, where he's supposed to be retired. In reality, he works just as hard as ever.

"Betsy Blue!" he said, happily calling me by a childhood name. "I'm so glad you called. Your brother's parole hearing is scheduled for early December and I know you'll want to be here. December tenth. Make your plane reservations now. And how's Roxie? Is everything going all right? I'm dying to hear."

I had spoken to my father only three days earlier and he sends e-mails daily, but he's the sort of person who prefers frequent updates. And given my family's propensity for unusual disasters, his concern isn't all that inappropriate. My mother, for example, was killed by a drunk driver on her way home from a Sierra Club meeting when my twin brother, David, and I were thirteen. Then five or six years later David began a descent into apelike behavior that would eventually earn him a stint in a Missouri state prison for attempted armed robbery. David's starting to shape up under the influence of his new wife, Lonnie, but I can't fault dad for maintaining eternal vigilance. Everything can change without notice, and my father knows it. What I know is that his need to be in touch is a form of not blinking.

"Everything's fine, dad," I said. "What I'm calling about is swords. In the Bible. Rox and I are about to be retained by the San Diego Police Department to profile somebody who wrote a letter three weeks ago threatening two women politicians. They've since died under unusual circumstances. The letter-writer signed as 'The Sword of Heaven.' I can't find it in the concordance. Do you know where it is?"

"Isaiah!" my father answered with the enthusiasm of a hound for a treed raccoon. "The author of this letter will turn out to wear white socks and a glow-in-the-dark cross lapel pin."

"Why do you say that?" I asked, gesturing for Rox to pick up the phone in the bedroom and listen. "Rox is going to listen in, okay?"

"Hi, Roxie," my father said politely, and then jumped back to the topic. "You'll find it at Isaiah 34, one of the early verses. Except I think it refers to a sword *in* heaven in most of the translations, rather than a sword *of* heaven. What's probably relevant to your inquiry is the nature of that particular text, however. I think you'll find this interesting, Blue."

"I'm listening," I told my father, who is professionally prone to the dramatic pause so common in sermons.

"It's one of those blood-and-guts apocalyptic tales in which God has a tantrum and wipes out a small nation, in this case a place called Edom. The author of this text was a poet, and the images of ruin are stunning. The stench of dead armies, mountains melting with blood, streams turned to tar, and a choking

black smoke covering everything. Only ravens and bitterns, dragons and owls would live among Edom's thorns once it was over.
The poet called Edom after the destruction 'an habitation of jackals.' Oh, and one other thing would live there, Blue. One other
entity."

"What entity, dad?" I asked, giving the response after which
he could go on.

His voice was at its basso-profundo pitch, and I could sense
his enjoyment of the moment. "Lilith," he pronounced.

"You're kidding!" I whooped. "This text goes back that far?
Wow! So don't tell me, let me guess. Edom was on the big guy's
hit list because the people hadn't quite caught up with the times
yet and were still worshiping the goddess, right?"

"Right. A number of pregnant female figures have been found
in excavations there. Edom was in a territory south of the Dead
Sea along the Araba Wadi that runs to the Gulf of Aqaba. Now
it would be in both Israel and Jordan. Excavations in both countries have turned up these female figures worked in clay and
stone, which certainly suggests—"

"Interesting," I acknowledged, halting the flow of archaeological data. "So the place had to be blasted, turned into a nightmare, and then the writer put Lilith there."

"Had to do *something* with her, Blue," he said with a chuckle.
"You know how difficult she was."

"Wait a minute," Roxie interrupted from the bedroom phone.
"What is this 'Lilith,' and what have you all just said that will
tell us anything about who wrote this letter?"

"My daughter can tell you all about the significance of Lilith,"
my father said proudly. "And at first glance what you've learned
about the letter-writer is that he or she has been exposed to
some rather screwball religious ideas—classes, sermons, the like.
This passage isn't used in traditional lectionaries—the predeter-
mined series of scripture on which weekly sermons are based
in every denomination. What I'm saying is, Isaiah 34 isn't in any
Protestant or Catholic lectionary I've ever seen, nor does it turn
up in the Jewish *Haftarot*. It's too ugly. But it is frequently used
by crackpots who want a biblical basis for their hatred of women."

"Are you saying you think the author of this letter is a woman? I mean, all we have is this one little phrase, this signature—'The Sword of Heaven.'"

"I have no ideas about the sex of the author," dad went on. "I can only guess that whoever it is, he or she has been exposed to some sort of religious experience in which a profoundly violent biblical text which fantasizes hideous punishment for a goddess-worshiping culture was used. I'm telling you that a mainstream denomination would never emphasize or even use this text, ever. A Lutheran auto mechanic or Methodist dentist would never have heard it from a pulpit. Your letter-writer either is or has been proximate to some fringe religious sect or cult."

"This is California, dad," I said. "There's a fringe sect on every corner."

"This one will probably bill itself as 'Christian' and 'Bible-based,' Blue. It will appeal to lower-class whites with little education. Probably it will be all-white, maybe even white supremacist. That sometimes goes with the woman-bashing."

I could hear Rox's snort of contempt. "We talkin' pointy hats and sheets here? 'Cause if we is, ole Roxie jus' remembered a previous engagement, y'all hear what I'm sayin'?"

In the two months of our relationship I'd never heard Rox do that patois. My dad took it seriously.

"I think the sheets are outré these days, Roxie. But if anybody has to go near these goons, let Blue do it."

"Oh, thanks, dad," I replied. "Just send me to the lions."

"Glad to help." He chuckled as we said good night.

After buckling on my waist pack, which among other things contains the Smith and Wesson I bought after my nine-millimeter Glock became a casualty of the Muffin Crandall case, I invited Rox to go with me on Brontë's nightly hike. This event is not a favorite of Roxie's, but I knew she'd go because she wanted to talk about the case.

"So what's this 'Lilith'?" she asked as we tramped through the rocks which comprise my property into the rocks which comprise the Anza-Borrego Desert State Park. A breeze moving across the desert floor made the spindly branches of an ocotillo writhe and cast snakelike shadows at our feet. Brontë raced ahead, her black fur reflecting moonlight. The setting, I thought, couldn't have been more appropriate.

"The name is an ancient Sumerian word meaning 'wind spirit,'" I began, smiling at my feet so Rox wouldn't see how much I relished this. There's nothing like a good ghost story. Lowering my voice, I went on.

"The mythological Lilith was Adam's first wife, but she didn't stay long because she insisted on total equality with him, including the right to be on top during sex. When Adam freaked, Lilith flew away and refused to return, preferring instead the erotic companionship of 'demons,' to whom she bore a hundred children a day, all of whom were killed every day by a deity annoyed at having to piece together another, more subservient wife for Adam.

"The word 'lilith' already meant a terrifying spirit that haunts wild places. After the Genesis story the word became a name, an embodiment of the wildness lurking just beyond civilization's control. Lilith became the 'night hag,' a woman whose beauty was equaled by her power. She always lived in wild places and was believed to drive men mad with her unrestrained sexuality. She's regarded as demonic by the men who wrote the Old Testament, but she's really the patron saint of every woman who won't be owned by *anything*. Her spirit is out here, Rox, in the wind and the rocks and the rattlers. She's the howling wilderness."

On cue, a gust of wind moaned as it moved through the shadows of a nearby slot canyon. I love the desert. Sometimes I think it loves me back. Like now.

"How *do* you arrange these sound effects?" Rox asked, glaring into the canyon as if sheer attitude could intimidate the wind. "And what does Lilith have to do with the Sword of Heaven?"

"Who knows? The sword is the destruction that wiped out Edom, and then the poet stuck Lilith there along with the jackals, dragons, and owls just to show that's where an untamable woman belongs. In a wasteland, a hell."

"Owls?" Rox said as something swooshed above our heads.

"Owls were sacred to the old religions, so the biblical writers had to make them look bad," I said. "But what you just felt flying above us was no owl. That was a bat, Rox."

Her ensuing silence was eloquent.

"From the size, I'd guess it was a western mastiff. Largest bat in the U.S."

"You can't know what this means to me," she said in a voice that was beginning to replicate the one she'd first used on Rathbone. The one that could cinderize cottage cheese. I know when to quit.

"They eat moths and sip nectar from desert flowers," I explained quickly. "Think of them as flying mice with elegant food preferences."

"I think of them as miniature vampires who carry rabies," Rox answered through clenched teeth.

"Myth," I said definitively, hanging a comforting arm over her shoulders. "There are only about five cases of rabies in the entire United States per year, and those cases are usually from skunk bites, not bats. I took some classes from the rangers when I moved out here from San Diego. That's where I learned to love them."

"The bats or the rangers?"

"The bats."

Rox cast her eyes dramatically toward the sky and rattled the beads in her hair. "What am I doing with a woman who loves bats?" she whispered.

I smiled to demonstrate my enormous tolerance for people who don't like bats and then ran a few hundred yards up a dry wash where Brontë was snuffing at something wedged in a crevice between two boulders. In the beam of the penlight I'd pulled from my waist pack I saw a small dark eye beneath a scaly brow ridge. An equally scaly five-fingered hand was pushing against the ground as the creature inflated one side of its body in order to push the other side farther into the crevice.

"It's a chuckwalla, Brontë," I told my Doberman. The bloated lizard looked like a small hot-water bottle with scales, trying to cram itself into the sort of thin box smoked salmon comes in. "Let's go. Leave it alone."

As I distracted Brontë by throwing a palo verde twig for her to chase, something occurred to me.

"Rox," I began after scrambling back down the wash, "what if Rathbone's hunch is right and there's some connection between this evangelist, Ruby Emerald, who wound up in the hospital tonight, and the deaths of Grossinger and Ross? What if Sword of Heaven did something to Emerald as well?"

"Rathbone's looking for pattern, Blue," she said. "It's what cops do, what we all do in one way or another. He's looking for m.o. in the same way I might look for diagnostic criteria or you for statistical similarities. Three prominent women on his beat dead or hospitalized with similar symptoms within weeks, followed by a threat against two of them would seem significant to him. That doesn't mean it *is* significant. Probably this Emerald woman just came down with a case of stage fright like the paramedics suggested. It's not unusual. Anxiety attacks in performers, I mean. Pretty common. Some of them say it's anxiety that gives them their edge, boosts their ability to project themselves to an audience. So what's your idea?"

"Just that dad said Sword has probably been around some fringe religious group. Maybe Emerald's revivals qualify as fringe."

"So Emerald's preaching this stuff from Isaiah about swords from heaven demolishing little countries because the little countries make statues of pregnant women," Rox began. "And somebody hears this and decides to start murdering women in a nearly impossible way, also announcing this decision to the police. This same person then decides to kill the preacher who's preaching the message in the first place. Blue, it doesn't make sense."

And it didn't. Although, I was sure, it would.

When we got back there was a message from BB on my machine, describing perhaps more colorfully than was necessary his thoughts on the appropriate fate of police in general and Detective Sergeant Wes Rathbone in particular. Incendiary devices and bodily orifices figured largely in the narrative. It seems he'd planned to meet the radical preacher from Kate's fundraiser for coffee, and Rathbone had left him in a holding cell at the police station for three hours until two other detectives interrogated him for another hour before allowing him to go. He'd missed meeting the preacher at the appointed time and was embarrassed to call and explain why the police could pick him up and hold him whenever they wanted to.

"What's the dude gonna think?" his voice growled from my answering machine. "Jus' the thing, right? Coffee with some nigga ex-con that don't show up 'cause he sittin' in some piss-smellin' tank with three winos and a crack pimp and ain't nuthin' he can do about it. Shee-it!"

Roxie had met BB when he was still in prison at Donovan on a drug charge. He'd been processed through her office for a routine psychiatric evaluation, but the two had connected in some way I never quite understood. They'd become friends, but despite that Rox never stepped outside appropriate professional boundaries with him. When he was released from prison she helped him find a job, which was where I came in. I was consulting on the redesign of a strip mall in a bad area plagued with crime and I needed a mall manager. Rox answered my ad and offered BB, who opened a resale clothing boutique called Death Row and policed the turf with an ex-con's edge. It was an experiment, but it worked. At least until tonight.

"Uh-oh," she said after hearing the rage in his voice. "Trouble."

"You'd better call him," I thought aloud. "BB's only twenty-seven. His testosterone levels are still too high for anything resembling rational behavior when he's humiliated and angry, given his history. He's likely to do something stupid and wind up back in prison."

Roxie gave me a look that suggested I shut up.

"Girl," she said with a vicious sweetness, "what did you think I meant by 'trouble'? That he might say something naughty over tea with the vicar?"

"Look, I care about BB, too," I snapped back. "You think I don't feel bad about what the police did to him? I do. But it's not my fault, Rox. And I can't always say things in just the way you'd like. I'm not black, but I'm not blind, either. I can see what's happened, how he must feel, and I hate it. All I said was call him. That's all I said."

With that I stormed into the inadequate bathroom off my bedroom and drained three inches of lukewarm water from the tank behind the motel into the tub. It's difficult to make dramatic gestures in the space of only two rooms without breaking something. In the tub I tried to compensate for that by elaborate splashing, an endeavor also doomed by the need to conserve water.

The reason I live in a half-built motel is that it has no piped-in water and so I was able to buy it for practically nothing. But trucked-in water is expensive, hence the three-inch bath limit. I felt like a giraffe in a wading pool as I strained to hear whether or not Rox was talking to BB. A miserable giraffe. This was our first real fight, and I wasn't even sure what it was about.

As I was drying off, Roxie knocked on the bathroom door.

"It's okay, I talked to him," she said. "He's not going to blow up any cops, although not because I called. Reverend Tie-Die called first. Wanna hear?"

"What I want to hear is what we're fighting about," I said after opening the bathroom door as if it were made of nitroglycerin. "Then I want to hear about BB."

Roxie looked equally miserable as she gestured toward the window and the tumble of moonlit boulders outside. She also looked lost.

"We're different, Blue," she said. "Do you know how weird this place feels to me, how scared I am of you sometimes? You're like mercury, like electricity or something. The way you think is intuitive, not rational, and even though you're usually on target, the way you put things sounds arrogant. You just talk and move around in life, any way or anywhere you want, and it works for you because you're marching to your own drum anyway. But it's not like that for me and never can be. Before I met you I thought my world, my way of thinking, was all there was. It isn't, but it's still my world, and sometimes you just barge into it like tonight with your half-baked analysis of BB. You weren't wrong, but you came *at* it wrong. Uppity. Do you know how many young black men are either in prison or on parole right now in this country, how many lives wasted?"

She was standing in darkness snapping and unsnapping one of the pockets of her bright blue cargo shirt, which looked gray in the gloom. Just a large, dark woman with big ears and beads in her braided hair. For a moment she seemed distant and two-dimensional, like a photo accompanying a newspaper article about black people doing something political. "Minority Business Leaders Launch Scholarship Effort." That sort of article. The sort you never actually read.

"Over forty percent of young black men in the U.S. are in prison or on parole right now," I answered her question. "But my brother's in prison, too, and he isn't black, and I'm not responsible for any of this, but I'm doing the best I can with him and BB, and I don't know if I can stop sounding arrogant to you, but I'll try, Rox. I'll let you teach me things I could easily live without ever knowing. Will you do the same for me?"

"I am letting you teach me. I am all the time," she answered as it happened again. That sense of walls dissolving and the slow, magnetic leaning toward something unknown. We stood that way in the dark for a long time, just looking at each other, not fighting it, rocking a little with the spin from a journey happening only inside our heads.

"Oh, shit," we said in unison as the phone rang.

It was Wes Rathbone.

"Sorry to call this late, but you're on the payroll now so get used to it," he said to my mumbled hello. "You're consultants now. It's approved as of tonight. This thing's blowing up, Blue. Get Dr. Bouchie on the other phone, please."

It was apparent from his tone that waiting until tomorrow wasn't an option.

"It's Rathbone," I said, gesturing for her to pick up the phone in the living room.

"What's happened?" I heard her ask him seconds later.

"Listen to this," was all he said. There was the click and whir of a tape being played, then a voice I recognized immediately.

A voice all Americans associate with the phrase, "What's up, Doc?" Bugs Bunny's voice. Only it wasn't Bugs Bunny.

"I destroyed Ruby Emerald because she was an abomination," it said. "I am the Sword of Heaven and she was an abomination to the law. The Sword of Heaven cast her down and killed her and will kill again."

After that there was another click as the tape was stopped.

"This thing came in to the local CBS affiliate shortly after the story about Emerald's illness aired on the six o'clock news," Rathbone explained. "It's illegal to tape phone calls without notifying the caller, but the woman at the desk where the call got shunted has a hearing impairment, so they let her tape calls as a backup in case she misses a name or phone number. We got lucky with this one. Not that it tells us much."

"What happened to Emerald?" Rox asked.

"Nothing," Rathbone answered. "That's what's strange. After the TV station called us with this tape, we called the hospital. She's fine, everything's normal. Her doctor says there's no reason she can't preach at this revival tomorrow. Her p.r. people are putting it out that she had a mild case of food poisoning. The doc says it wasn't food poisoning but declines to say what it was. Apparently our 'Sword of Heaven' thought she was a goner when the story hit at six, and called the station to take credit."

"Bugs Bunny called the station," I reminded him.

"That's a voice modification device you can buy all over, mostly from mail-order catalogues. They come prepackaged. Darth Vader, Homer Simpson, the president. You speak in your normal voice into a mike that funnels the sound through a distortion program. You come out saying whatever you said, but sounding like the program you picked. This one was Bugs."

Wes Rathbone was not amused.

"We've got a serious problem here," he went on. "CBS didn't keep this under wraps. The story will be on TV news tomorrow and in the papers on Monday. We're going to be under a lot of pressure. How soon can you get us that profile?"

"Tomorrow afternoon," Rox told him. "And we'll need a fax of the text from the tape right away. Send it here."

"Done," Rathbone said, and hung up.

Rox and I stood around watching the fax come in, saying nothing, thinking.

"Need to review the FBI profiling protocol for serial killers and then review all the data that says the FBI profiling protocol is a pile of crap," she muttered. "I'll need to be in my office by seven at least. This is going to take some time."

"I want to run vocabulary analyses of both the letter and the tape, but especially the letter," I replied. "There may be some clues in the language of the headlines selected to glue all over the page."

We were working, talking to ourselves, not to each other.

"Better get some sleep," Roxie said.

"You still didn't tell me about BB and the preacher," I reminded her.

"Oh, the guy sounds okay. He called BB after BB called here, told him he did a chaplaincy at Sing-Sing for five years and knows everybody who makes a mistake isn't necessarily toxic. Then he and BB went for an eight-mile run around Mission Bay, after which they had lattes and made plans to attend a gospel concert tomorrow afternoon. The run calmed our boy down. Right now he's in an agony of indecision over what to wear to a gospel concert. When we hung up he was leaning toward a Stokely Carmichael look. Black suit, narrow tie, you know."

We were doing okay, I thought as I felt Rox stretch and relax into sleep beside me in my queen-size bed. Everybody in my little world was doing okay. But somebody out there wasn't. Somebody out there was either killing or wanting to be seen as a killer. Somebody out there wanted to *be* a sword. The thought of that warped personality brought a bitter taste to the back of my throat. Just knowing it was out there made me happy about the Smith and Wesson now tucked snugly in my waist pack. You never know. You just really don't.

5

Profiles in Deadliness

Roxie was up at five, an hour I rarely acknowledge, much less see. For the record, in the Anza-Borrego Desert in late October, five A.M. smells like aluminum and seems to be deeply absorbed in a game that would turn out to be chess if you could see it. I sat up in bed feeling the clean desert chill and told myself a killer might strike again if I didn't get up. Then I curled under the comforter and began a delicious drift back into sleep. Brontë, stretched across the foot of the bed, was snoring softly.

"You and that dog were not raised on a farm," Rox noted as she applied makeup in the bathroom.

"Neither were you." I yawned from beneath the comforter.

"You and that dog do not understand the work ethic."

"Dogs do not have a work ethic," I muttered, well aware that some dogs do. Border collies, for example.

"I'll need your analysis of the clippings that were glued to the letter by ten-thirty, Blue. That will give me a couple of hours to mesh your findings with whatever I can come up with and get the profile over to Rathbone by one. We don't have much time."

"What are you going to give them?" I asked, opening my eyes in that way you know means you're going to get up. "FBI stuff on serial killers?"

Rox was bustling around my bedroom dramatically, moving the air in guilt-inducing patterns.

"Some," she said tersely. "Some of the Holmes serial killer typology, probably. More on the medical aspect. *If* somebody's manipulating blood pressure to murder people, then that person has had some medical training. Doctor, nurse, maybe pharmacist. Or anybody in a tech support position that involves knowledge of blood chemistry and systems. We're not looking for a dietician or an X-ray tech. We're looking for a medical professional familiar with the circulatory system who's cracking up. Probably not a true antisocial personality disorder, or the aberrant behavior would have shown up before or during medical training. This one's been repressing a big rage for years. But now something's triggered it."

"What about somebody who just learned about blood pressure by having it?" I offered.

Roxie laughed as she scrounged for a shoe under the bed.

"Blue, anybody who doesn't have blood pressure is dead."

"I meant high blood pressure," I said. I have never understood people who can use words correctly before coffee.

"Nah," she answered. "This is somebody who's learned how to push blood pressure dangerously, even fatally high in perfectly healthy people. That's not something you pick up from a pamphlet your doctor gives you as she tells you to exercise and cut down on fat."

I had managed to stand up and pull on a pair of sweatpants and a sweatshirt. My bare feet demanded more complicated behaviors. Finding socks, tying shoes. Feet are not something I easily deal with at five A.M. I ignored them and went into the kitchen to make coffee. Brontë followed me, clearly wondering how to feign alertness. She drank some water from her red ceramic bowl and then sat beside the refrigerator with the attitude of a dog on a mission.

"That's good," I told her. "Guard the refrigerator."

I noticed that her eyelids kept slipping downward, but she didn't go back to bed.

"I'm outta here," Rox said, taking a lidded car-cup of coffee with her. "You'll have your stuff to me by ten-thirty?"

"No problem."

The second Roxie's car started, Brontë stood and trotted straight back to bed. I wished I could, too.

Three hours later I still wished I could. Entering the texts of fifty-three newspaper article headers into my computer had given me a headache. But it had to be done manually since the little clips had been pasted all over the page in every direction and the computer program wouldn't be able to read the words from a scanned image.

What I found was nothing.

Sword of Heaven had no preference for any particular word or phrase in the article headers pasted on the letter. Certain verbs did show up forty-eight percent more often than would occur in the normal speech of a native American-English speaker with a high school education. But these were the "elocutionary" verbs journalists use to describe the speech of politicians. In newspapers public servants never "say" anything, but rather urge, call, issue, demand, and weigh. In dicey situations they may also answer, evade, dodge, or deny. I had just spent hours proving the existence of a linguistic usage pattern everybody knows and accepts without thinking about it. Only its absence would get attention. Something like, "Republican Leaders Clutch Funding Opportunity." Everybody knows the right word is "seize."

Sword, it seemed, had just cut out article headers randomly and stuck them on a page. Except, as every social psychologist will tell you, the behavior of an individual cannot be random. Never. Randomness is a mathematical concept, not a human one. People are programmed by species evolution and their own experiences to perform every act as a result of acts which have gone before it. Put simply, if there is no causal history to a behavior, if we haven't inherited it or learned how it's done, we can't perform the behavior because we can't think it. If we perform a behavior, it has an evolutionary or acquired cause. It is the result of something and is therefore not random.

After feeding Brontë I successfully negotiated the sock-and-shoe sequence and then took her out for a run. The desert was in morning neutral, nothing much going on. Instead of heading toward Coyote Creek I went south through Henderson Canyon toward the Los Coyotes Indian Reservation. The terrain in that direction is monotonous, just an expanse of snakeweed and creosote bushes. I didn't want to be distracted.

"The choices of clippings made by the author of this letter cannot be random," I lectured Brontë, who was watching a quail as it dashed between two rocks. "They *look* random, but they're not. What is it that I'm missing?"

The quail reappeared above the second rock and said, "Chicago," which is the only thing California quails say. There's another species, the scaled quail, that lives in states east of here and says "Pecos." I wondered why the calls of both species of quail should seem to replicate American place names. I don't believe in coincidence. Neither do I believe in attaching too much significance to these things.

"Chicago!" called the quail again, its black-feather topknot looking oddly Mayan against the pale blue sky.

I wondered what possible evolutionary function was served by quails' topknots. They seemed merely decorative, like plumes on hats Dorothy Parker might have worn to lunch at the Algonquin in 1926. That's when it hit me.

"Mary Harriet Grossinger and Dixie Ross were women!" I yelled to Brontë. "Come on, we're going back!"

It was the quail's topknot and the notion of hats, of fashion, that did it. Women politicians are subject to a type of scrutiny by the media that would be ludicrous if applied to their male counterparts. Imagine an article headed, "Port Commissioner Brad Thompson Opts for Black Velvet Cummerbund at Gala."

Back at my computer I went to the *San Diego Union-Tribune* archives, which are complete for the previous year. The analysis had to be e-mailed to Rox in two hours. I had no time to read all hundred and seventy-three article headers referencing

Mary Harriet Grossinger or Dixie Ross. This is where the concept of statistical randomness becomes useful. A random sampling of data makes it possible to draw conclusions about that data based on a very small number. I wanted to know about the article headers Sword *hadn't* selected to paste on the letter, and about the likelihood of those chosen being chosen by chance rather than design.

In the back of Blalock's *Social Statistics* are tables of random numbers. I picked a set of twenty-five and assigned them to the hundred and seventy-three articles, got twenty-five randomly, then fed the data into the same word-frequency program I'd used earlier. In minutes I knew that roughly fourteen percent of the articles printed last year about these two women politicians referenced clothing, hairstyles, and personal domestic routines. My favorite was "Senator Grossinger Changes Diaper on Road," an article about Grossinger having taken a grandchild with her on a trip to inspect irrigation ditches.

If Sword were choosing headers randomly from all available articles, then fourteen percent would involve references to traditional female interests because fourteen percent of all the articles did so. Fashion, cooking, cleaning, babies. Another analysis of the letter revealed no such references. None. This could not happen by chance, so I assumed the traditional female stuff had been excluded deliberately. Sword had told us that these women had to die because they were trying to be like men, and then pasted examples of their authoritarian pronouncements all over the letter in case somebody missed the point. Changing diapers was okay. Women were supposed to do that. But heading land use committees wasn't. Women who did that had to die.

I was running out of time, and had yet to address the big question. Was Sword more likely to be male or female? I was leaning toward male, but a mistake at this juncture would mislead the whole investigation. Sword might be a rotten speller, but he or she wasn't stupid. If things were as bad as they seemed to be, Sword had already managed to kill two people and endanger a third without leaving a trace. If the killing were to stop now, the odds against apprehension would be very high.

But Sword wasn't going to stop now. I didn't need a computer program to tell me that.

"Women are more likely to poison than men," I told Brontë. "But men are much more likely than women to demand acknowledgment for their accomplishments, including murder."

With her nose my dog nudged a yellow rubber ball toward my feet and smiled. I kicked it across the carpet with my foot and watched her run into a wall chasing it. Brontë has never grasped the constraints involved in chasing balls indoors. So I took the ball outdoors and threw it as far as I could fifteen times, making my Dobie's day. While throwing, I pondered the gender issue.

Social psychologists are supposed to be able to determine gender on the basis of very little data, but I didn't feel comfortable assigning sex to Sword. Not yet. Anybody intelligent enough to pull off the crimes suggested in the letter to the police and the Bugs Bunny tape might be intelligent enough to be misleading as to his/her sex. Already there were confusing markers. An "internal" kill method suggesting a female killer, and demands for attention suggesting a male.

Inside again, I looked at Rathbone's fax of the Bugs Bunny tape text. More biblical-sounding language. "Abomination." "Cast her down and killed her." There wasn't time to run more linguistic analyses, and they wouldn't have told me anything dad already hadn't. Sword was no stranger to violent and judgmental passages in the Bible and identified with them. Moreover, he or she was troubled by women in positions of authority, but not women in traditional roles.

Sword's choice of pseudonym was clearly phallic, which could be misleading. Research into the psychology of aliases and pseudonyms suggests that people often choose names reflecting qualities they lack or dimensions of themselves they believe others do not see. It is telling that the most common surname alias used by English-speaking prostitutes is "White." Sword could be a man conflicted about what a man is supposed to be, or a woman who sees herself as more like a man.

I documented my conclusions, arguing that Sword's gender

would have to remain open pending further information. "The subject is most likely to be a white male between twenty-five and forty," I wrote, "based on the pattern of killing or claiming credit for killing female Caucasian victims who do not conform to typical profiles for victims of female killers. That is, the victims are not children nor are they elderly or in any way disabled. However, the subject is intelligent and resourceful, perhaps sufficiently so that s/he is able to mask gender. Subject's need for attention from police and media, as suggested by the letter and tape, also suggest that subject is male. On the other hand, the presumed method of killing (introducing substance into body of victim) is typically female.

"My preliminary assessment is that the subject is either deliberately masking psychological features reflecting gender or is deeply conflicted personally over gender issues. In either sex, look for overcompensating behaviors. In both look for extreme and punitive religious beliefs. Suspect either is or has been associated with a religious context which stresses rigid sex roles and violent punishment."

I typed out another three pages of advice for the police, including warnings that victims were chosen from a population of women in positions of authority. I mentioned that newspaper coverage of these public figures might be a trigger to further attempts. Then I e-mailed my report to Roxie and called her at her office. It was precisely ten-thirty.

"Just e-mailed it," I told her. "What have you come up with so far?"

"Oh, just the obvious. High IQ, poor early schooling or else a learning disorder. Sword speaks well, but can't spell, may have had some negative experiences as a child due to difficulties with reading and writing skills. Doubt that there was ever a serious psychiatric disorder. This is psychological, not psychiatric. Rigidly controlled personality finally blows. God knows what the trigger was, but the murders were extremely well planned, if indeed they were murders. We still don't know that, Blue, although it seems likely. There are too many noncoincidental factors."

"What did you do about which sex this is?" I had to ask.

"Look for male, but don't rule out promising female suspects. Tidy, clean-cut person who's probably married or living with a mate. Financially secure, drives a fairly new car, is regarded as quiet and personable by neighbors and friends. May have a violent hobby of some kind."

"Yeah, I picked up on that, too," I said. "But how do you know about the *car*?"

"It's in the Holmes typology on 'organized' serial killers. I just threw it in."

"What did you do with the biblical language factor?"

"Same stuff your dad came up with, put in psychiatric terms." I sighed. "We really don't have much, do we?"

"More than you think," Roxie answered. "It's just that there isn't enough time to use it."

"What do you mean?"

I could hear her inhaling deeply and then whistling softly between her teeth.

"Sword will decompensate now, quickly, begin to fall apart. This person has probably kept a lid on very confused and violent feelings for a long time. Then something triggered those feelings, something intolerable. Sword had to act out and had to advertise the reasoning behind it. But our subject knows right from wrong and the conflict between that knowledge and the need to justify some personal confusion through killing will produce intolerable stress. There may be additional deaths in an attempt to reduce the stress, but they'll only produce more. The subject may commit suicide as the only way to stop the stress. That could happen at any time, and unless evidence is left behind, nobody will ever know that the subject has killed. I don't have a good feeling about this thing, Blue. It's weird."

We talked for a while, agreed to meet in town later for dinner, and then I'd watch Rox rehearse her country and western dance team. Brontë and I would sleep at her place. The wages of our deep commitment to nonenmeshment.

The phone was ringing when I hung up. Rathbone.

"We need somebody at Emerald's revival this afternoon," he said. "Can you do it?"

"Sure, but what am I there for?" I answered.

"Just get a feel for the thing. See if this might be where our boy got his Sword of Heaven ideas."

"How do you know it's a boy?" I asked. "Neither Rox nor I are sure about that from the available data."

"It's always a boy," Rathbone stated flatly. "Women just don't do this kind of crime."

Then I phoned to check on BB, who said the radical preacher had been called to a deathbed, so they'd had to cancel their plans for the gospel concert. He'd be happy to go with me to Ruby Emerald's revival, he said. He hadn't been to one since the summers he spent visiting relatives in Mississippi. We agreed to meet in the parking lot of a college stadium Ruby Emerald had leased for her event.

I went into my bedroom to search for whatever you wear to a revival. With my cropped hair, in sandals, black knit dress, and beige linen jacket, I looked too liberal. Roxie and I would pick me for a jury trying a death penalty case in a minute. The addition of a straw bowler with a flowered scarf tied around the crown helped. Now I looked like a liberal who ties scarves to hats. It would have to do.

6

A Green Paper

I had a few hours before meeting BB, so after I drove over the mountains and down into San Diego I went by Kate Van Der Elst's campaign headquarters to check in. Pieter Van Der Elst was overseeing four volunteers preparing a mailer as Kate talked on a phone at the back of the room. I noticed that Pieter had moved a Formica-topped desk near the door of the storefront so that anyone entering would immediately be seen by whoever was sitting there. At the moment, he was. And he seemed nervous.

"Just a small security precaution," he said, gesturing to the desk with both hands. "I've been in contact with Detective Rathbone and I know about the letter threatening Grossinger and Ross. He's told me that you and Dr. Bouchie are working on some kind of profile for the police. Blue," he asked, lowering his voice, "do you think Kate is in any danger? If she is I want her to drop out of the campaign immediately. I'm asking for your professional opinion. Is there really a killer stalking these women, or just some sick person trying to make everybody think there is?"

I'd come to know both Kate and Pieter fairly well while working on her campaign for city council and liked them both. In
addition to his European manners, Pieter is a listener. He takes
people seriously; he pays attention. I would do him the honor
of returning the courtesy.

"I honestly don't know," I said. "There is enough evidence at
this point to justify concern."

"Tell me more, Blue. What's going on? We heard that Dixie
Ross died of a cerebral hemorrhage as did Senator Grossinger,
and that a letter threatening these deaths was sent to the police weeks ago. How could someone commit murder without
even being present? Is there some kind of poison that does this?
And *why*?"

He was wearing a blue dress shirt with the sleeves rolled up
and a silk tie I knew cost at least as much as the four new ra-
dial tires on my truck. Yet he had a saintly aura that always
makes me think of monks. It wasn't just the tonsured look of
his prematurely white hair or those powder-blue eyes. It was a
sense that it would never occur to Pieter Van Der Elst to hurt
anything, that he was incapable of deliberate harm. He could
play St. Francis of Assisi without changing clothes and seem
completely in character. I wondered about the differences between Pieter and whatever called itself Sword of Heaven.

"So far the victim profile is women in positions of authority,
positions formerly reserved for men," I told him. "These may
be selected from coverage in the newspaper."

"Kate's in the paper all the time," Pieter said, his eyes scan-
ning the street beyond a plate glass window. "The election is
only a few weeks away. Of course the papers are covering all
the candidates. And more than a fourth of them are women!"

"There's no way to tell if the killer regards the city council
as a bastion of male power being taken over by women," I told
him. "There's no way to predict much of anything yet, except,
Pieter . . ." I made a fist and stared at my knuckles before finishing what I'd started to say.

"Yes?"

"It isn't over. There's very likely to be another . . . incident."

Color was rising in his pale cheeks.

"Another death, you mean. Blue, how can this be happening? I'm going to ask Kate to withdraw from the race. Dixie Ross died on her way to Kate's fundraiser, and both of them knew Mary Harriet Grossinger. There are too many connections. It's not worth the risk."

Kate had terminated her phone call and now stood behind her husband.

"Hello, Blue," she said, a thoughtful smile emphasizing the attractive contours of her face. "I suppose Pieter has told you he wants me to withdraw from the race two weeks before election day?"

I never know what to do with declarative statements pronounced as questions, so I merely smiled at a point just behind her head. Kate went on to answer the next question, which nobody had asked.

"It's out of the question, of course," she said. "And I love your outfit, Blue. Where did you find that hat?"

Real question.

"At a thrift store in Palm Springs. I'm going to a revival. Undercover, sort of."

It was clear that neither Kate nor Pieter had ever met a person who went to revivals. Or else they'd never met anyone who bought hats at thrift stores. Both faces went blank for the same fraction of a second, and then both said, "Really!" in unison. I assumed it was the revival thing that had brought them up short and decided to tell them what Rathbone apparently hadn't.

"A revivalist named Ruby Emerald was taken to a hospital with symptoms which might be the result of high blood pressure last night," I began. "Shortly after the news of her illness was aired on television, an audiotape was delivered to the local CBS affiliate. On the tape was a mechanically altered voice claiming to be the Sword of Heaven and claiming to have killed Emerald because she was an 'abomination,' although in fact she didn't die. I'm going to her revival this afternoon to get a sense of whether she may have any connection to Sword."

"But the taped message claimed that this person had killed Emerald," Pieter said, his voice thin.

"Yes. Obviously Sword thought Emerald was a fatality, but she wasn't. Her doctor won't tell the police what the diagnosis was and doesn't have to. All we know is that Emerald experienced some kind of cardiovascular event that may have been nothing more than anxiety. Sword may have nothing to do with Emerald's illness but just be grabbing for publicity. In the case of Dixie and Mary Harriet, however, the fact that the threatening letter was mailed to the police a week before Mary Harriet's and two weeks before Dixie's death is too compelling to lay at the feet of coincidence. Right now that's really all we know."

"It's enough for me," Pieter said, grasping the hand Kate had laid over his shoulder. "Please, Kate. You can run for another office next year when this monster has been apprehended."

I watched as Kate Van Der Elst stretched her neck and rubbed at the skin behind both ears as if something had clamped to her skull. She continued to stretch and turn her head as she answered.

"I've spent fifteen years managing our homes, hostessing parties and business events," she said evenly. "I've enjoyed it, Pieter. We've had a wonderful life. But I've never had anything of my own, never felt that I was important in the world as myself, only as your wife. Please don't ask me again to give this up. I can't."

"But Kate, it's only a city council seat," he continued, going squarely in the wrong direction.

I wasn't surprised when she repeated the word "only" with quiet anger and then walked away.

"You blew it," I told Pieter, who was again staring out the window.

"Blue," he said, not looking at me, "do you own a gun?"

"What?"

"A gun. Do you have one?"

"Yes," I answered. "I live alone out in the desert. I have a gun."

"Are you licensed to carry it in town?"

"No, Pieter."

I didn't like the desperation in his voice, and I didn't like where I knew this was going.

"Surely a license can be arranged," he went on. "I want to hire you as a bodyguard for Kate."

If he'd looked like a monk before, Pieter Van Der Elst now looked like the corpus in a pietà. A dead body, the slack posture of despair. In the weeks I'd been designing polls for Kate's campaign, I'd spent hours with this couple but hadn't seen the depth to which Pieter loved his wife. Of course, I wouldn't have. What I was looking at now seemed too intimate for anyone's eyes but Kate's, but there it was. He couldn't bear the thought of harm to her, of losing her. Love has that dark side. That intolerable fear of loss. I glanced down and pretended to be looking for something in my purse.

"Pieter, I have no training as a bodyguard and couldn't accept that responsibility," I said. "I'll be happy to refer you to some good agencies. But why don't we hold off for a few days? There may be no danger to Kate. We really don't know much yet."

He leaned forward to pull something from the hip pocket of his slacks. It was a fluorescent lime-green piece of paper, folded to a small rectangle. He ran a thumb along the folded edge and then looked at me.

"I got here first this morning and opened the office," he said. "Kate had gone to church with Dixie's sister and then back to their house to spend some time with the Ross family before the funeral on Wednesday. This had been pushed under the door."

He handed me the bilious green rectangle, which I unfolded. In the center of the page were words cut from newspapers.

"Kate Van Der Elst will die," it said.

"Why haven't you called the police?" I asked. "Why haven't you given this to Rathbone? How long have you had this, Pieter? And does Kate know?"

"I got here about an hour ago, and no, I didn't show it to her. I wasn't sure . . . There have been other things, Blue. A few phone threats, some nasty letters signed with names like 'Nietzsche.' Once someone spray-painted 'Die Jew Nigger Faggot' on the window. Public figures attract these things.

"The first time one of these incidents occurred I checked with ten or twelve of the campaign managers for other candidates, Blue. They all said these things are typical, that it's just part of the political scene and I shouldn't be concerned unless a threat was repeated. Then I should contact the police. This note under the door may just be another flare-up from some disaffected lout in the neighborhood whose father was killed in World War II and thinks 'Van Der Elst' is a German name. A man at a cocktail party only weeks ago asked me if my father had been in the SS. He thought my accent was German. I didn't know what to say."

I didn't, either. The man seated before me was sophisticated, European, accustomed to international travel. But not accustomed to the lethal riptides moving beneath the surface of American culture.

You have to grow up here to understand why a Maine hunter who shot and killed a housewife as she hung laundry in her own yard was acquitted on all charges. It's not just that the idiot mistook her for a deer, you see. It's that she and her husband had recently moved there. They were strangers, outsiders. Had they been insiders they would have known you don't hang laundry during deer season. The housewife, according to the community, deserved to die for not knowing one of many unspoken rules known only by the community. If she'd been part of the community, she would have known and would still be alive. In essence, she killed herself by failing to be born there.

It's this sort of thing I was certain Pieter Van Der Elst would never truly grasp. And in a huge city like San Diego there are thousands of such conceptual "communities," invisible to one another but just as deadly as that little town in Maine. Thousands of rules and closely held beliefs not obvious in the normal daily social exchange, but prone to erupt in the night, when no one is watching.

"I'm going to call Detective Rathbone," I said, and picked up a phone from one of the desks. "And you're going to have to show this green thing to Kate. You're probably right. It's probably not connected to Sword, but this is her reality and she has a right to know what the risks are. Stop protecting her, Pieter. Your wife is an adult."

After phoning in a message about this latest development for Rathbone, I approached Kate Van Der Elst at the back of the little storefront office. Red, white, and blue paper bunting tacked to the rear wall created a festive atmosphere not reflected in Kate's face.

"Pieter says you and Dixie Ross both knew Mary Harriet Grossinger," I began as she sank into a folding chair and scowled. "I want you to think about this. What, if anything, did the three of you share? What did you have in common? I don't mean your political beliefs. I mean did all three of you shop at the same grocery, go to the same church, use the same dentist? That kind of thing."

At "dentist" her shoulders moved uneasily beneath a washable silk blouse in a creamy color that precisely matched the lightest blonde streaks in her hair. Then she smiled a sincere politician's smile and said, "Let me give this some thought, Blue. I'm sure there are places—restaurants, theaters, and the like— where Mary Harriet and Dixie and I have all been, although not necessarily at the same time. That's what you mean, isn't it?"

"Anything," I answered. "But especially restaurants or other places where you might eat something. Also doctors, dentists, hairdressers, manicurists, gyms. Places where others touching you is normal. Did you and the other two go to the same gym?"

"Dixie and I played tennis at a club and worked out there as well," she said thoughtfully. "Mary Harriet didn't play tennis as far as I know. And If Dixie ever brought her to the club, I didn't see her. They did more professional things together, luncheons with business groups, speaking engagements. The only time I had dinner with the two of them was almost a year ago, and it was at Dixie's home. She'd made vegetarian chili and we had a lot of margaritas. That was the night they talked me into running for city council. I can't believe they're both . . . gone."

"I'm sorry, Kate," I said. "You knew Dixie Ross for most of your life, and Grossinger must have been something of a mentor for you. I know you must feel alone now, dealing with the campaign in their absence."

"Oh, Blue," she said, her hazel eyes determined, "that's why I can't quit now no matter what Pieter wants! He doesn't understand. He just wants me to be safe, but even if I wanted to bail out, and I don't, I owe something to the memories of Dixie and Mary Harriet. I was following in their footsteps. Now I *am* the footsteps."

I could see Pieter approaching, holding the bright green sheet of paper on which someone had pasted the words "Kate Van Der Elst will die."

"Keep thinking about places frequented by you, Grossinger, and Ross," I reminded her. "We'll talk later."

Outside again, I retrieved Brontë from my truck and snapped a leash to her collar. Then we made a wide loop through the residential streets behind University Avenue and came out on the corner next to the Aphid Gallery. I hadn't planned this, but since I was there I went in. A young man at a desk in the forward gallery, dressed from head to toe in fashionable black, eyed Brontë approvingly. His hair had been shaved to the skull and it was clear that he regarded my dog's choice of fur as a fashion statement.

"Are you interested in anything in particular?" he asked.

"The black-and-white photographs in the small gallery at the back. Do you have a sheet on the photographer?"

He opened a drawer in the desk and took out a file labeled "Current Exhibits."

"The photographer's name is Greave," he said.

"Yes."

"Black-and-white photos. An art critic for one of the local papers described them as possessing 'an eerie efficiency reminiscent of Edward Hopper.'"

"Is that all you have?" I asked. "What about the photographer? Who is 'Greave'? I saw the photos at a political fundraiser here Friday night and would like to know how old they are, where they were taken, the usual."

"Um, we don't seem to have much. The collection is part of a larger photography exhibit organized over a year ago by a company in Los Angeles. Apparently they bought the photographs for the exhibit and then went bankrupt. After the show, the bank holding the loan broke up the exhibit and leased it out piecemeal to a bunch of galleries, trying to recoup the loss. Some here, a lot to Laguna and the beach communities between here and L.A. The Greave photos go to Laguna after this. Guess the bank's just rotating the show in pieces through a series of Southern California galleries. There really isn't any way to get information on the artists because the original purchaser doesn't exist anymore. I'm sorry."

Brontë's nails clicked against the hardwood floor as we walked to the pocket gallery where Friday night I'd seen the photograph of a crumbling adobe building blasted by light. The photo was still there and still compelling. A card tucked into the lower right-hand corner read "$250.00." The young man in black had followed at a courteous distance and was making a production of adjusting one of the track lights.

"I'm sure Aphid has a discount policy for collectors," I mentioned, still inspecting the framed photo.

"We discount framing," he answered. "People usually don't want the original frame."

The original frame was a matte-finish metal, black. It looked fine to me.

"How about a discount for wanting the original frame? Saves a lot of negotiating."

"Two hundred twenty-five dollars," he said.

"Two hundred."

"Two-ten if you don't want it packed in a box. You walk out with it, as is."

"Deal."

In the noon glare on University Avenue I inspected my purchase. A roadside building at sunset somewhere in a high desert. The angle of light, the *blast* of light obliterating one side of the

building as the other lay in shadow. And the signature in spidery black ink. "Greave." Something about the photo continued
to frighten me. And something about it had the sizzle of my
own screwball philosophy. Fate, God, fortune, disaster—to me
these are just flashes from some huge grid on which everything
moves at lightning speeds. I do think this grid has a sort of
consciousness, although nothing like ours. I think its nature is
irony. And I was sure the strange photograph in my hands had
significance to my life in some way I might never know.

But then again, I might.

"Come on, Brontë," I said, "we're going to a revival."

7

The Land of Oz

The police department had reserved two press passes I was to pick up at a ticket kiosk. After allowing Brontë to run in a canyon near the community college stadium where Ruby Emerald would "revive" thousands, I picked up the passes, stamped SDPD in red ink. I tucked one rakishly into the scarf on my hat. Then I looked around for BB.

He was waiting near a sign that read FACULTY PARKING ONLY, his dreadlocks hanging wild over his shoulders. Were it not for the cream-colored V-neck varsity sweater he wore over a red polo shirt and tan corduroys, I was sure he would already have been arrested on suspicion of something. Anything. Or else it was the saddle oxfords.

"Don't tell me, let me guess," I said after hugging him. "You borrowed the outfit from a wardrobe for *Bye-Bye, Birdie*."

"Blue, you so retro," he replied, smiling broadly. "Try the stage show for *Rocky Horror*. This Brad's costume. You know, the ofay dude who—"

"BB, nobody has said 'ofay' in twenty years at least."

Framed by curly lashes, his brown eyes grew wide as he did

a Mr. Bones imitation. Both hands beside his face, fingers spread wide. I had no problem imagining the white gloves.

"That's the *point*," he said. "This a college, right? White folks' revival at a college. Figured the boy-cheerleader look the only way to go."

"But *saddle oxfords*? Bet you don't have the argyles to go with them."

"Wrong," he said, tugging up a corduroy pants leg to show red, blue, and cream socks in the traditional diamond pattern.

I should have known.

"BB, tell me about revivals," I said as we moved with the crowd into the stadium.

"They all about sex," he answered.

"Huh?"

"Sure. Figured that out down in Mississippi, used to go with my grandma and my aunt."

Like many blacks with southern roots, BB pronounced "aunt" as "ahnt." It sounded oddly Victorian and formal, coming from a Bob Marley look-alike in a cheerleader costume.

"Lotta things like that," he went on. "Get a bunch a people together, start slow, and then get 'em heated up, get 'em all riled and nervous, needin' somethin', needin' that *release,* y'know? Then come the screamin' and moanin' and touchin', folks cryin' and fallin' out. Hallelujah time."

"You mean it's like an orgasm," I said as we located our aisle seats in the sixth row. Where I come from, "orgasm" is not a word used in normal conversation, or any conversation. I wondered whether my casual use of the term meant I was incredibly worldly or merely gauche.

"Yeah, big O in the head," BB agreed. "Don't nobody understand sex ain't jus' a dick thing. Sex a head thing. Oughtta see some a them revival preachers they let in prisons! Same thing. Get goin' and pretty soon see hard-core killers with they eyes rolled back, twitchin' all over for the Holy Ghost. Hey. Sex be sex. Don't always have to come from the crotch, y'know?"

"Um," I answered as we took our seats and a small orchestra onstage began to play something I would have sworn was

"Danny Boy." BB was right, of course. Also right that very few people can deal with the information.

"BB, you're smart," I told him.

"Hey," he replied, grinning and stretching his long arms in front of him, "I been knowin' that!"

The orchestra segued into an upbeat rendition of "Come, Thou Almighty King" as a choir in brightly colored robes filled risers at the back of the stage, singing. When they were all in place the colors of their robes replicated a rainbow. Then a man with big gray hair in a tight black suit jogged onstage. I could see his lapel mike and knew it ran to a power pack clipped to the back of his pants under his jacket. No mike wires. Ruby Emerald had spared no expense in equipment for her show.

"This is the day the Lord hath made, and it is BEE-YOOTI-FUL!" he yelled, extending his arms toward the sky. The upbeat message was somewhat confused by the fact that the man was weeping. At the time I just chalked his tears up to some sort of religious fervor, an assumption that would almost immediately prove false.

At his wrists I saw white French cuffs and those lumpy gold cuff links jewelers make by melting leftover snips of gold together in clumps. The crowd responded by yelling, "Yes!" Okay, crying older man in Blues Brothers suit and garish jewelry saying, in essence, "It's a nice day." So far this didn't even seem interesting, much less threatening.

"My name is J. R. Jones and I'm here to introduce you to the world God means you to *have!*"

"Yes!"

"To join you in singing his praise!"

"Yes!"

He was almost convulsed with grief now, eyes streaming, nose running.

"To bring to you, right out here on this stage, none other than *HIS* messenger with everything you need to know about God's plan for *YOUR* prosperity, the Reverend . . . Ruby . . . Emerald!"

The man jogged offstage, his shoulders heaving with what

appeared to be uncontrollable grief, as the crowd cheered happily. Then the orchestra and choir lit into "Oh, Happy Day" as a woman in a pale green robe swept onstage. Multicolored pinlights directed at her mane of blonde curls refreshed my original impression of her as a Christmas tree angel.

"God loves you," she said, revealing several thousand dollars' worth of orthodontic work in a Glinda, Good Witch of the North smile. "And God wants you to PROSPER!"

I guessed she was between forty and forty-five, from anywhere except the Deep South, and in this line of work because it beat her last job as a receptionist for a large law firm.

As the choir hummed "Amazing Grace," she raised her arms and began a prayer that seemed to touch on issues of concern to the crowd.

". . . lead us to Your kingdom . . ."

"Amen."

". . . where we enjoy the riches You have placed here for us . . ."

"Yes!"

". . . because God's people are His emissaries of pure joy and great prosperity . . ."

"AmenYesss!"

I was beginning to get the picture, and it wasn't the one I'd expected.

"BB," I whispered, "is this the sort of thing you usually hear at revivals? This prosperity business?"

"No, but don't matter," he answered. "Idea is to get folks worked up. These folks wanna get worked up over gettin' rich instead a gettin' saved. Still the same. Look at 'em."

The crowd was predominantly white, although there were noticeable groups of Latinos and Asians. All were comfortably dressed in shorts, little denim dresses, sandals, and athletic shoes. Attractive, casual Southern California people accustomed to fast food and the fast lane. I didn't see anybody who looked capable of listening to Isaiah's tale of epic destruction. They didn't want to hear about dead armies rotting in heaps as streams turned to pitch. They wanted to hear that God's plan for them included a recreational vehicle, new PC complete with Photo-Shop and digital camera, and maybe a cruise to Guam or something. They wanted to hear that it was okay to be who they were. They wanted to hear it so much their eyes were glazing over.

After a sermon about accepting blessings, it became apparent that God would be particularly generous in the bestowing of worldly treasures to those who signaled their interest by giving money to Ruby Emerald. As the singers and musicians performed a medley of religious and secular numbers made popular in movies, cheerful teenagers collected checks. Apparently there was some kind of giveaway connected to the "offering" because from time to time someone would jump up and yell, "Microwave! I won a microwave!" or "Hey, got me a camcorder!"

"Here it come," BB said after the collecting of money. "Gonna get down an' dirty now."

Even in the bright afternoon sunlight the stage became different, darker. Like the turning down of lights in a theater. You know when that happens you're heading into an altered state, something better than usual, more interesting. Something more *extreme* than your own life. Ruby Emerald's head was bowed, a single white high-intensity pinlight illuminating her hair. The choir hummed chords in C minor.

"The Lord knows you have needs," she whispered after raising her head and flinging back her hair. "The Lord *gave* you those needs."

"Yes."

"So why shouldn't you *meet* those needs and prosper?"

She was saying absolutely nothing, but the staging and music were evocative. I could feel the hair on my forearms rise as the minor humming increased in volume. From the audience an older man stood and said something nobody could hear until out of nowhere one of the teenagers appeared with a clip mike and power pack. After attaching these to the speaker, the smiling boy dropped to one knee in the aisle and listened with rapt attention as the older man delivered in Shakespearian tones a tale of accepting God and then doing really well in a real estate deal. The proceeds, carefully leveraged, had enabled him to retire and devote himself to his ailing wife. Who had always dreamed of cruising to Mexico on their own yacht . . . which they'd been able to do . . . before she died of whatever it was. Praise God.

Emerald solicited more testimonials, and got them. At least half were scripted and performed by professional actors, I realized. The scripts had all been written by the same person. A person overly fond of the word "succor," which rarely occurs in the normal speech of anybody. The rest of the testimonials seemed real and involved less dramatic tales of success and financial reward. Not one of the real ones included "succor" of any kind.

And every time somebody near the stage stood to speak, the same three men and two women would position themselves along the stage apron, crouch, and watch.

"Cops," BB said without interest.

"The children of God have a right to happiness," Emerald insisted, pacing up and down now. "The righteous receive their reward."

"Yes."

The choir was loud now, the orchestra gradually joining. First the strings, then woodwinds, then brass and percussion. People were standing, holding their arms aloft as if they expected something to drop from the sky. Emerald continued to pace and shout, but I couldn't hear her over the music and the crowd, who seemed to be chanting, "Manna," over and over.

I didn't hear the shot.

But BB did. In one motion he pulled me to the ground, stuffing my head under the seat of the folding chair in front of me. I could hear a roar from the crowd as I hit my head on the chair seat trying to get up.

"BB, dammit!" I yelled. "We're *supposed* to see what's going on here. Let me go!"

"Roxie fry my oysters in hot lard, I let her lady get hurt at some honky revival," he noted. "Look like somebody shoot the preacher."

"Oh, God, it's Sword. And BB, nobody's said 'honky' in at least fifteen years."

"Jus' stayin' in character," he said as he scouted the scene. "Look like they got the dude already."

Waving my press pass with its police franking on it above my head, I made my way to the stage apron. Ruby Emerald was lying on the boards at the edge of the portable stage, surrounded by people. To the left, one of the women cops was snapping handcuffs on a man in a tight black suit. J. R. Jones, I remembered. The emotional emcee. He'd introduced Ruby Emerald through a flood of tears. Beside him one of the male cops was holding a small-caliber handgun wrapped in his shirt-tail as he dropped it into a plastic evidence bag. The smell of cordite hung in a cloud over the scene.

There was already a doctor tending Ruby Emerald, or somebody with medical training anyway, because I could see him directing members of the choir to apply pressure to the side of Emerald's neck as he clasped her wrist and nodded.

"Good, good," he said in a husky voice. "Paramedics should be here any minute. There's a hospital five minutes away. I don't think this is fatal if we keep the pressure on that artery."

His crouched stance and calm attitude seemed military. But with his free hand he smoothed the hair from Emerald's face and tucked it in back of her ear. The gesture was loving, maternal. And revealing.

Behind Ruby Emerald's ear and running along the base of her hairline was a fading reddish purple scar. I could see stitch marks where the long incision had been sutured. At the ear the scar literally ran inside, vanishing into folds of cartilage. The medical person supervising Emerald's emergency care seemed to notice as well and ran a finger along the healing wound.

"BB, somebody's tried to kill this woman before," I said. "Tried to cut her head off or something. Did you see that scar?"

"Blue, you dumber than soap. Ain't nobody try to kill you by cuttin' the *back* of your neck. Knife just run into bone. Take a meat cleaver and a mighty strong man, get the job done. That scar ain't from nobody tryin' to hurt her, no way. Too straight and clean."

Sirens, close by. Abruptly the person supervising Emerald's care stood and walked away, vanishing into the crowd. I hadn't paid much attention to him except to note that he seemed short for a man. I remembered dark glasses and a baseball cap. It seemed strange that he'd walk off just before the paramedics arrived.

One of the female cops planted her serviceable shoes directly in my line of view and barked, "Who are you?"

"Dr. McCarron," I barked back, using an academic title rarely useful for more than getting a decent table in restaurants. "The psychologist working with Wes Rathbone on the Sword of Heaven business."

Few people understand the difference between psychology and social psychology and I didn't see any point in confusing her.

"This is Bernard Berryman, who's working with me," I went on. "What happened?"

"What Sword of Heaven business, and why is Berryman in cheerleader drag?" she asked as BB shook his dreadlocks and scowled at her.

"My associate, Dr. Bouchie, a forensic psychiatrist, and I are on your payroll as consultants," I explained. "Somebody is sending threats that seem to result in death. Ruby Emerald is on the list. But it looks like you've got our man. So who is he?"

She looked over her shoulder at the man called J. R. Jones, who was crying again. One of the male cops was trying to take a statement from him and getting nowhere.

"Says he's in love with her. Says she was leaving him," the cop explained.

"Same ole, same ole," BB said, shaking his head. "Hard-hearted woman be the death of a softhearted man."

"BB, it's not the man who just got shot here," I pointed out.

Then to the woman cop I said, "Would you radio Detective Rathbone that I'll meet him at the station? He'll want Dr. Bouchie and me there for the interrogation, I'm sure."

I wasn't sure, but I was curious.

After calling Roxie at Auntie's from a pay phone, I dropped BB off at his shop and headed for police headquarters. He'd had enough of police stations, he said. On the phone Rox had confirmed what I suspected to be the usual reason for surgical scars along ventral scalp hairlines. Rathbone was already at police headquarters when I arrived.

"This is not our man," he said, ushering me to an interrogation room where J. R. Jones was drinking coffee from a foam cup in the company of three detectives.

"I keep telling you I don't know anything about swords of heaven," he said. "I don't know what you're talking about."

There was a smell in the room, metallic and musty at the same time. I'd noticed it before in the past. In prisons. Alleys where drunks sleep in cardboard boxes. Nursing homes where nobody ever visits. The smell of despair. It was drifting from J. R. Jones.

"This is Dr. Blue McCarron," Rathbone introduced me. "She's working with us on the Sword of Heaven situation."

"I don't know anything about that," he said again. "Just leave me alone. I don't care what you do to me. My life is over. Just leave me alone."

Up close I could see that his gray hair was heavily moussed and that contact lenses accounted for the startling blue of his eyes. His jawline showed no jowls or neck paunch above the starched white of his collar, but the hand holding the coffee cup was speckled with liver spots. J. R. Jones was a lot older than he looked.

"You must have been worried last night when Ruby was in the hospital," I said. "If you're not Sword, then you wouldn't have known what happened to her."

"I didn't know," he said softly. "She was so sick, her heart pounding like a little animal's. Like a bird. I'd kill anybody who hurt her."

Jones wasn't a big man, but he took up a lot of space. Some people are like that, like what's inside them spills over the boundaries of their bodies. People who know too much are often like that. And people who feel too much. I pegged Jones for category two.

"She's a beautiful woman," I went on. "And a charismatic messenger."

Rathbone was watching me, signaling the other cops with an imperceptible shake of the head to stay out of it and let me run with this.

"She's an angel, and anyone who would harm her should be put to death," Jones said with feeling. He seemed to have forgotten that he'd just shot the aforementioned angel with a .22 handgun.

"Have you been married before?" I asked softly, as if speaking of the dead.

"Thirty-five years. My wife, Crystal . . . the boys . . . well, the boys were grown when I left, when I first met Ruby and knew I loved her. She came to Indianapolis—Indianapolis, Indiana—did a revival. That's where we lived . . . I lived. I fell for her. She's so beautiful. I've been with her for six years now. I wanted to marry her as soon as Crystal gave me the divorce. But Ruby wouldn't, and then someone else . . . I'm sure there's someone else. She was dumping me. Today was going to be my last day introducing her, and I thought maybe, you know, I could just die up there onstage. I had this gun and I was going to do it, kill myself, but I wanted her with me. I couldn't go without her."

BB was right. Revivals *are* always about sex. The too-blue eyes were crying again, and I felt like a snake. He crossed his arms on the table and lay his head on them, sobbing. End-of-the-line despair. I hated seeing it because I have some idea of how it feels. Most people do.

"I'm so sorry," I said, walking around the table to put a hand on his shoulder. And that's when I saw it. A pale, thin scar running along his hairline in back and vanishing behind his ears. It explained the tight jaw, the absence of jowls.

"You probably even helped her pick out a plastic surgeon, didn't you?" I asked. "Everybody's doing it, but it's so hard to find somebody top-notch."

I don't think I've used the term "top-notch" in my entire life, but I had a sense Jones would find it appropriate.

"Oh, yes, she went to my surgeon for that," he said, half smiling blearily as he lifted his head. "Her base of operations is right here in San Diego, and so is the surgeon. She loved the way I looked and wouldn't have gone to anyone else. She just had it done three weeks ago, too. A whole face-lift. Just in time for this tour."

Just in time for this fill-in-the-blank. Tour, campaign, election.

I remembered Kate Van Der Elst rubbing at her neck as she talked to me earlier. Remembered her little twitch when I asked if she and Dixie Ross and Mary Harriet Grossinger went to the same dentist. My bet was it wasn't a dentist.

"I've been thinking of having a mole removed from my neck," I told J. R. Jones. "I'd love it if you'd give me the name of your surgeon."

"Rainer," he answered. "Dr. Jennings Rainer at the Rainer Clinic. They're top-notch. Everybody at Rainer is top-notch."

"Wes," I said to Rathbone in the hall, "I'm not sure, but I think I know where to find the Sword of Heaven."

8

Those Turkey Neck Blues

Rathbone and I agreed to meet at Auntie's, where Rox's line-dance team would be finishing rehearsal by the time we arrived. At this point, Rathbone said, the opinions of a forensic psychiatrist became critical. Not that my assessments leading to this point hadn't been brilliant, he hastened to add. But if I was right, the police would need special guidelines for continuing the investigation. Because it didn't look like any serial killer the police had seen before. It didn't even look like *anything* the police had seen before. He wanted Roxie's opinion before taking the next step.

When Brontë and I arrived he was already there, and if he felt the slightest discomfort at being in a gay bar, he didn't show it.

"Hey," he said, leaning comfortably on the rail surrounding Auntie's dance floor, "they're pretty good!"

Rox and the team were concluding a tricky routine that combined elements of both the tango and traditional square dancing. The choreography was Rox's creation, and I knew she had an eye on first prize at a big rodeo line-dance competition in

New Mexico right after Christmas. Her fringed satin blouse was drenched with sweat and all two hundred of her beaded braids flew out from her head as she executed the stomps and turns of the dance.

I thought she looked like magic out there under a strobing gold light. An image of everything bright and lively and warm. Her cowboy boots didn't miss a step when she saw me and smiled. I, on the other hand, managed to trip while standing perfectly still and wound up sitting on a stool I'd never intended to sit on. Sometimes just looking at Roxie causes me to lose track of basic things. Like maintaining sufficient muscle tension in my legs to keep from falling over.

Rathbone grinned.

"I get that way around Annie sometimes," he said. "It's ridiculous, but it keeps me from getting all wrapped up any more in the crap at work. I'm lucky."

"Um," I answered, embarrassed. "How long have you and Annie been married?"

"Almost a year. Surprised? Thought I was gonna say 'since high school' or something, didn't you?"

He seemed pleased with himself. I sensed a squadron of insights flying my way.

"Well, yeah."

"This thing with Annie, it changed the inside of my head. Used to be, I thought everything had to be one way. Cops are like that. But with Annie, well, she just loosened me up."

"That's great," I said, hoping not to hear more. "Looks like the rehearsal's over. Rox will join us just as soon as she changes her blouse. Do you two-step?"

I wouldn't have asked, but somebody had just put Mary Chapin Carpenter's "Down at the Twist and Shout" on the CD player. Impossible to sit still. There weren't many people around at dinnertime on a Sunday, but everybody who *was* there was on the floor.

"No, but I'm game to learn."

So while Roxie changed her sweaty blouse I led Wes Rathbone onto the dance floor and showed him how to do the simple steps shadow-style, both of us facing the same way. He caught on instantly and before the second chorus was able to lead from the traditional stance as well. By the song's end he was trying spins. Rox had changed to a pumpkin-colored sweatshirt and was watching from a table where she'd ordered iced tea for everybody.

"You're a natural," she told Rathbone when we joined her. "You'd be great for the line-dance team."

I was afraid he was going to say something like, *Aw, shucks, ma'am,* but instead he asked Rox if the invitation included his wife.

"Sure, if she's got half the moves you do," Roxie answered.

"More," he said. "Annie was a professional dancer when she was young, before her first marriage. Ballet. She's gonna love this! Let me give her a call, get her down here."

As he loped off toward Auntie's pay phone Rox looked at me over her tea and rattled her beads. The sound was questioning.

"So tell me what happened today," she said.

"You annihilate my equilibrium," I answered calmly. "And now you want to sit here and talk to a cop about serial killers. Is it just me, or is there something odd about this picture?"

"There's a lot odd about this picture, which is why it's interesting. What happened?"

"The preacher's boyfriend shot her because he loves her," I said.

"One way of handling it," Rox said thoughtfully as Rathbone returned and straddled a chair.

"Annie's on her way, can't wait to check this out," he said happily. Then to me, "This is what I meant, Blue. Annie 'n' me. She taught me never to pass up a chance, especially a chance for fun. World's full of mean people who put fun last, that's what she says. And you know, it's true."

I was beginning to think of Wes Rathbone as a New Age guru behind a badge. It was confusing.

"You wanted to talk about this case?" Roxie suggested. Down-to-business look.

"Both Jerry Russell Jones, the shooter in today's incident at the revival, and the victim, Ruby Emerald, have been patients at the Rainer Clinic, which specializes in cosmetic surgery," Rathbone replied happily, as if we were still talking about fun. "Emerald was the subject of one of Sword of Heaven's communications, an audiotape in which Sword took credit for Emerald's death even though in fact she did not die. Nor, by the way, is she dead now. Jones shot her in the left shoulder, smashed a bone. She'll be fine. And Jones claims not to know anything about the Sword communications."

"Wait a minute," Roxie said. "This Jones has just attempted murder in front of more than ten thousand people, right? This does not say 'reliable witness' to me. This says emotional lability, inflated sense of own importance, irrational need for attention, and to greater or lesser extents a break with consensual reality. Who here doesn't know that if you shoot an unarmed person in the presence of witnesses you're in deep okra? Get real, Wes. Just because Jones says he's not Sword doesn't mean he's not Sword."

Rathbone's easygoing smile did not diminish. "For the moment let's assume Jones shot Emerald because she was dumping him, just like he said. Let's assume he's not the sharpest tool in the shed, just an old guy who fell head-over-heels for a younger woman, left his wife of thirty-five years for her, followed her all over the country, and then she told him he was history."

I was curious. "How old *is* Jones?" I asked.

"Seventy-four."

"You're *kidding*! I would have figured early sixties, tops."

"Hey, he wanted to look good for his lady. Worked out, ate right, even had his face done. Hell, I might just do it myself one of these days. Why not?"

"Only vampires don't age," Rox said cryptically. "So where is this going?"

Rathbone leaned into the table and looked at me. "Blue has a notion that Kate Van Der Elst may also have had cosmetic surgery," he went on. "We don't know that yet, but for the moment let's consider the possibility. We do know that a threat was left at her campaign headquarters last night. Suppose Van Der Elst had a face-lift at this Rainer Clinic. Same place Jones and Emerald did. What have we got?"

"Three people who can't stop smiling?" Roxie offered.

"We have the first connection between two threats," I told her. "A common denominator."

"And you want me to do what?" she asked Rathbone. "Provide a typical psychiatric profile for serial killer cosmetic surgeons? Come *on*."

There are times when hard science and social science clash. This was one of them.

"I'll be right back," I said. Then I walked toward the ladies' room and detoured to the pay phone as soon as I was out of sight. After finding thirty-five cents I dialed the Van Der Elsts' home number and heard Pieter's voice answer. I'd correctly assumed they'd be at home on Sunday night, and I didn't mince words.

"It's Blue McCarron," I began. "I need to know if Kate has had any contact with a surgeon named Jennings Rainer."

His sharp intake of breath was a dead giveaway. "Why?" he said.

"Pieter, don't play games with me. This morning you wanted Kate to withdraw from the race because you were so afraid for her. You wanted to hire a bodyguard. A threat to her life was pushed under the door of her campaign headquarters. And now you're being coy about a face-lift? What's the matter with you?"

"I'd better get Kate," was all he said.

"Level with me," I told her as soon as she picked up the phone. "Ruby Emerald was targeted by the same person who named Dixie and Mary Harriet as victims before they died. Emerald had surgery at the Rainer Clinic three weeks ago. Did you?"

"Yes," Kate Van Der Elst said, her voice tremulous. "So did Dixie and Mary Harriet. Mary Harriet had gone to this place first, years ago. She told Dixie about it when she went back recently for an eye tuck, then Dixie and I talked it over for a long time and decided to do it together, have this . . . procedure done before the campaign crunch. It was a couple of weeks ago."

I felt a little dizzy, leaning against the wall by Auntie's pay phone. Also a little sick. Medical contexts—hospitals, ambulances, dentists' offices, even veterinary clinics—must engender trust. In these places we allow strangers a license unthinkable anywhere else in our lives. Medical personnel make mistakes, but rarely does any medical practitioner deliberately inflict harm. It just doesn't happen. And when it does, the perpetrator invariably reveals a darkness in the human soul best left unseen.

"Oh, Kate, why didn't you tell me this morning when I asked about places the three of you had been?"

"It isn't something you talk about, Blue. It's embarrassing, some people would even say shameful, to care so much about superficial appearance that you'll let someone cut your face off your skull and then sew it back on. But I was going to tell you if this . . . this *creature* sending all these threats wasn't found. Pieter and I talked it over. I was going to phone you Monday, tomorrow. But Blue, tell me . . ."

"What, Kate?"

"This Ruby Emerald, is she all right?"

I didn't want to confuse the issue by discussing Emerald's drama involving an aging lover and a gun.

"She's going to be fine," I hedged. "I'll want to talk with you tomorrow, and so will the police. We still know very little, but you've been helpful. Thank you."

Roxie and Rathbone were dancing when I got back to the table, where Brontë was wagging her stub of a tail and smiling at people as they returned from the bar with bowls of popcorn. My dog's priorities are clear.

And so were Kate Van Der Elst's, I thought. Southern California isn't the Hollywood hypeland everyone thinks it is. But neither are its cultural leanings characterized by stoic acceptance. Of anything. If there is a cultural mantra here, it's "Why hasn't that been fixed?"

Floods, earthquakes, fires, and mudslides regularly disrupt landscapes which within a year are rebuilt, replanted, and redefined.

The Southern California mind accepts the inevitability of disaster and death with a complacency almost Zen in its tone. The companion to such acceptance, however, is a fondness for beauty while we're still around to enjoy it. Freeway medians are planted with pink and white oleander. Streets are swept, houses painted, art purchased. An unattractive receptacle wheeled to the curb on trash day is a blight and must be replaced. The same goes for unattractive bags under the eyes or those drooping folds of skin at the neck. Why not have it all fixed? And who would vote for somebody who didn't?

"Kate Van Der Elst, Dixie Ross, and Mary Harriet Grossinger all had cosmetic surgery at the Rainer Clinic," I said when Roxie and Wes Rathbone returned from the dance floor. "I just talked to Kate."

"Hmm," he replied. "I did check out the Rainer Clinic Web site after what you told me at the station earlier. There are two surgeons—Jennings Rainer and Megan Rainer. From the photos on the Web site, I'd guess father and daughter. Pretty amazing all the stuff they can do."

A slight flush had crept up his neck and into his sandy hair at that last remark. Roxie grinned in a manner I can only describe as diabolical and said, "Yep, laser phalloplasty's the latest rage. Any good pictures on that Web site?"

Wes Rathbone's craggy cheeks were now bright pink. He looked like an aging English schoolboy.

"Phalloplasty?" I said. "Does that mean what it sounds like it means?"

At some point in my life I had learned that the correct term for a nose job is "rhinoplasty" because "rhino" is a Greek prefix meaning "nose." "Phallos" is also Greek, the end later Latinized to "us," and means the symbolic erect penis carried in ancient Greek festivals honoring the god Dionysos. "Phalloplasty" would have to mean a penis job.

"Penile enhancement," Rox said. "Longer, thicker, straighter. It's a gold mine, a total cash cow. Half the dermatologists I know are taking out loans to go back to med school, get a degree in cosmetic surgery just so they can do dick enhancements.

I've thought of it myself. It's such a moneymaker I could retire after two years."

"I couldn't believe it," Rathbone said. "Showed the Web site to a couple guys, they couldn't believe it."

"Hey, it's one of the biggest markets for cadaver skin around," Roxie said cheerfully. "So. what else did you get on this clinic?"

"An address in La Jolla," Rathbone answered after swallowing several times. "Tomorrow we'll have everything—an employee roster, bios on everybody who works there. Not enough evidence to bring Jennings in for questioning, or I would've done it. All we really have are threats."

"And two dead women," Roxie pointed out. "A third woman hospitalized for symptoms which may reflect a condition similar to the one that killed the first two. And a fourth woman in seemingly good health who has also received a death threat. Two dead, two alive, all threatened, and all patients at the Rainer Clinic. Seems like enough for a few questions."

"Not yet," Rathbone insisted. "Not until we have some guidelines for the investigation. That's where you come in. Dr. Bouchie, what are we dealing with here?"

"Could be coincidence, probably isn't. Could be somebody connected to the clinic, somebody with access to medical files on these women. Somebody aware of a preexisting condition in each of them that might be fatal, although that's an impossible stretch. This person wants the promised fifteen minutes of fame and goes after it by making dramatic public threats against high-profile women who are for some reason likely to die of natural causes anyway. Weird, but scarcely murder."

Rathbone stretched his legs and said, "Is that what you think is going on?"

Rox sat up straight, looking serious. "No, it's not what's going on, so I'm going to tell you what to look for. *If* there's a serial killer operating out of the Rainer Clinic, this is going to be one for the books. The Holmes typology breaks serial killers into 'organized' and 'disorganized,' which is rather obvious but makes a useful starting point. This person falls in the 'organized' category, holds down a professional job, is bright, educated, reads newspapers, has an adequate social life. In other words, there will be no flashing neon signs saying 'perp.'

"Your cops may be intimidated by the context at the clinic, the aura of wealth which is likely to surround it. They may also be snowed by the clinic staff, who will wear the same aura. The poor do not have cosmetic surgery, and the rich are most comfortable in medical surroundings which suggest that their doctors are also rich. The surface behaviors there are very likely to mask any pathology present in one of the employees. Have your detectives interview the Rainer employees someplace else, preferably places where the suspects feel out of place and uncomfortable.

"And there's no point in pretending the investigation is about something else. This person *wants* attention and will be excited by it. But tactically, the best way to elicit a revealing response is to go into elaborate detail about something only the perp knows is *wrong*. Refer to 'Heavenly Sword' instead of 'Sword of Heaven' repeatedly, for example. The author of that phrase may slip and correct it, and bingo, you've got a suspect.

"My guess is your suspect maintains enormous control and has for a long time. Probably feels a sense of pride in that. He or she thinks, 'You idiots don't have any idea of the terrible things I would have done if I didn't have such self-control.' The thing to do is attack that by constant references to weakness, impulsivity, childishness. Have your detectives say things like, 'Whoever did this is pathetic. Whoever it is, he or she is like a baby. An out-of-control brat.' At another time have somebody show cloying pity, which this person will hate. You get the picture?"

"Perp's a control freak. Insult him. Right?"

"Remember, 'he' may be a 'she,'" Roxie warned.

"Nah," Rathbone argued as a stocky woman in jeans and an embroidered pink denim shirt approached. Her blonde hair was short, curly, and shot through with gray, and she had the most beautiful skin I've ever seen. Also the most beautiful smile.

"Here I am!" she said to all of us, and I realized this was

Annie. Wes Rathbone's Annie, who had shown him the light. I could see it myself. She glowed.

It turned out to be a great evening. Before the place got crowded Rox taught Wes and Annie some variations on the two-step and a line dance called Whiskey River. Then BB and the radical preacher, whose name was Matt, showed up and we all went across the street to a Greek restaurant, leaving Brontë outside on a patio where she could see us and I could slip her bits of moussaka through the sliding glass door.

But in the back of my mind something nagged. Something about dancing and eating dinner as if nothing were wrong. When something *was* wrong. Something hidden in a fold of our own reality, our city. Something unseen except for its anger displayed in untraceable letters. I stabbed the last piece of cooling *saganaki* with my fork and wondered where the Sword of Heaven was at that moment. Not relaxing over dinner and conversation somewhere, I thought. Probably crouched in an attic hideaway, snipping at newspapers with surgical scissors that reflected the light of a naked bulb above. It was a movie image, and a first false step in a game of cat and mouse I didn't yet know I was playing. Although I would know. Soon. I would know in less than twelve hours that the mouse was me.

9

Blue Plates

On Monday morning I woke up just as a yellow-gray dawn began its urban seep through Roxie's blinds. I'm used to dramatic desert light, its sharp shadows and sudden illuminations. City light seems tepid by comparison. But this light had my attention. It had me awake. Only me, however.

Curling against Roxie, I nuzzled her ear and allowed my fingers a tentative slide down her arm.

"Mmmp," she said pleasantly.

There was no change in the rhythm of her breathing. No response. She was still asleep and clearly planned to stay that way. Brontë was draped across a rumpled silk patchwork coverlet at the foot of the bed, creating a sort of Chinese-style panorama which would have been called "Black Dog" during the South Sung Dynasty. I amused myself by mentally writing pretentious museum-pamphlet text about Taoist representations of the Doberman as an allegory for inner harmony. It was fun even though Dobies weren't bred until the nineteenth century in Germany, which would have made them *really* scarce in tenth century China. Then I got up.

I padded into Roxie's den and turned on her computer. There was nothing else to do that wouldn't wake everybody up. Coffee would have to wait. On the Internet I punched in the password ("dober1," what else?) which allows me to pick up my e-mail from anywhere. I was expecting dad's usual morning letter, which was there, but so was something else. A strange address in the boldface menu of new mail. Monday's date. Sent less than an hour before I turned on Roxie's computer. "Godsword@bluebay.com," it read. God's word? Or God sword? Bluebay was a local server used by all the Net cafés and public computers all over town. "Godsword" could have sent this message from anywhere and there would be no way to trace it. My hand was cold as I clicked on the address and watched. On the screen emerged two lines of text and a signature.

"Blue is no womens name and you will be sorry you have don this when van der else dye sun," it said. It was signed, "The Sword of Heaven."

"Roxie! " I yelled, abandoning all sympathy for those who slept. "Look at this!"

In the moments before Rox's den was filled with other presences, human and canine, I watched myself make a fist at the computer monitor.

"You don't know who you're messing with, you ignorant shit!" I whispered, every synapse thrumming in an adrenaline bath. I do not respond well to threats, and while I'll deny it, I'm territorial. Most women are. Like most women, I'm territorial about things I care about. And something had just violated a boundary, the borders of a space around Roxie Bouchie. Something had come into her home, even though it was meant for my home. Something ill-intentioned and murderous. I was disturbed by an awareness that if it came too close to Roxie or even Brontë, I might want to kill it.

"Blue, you're hyperventilating," she said at the door to her den. "What is it?"

"Look."

Rox had wrapped the silk patchwork coverlet around her shoulders and looked like a Gustav Klimt painting. She grimaced.

"Oh God, there goes breakfast. Blue, this is impossible. How could Sword know you were working on the case? Or get your e-mail address?"

"I don't know."

Something else about the message had captured my attention. Buttons. Little circles used in creating Web pages, you can download them free from hundreds of Web sites featuring buttons, bars, and background screen designs called wallpaper. Bars and buttons are just designators for where you click a mouse to go somewhere else in the Web page or to links to other sites. There must be thousands available in every color and texture, some of which look like actual buttons. The message before me had two buttons, one preceding each line. I clicked on them and nothing happened. They didn't go anywhere, but were merely decorative. They were also unusual.

Roxie has a real nine-to-five job as staff psychiatrist at a local state prison, after which she also maintains a private practice from an office she shares with another psychiatrist who's only there during the day. As a result, she hasn't spent the hours I have cruising around the Internet for no particular reason. I was sure she wouldn't grasp the significance of the buttons.

"Have you ever seen anything like this?" I asked.

"Like what?"

"These buttons."

"I've never seen them in e-mails," she said, catching something I'd missed.

There are no buttons in e-mail programs. To get them there would require work—a customized message. Sword was no novice with computers.

"Good point," I said, "but look at them closely. See?"

"They're plates. Little blue and white plates."

And they were. They were, in fact, photographs of ordinary dinner plates in a pattern called blue willow. The skill necessary to scan, tint, and size a photo and then file it to an e-mail program as a button was impressive. But why bother? Hours of work for what? So a threatening letter riddled with misspellings would look good? There was something peculiar about that, I thought, something ominous.

I made color duplicates of the letter on Roxie's printer, then forwarded it to Wes Rathbone's e-mail address at police headquarters with a note explaining exactly when I'd received it and how. Then I took Brontë out while Rox made coffee. When I got back we looked at the letter.

"Well, the concern over gender issues is consistent," Rox began. "It may even be escalating. Your name was apparently confusing. 'Blue' as a name is not a gender marker. Could be a male or a female. Not knowing seems to have caused some anxiety. I'm leaning toward male here, Blue. I think Sword is a man."

I inhaled the steam from my coffee as Brontë noisily crunched kibble from a bowl on Roxie's kitchen floor. I thought about the use of blue willow plates as buttons on a computer screen. Buttons that went nowhere but were just there.

"Because women don't typically experience anxiety over gender, right?" I asked.

"You rarely see pathological conditions in women related to it," Rox said, yawning. "Sure, there are a few female-to-male transsexuals, and women who simply prefer for any number of reasons to dress in men's clothing or even live as men. These women may be conflicted about gender, but not pathologically so. They know what they are. Menstruation is an inescapable reminder.

"But this is different," she went on. "Sword is made so anxious by gender ambiguity that it feels life-threatening. Unless a balance is restored, unless all references to gender fit into rigid categories, some kind of meltdown will occur. That's probably how it feels. Sword is nearly out of control with anxiety over this, trying to maintain equilibrium by single-handedly restoring the balance, the rigid gender categories. It would seem that this involves threatening or even killing women who have strayed beyond those categories. What I don't understand is how Sword knew you were working on the case."

I heard the thump of Roxie's newspaper hitting the door of

her condo. Then lesser thumps as more papers hit subsequent doors.

"You're working on the case, too," I said. "Maybe you got the same message."

I retrieved the day's news as Rox went to check her e-mail.

"Nothing," she said when I returned with the paper in its plastic bag. "I don't get it. Why are you the target? And how did Sword get your e-mail address?"

"It's not that difficult. All the servers maintain directories, listings of subscribers under their real names. There are ways of protecting identity—all kinds of Web services through which you can send e-mail anonymously or even have your own Web page without anybody being able to find out who you are. I didn't do that, although from the e-mail address I'd guess Sword did."

"Anybody could find my e-mail address in five minutes," I continued. "What I don't understand is how Sword knows I'm working on this thing."

"Maybe he works for the paper. Look." She'd unfolded the paper to the front page.

"Police Investigate Revivalist Threat," an article header told us. CBS had lost no time in disseminating news of the Bugs Bunny tape, but there was no mention of the previous letter threatening Grossinger and Ross or the green note pushed under the door of Kate Van Der Elst's campaign headquarters. I assumed that was because the police, while not hesitating to reference in an interview "forensic consultants Dr. Roxanne Bouchie and Dr. Emily 'Blue' McCarron, retained to profile the offender," had wisely chosen not to provide Sword any more publicity.

"He got your name from the paper," Roxie said. "And mine, although I don't seem to bother him."

"Roxanne is a woman's name," I pointed out. "No gender ambiguity to rile him up."

"Or else he's white."

"White?"

Roxie shook her head. "As in Caucasian, honey. You know, folks who sunburn? They have hobbies like owning plantations and naming their children for plants that grow in the Scottish highlands. Our boy isn't interested in me because I'm black. I could walk right up to him in a tux and introduce myself as Steven Spielberg and he wouldn't notice. Only the behavior of his own, of people with whom he identifies, is of interest to him."

"Three things," I said. "First, there's no way he could know you're black. Second, the e-mail was sent an hour and a half ago. It was still the middle of the night. The paper wasn't available yet."

"And third?"

"I sold the plantation in a leveraged buyout *weeks* ago, right after I legally changed my name from *Calluna vulgaris,* commonly known as heather, to the more serviceable 'Blue.' Rox, sometimes your racial jibes make me feel . . . I don't know, like you think I'd run out and buy a slave if I could find one on sale."

"Girl," she said in that way she knows is a guarantee of my total attention, "he could have read the paper on-line before it hit the streets and looked me up under the American Psychiatric Association membership roster for San Diego, found out I work at a state prison, and gotten the info off any of several different sites. Remember, I'm a government employee. Government agencies have to prove they don't discriminate on the basis of race, so everybody's race is documented in personnel data, which is all on the Internet. And I was just joking about the plantation. Sometimes I forget you aren't black."

It was hard to reply through the braids falling across my face as she hugged me, but I felt compelled to make a point.

"Nobody ever mentions that black plantation owners in the South *also* bought and sold black slaves," I lectured into braids. "Greed and cruelty are options for everybody."

"Good point," she said as she glanced at the kitchen clock. "Gotta handle an ethnic crisis this morning," she yelled after dashing to the shower. "Need to be there early. The Latino prisoners want to have a memorial service for some bullfighter who finally got gored to death in Tijuana last week. The guy was a kind of cultural icon to them. You know, *muy macho.* An artist, too. He painted pictures in the blood of the bulls he tortured and killed. Blue . . . ?"

I sensed a warning in the interrogatory use of my name.

"I won't," I said.

"Don't go anywhere near the Rainer Clinic today. Let the police do it and funnel information to us for analysis. That's our job. You hear me?"

"Huh?" I yelled back.

After Roxie had left, Brontë and I headed straight for my truck and drove to the coastal San Diego community called La Jolla, which is pronounced "La Hoya" and means "the jewel" in Spanish. Once an idyllic resort community favored during winter months by such East Coast luminaries as Ulysses S. Grant and the author Helen Hunt Jackson, La Jolla later became a magnet for movie stars who wanted someplace quiet in which to purchase weekend homes. Now it's the densely packed pinnacle of an area called the "golden triangle," and not for no reason. The village's rambling old streets are crammed with upscale shops, and a triangle of new office buildings, hotels, and shopping centers expands east toward its base at an inland freeway. Among those office buildings are numerous medical clinics, some of them featuring cosmetic surgery.

I had no intention of going *in* to the Rainer Clinic. In fact, my original plan had been merely to run Brontë along La Jolla's famous Coast Walk, a path through wind-bent juniper and sea spray along the spectacular edge of the continent. And I did. Then I found the clinic's address in a shell shop phone book and drove by. It was a new black-glass-and-steel monolith housing hundreds of discrete endeavors, none of which was obvious from the outside. I couldn't stand it. And I thought my long black dress and sandals were the sort of thing one would wear while popping into the offices of the place where Kate Van Der Elst had allowed her face to be, as she described it, cut loose from her skull.

The Rainer Clinic was on the ground floor of the building. The reason for this selection became apparent to me as I stood in the parking lot. From ambulance-bay doors emerged a young man with a thick bandage over his nose secured by gauze strips about his head. With him was an older woman who led him toward a tan Mercedes. The young man, really a teenager, seemed groggy. Then he doubled over to vomit beside the car.

"It's all right, Ian," the older woman said. "It's from the anesthesia. Let's just get you home, and you can use one of those suppositories Dr. Rainer gave you to control the nausea. You're fine, honey."

"Mo-om!" came the woozy response. "Don't talk about *suppositories*!"

Mother and son, I deduced. Rhinoplasty. The young man was being groomed for college and the marriage market. A Roman nose can be such a help.

Skirting the ambulance-bay doors, I entered the building's lobby from the front and looked around. Typical lobby. Black marble floor, textured walls, enormous flower arrangement on circular white marble table dead-center. The left rear door of four bore a brushed brass plate which read RAINER CLINIC. Pushing it open, I entered what seemed to be a small art museum.

Modern art. Minimalist in the reception area, but slightly more daring in two anterooms flanking a black marble counter. The carpet was gunmetal-gray and so thickly voluptuous it was like walking on a cat. An aquarium beneath a painting of black sticks on a background of white contained no fish, but a school of flat metal ovals that moved through the water in patterns determined by an almost invisible magnet on a clear plastic wire. The furniture was all black leather brightened by very thin pillows in shades of red chenille.

"May I help you?" asked an attractive woman behind the counter.

She appeared to be in her late twenties and was flawless. Porcelain skin, gleaming dark hair fashionably cut, pouty lips that whispered the word "collagen." Her suit, I noticed, was similar to the one I'd bought for Kate's fundraiser. Except hers was all black, the better to emphasize those deep red lips.

"Um, my husband has an appointment with an attorney on the seventh floor, going to be there for hours, I'm afraid, and the other car's in the shop, so I dropped him off and was going to go shopping but . . ." I said, mucking through my purse for the parking stub, "I forgot to have them validate my parking ticket and I was hoping you'd . . ."

"No problem," she said, smiling redly as she leaned to reach for the parking stamp beneath the counter.

Behind her I could see several glassed-in cubicles, each with what looked like a white Naugahyde dentist's chair. Also visible were stainless steel sinks and waste receptacles. Trays of surgical instruments. Oxygen tanks against a wall.

A woman in green surgical scrubs exited one of the cubicles, pulling a sterile mask from her face. About five-four, I guessed, ruddy and wholesome-looking. Cub Scout den-mother type. Wisps of straight, dust-colored hair drifted from the edges of her sterile green head covering. There was blood on the front of her scrub shirt. Megan Rainer, I thought. The daughter.

"I'll be meeting Chris for an early lunch at Samson's," she told the receptionist. "Think you can hold down the fort for an hour?"

"Only if Mrs. Austin doesn't show up," the receptionist answered, bringing a laugh from the woman in scrubs. "Dr. Rainer, I don't know how you keep from killing that woman, she's such a pain in the—"

At that point the receptionist remembered I was present and briskly stamped my parking ticket. Her look made it clear that I had no further business there, but I pretended to be searching for my keys as two men in scrubs identical to Megan Rainer's opened a cubicle door. On the reclining white chair inside I saw a woman in knit slacks and a blouse that buttoned up the front. She didn't move, and her entire head was wrapped in thick gauze bandages except for openings at the nose and mouth. Even her eyes were covered.

"Bettina will be ready to go in about twenty minutes, Mr. Ashe," I heard Megan Rainer say in another waiting room around a corner behind the counter. A door to this area stood slightly ajar to my right.

"She'll be woozy and will want to sleep as soon as she gets home. She'll probably sleep straight through until tomorrow morning once the nausea's controlled. We'll send some suppositories for that home with her, as well as antibiotics. Just help her through those double doors and out into the parking lot. It's not visible from the street. Nobody will see."

The name, Bettina Ashe, was familiar, but I couldn't place it.

"I'll just duck out this way," I told the receptionist, who nodded absently. I had ceased to exist in her mind, which was convenient. The closed waiting room, meant for those who would transport patients home after surgery, was also artfully decorated. In blue.

A lush quilt in shades of blue velvet, maroon satin, and gold lamé covered one wall, illuminated by gallery lights. On the opposite wall was an unusual collection. Plates. An antique blue willow design, a terra-cotta under an exquisite glaze the color of midnight. A Grecian key design in a mosaic of teal and sapphire bits of glass. A plate made of inlaid wood like a Chinese puzzle, every other piece a shade of blue.

I exited through the double ambulance doors to the parking lot without attracting further attention, blue circles haunting my field of vision.

10

The Cheese Blintz Connection

I was dying to get out of that black dress, but I knew once I got home I wouldn't drive back over the mountains into San Diego. And there was much to be done before I could afford the luxury of a swim in my pool. After stopping again to call Rathbone from a pay phone I began to see the value in having a cell phone.

"Did you get the employee roster and bios for the Rainer Clinic?" I asked.

"On my desk," he said. "Haven't had a chance to look at them. Where are you? I can fax them to you right now."

"I'm in a 7-Eleven parking lot in La Jolla where three Pacific Bell workers in a truck are blasting their radio so loud I can't hear you. Kenny Rogers's 'Ruby.' I'm going to buy a cell phone even though I think they're pretentious."

"Annie got one and loves it," he noted. "So where should I fax this file?"

"I'll just drive downtown and get it, Wes. Have there been any more threats?"

"Not that we know of. I'm on my way to the Rainer Clinic

right now. This thing isn't a high priority with the department as of last night, Blue. After this morning I'm not going to be able to spend much time on it. Threats are a dime a dozen, but with the newspaper coverage on the Emerald tape today we're under some pressure to investigate. Truth is, until we have some evidence that this guy's really killing people, he just goes in the kook file. I know you think the deaths of Grossinger and Ross weren't natural, but there's no medical evidence to support that. All we have is one letter and a tape that sounds like Bugs Bunny. I can't justify—"

"What do you mean, 'one letter'?" I interrupted. "What about the one on green paper shoved under Kate Van Der Elst's office door? Are you counting that one?"

"It's in a separate file," he explained. "Lab test showed the glue used wasn't the same as the glue in the first Sword letter. That was Super Glue and the green letter was Elmer's."

"So?"

"So they're not from the same guy. Van Der Elst's letter was probably just some local, like her husband said."

"You deduced this from *glue*?" I asked. It seemed silly. Most people keep more than one kind of glue around.

"Blue, there was a shoot-out just this side of Tijuana early this morning and a border agent was seriously injured. Looks like he's gonna make it, but he may never walk again. The perp fled into San Diego. We've got every available officer working on it. This letter-threat thing, it's just a minor felony—Section 422 of the California Penal Code, 'Threats to Commit Crime Resulting in Death or Great Bodily Injury.' A first offender would walk away with a few weeks of community service. We just don't have the manpower for a thorough investigation. But you and Roxie are still on the payroll. I agree with you that there's more going on here than meets the eye. Do what you can."

"Wes, what hospital is Ruby Emerald in?"

"Mercy."

After hanging up I headed toward the shopping center where the restaurant called Samson's is located, the restaurant where

Dr. Megan Rainer had told a receptionist she would meet someone named Chris for lunch.

The place was already filling up when I got there, and individual people are never popular with waiters during busy times.
I was escorted to a small booth for two in the main room and
handed a menu with the unstated expectation that I'd order
something simple and then leave. From my vantage point I could
see the entrance, and it wasn't long before Megan Rainer arrived with a thickly built man in jeans and a blue shirt. He wore
little round glasses and his frizzy dark brown hair hung in a
heavy braid down his back. Megan was speaking about something with great enthusiasm, but his eyes kept straying to the
menu he'd grabbed from a bin. They wore matching wedding
rings.

"I'll have a cheese blintz and coffee," I told the waiter as
Megan and what was obviously her husband were seated in a
booth diagonally across the aisle from mine. He faced in my
direction, and I could hear parts of his half of the conversation.
Things like, "Corned beef looks good" and "Love their matzo
ball soup, but I think I'll go with the Reuben." I wondered why
it is that TV sleuths in this position always stalk suspects who
graciously discuss their crimes over lunch. "Have you tried the
Caesar? And by the way, I hid the *real* emerald pendant in the
casket lining beside the false birth certificate. Maybe we should
split a dessert?"

I nursed my cheese blintz long enough to learn a few things,
though. For example, Josh, apparently their son, was going on
a school field trip to the Scripps Aquarium and wanted to take
his camera. This was a problem because the school had a rule
against children taking easily lost or stolen items on field trips.
It made sense to me.

It also became clear that something was wrong with their
dishwasher and some daffodil bulbs had been planted that nobody expected to grow. Megan Rainer and her husband laughed
a lot. More than once I saw her touch his hand on the table.
The only dissension involved something to which he kept saying things like, "It's only two more years, hon. We planned it

this way" and "Come on, you can do it!" After these remarks I could see Megan Rainer's right hand curl to a fist around the handle of her fork. Then she'd wave the fork around while saying things I couldn't hear. But I'd learned a little. Like, Megan Rainer and her husband, Chris, got along. They were concerned about their children's activities. And they had some sort of agreement which meant Megan had to do something for two more years because they'd planned it that way.

I would have eaten lunch anyway, I told myself. The time hadn't been a total waste.

After giving Brontë a saved sliver of blintz, I got on I-5 heading south toward the Hillcrest area of San Diego. Two sprawling medical complexes, the University of Southern California Medical Center and Mercy Hospital, contribute to Hillcrest's patchwork ambience. A single block boasts two sushi bars, a body-piercing shop, three narrow bookstores specializing in cookbooks, used medical texts, and Russian erotic art, respectively, a landmark deli, and an abandoned movie theater under whose marquee the homeless now sit on folded sleeping bags.

Some of the local merchants keep cans of dog food under their counters for the pets of the homeless population. Donations for this dog food are provided by Hillcrest's shoppers, who include highly paid personnel from both hospitals. There is no shortage of dog food in Hillcrest, a fact which says something about the nature of complex human societies, although I'm not sure what. I found a parking spot on the street in front of the theater and promised Brontë I'd be back within half an hour. Then I walked up to Mercy Hospital and asked at the information desk for Ruby Emerald's room number.

Mercy is a Catholic hospital, and although wimpled nursing nuns in starched habits are a thing of the past, Mercy has compensated for the loss with an abundance of crucifixes. They're everywhere. Brass and oak crucifix over a water fountain. Abstract stone and brushed-steel crucifix between rows of framed photos of hospital benefactors, all of whom look like corporate executives, which they are. The crucifix over Ruby Emerald's bed was sixties modern, aluminum and black wood. Ruby was reading the *Wall Street Journal* and humming "Don't Fall in Love with a Dreamer" with the radio when I walked in. Kenny Rogers again. I fought an urge to sing along.

"My name is Dr. Blue McCarron," I said, quickly adding, "I'm a social psychologist."

Ruby Emerald merely smiled brightly from her hospital bed and said, "I think you must be in the wrong room."

"No, I don't work here," I explained as she adjusted the position of her awkwardly splinted left arm. It was propped upward at an angle to her body, making her look as if she were hailing a cab. "I'm working with the police."

"Yes?"

"You know about the taped threat regarding you. I'm working on that investigation."

"I read about it in the paper is all," she said. "They called it the Bugs Bunny Caper! I don't think it means much of anything. As a psychologist you should know there are jealous, nasty people out there. I've gotten threats before." A smile pulled at the corners of her lips. "But let's face it, the dangerous guys are the ones you let in your bed."

"J. R. Jones. I was there when it happened, Reverend Emerald. It was horrible and I'm so glad your injuries weren't worse than they are. And I'm not a clinical psychologist, I'm a social—"

"You were there?" she interrupted. "What a disaster! And please call me Ruby. I should never have gotten involved with Jerry, but you know how it is. You don't think he sent that stupid tape to the television station, do you? I can't imagine Jerry doing that. He's a sweet guy, really, but you know how they are. Marriage and all that. He wanted to plant a flag through my head saying 'Property of . . .' you know?"

In the harsh California sunlight filtering through the window I could see that Ruby Emerald was not young. Pushing the outer edge of middle age in all likelihood. The skin of her arms was a mosaic of parched lines despite the expensive jar of herbal body cream on her nightstand. At her temples I could see that the blonde curls were gray at the roots. Early sixties, I guessed.

But her brown eyes sparkled with an ageless exuberance that probably accounted for J. R. Jones's murderous devotion to her.

"No, I think someone else sent that tape," I said. "Someone connected to the Rainer Clinic."

The brown eyes grew wide. "No! I can't believe that. Everyone was so nice there, you have no idea. I mean, they're really top-notch, just the best. And trust me, with what they get for a simple, old-fashioned face-lift, there's no reason for anyone there to be jealous of what I'm making!"

"The motivation might not be jealousy," I mentioned with some hesitation. There was no reason to frighten her with bizarre theories about gender-maddened serial killers. "Could you tell me a little about what happened the night before the revival? I know you were hospitalized."

"Now, that was strange," she answered, knitting her brow like a puzzled child. "That evening was very strange. Jerry was with me, very upset because I'd been trying to call it quits for months and finally I just told him, this is it. I let him think I'd met someone else, although I haven't. It was just a way to get him to back off. And in the middle of this a delivery service brings a deli tray I hadn't ordered, so I knew it must be from one of my followers. The card had been lost, but it was very nice. Red wine, caviar, several cheeses including my favorite English Stilton, a liver pâté with a little loaf of fresh bread, and beautiful imported chocolates all around the edge. Sometimes people send flowers and things, but this was *really* nice."

I wasn't sure where this was going, but I smiled encouragement.

"Well, Jerry was certain the goodies were a gift from this new sweetie I'd just made up because there wasn't any card. He was furious, storming around. I just went on nibbling at this and that, especially the Stilton. It was quite good. And then he grabbed the tray and threw it against the wall! Can you believe it?"

"Sounds like a waste of good food," I volunteered, hoping I didn't sound as dim as I thought I did. "So how did you wind up in the hospital that night?"

She seemed chagrined. "I guess I was more upset by Jerry doing that than I realized, because all of a sudden I just felt terrible. My heart was pounding, I felt dizzy and sick, and I started sweating something awful. And the headache! Just this terrible headache. Jerry called 911. He said he was afraid he'd killed me. Guess I should've listened to *that,* huh?"

"Do you remember the name of the delivery service that brought you the deli tray?" I asked.

"No. I didn't see the van. Just some guy at the door with the tray."

"What did the guy look like?"

She shrugged. "Just some guy, short guy. A deliveryman. I don't remember. Why? Do you think something on that tray was poisoned?"

"I don't know," I answered. "But as a precaution, in the future—"

"Don't eat strange food? No problem, Dr. McCarron. But I still think I'd do better to keep the overly devoted types out of my bed."

I couldn't think of anything to say to that.

"Here's my card," I told her. "Please call me if you think of anything else."

It was close to two when I picked up the copy of the Rainer Clinic file Wes Rathbone had left at the front desk of police headquarters for me. After grabbing an amaretto chocolate gelato at a drive-in, I took Brontë to Balboa Park and sat in the empty organ pavilion to eat it. Rathbone's file told me that Jennings Rainer, sixty-seven, had opened the Rainer Clinic twenty-five years ago at a different address and moved to the current location eleven years ago. Prior to opening his own clinic he'd practiced with a medical group and been on staff at a prestigious hospital in Boulder, Colorado. Rainer had been married for forty-five years to the former Marlis Hutchins at the time of her death from cancer two years ago.

I walked Brontë around the pavilion and along the wide pedestrian avenue which is the park's backbone. At the avenue's end a stream of water shot twenty feet into the dry autumn air and then fell into a pool at this base. When we got to the fountain I let Brontë splash in the water as I read on.

Jennings's daughter, Megan Rainer, forty-one, was his partner in the business. Also a plastic surgeon, she'd graduated from a California university and done her residency in San Francisco. Married ten years ago to Christopher Nugent, also forty-one, Megan Rainer was the mother of two children, Jenna, eight, and Joshua, six. Christopher Nugent wrote abstracts for scientific journals for a living and stayed at home with the two children. The file noted that Nugent was involved in several local ecology organizations.

The other medical employees of the clinic were Jeffrey Pond, forty-two, the clinic operating room manager, a registered nurse; Thomas Joseph Eldridge, forty, a surgical assistant and also an r.n.; and Dr. Isadora Grecchi, fifty-one, an anesthesiologist. All of which told me nothing except that the Rainer Clinic employed a lot of middle-aged people. In a small setting such as this, what that usually means is that the same professional staff have been employees for a long time. My guess was that all of these people had been with Jennings Rainer for years, which would suggest that they were well paid, well treated, and knew one another in the way that lifelong friends do. Scarcely a population from which to expect the eruption of a pathological killer.

"Maybe," I told Brontë as she shook water from her fur all over my black dress, "the person sending these threats is an ex-patient who wants to make us *think* somebody connected to the clinic is sending them. Maybe somebody who wasn't happy with a service performed there?"

Brontë was sniffing a breeze from the direction of a wheeled hot dog vendor and showed no interest in my suggestion.

A few people die each year from complications related to cosmetic surgery. These are invariably people who have tried to economize by turning themselves over to surgeons who lack board certification or have lost their licenses and are practicing illegally. You have to wonder about that sort of frugality. But all the medical personnel at Rainer were licensed. I didn't think the grieving spouse of a lethal face-lift sometime in the past was behind the threats. But I didn't dismiss the idea, either. Nor did I dismiss the possibility that a dissatisfied patient who'd wanted to look more like Leonardo DiCaprio than is possible might be behind them. In fact, I didn't dismiss anything. And I had an idea about what to do next.

Balboa Park is home to a number of museums and, I told myself, I was already there. Among other things, museums house curators, and curators often know a great deal about obscure things. Like china. As in plates. A curator might be just what I needed.

The Mingei International Museum specializes in folk art, but I started there anyway because I love the gift shop. A seventy-ish, deeply tanned docent wearing a gorgeous hand-woven dashiki in beiges and ecrus told me nobody at the Mingei would be able to answer my questions about blue willow plates, which do not qualify as folk art. But somebody across the park's carriageway at the San Diego Museum of Art probably would, she said.

She also told me that the dashiki was one of a collection for sale in the gift shop. I had tied Brontë to the wrought-iron railing outside the museum shop, and she watched through the floor-to-ceiling windows as I admired a rack of dashikis. One, a broad weave of deep purples and reds highlighted by bands of gold satin, just *was* Roxie. Christmas, I thought when I saw the price tag. I'd give it to her for Christmas.

After the Mingei shop staff happily took my credit card, Brontë and I and the dashiki crossed the old park street to the art museum.

"Of course," said a uniformed guard who looked like Santa Claus without the beard. "Just wait here and I'll get someone who can answer your questions."

The someone, an elegant gentleman whose name tag read HUTTON PIERCE materialized from behind a stone pillar and said, "Blue willow, of course!" He was wearing a three-piece suit and an expensive toupee which sat an eighth of an inch askew above his gold-framed granny glasses. I was sure he wasn't a day under eighty-five, and his aqua-blue eyes flamed with intelligence.

"Anyone referencing a 'blue plate' is talking about blue willow," he went on as if we were discussing one of the great veritics. "Please, follow me to the museum library."

"You see," he said after pulling a forty-five-pound book from a shelf and opening it reverently on an oak table, "here it is, the most popular china pattern *in the world*!"

"In the world," I repeated, trying to seem impressed as I looked at a picture of a plate.

"Absolutely! Look. Do you see the story? The pattern is always the same—a pagoda, a fence, three figures fleeing across a bridge beneath a weeping willow, a mysterious boat in the distance, and two birds hovering above. The fleeing figures are doomed lovers pursued by the girl's father or else by the wealthy old man to whom her father had promised her in marriage, depending on which version of the story you read. Captured and imprisoned in the pagoda by her father, the lovers become lost in the maze beneath it and tragically die. But so great is their love that they're transformed in death into the two birds flying above the scene.

"The tale is Chinese, but an English potter named Thomas Turner was the first to create blue willow dishes in 1780. The design was enormously popular, and as pottery began to be mass-produced in England, so did the design. It has since been reproduced in almost every country and continues to be popular today."

"But these plates aren't entirely blue," I insisted politely. "The design is blue, but the plate itself is white. Why are they called 'blue plate'?"

"I have explained," Hutton Pierce said as if speaking to someone who would never actually get it, "that this pattern *is* what is meant by 'blue plate.' You see, for a period of some two decades in the United States, roughly 1925 to the end of World War II in 1945, numerous manufacturers produced heavy porcelain plates in the blue willow pattern specifically for use in restaurants. The plates were divided into sections like this," he said, pointing to another illustration of a plate. This one was divided into three sections like a child's dish.

"There are minor variations in pattern depending on the manufacturer, of course. Some mistakenly included only *two* figures crossing the bridge. But such plates were quite commonly used in American restaurants from the 1920s through the 1950s," he continued. "They gave rise to the phrase 'blue plate special,' a term used to denote an inexpensive meal in which all courses are served together on one plate. The plate was this one, the divided blue willow. A collector's item now."

With that he snapped the book shut and returned it to the shelf. The gesture seemed definitive. Also final.

"Thank you," I said, walking backward through the museum library's double glass doors. I've seen people do this in movies when leaving the presence of royalty. It seemed appropriate.

Outside, Brontë wagged her stub of a tail beneath the plaster frescoes adorning the museum's facade.

"Somebody's playing a game," I told her as we walked to my truck. "And the pieces are blue plates."

11

Dog Art

When I got home I brought the framed photograph from the Aphid Gallery in and then went straight to the kitchen to look at my plates. Misha, an earlier love, and I had bought them at a pottery shop in Laguna Beach one weekend years ago. One of those weekends in the beginning of a love affair when you think something like dishes will make it last forever. Women are trained to equate things-that-can-be-bought with everlasting love by an advertising industry which, unlike Sigmund Freud, knows exactly what women want. Undying emotional and erotic bliss in a context of total security. Impossible. And for that reason a wish easily manipulated, over and over. Got a warehouse full of hideous orange birdcages you want to unload? Find a way to associate orange birdcages with enduring passion, and three out of twenty women will buy one. It's just the way we are.

Misha and I had been in an earth-tone mood that day and had gone for spatterware in a cream background with cocoa-colored spatters. I looked at the plates and tried to imagine attaching any significance to them beyond my memories of Misha. There was none. Without the memories, they were just plates.

Also coffee mugs and a few serving pieces. I still liked them and they went well in my desert decor, but I never *thought* about them.

Somebody was thinking about blue plates, though. Or thinking about blue willow plates, if Hutton Pierce's definition of "blue plate" was correct. But why? And who? I remembered the wall of plates in the surgical waiting room at the Rainer Clinic. One of them had been an antique blue willow design. Two women and three men comprised the medical staff at Rainer. Two women and three men who might be assumed to possess sufficient medical savvy to cause cerebral hemorrhages in patients through the deliberate manipulation of blood pressure. And if one of these five people really was a killer, it would be the one with a significant psychological link to *plates.*

I thought about that while holding the framed photograph against different areas on my living room walls. Beside the front Dutch door the photo was obscured in shadow, and the same problem applied when I held it against the wall on both sides of a picture window framing a desert corridor of broken hills. The photo needed its own wall and no textural competition. As I rearranged furniture in order to hang it to dramatic advantage, I tried to think about plates and got nowhere.

They're just there. Flat, round, slightly concave objects used for serving food. Descendants of the earlier *bowl,* I assumed. Somewhere I'd read that lead used in the manufacture of metal plates had probably contributed to the madness of countless kings and others privileged to eat acidic foodstuffs from metal tableware. Peasants, mopping their gravy from wooden plates throughout the ages, were presumably spared the inconvenience of lead poisoning. And so what? Mary Harriet Grossinger and Dixie Ross hadn't died from lead poisoning.

I don't like artwork in an eye-level band around rooms. I like it in odd places that force you to look up or down or into places you'd never look. The photograph of a light-blasted desert building looked best, I decided, below waist level. After hauling in one shelf of an old set of stackable shelves from my storeroom, I pushed it against the wall and set a lamp on it.

The light from the lamp illuminated the photo perfectly after I'd fastened it to the wall.

The entire arrangement was at Brontë's eye level, and she seemed to enjoy it. It occurred to me that nobody gives any thought to the possible esthetic needs of domestic animals. Maybe the artless and ill-lit realm below our line of sight is a psychological wasteland for our pets. After all, cats are always looking out windows, aren't they? I decided to research an article on the responses of animals to lighting and visual stimulation after this peculiar case was solved. *If* this peculiar case was solved, I reminded myself. Back to plates.

As a social psychologist I don't analyze the subconscious motivations and personal symbol systems of individuals. Clinical psychologists do that. A clinical psychologist can tell you what the American flag means to an individual. I can tell you what the American flag is likely to mean to members of various social populations (Veterans of Foreign Wars members, for example, as opposed to members of the Women's International League for Peace and Freedom.) Additionally, I can predict flag-buying and flag-displaying behaviors broken down any way you like. Want to know how many American flags are likely to be purchased by Presbyterian Korean females between thirty-five and sixty-five in Seattle during August? No problem. What I can't tell you is why Sharon Li, a fifty-three-year-old Korean grandmother who teaches Sunday school at Seattle Community Presbyterian, will buy that flag in August. Her personal motivations are not the concern of my discipline. And plates are more difficult to track than flags.

But I was getting paid a lot to do this, so I booted up the computer and went for the current sales reports of five U.S. china manufacturers who sell versions of the blue willow pattern. In half an hour I knew that sales of blue willow were evenly distributed all over the country, with predictable peaks in areas saturated with mail-order catalogues featuring blue willow items. I learned that a brisk mail-order business in blue willow accessories such as wall clocks, jewelry, table linen, and drawer pulls resulted in annual profits in the six-figure range, spread over the five manufacturers.

Clicking on another link, I wound up at the Web site of a restaurant in Georgia called the Blue Willow Inn. This is the problem with Internet research. It's so easy to get sidetracked. But the Blue Willow Inn was willing to share its recipe for fried green tomatoes, so I copied the page. I'd make fried green tomatoes for Rox, I decided. She'd never been in the South and it would be a treat. Although where was I going to find green tomatoes in the middle of the California desert in October? A challenge.

Clicking on another link, I found myself at the home page of a Phoenix car club. Old cars, lovingly restored and driven by steely-eyed men in plaid shirts who stared proudly from a color photo of them and their cars. The photo had been taken in front of a diner, and the Web page also noted that the Phoenix Crankshaft Club's Ladies Auxiliary filled its time while the men were retooling old combustion chambers by collecting blue willow china. Reading on, I learned that vintage car clubs across the country often meet at diners as a tribute to the old days when these very cars would have graced the parking lots of now-almost-vanished roadside Americana.

Out of desperation, it seemed, the wives of this particular club had decided to do something besides stand around pretending to admire corroded distributor caps. If they had to hang out at old diners, then they'd find something interesting to *do* about old diners. Eureka! Blue willow china.

The president of Crankshaft's ladies' auxiliary was listed as "Mrs. Ed Lauer," with a Phoenix phone number. I didn't know what I was looking for, but I called. Nothing ventured, etc. The woman who answered did not sound like somebody who hangs out in parking lots, which is the problem with assumptions based on group membership rather than on the individual. The practices of social psychology *never* work when applied to only one person.

Jackie Lauer, as she introduced herself, was sixty, had a Boston accent, and a Ph.D. in romance languages. She taught part-time at the University of Arizona, she said, but spent most of her time doing interesting stuff with her husband, Ed, a Vietnam vet who'd lost both feet to a land mine in 1968. Ed also suffered from depression, she mentioned, and fifteen years or so ago things had gotten really bad. Ed was sullen, then suicidal, wound up in a psych hospital. She'd left him during the sullen period, but went back during the hospitalization. They'd had to make some big changes. Medication for him, therapy and a different attitude for her.

I had that ice-water-on-the-neck feeling I get when total strangers insist on telling me after one minute of acquaintance things I would only tell my most intimate friend over a span of five years. This feeling approaches panic when the stranger seems to be heading toward some conclusion involving spiritual growth. Jackie Lauer, however, stopped mercifully short of that.

"What can I help you with?" she asked.

"I'm calling about blue willow plates," I explained, and then for some reason told her the whole strange story. Tit for tat, I thought.

"Wow," she said when I'd finished, "that's interesting. You know, I had my eyes done eight years ago, never regretted it. I had these pouches. God, I looked like Winston Churchill. But they just snipped the sag and sucked out all that fat, and I have to tell you I loved it! Went out and got contacts, had my hair styled. Ed said I looked twenty years younger and the truth is, I did. So anyway, what can I tell you about blue willow? What is it you want to know?"

"I'm not sure," I said. "A link between these blue plates and somebody who hates women in positions of authority enough to threaten them with death, maybe actually kill them. Somebody with the medical know-how to cause lethal fluctuations in blood pressure. One of five people on the medical staff at a clinic specializing in cosmetic surgery."

"Well," Jackie Lauer said, "all I can talk about is the plates. The club's been collecting and selling blue willow for years and I've noticed that people love these plates for two reasons. And I'm talking both men and women here. The first is when they get sort of drawn into the pattern. See, it's a little world, a scene where there's something happening, only it's frozen in time. It never changes. The little people are always running over the bridge, the birds are always flying above the pagoda, the willow is always there. Usually the people who get sucked into the pattern are women, and they'll buy anything just to have it around, look at it.

"The other group of collectors is where you'll find men as well as women. It's a business thing. The old restaurant plates haven't been made for fifty years or so, the ones divided into sections. They're prized as an investment. Leave-'em-to-the-grand-kids sort of thing. In another fifty years they'll be seriously rare. It's like anything. Keep it long enough and it's worth money."

"So do people buy and sell these plates a lot?" I asked. "What's an antique blue willow plate worth?"

"Oh, say one of the old English ones, circa early 1800s in fairly good condition with a potter's mark, you'd get up to two thousand in the right places. The mass-produced American ones, well, maybe five or ten dollars a plate with a manufacturer's mark on the bottom. But see, that's gonna go up, that amount. It's not a bad long-term investment. The club's made some good money selling these things. We support a battered women's shelter with the proceeds. Stock a nice children's library for the kids there, too."

"A women's shelter?" I said. "I thought this was a car club."

"Get real," Jackie Lauer told me, laughing. "That's what the guy's do. We provide the club with a 'community service' that allows it to have tax-free status. Boys and girls don't play well together, haven't you noticed? Only works if they play different games side by side. The boys strut around preening their cars and we ooh and ahh over dishes. But the guys are coming up with some mechanical innovations that have been useful, for example, to groups trying to help impoverished Mexican communities. A couple of our guys have gone down there to show people how to retool parts for old cars. Sometimes one car in a village can make a big difference in things like access to medical care, maybe even save a life or two. We do the same thing with our support of the women's shelter. It's just different, is all."

I was beginning to think of Jackie Lauer as a sort of pop-psychology encyclopedia. She was right about everything, but put a chipper, airy spin on it that was bewildering.

"I'm afraid I haven't been much help," she said cheerily. "But good luck with your serial killer."

Only Jackie could have said that.

Brontë was milling around near her dinner bowl, watching me impatiently. Past her dinnertime. I opened a can of Science Diet Beef and Chicken for her and shaved some cheddar over corn chips for me. Microwaving nachos requires split-second timing in order to melt the cheese before the chips get soggy, but I managed. Then I made myself a giant chocolate shake with a raw egg in it and sat at a counter stool to eat. One of the perks of living alone, I acknowledged, is the absence of someone pointing out that your food habits are weird.

After dinner I went for a swim in the pool and then phoned Kate Van Der Elst at home.

"I don't want to alarm you, but something's come up that may be significant," I began.

Her voice was strained. "What is it, Blue?"

"Ruby Emerald received a deli tray on Saturday night. It may be nothing, because there were a number of upsetting things happening around her that night, but she did develop symptoms and was taken to a hospital. She said she often gets gifts from her followers, so she assumed the tray was such a gift, although the card had apparently been lost. What we know is that a deli tray of rather exotic food arrived with no card. She ate some of the food, but her companion did not. She developed symptoms, and he did not. What I'm suggesting is—"

"Blue, somebody sent a tray with pâté and caviar and elegant little breads to my fundraiser! Remember? BB said a delivery service brought it to the gallery shortly before six. He asked me about it and I told him to just put it on the table with the other snacks. As I recall, the caviar was a hit, although BB thought the garnish of canned figs was odd and threw the figs away. Do you think somebody's sending poisoned food in these trays? Nobody got sick at my fundraiser, did they? It's so far-fetched."

I remembered watching the mayor of a suburban community scarfing up the last sturgeon egg from a blue willow plate with his finger. As far as I knew, he hadn't suffered any ill effects. For that matter, I remembered, I'd enjoyed a good bit of the caviar myself and I felt fine. Then it hit me. The blue willow plate.

"Something extremely unusual is going on," I told Kate as a small chill crept up the sides of my face. "This is going to sound strange, but it involves blue plates, anything with a blue willow design. You probably don't remember, but in the surgical waiting room of the Rainer Clinic is a wall of decorative plates. One of them is an antique blue willow."

"I remember," Pieter Van Der Elst's somber baritone interrupted. I hadn't known he was on the line. "I saw the plates as I sat there waiting to bring Kate home. What does this mean, Blue?"

"I still don't know," I said. "But Kate . . ."

"Yes?" Her voice was tight with anger now, and not at me.

"Don't eat *anything* at public gatherings between now and the election. Bring your own food, claim you're allergic to wine and cheese, it doesn't matter. Just avoid eating anything from deli trays at public gatherings."

"I never eat snacks like that," she said. "I'm on the Zone diet, carry my own snacks with me everywhere. It all has to be balanced, protein, carbohydrate, fat. I'd weigh three hundred pounds if I didn't stick to it. But if there's poisoned food, why aren't lots of people getting sick?"

The question was reasonable.

Pieter's voice answered. "This is insane," he said. "Kate, Blue has uncovered something important and you refuse to listen to her! This Emerald woman *did* get sick. She was hospitalized. Mary Harriet and Dixie are dead. Something horrible is happening and you're too selfish to care about anything except yourself and this city council nonsense. I'm going to have to . . ."

"You're going to have to what, Pieter?" she replied icily.

Even though we were on the phone I felt as though I were standing in the middle of their bedroom, an intruder in a bitter marital conflict.

"I didn't call to cause trouble or to become involved in your disagreement over Kate's candidacy," I spelled it out. "I called to provide Kate with some information she needs to have. That's all. Good night."

I hung up without engaging in further conversation, hoping I'd embarrassed them sufficiently that they didn't carry their dispute into public situations where it would be a detriment to Kate. There's nothing more damaging to a politician than the slightest hint of domestic turmoil. Nobody wants to see it. It's too close to home.

Roxie called as I was fastening on my waist pack prior to running Brontë.

"Long day." She sighed. "What've you been up to?"

I told her about Ruby Emerald's deli tray and my exhaustive research into blue willow plates, including my morning visit to the Rainer Clinic.

"Blue, didn't I specifically tell you not to—"

"I'm your partner, not your employee," I interrupted, echoing the spirit of Kate and Pieter's conflict. "I needed to see what was there."

The silence at Roxie's end was long, broken at last by another sigh.

"You're right," she finally said, "you have to do things the way you do them. I was out of line."

My heart melted. So few people ever listen. To anything.

"I got your Christmas gift today," I said, wanting to bridge the gap.

"What is it?"

"You'll like it," I went on. "Rox, let's do something special for Christmas. Let's go someplace."

"We are going someplace," she said. "We're going to St. Louis to spend Christmas with your dad and your godmother and your brother if he's out of prison by then, and your brother's wife,

Lonnie. We're going to stay at some inn that has fireplaces in the rooms and fantastic steaks in the dining room. What do you mean, 'let's go someplace'?"

When Rox is tired she becomes incapable of anything but the most concrete ideation.

"I was just fantasizing, thinking maybe Vienna, the opera, you know."

"St. Louis and a few blues bars will suit me just fine," she said. "Have you talked to Rathbone?"

"Not since this morning. I got the Rainer employee profiles from him, though. Haven't had a chance to look at all of them thoroughly."

"Well, look at them. We're having breakfast at Rathbone's place tomorrow morning. Six-thirty. The idea is to plan interview strategy. The department's keeping us on to profile all the medical employees."

She didn't sound happy about this.

"Why, Rox? Rathbone told me this case isn't a high priority. Something about a border patrol agent who got shot over the weekend. That's their priority."

"There's been another threat, another Sword of Heaven letter. Rathbone got it in his e-mail. Same format as yours. It had those little plates." Her voice was tired, ominous.

"Who is it this time, Rox?" I asked.

"Bettina Ashe."

The name was familiar, but it took me a few seconds to remember.

"Oh God, Roxie, she was there this morning! Bettina Ashe was the woman on the white chair in the operating cubicle with bandages all over her head. Her husband was in the surgical waiting room. I heard Megan Rainer talking to him."

"But do you know who she is?"

I'd heard the name. Bettina Ashe. Betsy. The Ashe Foundation. Charitable contributions everywhere.

"Not exactly," I admitted. "But it's her husband who's the bigwig, right? I heard Megan Rainer call him 'Mr. Ashe' this morning."

"His name is John Harrington, and he's probably used to being called 'Mr. Ashe,'" Rox explained. "Old Southern family, lots of class but no money. He married Betsy Ashe fifteen years ago, and while it looks like a marriage of convenience, Rathbone says they're crazy about each other. But she's the Ashe, not he, and she's worth millions."

"Rox, there's something about deli trays. It may be nothing, but both Ruby Emerald and Kate received deli trays from which the card had apparently been lost. Nice stuff—caviar, pricey cheeses, designer chocolates. Kate's can't have been poisoned, though, because I ate quite a bit of it and didn't get sick. Still, I think Bettina Ashe should be warned."

"The police will take care of that," Rox said. "The husband, Harrington, has hired extra security around Betsy and is putting major pressure on the police to beef up the investigation. The Ashe Foundation supports a number of police charities, especially a scholarship fund for children *and* wives of officers killed in the line of duty. You can imagine the response down at headquarters. Politicians and preachers are one thing, but Betsy Ashe is another. You're going to be working on this around the clock, Blue. Sorry I can't do much, but I have a job."

"Rox, these interviews Rathbone wants done. They're really your sort of thing, not mine. I'm not feeling comfortable with this. I'm *not* a clinical psychologist. And you're the psychiatrist."

"Don't worry," she told me. "Dr. Bouchie's crash course in interviewing serial killers is all you need. Plus I'm sending BB with you."

"BB?"

"Yeah, I've got a plan," she said, chuckling. "Don't worry, Blue. Crunch a few numbers in your computer and get some sleep. You'll have to get up at four-thirty to get to Rathbone's house by six-thirty. G'night."

"Night, Rox," I said.

But I didn't crunch numbers and go to bed. What I did was take Brontë for a long walk in the chilly autumn night, through shadows of ocotillo cactus and rocks so old they'd known the footfalls of prehistoric camels eighteen feet tall. Now these rocks knew the lesser, scritching footsteps of lizards. I thought about the chuckwalla Brontë had found two nights ago. A strange lizard that inflates one side of its body in order to compress the other side into rocky cracks and fissures. Sword seemed like a chuckwalla, I thought. The righteous biblical language of the letters was the inflated part, but what part was being compressed into hidden places behind it?

When we returned over an hour later there was something on the front step, something wedged against my Dutch door. It gleamed oddly in the waxing moonlight. Something pale and round. I didn't think much of it until I was right on top of it. Stuff blows around in the desert. Tumbleweeds. Trash left by occasional picnickers. I suppose I thought it was going to be a foam container that had once held a Big Mac and fries, blown two miles across the desert from the road. But it wasn't.

By the time I was fifteen feet from it I knew what it was. A shining white plate with a blue design. A fence, a pagoda, three little figures running over a bridge, a boat, a willow tree, and two birds hovering above.

"Oh, my God," I said as I pulled the Smith and Wesson from my hip pack and released the safety. But there was nobody there. Nothing but desert wind and the sound of my own heartbeat.

12

Chocolate Chips at Dawn

I picked up the plate with the cuff of my sweatshirt, not that I really thought there would be fingerprints on it. Then I dropped it in a plastic freezer bag, zipped shut the top, and looked at it. A cheap import, brand-new. Not an antique English plate or even one of the mass-produced American restaurant blue willows. Sword wasn't wasting the good china on me, a fact I found oddly insulting.

Also creepy. I don't keep my blinds closed at night. Why should I? There's no one beyond my windows to watch me grating cheese. The paved road is two miles away and the dirt track to my place is guarded by a locked gate. There's nothing out there but rocky hills crumbling under the weight of time. Desert plants, seemingly dead now in the dry season but capable of blooming overnight after a deep rain. Lizards, jackrabbits, coyotes, snakes. From outside, the light from my office spills in a hazy yellow pool through only a few feet of darkness. Beyond that, there's nothing human. Usually.

The little Smith and Wesson .38 Special revolver I bought after my Glock nine-millimeter became a necessary loss during

September's Muffin Crandall case is a lot lighter than the Glock. Only fifteen ounces in the aluminum alloy and carbon steel model I chose. The barrel's just an inch and seven-eighths long. Not a gun for shooting things at a distance. But distance wasn't what I was worried about. What I was worried about was what might still be out there, watching. What might decide to come *in*.

I took the gun into my bedroom and checked the cylinder. Rounds in all five chambers. Then I curled up to sleep with the weapon's reassuring blue-black presence inches from my hand on the nightstand. Brontë would bark if there was the slightest unusual sound anywhere in or near the motel, and I would grab the .38 and shoot anybody who happened to be standing around in my living room doing something strange with china. The thought was comforting. Most women are uneasy around guns. But the way I look at it, women are usually the people who need them.

I had no need of mine that night, although I couldn't have known it when I went to bed. As a result I didn't sleep very well and had no problem getting up at four to run Brontë and then drive over the mountains and down into San Diego for breakfast at Wes and Annie Rathbone's house. Annie was making chocolate chip pancakes when I got there, and the aroma obliterated everything else from my consciousness.

"Blue, why are you carrying a plate in a plastic bag?" Roxie inquired from one side of the Rathbones' pine-plank kitchen table. It was apparent that somebody had knocked out a wall to create this room, because Southern California tract houses do not boast kitchens in which you could moor a tugboat. A fireplace in the rear wall was the clue. A "family room" had been sacrificed for the expansion of the kitchen into a usable space. Wes poured coffee into a bright yellow mug for me and glanced meaningfully at the worn vinyl floor.

"Um, Sword paid me a visit last night," I said. "Left a calling card. By the way, Annie, Wes tells me you're thinking about Pergo for the floor. I've got it. and I really like—"

Roxie, dressed for work in a cork-colored business suit that would've made her look dead except for a brick red blouse and gold hoop earrings I could put my foot through, raised her eyebrows and leaned forward across a yellow raffia placemat.

"Blue," she said, "don't talk about the *floor.* What do you mean, he paid you a visit? When? What happened? Did you see him. What?"

"I didn't see anybody, Rox. I was out running Brontë for over an hour, maybe until eleven or so. When I got back this plate was propped against my door."

To Rathbone I added, "I didn't touch it."

Annie, still in a sky-blue chenille bathrobe and house slippers, put a stack of steaming pancakes in front of me and then sat down to eat her own as Wes made another batch for himself.

"I don't understand why this creep is harassing you and not Roxie or Wes," she said. "And what's with the plate?"

"There's a connection to blue willow plates," I answered. "It doesn't make any sense."

"Oh, it makes sense," Rox interjected. "Not everyday sense, but a particular, personal kind of sense. Sword attaches great significance to the plates or the pattern or something else about them. To him this significance is simple, obvious. He's using the image to draw us to him, and is probably a bit frustrated by now that we haven't figured it out. He thinks we're stupid."

"So he wants to get caught?" Rathbone asked from the stovetop where he was expertly flipping pancakes.

"He wants to play for a while," Rox said. "My concern about Sword is that he's nothing typical. Certainly not the typical serial murderer, if there really is such a thing."

"What do you mean?" Rathbone demanded. "Of course there's such a thing. Ted Bundy, John Wayne Gacy, Berkowitz, *Dahmer,* for God's sake."

"Um, a number of people in my field would argue that there have always been people who killed over and over," I jumped in. "But they were either just seen as 'murderers' with no special title, or not seen at all, as in the case of military or law-enforcement workers whose 'serial killing' is perceived as okay as long as we don't call it serial killing. The concept is that in creating the term 'serial killer,' society has literally created a bogeyman, a powerful myth on which to project all our own dark and unacceptable impulses. It's a very new cultural myth, exclusively American and less than twenty years old. When we were all kids, there was no such thing."

"That's true," Annie Rathbone said, relishing her pancakes. "But maybe that's because the police and FBI have computers now and can track all the different things—the m.o. and where the murderer leaves the body and all that. They can track all these little details all over the country now, where before it might seem like something that just happened one time in Iowa, for example. And the killer goes to prison in Iowa, and that's that."

"The serial killer phenomenon can also be seen as a way of avoiding certain unpleasant truths psychiatry turns up," Roxie said. "People need to believe that such killers are utterly unlike themselves, that a Jeffrey Dahmer, for example, was an alien being beyond all human comprehension, like a god of pure evil. Psychiatry steps in and says, 'No, this is just a guy like you and me in whom a combination of brain function and life experience produced some pretty disgusting behavior.' For example, recent studies have shown a stupendously high incidence of childhood brain injury in the medical histories of men imprisoned for violent crimes. Coupled with poverty and illiteracy, it looks like brain injuries contribute to violent behavior, but nobody wants to hear it."

"Why not?" Annie asked.

"Because then it could happen to anybody," Rox explained. "No more comforting bogeyman. Plus, parents might be reluctant to let their boys play violent sports in which head injuries are a risk. And there goes the American way of life. Where would we be without football?"

Wes Rathbone was rolling his eyes. "All very interesting, but it doesn't help me catch this guy."

"Okay," Roxie went on, "so far all we have is a series of threats and two dead people who might have died from natural causes even though that's statistically impossible. But if he *has* killed, then I think he doesn't 'want' to be captured as much as he believes nothing else can happen. To him punishment for wrongdoing is swift and certain. It's inevitable. That he hasn't been captured yet is probably confusing to him."

"How can there be a 'typical' serial killer?" Annie asked, pushing butter and a jug of real maple syrup toward her husband.

"FBI has done some profiles," Wes began. "Things about disorganized crime scenes and dump sites, who dismembers the body and who doesn't, souvenirs, that sort of thing. It was a way of getting a handle on these guys, putting their behaviors in words cops can understand rather than a bunch of psychiatric mumbo-jumbo. No offense, Rox. But any cop, FBI or otherwise, will tell you every one of these weirdo killings is different from every other one. The profiles don't help much. The only way to get two steps ahead is to get into the killer's mind, figure out what he's thinking. This guy thinks he's God's own vengeance and has a fetish for plates. Now he's threatened one of the wealthiest women in the region. None of this is fitting together for me, I have to tell you."

I'd finished my pancakes and was feeling useless. Profiles are the kind of thing I do, the way I think, and Wes had just said they didn't help. Getting into Sword's mind wasn't something I could do.

"Before we scrap the FBI profiling system completely," I began, "let's look at the salient features. Maybe there are a couple of things we need to be looking for."

"Salient would, in my opinion, concern the killer's need for validation," Rox answered. "According to the FBI that means dump sites and souvenirs, mostly. A lot of male killers will return to the site where they dumped the body, over and over. The theory is that reliving the kill is pleasant, even sexually arousing to them. But whether that's true or not, what's absolutely true is that the actual, physical existence of the site *validates* the reality of the kill and therefore validates the killer. He goes there to feel real.

"Also typical among male serials, according to the FBI, is the keeping of souvenirs. Articles of the victim's clothing, body parts, scrapbooks of newspaper clippings about the crime. Again, these may be sexually arousing or not, but they are always a source of instant validation. He will cherish these and need to see or touch them often because they are the trophies that prove he has a function in the world, that he's important.

"And while there are a few females who kill more than one person in sequence, their motivations are entirely different. They don't return to dump sites and have no need for souvenirs. Am I right, Blue?"

"Women serial murderers are usually 'black widow' wives who kill their husbands or boyfriends, or Munchausen moms who sequentially kill their own children in order to be seen as heroic in the face of illness and death," I explained to Wes and a fascinated Annie. "The female killer chooses people close to her as victims, people who are extremely vulnerable to her. A sleeping husband, children. The other typical profile is the woman who takes in orphans, the elderly, or the sick for pay, and then kills them for their Social Security payments, insurance, or pension benefits. These victims are also in vulnerable positions relative to her. In both cases the killers show disinterest in their crimes, as if the crimes had been committed by someone else. These women killers would recoil from souvenirs or visiting dump sites. They get no sense of power from the kill and in fact don't think about it at all. What they get is either financial gain, to which the female 'serial killer' often feels entitled, or the praise of others, in the case of the Munchausen moms, for their seeming courage and fortitude.

"Which leads me to make this point," I went on. "Rox, you and Wes have concluded that Sword is a man. But notice . . . these killings have no dump sites to visit. The killer isn't present when death occurs, so there can be no taking of souvenirs from the kill. Neither of these profiled male behaviors is possible in this case. But what is possible is the female profile—disinterest, distance."

"Okay," Roxie agreed, "except for the attention-getting behavior. Sword is advertising himself everywhere—to the victims, the police, and the media. He *has* to have attention, and that's the gender marker. It's a male. And he'll do something to approximate visiting dump sites and collecting souvenirs. This is where you come in, Blue."

"I do?"

Rathbone turned his chair around and straddled it, his version of a down-to-business posture.

"Rox and I worked this out yesterday on the phone after I went to the Rainer Clinic," he explained. "It was pretty much the way she said. Everybody was polite and aloof, nobody knew anything. I couldn't spare a detective from the border-agent case, so I had to go alone. Insufficient cause to haul anybody down to headquarters for questioning, so I was on their turf. About all I found out was that the old guy, Jennings Rainer, thought his daughter would take over the clinic when he retired, but apparently it's not gonna happen. She was out to lunch when I was there, so I didn't talk to her."

"She had lunch with her husband, Chris, who looks like Smokey Bear with an Indian braid down his back," I said, not looking in Roxie's direction. "He ordered a Reuben and is worried that their son, Josh, may be traumatized by not being allowed to take a camera on a school field trip. I'd ducked into the clinic for a minute on a ruse, overheard Megan say she was meeting somebody at Samson's. So I checked it out."

Rox studied her coffee cup as if it were an archaeological find when Rathbone said, "Good work, McCarron! You've got the heart of a cop. So what else did you learn?"

"Not much. Except they have some sort of agreement, something Megan has to do for a couple more years because that's the agreement. Apparently she doesn't want to do it, but he's encouraging her to go on."

"Megan is the daughter, right?" Annie said thoughtfully. "Plastic surgeon daughter of plastic surgeon father. Father wants her to take over the business but she's not interested. Wes, how did the old guy seem to you when he said that? Sad? Bitter? Hopeful?"

"I dunno. None of those, I guess. I thought it was just a way to get the questioning off track. He kept gesturing around, like the place meant something to him. It's like his little kingdom, all fancied up with art and fish tanks. But he didn't answer—"

"Wes," I had to interrupt, "did you look at the fish?"

"No," he answered, glancing at his watch. "What about 'em?"

"They're metal. Flat metal fish shapes that follow a magnet through the water. They're not real, but they look like they are."

"In the right lighting," Annie said with a grin.

"*And* with the right accessories," Rox added. Similar grin.

Three women understanding precisely what they're talking about.

"Huh?" said Wes Rathbone.

"Never mind, sweetie, it's a girl thing," Annie cooed across the table. "Has to do with illusion, what used to be called 'glamour' when witches were burned at the stake for it. Looks like you walked right into its den and didn't see it, which is the point, isn't it?"

Roxie had rolled her head back and was saying, "Girl," in a way indicating deep appreciation as she shook her braids back and forth, laughing. Rathbone still didn't get it.

"So, the plan we came up with," he began, ignoring us, "will use Blue for in-depth interviews with all five of the Rainer medical staff."

"But I don't *do* 'in-depth' interviews," I insisted. "I don't even do shallow interviews. I don't do *interviews*! That's Roxie's thing. I do data. Is there some reason nobody understands this?"

"We understand," Rox said. "You're terrible at interviews. But you're not terrible at picking up details, thousands of them, and then fitting them into patterns and drawing conclusions. Look what you did with the fact that two politicians died within weeks of each other. What we want you to do is just talk to these people, go into their homes, look for those details. It doesn't matter what you say to them."

"Here's the setup," Rathbone went on. "The department has arranged interviews with individual medical staff members from Rainer for today. They are to be held in the homes of the subjects, fifteen minutes apiece. I have a list of appointment times and addresses for you. The idea is that these in-home interviews are a convenience to them, a courtesy."

"So what am I looking for?" I asked.

"Whatever it is you look for," Roxie answered briskly. "And BB's going with you."

"Okay, but why?"

Rathbone beamed at Roxie. "Her idea," he said. "The subjects are all white professionals. Your friend Berryman can make them uncomfortable simply by being present, throw 'em off. You'll introduce him as your bodyguard and then ignore him. But they won't. His presence, if Roxie's right, will make 'em nervous and give you an edge."

Annie was eyeing a wall clock featuring Betty Boop in biker gear. Seven-fifteen.

"Wes learned the surgery schedule yesterday," Annie said. "They're doing it right now. All the major surgeries are done early in the morning, the ones requiring an anesthesiologist. Every weekday they're all there at six A.M. Afternoons are the simple stuff that can be done with a little shot of local anesthesia any r.n. can administer—wart and mole removal kinds of things. So the anesthesiologist leaves around noon, and everybody else is finished by two. After that there's nobody there except the receptionist, unless one of the doctors is interviewing prospective clients. The office closes at four. Hard to believe enough women are having face-lifts to keep them busy five mornings a week, isn't it?"

"Rainer told me about ten percent of the face-lifts are for men, and maybe twenty percent of the liposuction," Wes noted.

Now he was blushing. "I didn't ask him about this phalloplasty thing, but I assume that's one of the ones they do in the morning."

"Really, hon?" Annie said with an impish grin. "And here I thought that was something they could handle with a little local anesthesia. You know, novocaine, big shiny syringe like at the dentist, long needle. . . ."

Wes Rathbone was turning gray. "Stop!" he begged, trying to laugh. "Gonna lose my pancakes otherwise."

"Ycchh!" the rest of us said in unison.

I hung around to look at flooring samples with Annie after Roxie and Wes had gone to work, Wes taking my blue willow plate in its bag for fingerprinting. Annie and I agreed that planked natural pine was the best choice, since its light color wouldn't diminish the effect of the large room. Over a third cup of coffee she asked me something.

"How do you think these medical people feel about doing plastic surgery?" she said. "I mean, wouldn't you think they'd feel like a joke compared to other doctors and nurses who're saving lives every day? All they do is tuck up sagging chins and suck fat off stomachs."

"Rox says there's a lot of money in it, Annie. And I don't think it's all face-lifts. They do reconstructive surgery for people who've been burned or gone through windshields, that kind of thing. And I don't know how I feel about cosmetic surgery, but basically I guess my view is—why not? I wouldn't hesitate to do it if I wanted to. Would you?"

As she walked to the sink and began rinsing her cup I noticed that she kept her left arm tucked close to her body, across her chest.

"I guess I'm asking for an opinion, really," she said nervously. "See, I'm thinking about having something . . . some surgery like that. The insurance will pay for most of it, and the rest, well, it's either that or a new floor. I know it's silly, but . . ."

After drying the cup more thoroughly than was necessary, she turned around. Wes Rathbone's Annie, who had changed his life, he said. Her arms were at her sides and I could see that one side of her chest was flat.

"Cancer. A mastectomy," she announced. "What I'm talking about is breast reconstruction. I've read all about it, seen pictures, everything. My friends say do it, but all they care about is men and they think, you know, I'd be doing it for Wes. But Wes never cared. I'd already had the mastectomy when we met. He says it's my heart he loves, not my breasts. So I was wondering what you think."

She was folding and unfolding a dish towel and her blue eyes were shy.

"You want my opinion because I'm gay and therefore not obsessed with men?" I had to ask.

"Well, yeah. I did talk it over with my younger sister. And I liked what she said, but maybe that was just because she's my sister. So I thought . . ."

She was so sweet about it and so miserable I felt I had to come up with an answer, but I'm not much good before ten A.M. and it wasn't quite eight.

"I guess what it comes down to is what you really want more," I blundered gamely, "a breast or a floor."

Attila the Hun would probably have been more subtle. After a second of dead silence we both laughed.

"So what did your sister say?"

"She said it's just about me, nothing else. If I feel like I need a reconstructed breast, then that's what I need and I should go for it. She said women have a relationship to their bodies that has nothing to do with men, and that a lot of women just use the man thing as an excuse to look the way they want. She said what's important is that I feel attractive to *myself.*"

"So then what's the problem?"

Annie Rathbone held out the flooring flyer, doubled over with laughter now. "I'm not sure I wouldn't feel more attractive to myself standing on this than I would filling out a bra again," she said.

It was a difficult call, and I had a feeling the floor was going to win.

"Annie," I said, giggling along with her, "Wesley Rathbone is one lucky cop."

"I'm lucky, too." She grinned. "Not only do I adore him, but he knows how to lay flooring."

Some marriages are made in heaven.

13

The Library Girl

In my truck I looked at the list of Rainer medical staff appointments. The first was at twelve-thirty with Jennings Rainer at his condo near the clinic. I was supposed to pick BB up at his shop at twelve. Since it was only about eight-fifteen, I couldn't decide what to do. Sleeping for a few hours at Roxie's was an option, but I wasn't tired. I'd left Brontë at home in her rarely used chain-link run, so a romp along the beach with a Doberman wasn't possible. The library, then, I decided. I love libraries on principle, and besides, I could do a little research.

San Diego's downtown Central Library was built in 1954 and it shows. The flat facade of rectangular Santa Maria limestone slabs looks from a distance like old yellow and brown siding. The kind you see on the backs of houses in the Midwest as you watch from a train window. But I've always liked the two Donal Hord cast-cement bas-reliefs decorating the California limestone. Intellectual traditions from East and West. Each sculpture portrays three figures above a presumably American youth, reading.

The "East" sculpture depicts a Chinese Mandarin holding a

scroll, a Persian holding a harp, and a nude tattooed figure representing India holding a palm-leaf book. Beneath these is a lotus blossom, a duck, and an American girl with those defined abdominal muscles that are only possible if you're a statue. She sits cross-legged forever, ignoring the parking problems on E Street, reading a book. Say what you will about Southern California, even in 1954 it was understood here that women account for more than fifty percent of the world's population and therefore should not be overlooked when commissioning sculpture for public buildings. I also like the duck.

But for the moment I was interested in the two women on Rainer's medical staff, both doctors. Few medical schools admitted women students until the middle of the twentieth century, and for years the experience for women was harrowing. Med schools, like law schools, were boys' clubs, and women had to work doubly hard to prove themselves while enduring incessant harassment, sometimes outright psychological torture, from male peers during their residencies. Those who survived were often permanently scarred by it.

Rainer's anesthesiologist, Isadora Grecchi, was fifty-one. That meant she would have been in med school in the early seventies. Still a dicey time for women. I looked at Grecchi's bio in the folder Rathbone had given me as I sat down at one of the library's computers and typed in "Ohio State University College of Medicine," where Grecchi had gotten her medical degree. Nothing. At least nothing to support my feeble hypothesis that a woman brutalized by her experiences as a medical student had thirty years later decided to retaliate by killing her patients.

If anything, the medical college looked like heaven. Its faculty director wrote books for women about how to get decent health care in a medical system designed by and for men. On the other hand, only seven of the college's thirty-eight faculty members were women. Numbers don't lie. The nice faculty director might be window dressing behind which lay a mined field of male supremacy. And what was it like in 1971 when Isadora Grecchi in bell-bottoms first practiced sticking needles in cadavers? My hypothesis was still intact, but I wasn't getting anywhere.

From the shelves I took five or six books on Columbus, Ohio, and continued to learn nothing useful. It seemed like a nice town. The capital and largest city in the state, it had the requisite schools, art museums, a symphony. Smack in the middle of Ohio.

I gave up and went for a glass of iced tea at a diner up the street with fading place-mat art on its grimy walls. And a lot of men coming in to buy something at the cash register and then leaving. Off-track betting on horse races is illegal in San Diego County, but I didn't mention that as I ordered my iced tea and a bag of chips. One crime at a time.

The diner was called Becky's, and might actually have been the pride and joy of somebody named Becky a half century ago. Now her name in a once-black script across the front window was so chipped and faded that the old-fashioned lettering seemed nothing more than a discoloration in the glass. The place was a storefront, long and dark inside. In the wall behind the counter were round window frames, some still holding jagged bits of mirror. Where the maroon and black asphalt floor tiles had worn through I could see the old plank flooring, probably salvaged from a no-longer-seaworthy ship, as was the custom here. San Diego has always had to scrounge for its lumber.

With my canned tea I was given a scratched red plastic glass half full of melting chipped ice and a straw in a paper wrapper. A very old woman in a long green coat and orange gloves sat at the counter drinking coffee from a thick white cup and talking to herself. The coat was worn and grimy at the cuffs, and most of the gloves' fingers had come unstitched. She didn't take the gloves off, even when she lifted the saucer to pour an ounce of spilled coffee back into her cup. The saucer didn't match the cup. The saucer had a blue design. Pagoda, willow, three little figures on a bridge.

I was at her side in two seconds.

"Isn't that the blue willow design?" I asked. "Do you remember this place from the old days? Did they use the blue willow restaurant plates here?"

The woman's wispy white hair was dyed a pinkish orange and she wore a musty sailor's watch cap. Her old eyes regarded me with curiosity, but I could see that I'd scared her. Her hands were shaking.

"You see," she said as if we'd been talking all along, "they always do that. They always say they'll get you the best deal and then just you wait. Then's when, then's when . . ." Her eyes grew cloudy. I could see it happen, like a shadow cast from inside her head.

"Fuckers fuckers," she mumbled. "Goddamn fucking fuckers-fuckersfuckers."

In her orange hands the coffee cup rattled against an old blue willow saucer.

"Oh, my God, I'm sorry," I whispered. I'd upset her, shattered her fragile space with my blundering. She hadn't been bothering me. It was I who bothered her. I was bothering one of the army of mentally ill people who just barely exist on the streets of any city. I thought she probably lived on Social Security in one of the nearby old hotels converted to "Single Room Occupancies" for just such unwanted people. And even though the skin of her face was so pale I could see through it to the veins and capillaries below, I couldn't help thinking of Roxie's mother.

"Here," I said, slipping two ten-dollar bills into her coat pocket. "You go to a movie and have dinner. Whatever you want. I'm so sorry I upset you."

"Fuckers!" she replied, glaring into one of the empty round windows behind the counter as her lower lip began to tremble and tears filled her eyes.

She'd just lose the money or somebody would steal it from her, I knew. I wanted to shoot myself.

Instead I went back to the library and bombed completely in my attempt to identify the origins of the term "blue plate special." A good library, it would have held the information I wanted if the information existed. But the four highly trained librarians found nothing about blue plate specials.

Then I spent two solid hours researching *diners* in the home-towns of all the Rainer Clinic staff. There were hundreds of diners in Denver, where Isadora Grecchi grew up. Also hundreds in San Diego, where Megan Rainer grew up. Jennings Rainer had spent his early years in Chicago, also hundreds. The two Rainer r.n.'s, Jeffrey Pond and Thomas Eldridge, were children in Bakersfield and Riverside, respectively. Plenty of diners in both places. I made notes of some diner names and street addresses in each locale. It was a shot in the dark. Blue willow plates, diners, death. There would be a connection. And it would exist in the mind of one of the people BB and I were about to visit.

He was in his shop, Death Row, when I arrived an hour early, working on a wall hanging which seemed to be swags of ordinary burlap fastened by tooled leather belts.

"Dude from the High Noon Boot Corral came in Auntie's, hired me to do a belt display," he said, eyeing my jester suit uneasily. "Blue, that what you gonna wear to catch a killer?"

"What's wrong with it?" I asked. "Other than the fact that I look like a bowlegged bit player from a Shakespearian touring company?"

"That do it."

"I hate to say it, BB, but the hip-hop pants and the low-rider undershirt you're wearing don't exactly say 'fashion statement' to me, either. They don't even *go* together."

"Ain't seen my do-rag yet," he said, grinning. "See, I be *knowin'* how to play this party. Give 'em what they want. Hey, criminal drag—it be *in*."

What BB was calling "criminal drag" was baggy hip-hop pants in chino, popularized by black rap groups, worn low on the hips with at least four inches of designer Y-fronts showing. These were topped by the heavy white cotton athletic T-shirt worn by Latino gang members. With a ratty cloth "do-rag" on his head, the manner of its tying a mark of black gang membership in Los Angeles, BB would be a walking billboard of multicultural threat. I wasn't sure what the military-style boots meant, but they looked dangerous, too.

"See, Blue," he went on, "party like this, you need to distract these fools. Give 'em a picture."

I could tell from the way he was circling me, eyes narrowed, that my jester outfit wouldn't do. That was okay. I hated it, anyway.

Grabbing a lump of black wool from a bag of used clothes BB buys by the pound at a distribution center down at the border, he held it to the light and grinned. It appeared to be a skirt. In minutes he'd located a brown and black pinstriped men's suitcoat with wide lapels and an ungodly mustard-yellow polyester blouse that would have fit a cow. The kind with the floppy bow at the neck. Something had chewed holes in the trailing ends of the bow. The blouse came to my knees.

"Just the thing," BB said. "Do this first," he added, trimming the blouse around me with pinking shears, then removing the attached scarf pieces with what looked like a scalpel. He'd found thread in a mustard-yellow match and it hung from a needle clenched between his teeth. A cut up the back of the blouse, five minutes of stitching, and the blouse fit perfectly, except for the sleeves. These he bunched above my elbows and secured with ordinary tape.

Next, the black skirt was altered, and then the suit jacket, which took longer than anything else. When he was finished, he steam-pressed everything and a greasy odor filled the air.

"Steam get some of the smell out," he noted.

"That's wonderful," I said, "but BB, what are you doing?"

"Got to look like a cop," he explained as he helped me into the freshly pressed jacket. "Scare 'em a little."

I didn't think I looked like a cop as much as like Mary Poppins. The black skirt grazed the tops of my shoes. All I needed was an umbrella with a parrot-head handle. Although I did like the brown-and-black pinstriped jacket. Very k.d. lang. The blouse was still hideous.

"Need somethin' else," he said.

Several scarves were rejected until he hit upon the idea of a string tie made of scraps from the jacket alterations. In seconds my collarless blouse was accessorized by a wool string tie fastened at the neck with a big brown coat button. Then he approached with a brown felt hat. A fedora, it looked as though very small mammals had lived in it. For years.

"No!" I said.

"Jus' try—"

"No."

We compromised on a brown corduroy tam he whipped up from an old pair of pants in the rag pile. I was afraid we were going to be late for our appointment with Jennings Rainer, but BB insisted on sewing another brown coat button to the tam's band.

"Now!" he said proudly.

I looked in all three mirrors and saw a combination of Annie Hall, Eleanor Roosevelt, and Cruella De Vil. In a newsboy's tam from 1920.

"If the idea is to frighten the people we're interviewing, this works," I told BB. "Now let's go."

In the car he fussed with his do-rag, a dirty black bandanna, all the way to La Jolla.

"Got to get the tie right," he insisted. "Get it wrong, gonna look like I'm tryin' to join the Aryan Nation."

"BB, there's no way," I said as we pulled into Jennings Rainer's gated condo parking lot. "It's a closed club."

The guard at the condo looked askance but let us in after phoning Rainer. It wouldn't be the last time we'd get funny looks, I thought. It's not every day you see a Gibson girl with cropped hair running around trendy neighborhoods with a black gangbanger whose entire life is probably devoted to selling your toddler drugs.

"I can't imagine why this is necessary, Dr. McCarron," Jennings Rainer said as he opened the door to a seventh-floor condo with a view of other condos. "And who is this?"

"Mr. Berryman is my bodyguard," I said in somber tones. "The police are concerned with their liability in this case. As an outside consultant, if I were to be hurt . . ."

"Ah," he said.

Doctors understand anything involving insurance.

BB stood conspicuously just inside the door and scoured Rainer's living room with his eyes as if assassins lurked behind every piece of furniture. Not that there was that much furniture.

Rainer's condo had obviously been done by a decorator who felt strongly about chrome. The glass-topped coffee table had a chrome frame, as did black leather director's chairs flanking a white leather couch on which I was sure nobody had ever sat. The railing of a small balcony beyond sliding glass doors was woven with chicken wire. I could see that each honeycomb was snugly fastened to the bottom of the rail with baling wire. There was no furniture on the balcony, but there was a double dog dish, one of those plastic igloo-shaped doghouses called Dogloos, and a cat-litter box containing two squares of grass turf.

"What's your dog's name?" I asked as Rainer and I sat in the black chairs.

"Um, Snuffy," he answered, tugging at the red plaid vest he wore over gray flannel slacks with a navy blazer. "He's upstairs. May I offer you something to drink—you and Mr. Berryman, of course?"

Jennings Rainer had well-trimmed white hair and the look of a very old choirboy. A few broken capillaries across his nose and cheeks might mean a drinking problem, or might mean he'd spent a lot of time crying. Hard. On a black enamel sofa table I saw a silver-framed photo of Rainer and a pleasant-looking woman with tinted red hair. The photo seemed fairly recent, and the woman did not appear to be well. The red hair was sparse and much shorter than that particular woman would ever wear it. Chemotherapy.

"No, thank you," I answered. "And I'm so sorry you have to go through this unpleasantness, but it has to be done. I'm aware that you lost your wife only two years ago. What a difficult time for you. We'll make this as brief as possible."

"I don't know what the police are talking about, Dr. McCarron," he began. "All my medical staff have been with me for years. No one at my clinic is sending these letters, and certainly no one at my clinic is killing our patients by somehow causing them to have cerebral hemorrhages. I do understand that the only common denominator among these women is that they've been our clients, but that is coincidence. What more can I say?"

At the top of carpeted stairs there was a *whuffing* sound.

"Snuffy," Jennings Rainer explained. "Do you mind?"

In a minute he returned holding a young schnauzer in his arms. The dog regarded me and then BB with interest but didn't bark. Instead, he licked Rainer's face and cocked his head as if expecting something.

"His walk," Rainer explained. "We always have ourselves a nice long walk when I get home, don't we, boy?"

"Snuff was Mar's dog, that's my wife, Marlis," he went on. "I got him for her when we knew, well, when the cancer came back. She adored him. Snuff was right there on the bed with her when she . . ."

"I'm so sorry, Dr. Rainer," I said, and I was.

In the remaining fifteen minutes he gave me thumbnail sketches of the rest of the medical staff. Megan, of course, had been expected to take over the clinic. But she and her husband, Chris, had bought some land in Northern California and wanted to move there, build a house, raise the kids in a small community. Chris had some ideas about land management, tree farming, sustainable agriculture. He wanted to grow trees and herbs, Rainer said with disbelief. Organic herbs. Her father was sure Megan was neither threatening nor murdering their patients.

"Jeff and T.J.," he went on, "both have been with me for years. Both r.n.'s, trained in the service. Jeff's my operating room manager, Jeff Pond. He was Navy. T. J. Eldridge is the surgical assistant, came out of the Army."

His eyes crinkled a little at the edges as he smiled. "Now, you're going to find both of these boys a little out of the ordinary, but they're not killers."

"Out of the ordinary?" I said as BB moved quickly to the kitchen door for no apparent reason and glared at a microwave oven. Rainer watched him, puzzled.

"Um, yes," he went on. "Pond's a weight-lifter, what do you call them? Bodybuilder. Good-looking man, though. And excellent in a crisis. Pond's got nerves of steel, just like those beefy arms of his.

"Now, T.J., he's a family man, a little old-fashioned like me. Completely dependable. Got two of the cutest little towheaded kids you ever saw. Mar always thought his wife was kind of 'slow,' if you know what I mean, and tried to help her out at clinic parties and what have you. Then come to find out Kara Eldridge has been going to school during the day without telling anybody and gotten herself a two-year degree in computer programming from a community college! Apparently she just finished her course of study a few months ago. She'd be so surprised, Mar would."

"Do you have a computer here?" I asked.

"It's my wife's," he said sheepishly. "To tell the truth, I meant to learn to use it, but I just haven't gotten around to it."

"Do you mind if I look at it?"

Upstairs the second bedroom had been made into a sort of office. The antiqued pine desk and chair had been his wife's, I thought, brought here from a house where they had lived and raised a little girl. As I booted up Marlis Rainer's old Macintosh computer, BB stood at the door and dramatically glanced back and forth through both windows as if snipers were stationed on every balcony in the facing building. Under his right sock was a gun-shaped bulge. As a parolee BB couldn't carry any weapon, much less a concealed one. But we figured the transparent green plastic squirt gun in his ankle holster wouldn't really qualify as a weapon or even an equally illegal facsimile. Rainer didn't seem to notice it.

The computer revealed that Marlis Rainer had collected recipes from the Internet, maintained interests in counted cross-stitch embroidery, organic container gardening, and child portrait photography, and spent a lot of time e-mailing friends, none of whom lived out of town. The last message, written over two years in the past, was to someone with the e-mail name "bettybun."

"I want you to have my mother's recipe for creamed chipped

beef," it said. "Megan and Chris are vegetarian and will never use it. Enjoy!"

Before the final stages of her illness, Rainer's wife had given away her recipes.

The computer's modem wasn't connected to any Internet service provider here, where Rainer had moved after his wife's death. There wasn't even a phone jack in the room. I turned Marlis Rainer's computer off. Quickly.

"And what about your anesthesiologist, Isadora Grecchi?" I said too loudly in the quiet little room.

Jennings Rainer had been watching as I invaded the now-lost world of his wife's days.

"Mar's creamed chipped beef was the best in the world," he said, sighing. "I suppose I should get rid of her old computer, get a new one for myself, learn all the things you can do on them. But you see, it's as if some part of her is still in there, in that wiring. Parts of her life, things she said to her friends, all her interests. I know she's gone, but part of her isn't. It's in there. So I just keep it, let it sit there."

He turned to face me, shoulders back.

"Dr. McCarron, I'm aware that the grieving process can be dangerous if it goes on too long. I'm thinking of seeing someone, a professional. This nonsense you're investigating has nothing to do with my clinic, but we're going to be ruined by it. I've already decided to close. And do you know? I don't care. Megan was not going to take over, anyway. My career is finished, my wife is dead, and I'm afraid to get rid of her computer. Can you recommend someone? I assume that in your line of work you have occasion to meet psychiatrists and other psychologists."

I didn't even bother to explain the difference between clinical and social psychology.

"The best person I know is a forensic psychiatrist," I said. "She's the staff psychiatrist at a state prison, but she has a private practice as well. She's also my partner in a consulting business. Let me give you her number."

"Forensics?" Rainer said, smiling for the first time. "That sounds rather interesting."

"I think you'll like her," I said. "I do."

As we made our way soundlessly back down the heavily carpeted stairs, Rainer said, "Oh, yes, you asked about Isadora. She's quite competent, has a number of interests outside work. Art, volunteering, that sort of thing. Isadora became a sort of mentor for Kara Eldridge after Mar's death, tried to help her as Mar had done. Isadora never married, seems quite content to live alone."

BB was listening, intently.

"She's quite involved in women's health issues," Rainer concluded.

"Uh-HUH," BB said softly as I nudged him out the door.

14

Real Art, No Art

Can't believe you send that dude to Roxie," BB said in my truck after he'd stopped giggling over Rainer's finding a woman who never married unusual.

"Rainer is from another time, BB," I said, addressing the issue of Grecchi's marital status. "In his day it was assumed that all any woman could possibly want was to care for a husband and family. And don't assume—"

"This Grecchi gonna turn out to be our man," he conjectured.

"Don't assume that," I insisted as we sped south on 1-5 toward the heart of San Diego and a one-thirty appointment with Isadora Grecchi. "And why wouldn't Rox be a good shrink for Rainer? He's depressed and he knows it. I think she'll be wonderful with him."

I did think Rox would be helpful to Jennings Rainer, and I didn't think Jennings Rainer had sent threatening letters *or* poisoned caviar to anyone. But I'm not renowned for my abilities with people, only with numbers.

"What did you think of Rainer?" I asked BB.

"Sad old dude. Loved his wife, she gone. His daughter ain't gonna take over the business. All he got is that dog."

I equate the love of animals with a sort of core decency which precludes the murder of other species, such as our own. But that isn't remotely true. Any number of murderers have been apprehended in the company of a pet, and there are regulations regarding what must be done with pets taken into custody because their owners are on their way to death row. I thought Jennings Rainer was exactly what he appeared to be, but that didn't mean he was. What if Snuffy was just a prop? A borrowed dog meant to create precisely the illusion I'd fallen for? But Snuffy had seemed happy in the arms of Jennings Rainer and had clearly expected the walk Rainer said they took every day. Had I been conned by a schnauzer?

And the wife's computer. Rainer couldn't have faked that without a lot of work. It was real, as were his feelings. And the computer couldn't have been used to e-mail me or Rathbone because it wasn't connected to a server. It was only a dusty electronic ghost Rainer would need help exorcizing. Rainer and thousands of other people in coming years, I thought. People who could return in time to the lost world of a dead loved one with the flick of a mouse, perhaps discovering things they were never intended to know. And then perhaps not being able to get back. I wondered if dad had given this problem any thought. It would make a terrific pastoral counseling workshop.

BB seemed unusually thoughtful. "Dude really loved his wife," he said.

"Yeah."

"Blue, you ever love anybody like that? Like if they gone you just *empty*?"

I didn't know what to say. BB is eight years younger than I am, and while a friend, he's also a former patient of Roxie's from his days in prison. There were boundaries, I thought. But he wasn't being nosy or intrusive. He just wanted to know something.

"Yes," I said, forgetting about the boundaries. "It took me a long time to get back to myself after she was gone. For a while, for a few years, I felt empty like that and kept emptiness around me. It's hard. And nobody tells you how hard it's going to be. There aren't any songs on the radio about that emptiness, no books or movies. But sooner or later most people find out, and then they don't talk about it, either. Why, BB?"

"I never cared that much about anybody," he said quietly. "But I'd like to."

Isadora Grecchi lived in an old Craftsman bungalow in San Diego's Mission Hills district. Built in the thirties, these architectural gems can be found all over central San Diego. Grecchi's had been restored but with modern features where advisable. Its long-eaved roof had been done in synthetic, fireproof shake shingles, and a deck cantilevered over a canyon rim in back was visible from the street. I parked in her driveway and saw the front door opening. Even from her porch, it was clear that Isadora Grecchi wasn't happy about our visit.

"What's *he* doing here?" she yelled.

BB flexed all the muscles in his upper body and then stood glowering beside my truck with his arms crossed over his chest. He was truly formidable, unless you knew him. And so was Isadora Grecchi. I was certain no one had ever described her as "pretty," but with her coarse, unruly black hair and huge brown eyes, she was *interesting*. Wide cheekbones, aquiline nose, too-large mouth. She was wearing jeans and a paint-spattered tan corduroy shirt, no shoes. Big bones, about five-five, but not an ounce of fat.

"And who does *your* hair?" BB said under his breath.

"Mr. Berryman is my bodyguard," I said for the second time that day. "I'm Dr. Blue McCarron."

"I know who you are. The police said it would be necessary to talk to you in order to avoid being interviewed by one of them at the police station. I had no idea they'd send a bag lady and an apprentice pimp. I want you to get this asshole off my property."

Her voice was deep and projected like a trained singer's. I could have heard her a block away.

"I'm sorry," I said. "It's police policy to ensure the safety of consultants in the field."

"Bullshit," boomed Isadora Grecchi, quite correctly. "All right, come in. Let's get this over with."

Grecchi's opening remarks were no indication of her taste. The interior of the house had been gutted, providing a spectacular view through the structure and out to the deck and canyon beyond. The original woodwork on walls and ceilings had been kept and refinished in an eggshell varnish that emphasized the grain. Ditto the hardwood floors, rarely seen in any but San Diego's oldest homes. A fireplace in the north wall also retained its original Italian glazed tiles in a deep celery color Grecchi had repeated in silk throw pillows strewn on two couches slipcovered in buttery yellow canvas. On the east wall was a stark black and white abstract I suspected was an original Franz Kline. The only thing in the room that didn't exude artistic taste so understated you almost missed it was a shabby brown corduroy teddy bear on the mantel. The toy was missing one of its black button eyes and lent a sense of sadness and disarray to the impeccable surroundings.

"Sit down," Grecchi told me.

To BB she said, "What kind of statement are you making by displaying your underwear? You look like a fucking two-year-old."

BB merely stood by the door and glared, although I could tell he was warming to her. To the right of a kitchen/dining area at the back of the house I could see an easel under a skylight. The scent of oil paint was everywhere and she held a brush in her left hand.

"You do abstracts," I guessed aloud.

"And you don't," she answered.

A comedian. But there was an edge to Isadora Grecchi that wasn't funny. Something jumpy and bitter. Maybe dangerous.

In fifteen minutes I was told several times that she knew absolutely nothing about threatening letters or murders connected to the Rainer Clinic, where she had worked for fifteen years. All other questions were answered cursorily. She'd had a decorator select her china and didn't know what a blue willow plate was, she said, opening a kitchen cabinet door to display elegant plain black dishes and pale green Hungarian stemware. She had never belonged to a church and in fact couldn't be paid enough to set foot in one. I could tell she was enjoying my incompetence, which made me feel even more incompetent. Until I mentioned Jennings Rainer.

"Dr. Rainer mentioned that you're involved in women's health care issues," I said, fishing awkwardly. "And yet you're doing breast implants and—"

"I don't do breast implants or any other form of surgery," she interrupted. "I'm an anesthesiologist. I anesthetize."

But I'd seen it and so had BB. A leap of emotion at the mention of Rainer's name, a softening of those dramatic facial features. The impression, oddly, was one of motherliness. Isadora Grecchi seemed to feel, for a split second, *protective* of the aging surgeon. But why?

"When the clinic closes, I plan to join the staff of a hospital which specializes in breast cancer," she went on in obvious defense. "In the meantime, I donate two afternoons a week to surgeries at a women's reproductive health center."

The politically correct credentials were clearly important to her. So why had she stayed on the staff of the politically incorrect Rainer Clinic for fifteen years?

"Is the clinic definitely closing?" I ventured. "Dr. Rainer seemed to hold out hope that his daughter might take it over."

"Megan," Isadora said coldly, "hates the money with which she supports a husband and two children. She wants to go live among towering pines and eat tuberous begonias. She will not take over the practice when Jen . . . when Dr. Rainer retires. Which will happen in a matter of days, thanks to you and this demented crap about one of us killing our patients. Once a rumor like this gets out, the clinic is finished. Jennings isn't ready to broadcast the information, but yes, the Rainer Clinic will close this week. He and Megan and I have already canceled all procedures scheduled after tomorrow, when the story will hit the press. The police said this interview would take about fifteen minutes. Your time's up."

"Mind if I use your bathroom?" BB asked, already moving toward a hallway off the main room. "Gotta—"

"Just use the bathroom and then get out of here," she snapped, really angry now. She didn't want BB in her house, especially in her private space. I could see that his request to use the bathroom was, to her, an invasion. Women don't react to men the way Grecchi did for no reason.

"We'll be gone shortly," I said. "I know this is unpleasant for you."

With BB out of the room there was a difference in the woman facing me. A sliver of openness. And a look.

Don't go any further, it said.

I wanted to put a hand on her shoulder but there was something about Isadora Grecchi that wouldn't be touched. Instead I suggested that she return to her painting while BB and I made our exit. She agreed, and as we left I saw her dabbing at the canvas with the brush in her left hand, while with her right she held up the middle finger at our retreating backs.

Outside, BB said, "Computer in the bedroom *with* a phone line, so our lady of the bad hair can send e-mails. Lotta pills in the bathroom."

"Pills? Did you get any of the names?"

He rolled his eyes and then said, "Klonopin, Prozac, Zoloft, Paxil, Celexa, Neurontin, Nardil, Parnate."

"Write them down once we get in the truck. I don't know about the rest of them, but Prozac's a popular antidepressant. Rox will know what they are. Looks like we might have a suspect. Grecchi's a ticking bomb."

"The lady don' like men, tha's for sure," he said while writing. "But she ain't no dyke. Hard to get a call on that one."

I wasn't sure I wanted to get a call on Isadora Grecchi, in whom something painful lay tightly curled. Then I remembered my conversation with Roxie when Rathbone first asked us to work on the case.

"What if we're tracking down a woman?"

What if we were?

Our next appointment was for three-thirty with Thomas J. Eldridge, the surgical assistant, at his home in Carlsbad. To reach the northern coastal suburb we had to go back up 1-5 past La Jolla and a sequence of beach communities. By Del Mar, the first village beyond La Jolla, BB's stomach was growling.

"We'll find someplace in Del Mar to get a sandwich," I said. "I need to call Rathbone anyway."

Del Mar's main street, Camino Del Mar, is part of the old Coast Highway, originally a horse path with breathtaking views of the Pacific. The current population far exceeds what the street can offer in the way of parking spaces, so I headed for Del Mar Plaza. The new and relentlessly upscale shopping center has an underground parking lot. My satisfaction at being able to park obscured my judgment, however. I'd forgotten that BB and I looked as if we'd wandered off the set for a movie involving black ghetto criminals in Jane Austen's England. The maître d' at my favorite restaurant tried valiantly not to scream when we approached his podium at the door of the restaurant.

"Two, please," I said.

BB pulled his pants up to his waist, although since they weren't supposed to be there, they didn't stay.

"Of course," we were told, and then escorted to a table in the rear near a small bar not currently in use. The bar acted as a wall between us and the other patrons.

"I'd prefer a table with a view," I said.

"I'll see if one is available."

At two-ten in the afternoon most of the tables were empty.

"Look like about sixty available," BB noted, giving the man a sizing-up look I was sure he'd learned in prison. "The lady want a *nice* view."

The maître d' sighed in a way which suggested that escorting people to tables in restaurants was an exhausting job with weighty philosophical ramifications.

"Will this do?" he said into a space of thin air between us, indicating a window table with a presentable view of the Pacific Ocean.

"Sho nuff," BB said. Menacing grin. Lots of teeth.

"Don't overdo it," I told BB, and then ordered the restaurant's signature salad—a salmon jerky Caesar with wonton croutons.

BB ordered a salad of greens, apples, caramelized walnuts, sun-dried cranberries, and balsamic maple dressing topped with goat cheese fondue. We decided to split the entree, barbecued sugar-spiced king salmon with garlic mashed potatoes. BB was impressed with the food.

"Don't get nuthin' like this in prison," he joked. "Or nowhere else. What kinda food *is* this, Blue?"

"California cuisine," I told him. "What that means is a creative chef and a mix of styles ranging from Tex-Mex to Pacific Rim. I'm going to call Rathbone, see if there's anything new we need to know before the Eldridge interview. I wish I knew what I'm doing."

"Two outta five," he said. "So far my money on Grecchi. Somethin' *off* about her."

I agreed with BB. Isadora Grecchi was wound as tightly as the mile of rubber band inside a golf ball. Had something cracked the tough surface, causing her to unravel? And even if so, would a woman to whom the plight of women is so important threaten and possibly kill women?

Rathbone wasn't in when I called but had left a message. "Background checks on Rainer personnel indicate the following," I was told by a clerk. "Isadora Grecchi made ward of family court in Denver, Colorado, 1958. No further details, as juvenile files are sealed. Jeffrey Alan Pond, suspicion of rape, San Diego, 1997, charges dropped. Megan Rainer, suspicion of carrying concealed weapon, Riverside, California, 1999, charges dropped. A ceramic plate with a blue oriental design was dusted for fingerprints and was clean. Detective Rathbone wants to talk to you after you've interviewed all suspects," the clerk concluded.

So at least three of the Rainer employees had come to the attention of legal authorities, two of them recently. Accusations of rape and of carrying a concealed weapon. The operating room manager and Rainer's daughter, respectively. And of course the plate Sword left at my door had no fingerprints, I thought.

He, or she, wasn't stupid. Unless driving for hours through mountains and deserts in order to prop a cheap plate against the door of a stranger could be construed as stupid.

Which it couldn't. Unusual, yes. Strange and threatening. But nothing connected to this case or the people involved in it seemed particularly harebrained. With the exception of Sword's bad spelling, so far I felt as if I were wandering in a symbolist play written by somebody whose native language is not English. That jarring sense that all the lines being read are awkward translations of something that might otherwise make sense.

BB and I arrived at the Eldridge home at precisely three-thirty, reeking of salmon. Eldridge's wife, Kara, met us at the door.

"I took the children to a neighbor's because I was afraid something like this might make them afraid of the police," she said. "I think it's so important that children understand the policeman is their friend, don't you?"

At his post by the door BB stifled a laugh. I remembered that Jennings Rainer had said his wife regarded Kara Eldridge as perhaps a little slow and had tried to help her navigate social situations. She did seem childlike, with wide hazel eyes under a mop of long blonde hair parted in the middle and held at the back of her neck with a sparkly pink clip. She was wearing no makeup and a white sweatshirt with a painted cat on the front, its left front paw on a ball of chartreuse yarn. Instead of pants she wore navy blue culottes, which, as is invariably the case with culottes, made her look heavier than she really was. I couldn't pinpoint why she looked familiar to me until I realized that she resembled the girl on the library bas-relief, forever unaware of anything but her book. That sense of oblivion.

"We aren't police," I explained as I took a seat at the end of a pink and green plaid couch. "I'm a social psychologist consulting with the police on a case involving patients at the Rainer Clinic. Mr. Berryman is my bodyguard. I'd like to speak with your husband, Thomas Eldridge, please."

If Kara Eldridge felt any discomfort at BB's presence, she didn't show it.

"He's in the garage," she said. "Let me get you some coffee

and I'll call T.J. I made some lemon bars, too. Low-fat. The kind you mix with applesauce instead of the cooking oil. T.J.'s very careful about what we eat. I mean, he'll *only* eat things I make for him special except for his baloney and cheese and crackers. Has to be cheddar, extra-extra sharp. T.J. never goes *anywhere* without his little Baggie of extra-extra sharp cheddar I cut up for him, and baloney and some crackers."

I had no idea what to say to that, so I just smiled.

"But you don't look like you need to worry about your weight," she said to BB. Perfectly at ease with an apparent street savage in her living room.

Then I remembered Rainer saying Kara had gone to a community college, just finished a two-year degree in something about computers. San Diego's community colleges are melting pots, drawing students from diverse ethnic populations. Kara Eldridge would have been around plenty of people who looked just like BB there, as well as Vietnamese fishermen, Latina hairdressers, and Iraqi cab drivers getting degrees in hotel/motel management.

"Lemon bars sound good," BB said, eyeing the mantel, which bore a collection of studio photos of Kara, a man with short brown hair, and two blonde children.

In the space above, normally reserved in American homes for a single piece of art that embodies the taste of those who live beneath it, was a small framed poster. One of those lists of aphorisms urging adults to like children. "No man stands so tall as when he stoops to help a child" kind of thing. Around the little poster were pale rectangles of paint, their edges clearly defined. A collection of pictures had hung there until recently, then been removed. The cardboard poster was a stopgap measure.

"Gonna check around," BB said pointlessly, since there was no one there but me. Then he loped into the kitchen and I heard a door opening. To the garage, I thought. Then a rumbling conversation I couldn't hear.

"My wife will serve us in the living room. Please follow me." Door closing, firmly.

The man who preceded BB into the room was the man in

the mantel photos. Close-cropped dark hair, slight build, brown eyes with heavy, drooping lids. The plates from which Kara served the lemon bars were plain white with an embossed leaf pattern on the rims. The cups and saucers matched.

"I have no ideas about this business you're here to investigate," T. J. Eldridge said from a standing position before the fireplace, his arm on the mantel. "But of course we support the police in any way possible. What is it we can do for you?"

"I understand you were in the Army, Mr. Eldridge," I said, having as usual no idea what I was doing.

"Medical corpsman." The answer was itself snappy, military. *Next?* it implied.

"How long have you and Mrs. Eldridge lived here?" This question is common on credit and loan applications and was at one time a good indicator of stability. Now people move around so often that it's meaningless, but I couldn't think of anything else to say.

"Four years. Our daughter, Ann, was six and we wanted a good school district."

Kara's look when he said "Ann" was strange, as if he'd forgotten their child's name. But she quickly covered it and continued to smile at her husband.

"Tell me what you do at Rainer," I went on, and then pretended to listen as he detailed his schedule and responsibilities, which largely involved assisting in surgeries, clamping, "tying off bleeds," he said, as well as post-operative monitoring and follow-up appointments. After five minutes I turned to Kara and said brightly, "Does Ann collect miniature tea sets?"

"Who?" Kara Eldridge answered.

"Your daughter."

"Oh, Namey's such a tomboy she's more interested in action figures and soccer than tea sets," Kara began. "Of course, T.J. insists that the children be home-schooled, but she's allowed to play soccer with a girl's team at the Y. She has practice on Thursdays, and—"

"You don't need to know about our children," T.J. interrupted defensively, rocking back and forth on military-style black leather shoes equipped, I noticed, with lifts. T.J. wanted to appear taller than the five-six or so I guessed him to be in his bare feet.

In the next ten minutes BB gazed piercingly out windows and into bookcases full of ceramic kittens as I learned the Eldridges were members of Memorial Methodist Church, volunteered at a food bank once a month, and enjoyed hikes and rock collecting along Carlsbad's beaches. There was no television in the family room where we were talking, and I mentioned it.

"Oh, T.J. thinks—" Kara began, and then stopped as her husband finished the sentence.

"There's so much junk on television," he said. "We want the children to enjoy reading, develop their imaginations that way instead."

It was a noble thought, but there wasn't a single book visible in the room, either. Not even a magazine.

"Mr. Eldridge, is there anyone connected to the Rainer Clinic who in your opinion might be capable of the terrorist acts we're investigating?" I asked.

"Absolutely not," he answered, glancing at a clunky watch that dwarfed his wrist. One of those Swiss Army-knife-type watches that also has a compass and a stopwatch, tells you what time it is in ten world capitals as well as everywhere the U.S. has military installations, and hides a tiny manicure kit in the case. "We have plans, so if there's nothing else . . . ?"

"One more thing. Do you own a computer, Mr. Eldridge?"

"Three," he answered proudly. "The children have one which they use for their schoolwork. Some years ago I gave Kara an old one of mine, and she's developed quite an interest in them, even gotten some training. Of course I have one as well. We're all on-line. Why?"

"So many people find them useful," I answered vaguely. "Thank you. We'll be going now."

The Eldridges stood on their steps as BB and I drove away. They seemed posed, standing there as if they expected to be photographed.

"The pictures that was over the fireplace before they took 'em down?" BB began.

"Yeah?"

"They out in the garage, hung on a wall over T.J.'s computer setup. Buncha pictures of his wife. Pretty nice. Wife in the kitchen, cookin', mostly. Wife sayin' prayers with the kids kneelin' beside their beds. Wife all dressed up and smilin' with a corsage on her dress, look like Easter. Guess he love her, take all them pictures. Glass broke in the one with her prayin'. Guess they took 'em down to get it fixed. Maybe he's got some new ones. These looked like from a long time ago, kids just little chubby babies."

"There's something weird about those people," I told BB. "Like T.J. called their daughter Ann and then Kara called her Namey. Seems like an odd nickname, doesn't it?"

"I got a cousin called Namey," he replied. "Her real name Naomi. She got two brothers name Joshua and Nehemia, too. Whole family get baptized every year at Easter. They mama, my aunt, she say it wear off after a while, have to keep doin' it. You think that's right?"

"Fine with me if it works for her," I answered. "But the traditional thing is to just do it once. Isn't it strange that a mother and father don't call their daughter by the same name?"

"Nah, my daddy call me Bernard when I used to see him, 'fore he got killed. Mama, she always call me Bernie. And what *strange* was the lemon bars. Taste like water and paper."

"Must have been the applesauce," I said, wondering for the hundredth time that day what I was doing.

15

Shadows

Jeffrey Pond came to the door of his apartment in a blinding Hawaiian shirt and navy blue sweatpants. His bare feet were still pink from a hot shower and he smelled like Dove soap.

"I'm Dr. Blue McCarron and this is Mr. Berryman," I began.

"Dude," Pond said to BB as if they were surf buddies. To me he said, "Hey," as he gestured for us to enter. I remembered that he was forty-one. Why was he speaking in the one-syllable code used by teenagers?

"Thank you," I pronounced slowly, hoping to introduce the idea of two-syllable speech. Otherwise, I thought, this interview could take all night.

BB stood by the door as usual, eyeing Pond's overdeveloped muscles. The biceps pushing against the man's flowered sleeves as he picked up an upholstered chair and set it down facing the couch were the size of softballs.

"So," he said amiably, flopping into the chair and grabbing what looked like a huge wad of Silly Putty from the coffee table, "what's this about?"

I watched as he crushed the Silly Putty in his right hand,

making all the muscles in his forearm stand out like an anatomy illustration.

"The police will have explained to you that someone has threatened to kill at least four women who were patients of the Rainer Clinic," I said. "Two of these women are dead. Can you spell the word, 'encyclopedia,' Mr. Pond?"

For a split second I felt shrewd. The author of the Sword letters was a rotten speller. I wished I'd done this with the others. Jeffrey Pond switched the Silly Putty to his left hand and spelled "encyclopedia" correctly. I no longer felt shrewd.

"I think it can also be 'p-a-e-d' in the old spellings," he noted. "Is this a trick?"

"No. Why are you squashing Silly Putty in your hands?"

"Bodybuilding. Got a competition coming up. Builds the forearm."

I remembered Roxie mentioning that the killer, if male, might have a super-macho hobby. Did bodybuilding qualify? I couldn't quite see posing, oiled, in a thong as macho. John Wayne wouldn't have done it, I was certain. Jeffrey Pond's bright blue eyes were as guileless as a puppy's, but not unintelligent.

"You want some o.j. or something?" he asked. "I've got some mango-guava juice, too."

"Thank you, but we don't have much time. Do you have a computer, Mr. Pond?"

"Jeff," he answered. "You can call me Jeff. And I haven't killed anybody. Sure, I've got a computer. You wanna look around? I don't care. Come on."

With that he launched himself out of the desk chair and led us through the small, tidy apartment. Dining area, kitchen, half bath. Then the hall, a full bath done in tan ceramic tile still steamy and littered with body oils, and two bedrooms. The smaller bedroom contained a double bed and matching dresser. The larger one held weight-lifting equipment and a computer on an inexpensive student's desk.

"Lotta bodybuilding sites on the Web," he said. "Good place to find out about competitions. And my son downloads games when he's here on weekends. I'm divorced. My son visits on weekends. Steve. He's fourteen."

The information was presented casually, but I hadn't asked for it. So what did that mean? Jeffrey Pond seemed to have nothing to hide. In fact, Jeffrey Pond seemed to be dying to talk.

"You were arrested on suspicion of rape in 1997," I mentioned as we moved back into the living room. "I am not a law enforcement officer, but a social psychologist consulting with the police department on this investigation. And even if I were an officer, you wouldn't have to discuss that arrest without an attorney present."

He flung himself into the upholstered chair again as I resumed my seat on the couch.

"It was the divorce," he answered, grabbing the Silly Putty again. "I really got screwed. My ex-wife wanted custody of Stevie and my little girl, Beth. She wanted to make me look bad in court. So she had this friend of hers claim I'd tried to rape her. Cops came and took me downtown, interrogated me, the whole nine yards. Only thing is, the night this woman said I'd tried to date-rape her after taking her home from a club, I was at an all-night gym working out. I mean, I *did* give her a ride home from this place we all used to hang out on weekends sometimes, but I didn't even go in. Just dropped her off and went to the gym.

"Gwen, that's my ex, didn't know I'd started working out. At first lifting weights was just a way of dealing with the stress, you know? But then I really got into it—bodybuilding, I mean. Anyway, they'd set this whole thing up, Gwen and her pal Jeri. But five guys told the cops I was at the gym from ten-thirty to one o'clock that night. This woman said I jumped her at eleven-thirty after drinking up her flavored vodka. Shit, all I had that night was one beer at the club. I don't even *like* vodka, especially if it has flowers in the bottle.

"After that Jeri admitted it was a setup and dropped the charges. But you know what? It's on my record now, 'suspicion of rape,' and the damn judge won't let me have Beth here overnight. Never. I can only have my daughter with me during the day unless we stay over at my parents' so there's 'supervision.' My daughter is *eight*!"

BB and I watched as Silly Putty squirted in four explosive arcs from between the fingers of Jeffrey Pond's clenched fist. I had no idea what to say next.

"Did you get your r.n. training in the Navy?" I ventured.

"Some of it," he answered without interest. "I'd gotten a job as an orderly at a state psych hospital right out of high school. They provided training and then paid half your tuition if you wanted to go to a community college at night for more medical training, so I did and then I went into the service as a registered practical nurse. Finished my r.n. in the Navy. Wanted to go back to school on the G.I. Bill when I got out, become a doctor's assistant. But by then Gwen and I were a thing, and then she got pregnant, or she said she did, and we got married, but she lost the baby in her second month. At least that's what she said. I don't think I believe it now. I think she just wanted to get married, and there I was, this dumb stooge who thought that was the Christian thing, you know? Marry the woman if you loved her enough to knock her up. But everything was okay for a long time. We had Steve, and then Beth. I *thought* everything was okay. Right."

Christian thing.

"So you trained as an r.n. instead of as a doctor's assistant?"

"Yeah."

Jeffrey Pond seemed to have very little interest in discussing his work. And a lot of interest in discussing his ex-wife.

"How did you come to work at the Rainer Clinic?"

"Answered an ad in the paper ten years ago, liked the hours. I'm off at two. Gave me time to do some temp jobs at night out of the nursing registry. Made enough to buy us a nice house, get Gwen the things she wanted. Furniture, new carpeting, her own car. So now she's got the house and the furniture and the car, and I'm still paying for all of it plus child-support payments and alimony. Hell, I can barely afford this place, which you've probably noticed is a dump."

"Do you—" I began, but was interrupted.

"You know what I'd like to do?" he said, mashing the Silly Putty flat between both palms. "I'd like to just *leave,* take off and start all over again someplace else with a new identity and a clean slate. Someplace away from Gwen. But I can't. My parents are getting old. Dad's not doing too well. Emphysema. Heart problems, too. I have to do things for them. Supposed to honor thy father and thy mother, you know? And how would I ever get a job? All I know is nursing, and it could be traced if I got a job in any hospital. Gwen could find me, track me down. And the kids. They're my kids. I can't just leave my parents and my kids. I'm stuck, as in *stuck pig,* you know?"

His jaw was clenched in what looked like anger, but I was afraid he was going to start crying. Again, I had no idea what to say, but BB leaped to the rescue.

"Dude," he said, somehow communicating masculine sympathy. The single, meaningless syllable seemed to help Pond, who relaxed and stood up.

"So anyway, I don't know anything about threatening letters or what happened to those patients who died of cerebral hemorrhages," he said. "I wish I could help you, but I can't."

Our fifteen minutes were up.

"Thank you," I said as BB halfheartedly placed himself between me and Pond as I walked out the door.

In the truck he said, "One miserable dude. Kind of makes you glad to be gay, never have to do all that divorce business."

"Did you hear him say 'the Christian thing' about marrying Gwen after she said she was pregnant?" I asked. "And quoting the Ten Commandments about honoring *thy* father and mother? Biblical language, like Sword's letters."

"Blue, lotta people talk about Christian this and Christian that. Say 'thy' and 'thou,' too, if they raised to know the Ten Commandments. Didn't you have to memorize all that when you was a kid? I did, in Sunday school. Still know 'em, too. 'I am the Lord thy God and thou shalt have no other gods before me. Thou shalt not make any graven image—'"

"BB, please," I interrupted. "My father is a clergyman and you're black. We're both from backgrounds where we'd memorized the

Ten Commandments as children. But Pond's the first Rainer employee so far who's used biblical language."

"Don't mean nuthin'. Fact he been screwed by his wife maybe do, though. Dude's hurtin' and he's mad."

"And talking," I said. "Surely he wouldn't talk so much if he knew how suspicious it makes him look. He can't seem to stop, though. I always get stuck on airplanes next to somebody like that who insists on telling me boring personal stories. It's some kind of syndrome."

"All you supposed to do is remember and tell Roxie," BB said. "All I supposed to do is scare white folks. Didn't scare this dude, though. Shit, he didn't even know I was there once he got goin' on how baaad his wife be."

"That does seem to be his sole topic of conversation," I agreed. "But I wonder how much of what he said is true."

It was time to visit Megan Rainer and her husband, Christopher Nugent. I'd have to drive through Julian, where they lived, on the way to my desert hideaway, so I dropped BB off at his shop before heading east on I-8. I let the truck idle as we sat outside for a few minutes.

"I been locked up with a lotta killers," he said, drawing X's in the dust on my dashboard with the edge of his thumb. "Premeditated, manslaughter, drunken brawls, guys catchin' back for some dude ballin' their wife, all that. Course, they all act like they ain't done nuthin', they innocent, somebody else did it, and all that shit. But they did and you be *knowin'* they did. Jus' somethin' you can tell, be around these guys all day and night for a year or two."

He quit drawing in dust and stared through my windshield into the distance.

"Don't nobody talk about it. Nobody ever say, 'Oh yeah, I'm in this shithole for thirty years 'cause I s'posed to kill my old lady with a baseball bat, only I didn't kill nobody, y'see. I got framed, man!' Nobody ever say nuthin', but after a while you kinda know. It's like you can see it, how this guy would do some crime, and this other guy would do another. It's like the crime leave a shadow on 'em, y'know?"

BB rarely says that much at one time, so I knew he'd been thinking about it. I also knew he had a sixth sense about crime and criminals you can only get in prison.

"So what do you think?" I asked. "Of the people we've seen today, who's got a shadow that looks like murder?"

"That's what so funky," he answered as he opened the door. "'Cept for the old doctor, they *all* do."

I thought about that as I drove up from San Diego's coastal basin and into the mountains. Isadora Grecchi was angry at the world about something I suspected would turn out to involve rape . . . but angry enough to betray her oath as a physician and "do harm" to her patients? And if she was a rape victim, why would she victimize women? The nurse, Thomas Eldridge, hadn't seemed murderous to me, merely stuffy and rigid. A world-class bore. But that might be a facade covering something else. And while Jeff Pond was obviously angry at his ex-wife over a messy divorce, did that mean he was taking out his anger by killing prominent women clients of the Rainer Clinic?

BB had said he didn't see the shadow on Jennings Rainer, but maybe he'd been blinded by the older man's grief as I had. Or by adorable Snuffy, the schnauzer. What if Rainer was really the killer? After years of working with the same staff, he'd know them intimately. He'd know all their personal problems and how suspicious each one might look to someone seeking motivation for this strange sequence of murders. And Jennings Rainer had plenty of time to construct a presentation that would make him appear as harmless as Gandhi.

All of them, I realized, had plenty of time to construct such a facade. None of them was stupid. All possessed sufficient medical training to manipulate blood pressure. All had opportunity to do things to the bodies of anesthetized patients. But what "things"? If one of these people was killing Rainer Clinic patients, how was he or she doing it?

I kept driving and wondered how I'd gotten into this. Nobody is worse at interviews than I am, and nobody knows less about blood pressure.

The home of Megan Rainer and Christopher Nugent looked

like a "before" illustration from a manual on restoring quaint old houses. A little outside the village of Julian but visible from the road, it sat about a quarter of the way up a steep, rocky hill. Once a cream color with navy blue shutters and porch railings, the two-story frame house now seemed merely a two-tone gray. Curls of peeling paint shivered along its eaves in a wind I was afraid meant rain. I wanted to get down the eastern slope of the mountain before it hit.

"Hi, I'm Chris Nugent," Megan's husband greeted me in the pool of yellow light spilling from the front door as he opened it. I could smell pizza baking. "Jenna, that's our daughter, had an accident with a neighbor's horse and Megan took her down the hill for an X ray. Horse stepped on Jenna's foot. I'm afraid Megan won't be back in time for you to interview her, but I'll be happy to answer any questions I can. Why don't we go in the kitchen, have some coffee while we talk."

Unlike the forbidding exterior of the house, the interior was bright and pleasant with overflowing bookcases, a huge braided rug, and a stone fireplace in which a small blaze flourished. A doorway to the right of the fireplace led to a large kitchen in which a small boy who looked like Jennings Rainer was washing and tearing romaine lettuce for a salad.

"Joshua, this is Dr. McCarron, who's a social psychologist. What they do is predict things. Dr. McCarron, Joshua."

"Hi," he said, jumping down from the stepstool where he'd been standing to work at the sink, and holding a dripping wet hand in my direction. "Can you predict stuff like when asteroids will crash into earth?"

"Um, no," I said, shaking his wet hand. "But I can probably predict how many people in Fresno will think the asteroid is really a robot spaceship sent by aliens from another galaxy when it does hit," I offered.

He wiped his hands on his jeans and grinned, revealing the absence of a front tooth.

"Wow!" he said. "Guess you could write some great stories."

"As long as they're written in numbers," I agreed.

"I'll finish making the salad," his father said. "You and Elsa can go play until the pizza's ready. Dr. McCarron and I have some things to talk about."

After the boy and a sedate Boston terrier I hadn't seen curled in a basket by the back door were gone, Chris Nugent poured coffee into brown pottery mugs for us both and then continued to wash romaine lettuce as I sat at the table. The dishes I could see through glass cabinet doors were Fiestaware in various colors. No blue willow.

"Megan has told me about these threats to Rainer patients, and the two deaths," he said. "Of course Jennings will have no choice but to close the clinic. What's your take on it?"

I hadn't expected to be interviewed, but he seemed genuinely interested.

"I think it's possible, even likely, that one of the medical staff at the Rainer Clinic is killing patients," I answered. "You must know these people from social events over the years. Have you seen anything that would indicate—"

"—the presence of a maddened serial killer?" he finished for me. "It's ridiculous. It would have to be Megan, her father, Isadora Grecchi, Jeff Pond, or T. J. Eldridge. The receptionist and clerical staff have no contact with the patients. And I can assure you that my wife doesn't run around killing people. I can also assure you—"

"Your wife has been arrested on charges of carrying a concealed weapon," I mentioned.

He let the romaine fall into the sink and spun to face me so fast that his long braid whipped over his shoulder and fell across the front of his blue shirt.

"For crying out loud, Dr. McCarron," he said angrily, "surely you know how much credibility to put in arrest reports! I want to show you something."

He walked to a third door in a far wall of the kitchen and opened it, gesturing for me to follow. After he turned on the light I could see that the room was an office, obviously his. The clean smell of new textbooks was evident, and the books themselves were stacked everywhere. On a desk which was really a door on sawhorses sat a computer. I could see the modem wire running to a wall jack.

"I have a Ph.D. in comparative physics and write abstracts for professional journals," he explained. "But this is what I want to show you."

He unlocked a closet, reached to its top shelf, and withdrew what looked like a big plastic jar of red bath oil beads. The kind that are usually egg-shaped. The waxy shell melts in hot water, releasing the bath oil inside. These weren't egg-shaped, but round. He threw the jar on a battered plaid couch.

"Know what those are?" he asked.

"Bath oil beads?"

"I didn't think you'd know. Now look at this."

I wasn't expecting to see a gun, but that's what he pulled from the closet next. It looked like an odd semiautomatic rifle. Lightweight and black with a rectangular bin where a scope would go. It looked real, but there was also something about it that said *toy*. The cozy room suddenly felt cold.

"I am unfortunately not armed," I said, backing toward the kitchen door and wishing I'd brought the Smith and Wesson. "The San Diego police arranged this interview and know I'm here. Put that thing down."

Chris Nugent shook his head the way people do when confronted with hopeless idiocy. He also put the gun on the couch beside the plastic jar of red balls.

"It's a *paint ball* gun," he said. "Those are paint balls in the jar. At point-blank range that gun will produce a sharp sting and maybe a bruise, but the paint ball won't even break your skin. The police who stopped Megan for going thirty in a twenty-five-mile-per-hour zone in Riverside felt compelled to open her trunk, saw the paint ball gun, and made the same mistake you've just made. She was on her way home from a competition. This was the 'concealed weapon.'"

"It looks like a gun," I said. "And what is your wife, a *doctor,* for crying out loud, doing running around with a bunch of dimwit survivalists in camo gear who play soldier by shooting each other with paint?"

"You surprise me, Dr. McCarron."

"In what way, Dr. Nugent?" I replied. We were playing doctor.

"It shouldn't, but prejudice in educated people always surprises me," he said. "You don't know anything about this sport or the people who engage in it, but you think you do. For the record, I tried it once and found it utterly pointless. But Megan and a lot of other people who thrive on competition and at least the illusion of risk enjoy it. They aren't a 'bunch of dimwit survivalists,' as you say, but a mix of all sorts of people. Young men, of course, but also bored account executives and sixty-five-year-old housewives. One of Megan's paint ball teams even includes a nun who just retired after a missionary stint in Guatemala. We had her over for dinner. She said paint ball gives her a way to get rid of her aggression. She was, incidentally, the only survivor of a political raid on a mission school twelve years ago. Two other nuns and twelve students, both adults and children, were murdered."

"You're right," I said. There was nothing else I *could* say. I'd just done one of the things I swear I'll never do. I'd made a judgment based on nothing but vague impressions picked up from sources I could neither identify nor remember. And Christopher Nugent had justifiably nailed me to the wall for being a dolt. I deserved it. However, nothing he'd said diminished the possibility of his wife's being a killer.

"What will you and Megan do now that the Rainer Clinic is closing?" I asked as he carefully replaced the paint balls and gun and locked the closet.

"It's no secret that Megan never wanted to be a cosmetic surgeon," he said as we moved back into the kitchen. "But as the only child she wanted to please her parents, especially Jennings. They're very close. By the time she realized it wasn't for her, she was through med school and residency, up for board certification. We were already married then, and we talked it over for months. We wanted a family. Sometimes it's necessary to punt."

"Punt?"

"Just kick the ball when you've got your hands on it rather than throwing for some elaborate play that may not work."

"I went to high school," I said. "I know what it means in football, but not what it means in cosmetic surgery."

"For us it meant going with what we already had. Megan could work at Rainer, even when she was pregnant, and amass enough income to buy our dream, make some investments. I'd stay home and care for the children, doing my own work around those responsibilities. We've got a tract of land in Northern California. It's paid for. We'll build a house there, maybe have another child. I've got some ideas about sustainable forestry I intend to try. We would have moved there within two years in any event. Since you and the police will soon succeed in destroying the clinic's reputation with this nonsense, forcing Jennings to close, we'll go now. This house is a rental. We can leave at any time, and Megan's more than ready. Our only problem is that Jennings refuses to go with us, and I don't think Megan and the kids will be happy without him nearby. That's the difficult part."

I could hear the wind whipping tree limbs outside, its velocity increasing. There are some dramatic, thousand-foot drops on the switchback road down into the desert from Julian. And pickup trucks with camper shells are notorious for blowing off course in high wind. I wanted to get going.

"Thank you," I told Christopher Nugent. "The police will probably want to speak with your wife at another time."

The house looked like a rectangular gray balloon full of yellow light as I drove away. Like something about to pull loose from old moorings that could no longer hold it. I wondered how much of what her husband had told me of their "dream" was also true for Megan Rainer. And how much was the desperation of a bright and educated human being trapped for years in a house with small children, ceaseless domestic chores, and no way out.

16

Hangdog

Julian sits on the crest of the long Laguna Mountain Range, so there's nowhere to go from there but down. Locals refer to a western descent toward San Diego as "going down the hill." There is no equivalent phrase for the eastern trip down a road called the Banner Grade and into the desert below. I choose to think this lack reflects a sense of mystery proper to the desert. If that's where you're going, you probably don't need to talk about it.

Usually the Banner Grade is a delight. A twisting road through forests of Jeffrey pine and coast live oak near the summit, it then descends through chaparral and finally the rocks and peculiar plants of the desert. Gold was discovered in the area in 1869, and by 1870 there was an influx of prospectors who created the town of Julian almost overnight. Within steep-sided Chariot Canyon off the Banner Grade are seven old gold mines, including the legendary Golden Chariot Mine, from which two million dollars' worth of bullion was taken before it closed. Golden Chariot and two others, Cold Beef and Golden Ella, are now mined for the granite blasted apart in the search for gold over a hundred years ago. One of the uses for this granite, I remembered as the wind howled down Banner Grade, is the making of tombstones.

"Don't," I said to myself as I felt the truck lurch and sway in the wind. Melodramatic thoughts are unwise in situations of danger. But I can never drive the Banner without thinking about the silent honeycomb of mining tunnels, some collapsed now, most blasted shut and forgotten, hidden inside the mountain. Once in a while hikers stumble over a tunnel entrance half buried in rubble. Occasionally these hikers wriggle inside to explore, only to find mountain lion scat near the entrance and a skeleton in century-old rotting leather boots deep inside. The County of San Diego provides these skeletons traditional burial in a potter's field, and a handful of strangers always show up for the brief ceremonies. But no one ever knows who the skeletons were.

The train of thought seemed appropriate. I was beginning to think we'd never figure out who the Sword of Heaven was, either. None of the four people I'd interviewed seemed capable of murdering anybody, although none of them was exactly a poster child for stress-free living, either. And although Megan Rainer's paint ball hobby seemed particularly weird for a professional woman and mother of two, I thought my feeling about it probably reflected nothing more than my own bias. Shooting bullets of paint at people in order to capture a flag before they do is definitely on my list of the Top Ten Most Boring Leisure Activities on Earth. But then, I'm not naturally aggressive and/or waiting for the day I can leave a job I don't like to go live in the woods and raise herbs. Dreams deferred can make people hostile. But they don't usually make people murderers.

The first teacup-size splatters of rain blew against my dusty windshield ten minutes later. And at the worst possible point along the lonely two-lane desert road between the Banner Grade and Borrego Springs far below. Yaqui Pass. I'd been afraid of this.

Yaqui Pass is a narrow cleft in the seven-mile-long Pinyon Ridge Mountains below which lies the valley I call home. The first non-natives to struggle through it with horses and wagons were the Mormons, followed much later by General Patton's troops trucking across the desert and down into San Diego as a defense against possible attack by sea during World War II. Yaqui Pass is at an elevation of 1,750 feet. Just a hill, really. Unless you're looking straight down all 1,750 off the side of a mountain road while driving a pickup with a camper shell in high winds and rain. Under those circumstances the bottom of 1,750 feet looks as bad as the bottom of two miles. Not that I could actually see the bottom through the black torrent lashing my windshield. But I knew it was there.

There's no shoulder on the stretch of road through Yaqui Pass. There's not enough room for a shoulder between a sheer rock wall on the north and a sickening drop on the south. You can't just stop and wait out a blinding downpour because another vehicle coming from behind would be sure to hit you. Pushing you through the cable-strung guardrail to fall end over end through sheets of ebony glass until crashing below into scenic outcroppings of what geologists call crystalline basement rock. I tried to stop thinking about that as I edged along, tacking the truck against the howling wind.

Instead I tried to remember if I'd seen pictures of a mountain-pass saint in any of dad's religious books I'd loved as a child. None came to mind, and it seemed an oversight. There are saints for wells and gardens, barbers and drunks. Also barren cattle and balding women. Why not mountain passes, I thought, which are traditionally hotbeds of human drama? But there was one mythological figure I was sure I could count on.

"Lilith!" I yelled to an Old Testament figure who'd *love* a night like this. "My dog's outside in a chain link run with only a partial roof for shelter, and storms make her nervous. Really, I *have* to make it home!"

In the racket outside I imagined I heard the throaty laughter of an ancient demon who hangs out in wild places because she hates hassles. My kind of demon. The laughter was not unfriendly, merely distant. Like the song of coyotes, I thought. And then I was out of Yaqui Pass and on the easier grade down, down to the desert floor. In another twenty minutes I'd be home.

When I got there the rain had blown over, although the wind continued and tumbleweeds rolled across the road like stampeding beach balls. One hit the truck as I approached the motel, stuck to the side for a few seconds, and then was blown loose with a sound like ripping silk. About twenty of them were jammed against the chain link surrounding Brontë's run when I ran to get her before going inside. That's why I didn't see the pink froth at her mouth right away. Or the blood on her front paws and chest. I just reached over a mound of prickly tumbleweeds without looking and opened the gate to her run.

"Come on, girl," I said, turning back toward my front door. "Let's get you inside."

It wasn't until I switched on the lights that I saw pinkish foam hanging from her jowls and a strange look in her eyes. Confusion. Rage. Shame. On the carpet were sandy wet pawprints threaded with blood.

"Brontë, what *happened*?" I said, kneeling to inspect her and seeing bloody scratches on her chest as well. No response but that look which in humans is called "hangdog." In dogs it says "humiliation." But I thought I knew what was behind it.

"You saw something, didn't you?" I said gently as I washed her front paws and chest in the kitchen and then smoothed antibacterial cream on the scratches. "In the storm a jackrabbit or a coyote or something came near the building, using it as a windbreak, and you barked until your throat bled, right? You just went bonkers out there, barking and trying to climb the chain link, throwing yourself against the fence trying to get at whatever it was. Tell me I'm wrong. That's it, isn't it?"

The dark eyes still had that odd look, but she ate her dinner with enthusiasm as I scrubbed her thready bloodstains out of the carpet. Then she stood by the front door and whined.

"Forget it," I told her. "You've been outside all day, you're still wet from the rain, and there's nothing out there but wind and tumbleweeds. Why don't I put on a nice CD to calm you down? Humperdinck's *Hansel and Gretel* should do it, huh?"

Brontë is fond of opera, and although this one isn't a favorite, it does seem to put her to sleep. I, on the other hand, can't hear "The Children's Prayer" from it without crying because it makes me think about my twin brother. But neither response was going to occur that night. She ignored the music and continued to jitter near the door, whining angrily.

Maybe something was still out there, I thought. Maybe an animal wounded in the storm. A reptile, probably, flushed from a flooded underground lair and now sluggish and nearly paralyzed with chill. Something cold-blooded and thus unable to regulate its body temperature, stunned into immobility by rain, wet ground, and the evaporative effects of the wind. I had it all figured out by the time I pulled on thick leather boots and snapped the clasp of my waist pack.

"Brontë, stay," I commanded as I opened the door and ducked my head against the wind. In the beam of my flashlight I saw the tumbleweeds massed against the fence, but nothing else. No half-dead snake, no chilled-out chuckwalla, no baby bighorn sheep lost in the storm and bleating to be fed warm milk from the fingers of a rubber glove. There was nothing there.

Dodging tumbleweeds, I walked to the other side of Brontë's run just to be sure. The flashlight's yellow beam captured little pictures set in stark relief. A palo verde limb suddenly white against a tangle of shadows. A cracked granite boulder sparkling with flecks of iron pyrite, seeming to float on the blackness behind it. Cholla cactus and rabbitbrush springing up and then falling into obscurity like puppets on a darkened stage. And then I saw it. Or I saw *something*. A disturbance in the sandy dirt beside the back of the dog run about three feet from the fence. Something had been there, but I couldn't tell what. The ground was merely disturbed, not smooth like that adjacent to it.

Animals leave tracks. Foxes, coyotes, lizards, even snakes leave tracks. Especially in wet sand. Falling tree limbs and dislodged rocks can also leave marks in sand, but the limb or rock will still be nearby. There was nothing near the rumpled patch of ground. There were no tracks. A chill spread across my eyes, causing them to narrow as I took the little .38 from my waist pack and thumbed the safety off.

Gun in my right hand and flashlight in my left, I moved past the patch of earth somebody had smoothed, staying several feet away. It wasn't hard to see the footprints leading from behind a creosote bush toward Coyote Canyon. Human footprints. Wearing shoes. The ground was saturated and soft. Somebody had stood there while Brontë barked and flung herself against the fence. Stood there long enough for her to bloody her paws and chest and throat trying to guard her property, which is the nature of Dobies. They're atrocious swimmers and mediocre trackers even when trained, but a Doberman will guard its home to the death.

"Good girl," I told my dog somberly two minutes later. "There *was* somebody there."

She continued to pace at the door, but she'd stopped whining. The look in her eyes was now expectant.

"Whoever it was has a fifteen-minute start on us," I said. "There's no point."

Hangdog again.

I tried to think like Roxie and the rest of the world, tried to be practical. The person who had stood by Brontë's run in a desert storm might be some inebriated camper driven out of Coyote Canyon by the rain, and might be a murderer. Sword knew where I lived, had been there before, and seemed to have some special interest in me. Either way, tracking that person into Coyote Canyon in the dark made no sense. There are a million places to hide out there. Hide and wait. Brontë and I would be like cardboard ducks in a shooting gallery. Or worse.

"Absolutely not," I told her.

Broken spirit, broken dog. A dog who had failed the charge of her breed. Head down, ears laid back. A dog in ruins, and an Academy Award performance. I couldn't stand it. In her place, I would want another chance, I thought. Sometimes love means helping a good soul save face. Even when it involves a bit of risk. So much for the rational approach. Which just doesn't work. At least not for me.

"Oh, for God's sake, all right. Just give me a few minutes to get less white," I said.

After changing to black pants and shirt I burned a few pieces of typing paper in the sink and ground the ashes to powder in a bowl. Then I stirred in some vegetable oil, making a black paste, and smeared it on my face and the backs of my hands. The process took an extra ten minutes, which was fine with me. Brontë's spirit was what mattered. I didn't want to catch up with the prowler. This would be a charade, nothing more.

High clouds were still blowing west over the mountains, obscuring the light from a quarter-moon. Brontë and I had no problem staying in shadows as we sprinted toward Coyote Canyon. I'd taken only the flashlight and gun and could have left the flashlight behind. The prowler's tracks were clearly visible in the wet desert dirt. Even in the dim light the tracks held deep shadows. It was too easy, I thought. Almost as if whoever it was *wanted* to be followed.

Brontë moved swiftly across the familiar terrain, seeming to know what she was doing even though she's no tracker. From time to time she stopped to make sure I was following, then dashed ahead. At the entrance to Alcoholic Pass, which connects Coyote Canyon at its mouth to Rockhouse Canyon on the eastern side of Coyote Mountain, she stopped again. The shadowy tracks, about the same size as my own, vanished into the pass's rocky, difficult terrain.

Brontë was happy, no doubt having convinced herself in some canine way that she'd driven away danger and secured the perimeters of her territory. I knew she'd be content to go home now. The purpose of the outing was fulfilled. But I wasn't quite ready to go.

Alcoholic Pass is a jumble of broken rock that can only be crossed on foot. It opens into Rockhouse Canyon, where there is a dirt road. It seemed likely that whoever had been hanging around my place had left a vehicle on Rockhouse Road, hiked through the pass, and returned by the same route. But why?

My place wasn't broken into, Brontë wasn't really harmed, nothing was done. So why would somebody clamber through a desert pass over cracked boulders, stand around in a storm enraging a dog for a while, and then clamber back over the same boulders? The behavior, I thought, was that of a child. That aimlessness.

Maybe it was just the adventuresome child of people camped over in Rockhouse Canyon, I thought. Maybe the child had wandered onto my property and seen Brontë in her run. Most children like animals, especially girls, and I remembered that my feet had been the size they are now since I was eleven. Maybe the child had wanted to pet Brontë or play with her. Maybe the child had stayed near Brontë during the storm in an attempt to reassure her. I conjured up a vision of a big-footed eleven-year-old in jeans, an experienced desert camper whose parents let her roam free out here, hovering near Brontë and whispering, "It's okay. I won't hurt you."

But why would a child erase her footprints?

"Let's just go a little way in," I told Brontë.

It was darker between the crumbling walls of Alcoholic Pass. And the wind made strange sounds as it blew through a thousand rocky crevices. At one point it seemed to be the mewling cry of a cat or human infant. At another it was a sucking roar like a huge whirlpool into which only a fool would look. And that fool, I reminded myself, would never be seen again.

Brontë trotted beside me, almost invisible in the gloom. Twice I tripped over unseen rubble, the second time falling painfully on my left knee. I didn't want to switch on the flashlight, making myself a well-lit spectacle for anybody who happened to be watching. And I didn't want to go back. Not yet. Then through the grit blowing in my eyes I saw something familiar in the middle of the trail ahead. Something that did not belong in Alcoholic Pass.

Nothing is perfectly round in the desert, and nothing is white. In other areas of the Anza-Borrego there are cannonball-shaped concretions of mineral in the rock, but they only look round from a distance. Up close their surfaces are lumpy and uneven. And while the desert palette contains infinite gradations of beige ranging to the palest creamy ecru, nothing is bleached to real white. Yet there was something perfectly round and white on the trail ten feet ahead, reflecting the minimal light like a beacon.

Brontë loped closer to the object, sniffing the air and then the ground as if she were a bloodhound. Then she stopped. I could hear her low growl as I caught up with her. The thing on the narrow, desolate trail was a blue willow plate.

Quickly I pulled Brontë into the dense shadows beneath a tilted slab of granite that probably had broken away from Coyote Mountain long before any human eye had evolved to see it. The Smith and Wesson tucked in the waist of my pants gouged my side reassuringly, and I curled my hand over its grip but didn't pull it up to firing position.

There was nobody in Alcoholic Pass but me and Brontë, and I knew it. No sense of another presence, no sense of danger. Brontë, tense and alert beside me, seemed to know it, too. Her growl had been in response to a visual anomaly. Round white thing where there have never been round white things before. Dog version of my own reaction.

"Brontë, stay," I commanded. Then I walked to the plate and picked it up.

It was one of the old restaurant blue willows, divided into three sections by raised ridges. In a diner the three sections would have held a main course and two vegetables. Meat loaf, mashed potatoes, and corn, maybe. Now it held nothing but wind.

"Come on, girl," I called, tucking the plate under my left arm and switching on the flashlight. "Let's go home."

Against my ribs the plate was a not-uncomfortable burden, like any awkward thing we nonetheless carry around. Like the clutter of awkward things we eventually carry home. Cuckoo clocks, pressed flowers in frames, sorrows.

The prowler had been Sword, I realized, but the purpose of the visit had not been to harm me. Despite my precautions I'd been an easy mark for anyone waiting in Alcoholic Pass. The purpose of the visit had been a child's game of hide and seek within the corridors of this ruined cathedral few visit and fewer love. Nothing more. A strange night game in a place where nobody goes.

I thought about that as Brontë and I made good time getting home. Sword had come out there twice, each time leaving a gift. Blue willow plates. The first a cheap contemporary product, the second more valuable. Was I being rewarded for something? I wondered. Or was I being given clues I was expected to understand? That sense of childlike desperation followed me like a ghost in the wind.

Play with me, it demanded. *I know a neat game. Come on, play.*

The lights from my place cast a hazy yellow bubble that didn't move in the wind. In minutes we were inside and it felt good to be safe, have some coffee, take a bath. But I couldn't shake a sense of inexplicable sadness that seemed to lash about outside in the wind. It felt like the sadness of a child who cannot understand what's happened, why no one wants to play. And I wondered if there would be a third plate, and what that would mean. In the chants of childhood games, three is a final number. Everything ends after three tries. The third time, I remembered, is the charm.

17

Saints Fallen and Intact

It was nearly eight when the phone rang. It would be Roxie, I thought, feeling a little guilty for not having called her earlier. She'd want to hear my take on the interviews, having no doubt already received a report from BB.

"Hi, hon," I answered.

Wes Rathbone didn't even chuckle at the gaffe.

"Get a cell phone tomorrow, Blue," he ordered. "Rox and I have been trying to reach you since you left Christopher Nugent. Why haven't you picked up the messages on your machine? Bettina Ashe died this afternoon. Her husband authorized an autopsy, which was performed immediately. She died of a cerebral hemorrhage."

"Oh, my God," I breathed into the phone. "Wes, did somebody send a deli tray? Did somebody send fancy food to her house today? She should have been warned about that, but—"

"Nobody sent anything to the Ashe mansion, and the staff would have thrown it out in any event. Her husband, John Harrington, had been warned about the possible connection to unusual foods. He'd also hired a squad of security guards to patrol the place and never let Betsy out of his sight. He was with her when it happened. Her head was still wrapped in bandages from the surgery yesterday, but they'd uncovered her eyes so she could watch a video. He said they were watching *Dr. Zhivago* when she complained of a terrible headache, became dizzy, then collapsed on the floor of their bedroom. Death was apparently instantaneous.

"I don't have to tell you he's beside himself, threatening to sue everybody including us, and I don't blame him. I've already talked to Berryman about your interviews today, but I want a written report from you tomorrow morning. Right now I just want to know what you think. Which one of them is doing this, Blue? If you've got a good idea I'll have whoever it is brought in and interrogated. Keep him in a tank all night with some undercovers who'll scare the shit out of him. We can break him, Blue. But who the hell *is* it?"

The words pushed me against a wall. The words and the panic behind them.

"I don't know, Wes," I said. "I need to look at some data on behaviors connected to grief, also rape victims and divorce, before I can sort any of it out. Isadora Grecchi's a time bomb, but it's men she can't stand. I'm almost certain she's been the victim of some kind of sexual assault. But that shouldn't predispose her to kill women. Doesn't make any sense."

"Berryman pegged Grecchi, too," Rathbone said. "We've got a subpoena to get her juvenile records from Colorado, but it'll take weeks. All we know is that she was made a ward of the court in 1958. Everything else is sealed. It's not enough to bring her in, but I've got a surveillance team watching her house."

Brontë was lying on the floor beside me, licking the scratches on her chest.

"Wes, Sword was out here again tonight and left another blue willow plate. Has Grecchi been home tonight? Say, for the last five hours?"

"Not for the last hour and forty-five minutes," he answered dismally. "Surveillance was set up by six-fifteen, and the house has been dark since then. She's not there. But it's still not enough to pick her up. Blue, did you *see* her out there? Did you see *anything*?"

"Just footprints, then the plate on the ground. The footprints are about the same size as mine."

"Which is?"

"Nine and a half. I've got huge feet."

"Great. So how big are Grecchi's feet?"

I felt inadequate, sloppy, a bad detective. "I didn't look at her feet," I admitted, then remembered she'd been barefooted when BB and I arrived "Well, actually, I guess I did. She didn't have any shoes on, and she was painting. The place smelled like oil paint."

"Her *feet*, Blue," he insisted. "Did she have big feet? Could those have been her prints you saw?"

"Wes, I didn't notice," I apologized. "I didn't know I was supposed to look at feet. I just can't answer. Feet all look the same to me."

His sigh was irritable and tired. "What about Megan Rainer? Berryman wasn't with you for that one, so I haven't heard anything. What was your take?"

"She wasn't home," I answered. "Their daughter had been stepped on by a horse and Megan took her down into San Diego to have her foot X-rayed. I talked to the husband, Chris—"

"Did you confirm that?" he interrupted. "Where did she take the daughter? What hospital? What time? All you have is the husband's word on it. Maybe the daughter was at a friend's and there was no horse. Maybe Megan was someplace else, like out at your place strewing plates around. Maybe Nugent's lying to protect his wife."

I remembered Christopher Nugent, stuck for years in a trap usually reserved for women. He wanted out, wanted to move to Northern California and grow things. If Megan was the perp in this string of murders, then he was doomed to domestic slavery forever. Megan would go to prison for the rest of her life and he'd have to raise two children alone. Good-bye, dream. It dawned on me that Chris Nugent had some very good reasons for lying.

"I hadn't thought of it, but you may be right," I told Rathbone. "He wants to get out of here; they both do. Move up north and do something with sustainable agriculture. Trees and herbs. They'd planned on leaving in two years, anyway. Megan would work at the clinic until they had enough of a nest egg that they could live frugally off their investments. That was the plan, except they were both tired of waiting. But Wes . . . ?"

"Yeah?"

"I can't believe Chris Nugent would look the other way if he knew his wife was killing people. He's an intelligent, thoughtful man. Who could pretend not to see something that serious?"

Wes Rathbone sighed. "You'd be surprised at how easily people don't see what they don't want to see. Nugent may not 'know' Megan's the perp, but maybe he senses something's terribly wrong with her. He thinks she's just nervous, unhappy. He thinks whatever's wrong will go away when they get out of here, when they get to their dream. That's all he can let himself think. It's not unusual; people are like that. Cops call it 'blind in both ears.'"

"He was pretty defensive about her concealed weapon arrest," I agreed. "He showed me her paint ball gun and a big plastic jar of paint balls. He said they have a friend who's a nun and she likes to play paint ball because it relieves her anger over a school massacre she was involved in. Guatemala. It made a sort of sense."

"Megan Rainer hasn't been in Guatemala," Rathbone said. "And her husband knows there's something not quite right about her passion for shooting at people, or he wouldn't have been defensive. What about these damn plates? See any of 'em anywhere?"

"No," I answered. "But Jeffrey Pond used a lot of religious language and he's just been through a nasty divorce. Hates his ex-wife, who set up a friend to accuse him of rape. I'd say he's got some motivation to hate women."

"Yeah, we checked that thing out. It was a setup. Goes on all the time in divorce cases. The guy got royally screwed."

"So has he been home for the last five hours?" I asked, trying to imagine muscle-bound Jeffrey Pond lumbering around the desert in order to leave a blue willow plate on the ground.

"None of them are home, haven't been since we got word of Bettina Ashe's death. Or else nobody's answering the phone. The only house we've got surveillance on is Grecchi's. So what's your take on Eldridge?"

"Strange as the rest of them," I told him. "Stuffy. The wife seems odd, too. Something out of *Stepford Wives*. She lets him interrupt everything she says, and at one point it seemed like he didn't remember their daughter's name. He called her Ann and then later Kara called the girl Namey."

"Namey?"

"Yeah. Wes, I haven't had time to organize anything from today. I need to look at some stats before I can give you anything usable. If you can just wait—"

"Betsy Ashe is dead, Blue," he said. "One of the most prominent women in San Diego, as well as one of the wealthiest, and a good friend of this police department. We knew she was in danger and we let her die. The next one could be your friend Kate Van Der Elst. She's the last of the Rainer patients known to have received a threat. We can't wait."

His voice sounded like a mooring cable groaning against an enormous burden. Wes Rathbone hadn't wanted to be a cop's cop anymore, just wanted to enjoy life with his Annie. Circumstances had pulled him back to that earlier persona. I could tell he didn't like it, but I knew he didn't have any choice.

"I'm going to help you with this thing," I told him. "Just give me time to talk to Rox, look at some data, pull it together. What we need to know is right in front of us. We just can't see it."

"Yeah, right," he answered. "Now, what about the old guy? Do you think he could have done it, done something that's killing these women?"

I continued to feel pushed, unprepared. I didn't know what I was talking about and yet I knew at least as much as anybody else. It felt silly until I realized the silliness was just a skin over my fear. Three women dead now, no end in sight, and the killer luring me to play a child's game amid prehistoric rubble. The killer leaving me gifts in the dark.

"Rainer had the same opportunity as everybody else, Wes," I said. "And he's depressed over his wife's death and Megan not wanting to run the clinic, and now having to close it. But of all of them I think he's the least likely. He's just an old-fashioned guy, a traditionalist. His life's in shambles and he doesn't know which way to turn right now. He's afraid to get rid of his wife's *computer*, you know? He's lost."

"Probably our man," Rathbone said bleakly. "In the movies it's always the one you least suspect."

"This isn't a movie," I said unnecessarily. "Tell Annie hi for me. I want to call Rox now, go over the interviews. If we come up with anything I'll call you back."

"Do that," Rathbone said tersely, and then hung up.

I phoned Rox, who didn't answer. Probably in the bathroom, I thought, and left a message asking her to call right away. Then I listened to the messages on my answering machine.

The first was from my brother, David, nothing but a taped female voice saying, "This is a collect call from a prisoner at . . . the Missouri State Penitentiary. The prisoner placing the call is . . ." Here I heard my brother's voice saying, "the Apeman of Alcatraz," a joke about my doctoral dissertation, which had been a failed endeavor to explain David's self-destructive behavior by comparing human males to other male primates. I learned a lot about apes and still don't know why my twin brother chose to behave like one.

Prison phone systems are automated so that if you're willing to accept the call you have to push a number. Even if you don't, you're billed for the call. One of the thousand ways everybody makes money off people who have no choices. I hoped David would call back. He might, I thought, have some insights into Sword. After all, he lived with killers.

The next message was from Kate Van Der Elst, who seemed to be crying.

"I need to talk to you as soon as possible, Blue," she said. "I just heard about Betsy Ashe's death. It was on the six o'clock news. They didn't say anything about the link to the Rainer Clinic, but I'm sure that's where Betsy would go for that kind of thing, and I'm sure that's what happened. Just like Mary Harriet and Dixie. Somebody at Rainer did something to all of them that killed them. And I may be next."

Here she breathed a shuddering sigh and then went on.

"When Pieter heard about Betsy Ashe, he gave me an ultimatum. Either I withdrew from the race or he'd leave me. I refused to withdraw. He's gone. Moved into a hotel downtown. He said he was flying back to Amsterdam tomorrow if he could make the arrangements. He said he didn't want to stay just to watch me commit suicide. Please call no matter what time you get in. I don't know what to do. I'm scared."

So Pieter Van Der Elst wasn't the saint I'd imagined him to be, I thought. Nobody ever is. But what could he be thinking, leaving Kate alone now? That she'd knuckle under to his demands, crumble under the terrible weight of his love for her? Did he think he could preserve her life by breaking her spirit? Why couldn't he see that what would remain of Kate after he broke her would be worthy only of his contempt? Yet I'd seen it before. Couples, parents with grown children still under their control. One broken by the exertion of the other's will, the other now bored and bitter and trapped. Pieter Van Der Elst, I realized, had just made an epic mistake that could cost him what he valued most.

The rest of the messages were from Rox and Rathbone, frantic to reach me. As I erased them the phone rang.

"I'm at a pay phone in Borrego," Roxie's voice told me without preamble. "Unlock your gate."

Rox does not come out here unless she has to, and she's never come alone. Even the little desert town near my place feels like Mars to her with its easy-going middle-class assumption that we all know the rules. And in reality, we all do. From the tanned and lusty golf pro at Borrego's big resort to me, the reclusive social psychologist who lives in a half-built desert motel with her dog, everybody here knows exactly what to say when bumping into the Methodist minister at the grocery store. And exactly what not to say when bumping into the minister's wife with the golf pro in her car behind the same grocery at midnight. The rules of white middle-classness are invisible but as dense as a web of lead.

"Okay, I'll see you in a few minutes," I agreed. No questions. But something was wrong. Seriously wrong. I felt a tidal wave of uneasiness as I drove out to unlock my gate.

"What?" I asked through her car window as Roxie navigated the bumpy entrance to my property. In the dark she looked angry. Or determined. Or sad. I couldn't tell which.

"I need to talk to you," was all she said.

So I relocked the gate and followed as her car bounced along the damp road. In my living room she flung herself on the couch and looked distraught.

"What?" I asked again, pacing beside my desk.

"Something's come up. Not something I wanted to talk about on the phone. And I couldn't reach you anyway. Rathbone, either. We've both been—"

"Roxie, you drove all the way out here for a reason. And if you don't tell me pretty soon I'm going to explode. Or implode. What *is* it?"

I thought it was going to have something to do with Sword. Something she thought would upset me, like she'd figured out that Jennings Rainer had not only murdered his patients but thirty other people as well. And been a Communist double-agent, too.

"Some folks in Philadelphia called today," she began.

Philadelphia?

"Okay. What did they say?"

"Wanted to talk about a research project. Good funding. Has to do with analyzing a possible relationship between brain trauma and the onset of major psychiatric disorders in people with the genetic history for it."

Oh, no.

"So? People call you about this stuff all the time, don't they?

What did they want? For you to provide medical histories on head injuries for all the psych clients at Donovan? I suppose each prisoner would have to sign a release, right?"

Nice try, McCarron, but who are you kidding?

"They need a project director," she said, looking at me as if from a gallows. "The job includes an impressive salary, a staff of fifteen, and extensive lecturing at universities both here and abroad. They want me."

Train wreck, atom bomb, end of life as we know it.

She was wearing jeans, a black turtleneck, and tennis shoes. I noticed those things suddenly, as if my mind were taking snapshots of her sitting there on my couch. As if I would want to remember her someday. *Click.* Roxie sitting on my couch on an October night. *Click.* Roxie's hair in a hundred braids, the wooden beads silent as she sat there. *Click.* Roxie the way she looked the last time I ever saw her.

"Oh, God," I said, and sat down beside her.

For a while we just sat there. Soon, I knew, we'd say a lot of things. But for that moment we just sat inside the news and let it be. It was one of those moments when the barriers that always exist between people just dissolve. That sense of being drawn through an open window to someplace unknown. Airy, dizzying, scary because there are no lies there. I noticed that we'd grabbed each other's hands, our fingers laced and holding tight.

"Blue, I don't know what to do," she said. "That's why I had to see you, had to come out here tonight. They want me to fly to Philadelphia next week for an interview. I said yes, but I'm not sure. They're going to offer me the job. The interview's just a formality. But I'm not sure I can live without you and I can't ask you to—"

"Shh," I said against her braids as I held her and we both cried. My face hot and wet against hers, hands in each other's hair now, a terrible anger beneath it all. Then words.

"Oh, shit, Roxie. This is just *shit!*"

Me up and pacing now, banging things around on my desk. Me feeling like I'm supposed to act like this, but what I really

want to do is go back in time to the point before I met Roxie
Bouchie and then *not* meet her.

"I know. I can't go. How can I? But . . ."

I suspected Roxie was having feelings similar to mine. Her
goals had been clear since she was a kid, and this career opportunity fit her goals. She hadn't wanted me in her life; it just
happened.

"Of course you'll go," I said gamely. "You have to go. I'll go
with you. Where is it again?"

"Philadelphia. Pennsylvania. You'd hate it. It's a city."

"I don't hate all cities. Isn't that where the Liberty Bell is?
Have you ever been there?"

"You never told me you were dying to live near the Liberty
Bell, and no. Have you?"

"No. Oh, Roxie, why now?"

After several repetitive cycles of this we were still crying but
laughing at the same time. Two competent adults revealed to
be dim-witted adolescents inside, unable either to cope with the
bond between us or to place a major American city on a map.

"There's still a killer on the loose," I said, sniffling and giggling. "Can we table this? I have to call Kate Van Der Elst.
Pieter's left her because she won't drop out of the city council
race. He's moved into a hotel until he can run home to the
Netherlands. Kate's alone and scared."

At "alone and scared" we both burst into tears again, then
laughter.

"Call her," Roxie said, standing and heading for the kitchen.
"I'm going to make a sandwich."

As Brontë followed her I looked at Roxie's braids tumbling
over broad shoulders, the straight, strong line of her back. She
hadn't played games with me over her Philadelphia job offer,
hadn't ducked her own pain and confusion about what it might
mean. But most importantly, she hadn't left me alone with it.
She'd come to me and told me and let the shock be absorbed
in us, together. She didn't hide. Roxie was no coward. I loved
her, but in that moment I felt something more. I felt a deep respect for her. I could never be as rational and businesslike, but

I knew I'd spend the rest of my life trying to be as brave as Roxie Bouchie was with me that night.

"Rox," I said as I picked up the phone to call Kate, "thanks."

She'd turned from pawing through my refrigerator and her head was backlit by its fifteen-watt bulb as she nodded. The nimbus of light behind her clattering braids made a sort of halo. She knew what I meant. There was nothing else to say.

18

The Roadkill Connection

Oh, Blue, I'm so glad you called," Kate Van Der Elst said when she heard my voice. "Pieter's gone to the Marriott downtown, the big one next to the convention center. He won't take my calls. Or else he's *swimming*. You know, they've got all those beautiful pools and you can swim from one into another under bridges and down little waterfalls. Sometimes we'd spend a night there just to swim from pool to pool. That's probably what he's—"

"Kate," I interrupted, "is there anyone at your house with you? Are you alone there?"

I didn't like the way she sounded. Her voice was reedy and her remarks had a giddy tone that suggests panic.

"There's no one here," she answered in the same strained, high voice. "Who would be here? Dixie Ross was my best friend, but someone killed her and her funeral is tomorrow. I can't very well call her to come over and hold my hand, can I? She's in a *casket,* Blue. And my husband has turned into a man I neither like nor even know, who walked out on me because he loves me, he says. I *can* call him and I have, but he won't talk to me. Blue, I'm just undone by all this. Could you possibly come over?"

"I'm sorry, Kate," I said in quiet tones I hoped would help diminish her anxiety, "but I can't drive into the city tonight. It would be best if you weren't alone, though. Surely there's some- one else you could call. Maybe one of your campaign staff?"

"I don't want anyone connected to the campaign to know . . . to know what's going on between me and Pieter," she said, making an obvious effort to calm herself. "I'm going to say he's been called to Amsterdam due to illness in the family. Less than two weeks remain until the election. I can't have it all over town that my husband has left me."

She was right. Not that being right ever got anybody through the night.

"Kate, I just can't believe Pieter would do this," I said. "I know how much he wanted you to drop out of the race, but to leave you when there's danger, leave you tomorrow to at- tend the funeral of your best friend alone? That's not the Pieter I know."

"He hasn't been himself since the day he found that threat- ening note pushed under the door of my campaign headquar- ters," she said, sighing. "You know, the one on green paper that said I'd die? It did something to him, Blue. Since then he's barely eaten and tosses all night. He looks terrible. Maybe I should just have done what he wanted."

"But you didn't," I pointed out. "And so you have to plan a course of action that deals with the way things are now. You need to get out of there, go someplace with lots of people around. The hotel where Pieter is will have a good security staff, since it services conventions. I want you to pack a few things and check in there. You'll be near Pieter and you'll feel safe. It may sound silly, but it's not."

"Blue, I'm not going to chase after Pieter and I hate being away from home anyway, because the food thing is a prob- lem," she said. "You know I'm on this diet, and talk about sounding silly, but it's almost impossible to get the right com- binations of carbs, protein, and fat in a restaurant. They just load you with bread and pasta and there's never enough protein."

"Kate!" I heard myself yelling. "Stop worrying about that stupid diet and get yourself somewhere with people around you. I can't believe you—"

Roxie had been listening to the conversation from the kitchen, but now hurried toward me.

"Let me talk to Kate," she said urgently.

I couldn't quite peg the look on her face as she took the phone, but it was serious.

"Kate, this is Dr. Bouchie," Rox said professionally, talking fast. "I want you to tell me *exactly* what you eat on this diet and what you don't. It may be very important. Please leave nothing out."

For a while there was no sound but the scritching of Roxie's pencil on a sheet of paper she'd pulled from my printer's feed tray. From time to time she drew deep breaths, then nodded.

"Mostly fruits and vegetables, then. Do you *ever* eat meat? Turkey breasts and fish that you buy fresh. Okay. Are you taking any antidepressants or cold and sinus medications? Good. Don't take any."

I could almost hear Rox's mind working, a sound like lockpins dropping in cylinders. Hundreds of them, one after another.

"Here's what you *must* do," she told Kate Van Der Elst. "Don't eat anything but fresh fruits and vegetables until I get back to you. Nothing else. Especially nothing dried, pickled, or fermented. Do you understand? No, no raisins. They're dried. I can't explain right now. I have to check some things. I may be wrong. Meanwhile, these precautions won't hurt you and may save your life. If I'm right it won't matter whether you stay at home or in a hotel tonight, except that you'll feel more comfortable if you're not alone. Either way, I'll want to talk to you tomorrow morning, so I'll need to know where I can reach you.

"And don't worry, if what I suspect is true, you're in no danger unless you eat certain things like fava beans, a lot of imported chocolate, salami, there's a long list. Just eat nothing except what I told you. I need to make some calls right now, so I'm going to hang up without giving you back to Blue. But leave the number where you can be reached tomorrow morning both here and with Detective Rathbone. You'll be hearing from me."

"Rox, what?" I asked the second she hung up, but she was already punching Rathbone's number.

"Wes," she said seconds later, "it's Roxie Bouchie. Do you know what Bettina Ashe had to eat today? Find out and call me back immediately. I'm at Blue's."

He hadn't asked why she wanted to know, merely understood that the question was important and agreed with her request. But I wasn't Wes Rathbone.

"Roxie, what is it?" I begged. "What's the food connection? What have you figured out?" I can't stand not knowing, being in the dark. Not knowing makes my ears ring.

"It's so obvious I should have seen it," she muttered, moving back to the counter to take another bite of her sandwich. "Nobody else would be likely to, but *I* should have. A psychiatrist should have."

"You should have seen *what*? What are you talking about?"

"MAOIs," she answered, pronouncing the letters slowly as she wandered back across my living room to look through the picture window at tumbleweeds blowing by. Deep in thought, she continued to munch on her sandwich, dropping crumbs on the carpet. Brontë hovered beside her happily, consuming the crumbs. I sat in my desk chair and bit my lower lip.

"MAOI means 'monoamine oxidase inhibitor,'" she finally explained. "It's a drug used in the treatment of depression, although it's not used much these days. Patients don't like the dietary restrictions associated with it, and most doctors prescribe everything else available before trying MAOIs."

"Dietary restrictions," I said, trying to find a thread. "Is Kate taking this stuff? Why did you tell her not to eat anything but fresh vegetables?"

"It's a long story, Blue."

I love long stories.

"Tell me," I said as she flung herself on the couch and looked longingly at the phone. "Wes will call you back as soon as he knows what Bettina Ashe ate today. There's time."

"We're omnivores," she began. "We evolved eating anything we could find, and our distant ancestors couldn't afford to be picky about freshness, to put it mildly. If it hadn't turned to ooze, they ate it. Even if it *had* turned—"

"I get the point, Rox," I said. "But Bettina Ashe did not eat ooze today. I'm sure of it."

"No, but her stomach should have been ready if she had. We all produce a monoamine oxidase in our gut, an MAO. It's there to oxidize a substance called tyramine, which is found in rotten foods and even some that aren't spoiled, especially liver. We evolved, you might say, with a roadkill palate."

I thought of vultures feasting unspeakably in the desert. And crows. And us.

"Then about forty years ago somebody discovered that inhibiting the chemical effect of MAOs helped reduce the symptoms of clinical depression by altering certain chemical patterns in the brain," she went on. "For a while these MAO inhibitors, or MAOIs, were widely prescribed for people suffering from chronic depression, but patients taking them had to watch their diets very carefully."

"No roadkill?" I said, tracking the explanation although it still made no sense.

"A number of foods are actually somewhat spoiled and meant to be," Rox went on. "The process of spoilage gives them their distinctive flavors. Fermented drinks like red wine and beer are made from rotted grapes or hops. Miso is fermented soy mush. Pickled foods like herring or sauerkraut, same thing. Hard sausage, bologna, salami. They all contain substantial quantities of tyramine, which we can oxidize, or digest, because we're producing MAOs.

"But if we're taking something that inhibits the MAOs, what happens?"

"In extreme cases," Rox said, her brown eyes bright, "a hypertensive crisis. Blood pressure shoots way up, the heart races at over a hundred beats per minute. The person experiences sweating, dizziness, nausea, a sudden, agonizing headache, and then blam! An artery bursts in the brain and death occurs."

"Rox, that's what happened!" I cheered. "You've figured it out! Dixie Ross must have had this stuff in her somehow, this drug, and then she must have eaten pickled herring or one of those things, and it killed her. Same for Mary Harriet Grossinger. And Ruby Emerald. Somebody delivered a deli tray to Ruby the night it happened, Rox! A deli tray with caviar, liver pâté, European chocolate, and red wine. All the bad foods. Poisons, for her. Except her boyfriend threw the whole tray against the wall in a fit of jealousy before she could eat much of it."

"Probably saved her life," Rox said thoughtfully.

"And then he tried to shoot her the next day," I finished the strange love story. "But what about Kate, Roxie? She's been threatened, but nothing's happened to her. She's fine."

Rox stood up to pace beside the telephone.

"That was the tip, Blue. When I heard you tell her to forget about this diet she's on. She eats a lot of broccoli, vegetable salads, fresh meats she buys and cooks herself. This Zone diet is based on a strict balance of carbohydrates, protein, and fat. Every time she eats, her food is fresh and perfectly balanced, and she doesn't eat anything that upsets the balance. She wouldn't eat salami, for example, which is full of tyramine and could have killed her. Too much fat. Kate Van Der Elst is protected from the danger of inhibited monoamine oxidation by her diet!"

I remembered carrying Kate's snack in my purse at the fundraiser. Half an apple, a stick of low-fat skim-milk string cheese, and two macadamia nuts. It had seemed ridiculous at the time. Who can eat only two macadamia nuts? But Kate Van Der Elst was alive.

"How did Sword do it?" I began as the phone rang. Roxie grabbed it before the end of the first ring.

"Wes?" she said. "Some liver pâté? Oh, God. What else? Grilled cheese sandwich her husband made for her himself. What kind of cheese, Wes? Aged sharp cheddar they order from Vermont, with a little strong Romano. Got it. Anything else? Miso soup. That's enough to do it, Wes. Liver pâté, aged cheese, miso.

That's enough to kill her. And a couple of imported chocolates. Couldn't be worse. She never had a chance even without the chocolates. Yeah, I'll explain."

I listened as Roxie outlined the roadkill chemistry again to
Rathbone, but I was already thinking. We'd need to chart what
each of the victims had eaten immediately prior to death, I
thought. In Ruby Emerald's case, prior to a hypertensive crisis
that could have killed her except that seventy-four-year-old Jerry
Russell Jones had smashed the lethal delicacies against a wall
in a fit of jealousy that saved her life. The irony of Jones's behavior was stunning and reminded me of my personal philosophy. The grid. It just *loves* stuff like this. "Man Accidentally
Saves Life of Woman He Will Try to Murder the Next Day." Film
at eleven.

Rox was going into exhaustive detail with Rathbone about
MAOIs, but I ignored her and booted up my computer, which
has its own phone line. Research. Something I know how to
do. It felt good to be useful.

First I activated the word-finder program that's in all word-
processing software and told it to locate all variants of "eat,"
"lunch," "dinner," "snack," and "deli." Then I went to the file
containing my notes on Dixie Ross. Immediately the word "dinner" was highlighted within the phrase "bean-growers' dinner."
Just before her death Dixie Ross had been at a dinner spon-
sored by the North San Diego County Organic Bean Growers'
Cooperative. She'd been driving from that dinner to Kate's
fundraiser at the Aphid Gallery at just after seven on Friday
night when a cerebral hemorrhage took her life.

Rox was still talking to Rathbone, so I checked out the bean
growers' Web site, which had a link to an article in a north
county community paper about the dinner. "Growers Celebrate
With All-Bean Feast," the header announced. Among the dishes
served were a fava-bean-pod bisque, pinto bean salad with
tomato and garlic dressing, bean-thread noodles in peanut sauce,
pineapple-orange Honolulu skillet beans, black bean and onion
cornbread casserole, and Belgian chocolate cake baked with

white bean flour and topped with soybean ice cream. All organic, of course.

I highlighted the dishes from the article, copied them over to my file on Dixie Ross, and interrupted Roxie.

"Take a look at this," I said, pointing to the screen. "Dixie Ross was at this dinner Friday afternoon before her death, but I don't see any fermented or dried foods."

"Just a minute, Wes," she said. "Blue's got something on the computer."

"It's all beans, Rox."

"Beans *are* dried, Blue. Ever see them in bags at the grocery? And broadleaf beans like favas are high in tyramine whether they're dried or fresh. The soup course alone could have killed her. Wes, Blue may have found your murder weapon for Dixie Ross. Beans. Yeah, I'll explain that."

Rathbone's interest in the details of Roxie's theory was clearly greater than my own. She seemed to be providing a list of all the foods containing tyramine in quantities sufficient to be dangerous.

"All kinds of liver," she recited. "All pickled fish, meat, or vegetables. Caviar, snails, corned beef. Bean pods, Chinese pea pods, some beans, definitely fava beans, dried fruit, canned figs, red wine, champagne, sherry, brandy and cognac, all aged cheese. . . ."

She stopped and looked at me quizzically. "What is it, Blue? You've got that spacey look again."

"Didn't you say canned figs?"

"Yeah."

"Rox, a deli tray was sent to Kate's fundraiser. BB took it from a delivery service. He said the card had been lost. It had a liver pâté and a huge mound of domestic caviar with little toast rounds and a tiny spoon. The caviar was good. I ate a lot of it myself. But I remember BB telling Kate that there had been canned figs on the plate as well, and that he'd thrown them away because he didn't like the way they looked. Roxie, nobody puts canned figs on an appetizer plate with caviar or anything else. It had to be deliberate. Sword meant that tray for

Kate, Rox. Kate was supposed to eat pâté and canned figs and caviar and then die."

"You hear that, Wes?" Roxie asked. "Okay, here's my guess. Somebody at Rainer introduced a quantity of MAOI, probably in a timed-release form, into the incisions of the victims while they were anesthetized. It wouldn't be difficult to do. Traditional, not laser, cosmetic surgery on the head is bloody even though patients take a clotting agent the night before. Head injuries are just always bloody and Rainer's old-fashioned, doesn't use lasers for face-lifts. In the bloody mess any one of the medical staff could slip something under a muscle or loose flap of skin at any point in the four-hour surgery or the sewing-up. Something with a coating that would dissolve over time, releasing its contents to be absorbed into the bloodstream of the victim. In this case an MAOI.

"Nothing would happen for days, even weeks, until the coating dissolved and the MAOI was released. Then if the victim ate the wrong thing or took another kind of antidepressant called an SSRI, or got a cold and took a decongestant or a sinus pill, a hypertensive crisis could occur. Right, *did* occur. And no, an MAOI wouldn't show up in a blood analysis unless somebody knew to look for it specifically. Okay, Wes, we'll get back to you.

"Something came up," she said to me. "A crisis, everybody yelling. He had to get off the phone. What *we* have to do is figure out which one of them did it."

I felt suddenly edgy and restless. It happens to me when I haven't had time to process things that seem to be happening around me at cartoonlike speeds. And the evening had been like that. Rox and the job she might take in Philadelphia, a little-used antidepressant that kept people from digesting spoiled food and then killed them by blowing up their brains if they ate spoiled food. It occurred to me that I could have lived happily forever without knowing my body produces a chemical that will let me eat all the dead things I want. Then I thought about the things I *do* eat and realized they're all dead. I hate it when this happens.

"Rox, the Rainer Clinic is for all practical purposes closed," I said. "There won't be any more major surgeries there, so Sword can't strike again. I don't think I want to talk about this anymore right now. I need some time."

"Great," she answered, rattling her beads ominously. "The Rainer staff are free to disperse all over the country now, get new jobs. Let's just let the killer go and hope it doesn't happen again because you're feeling moody and can't be bothered. Is that what you're saying?"

Her dark eyes had narrowed and I didn't like what I heard in her voice. The beginning of contempt. Behind it was everything I knew about Roxie Bouchie. The sacrifices she'd made to get where she was, the years of grueling work in which she'd learned a self-discipline I admired but didn't particularly want for myself. It's not the way I operate and the truth is, I don't have to.

"Please, I don't want to fight with you," I said, looking around for the keys to my truck. "I've been up since four A.M. and spent the day running all over San Diego County trying to do psychological interviews for which I have no training and at which I'd be lousy even if I did because, as you say, I'm not rational. Then I damn near got blown off Yaqui Pass and came home to find Brontë half crazy because one of the people I interviewed, the one who's been killing women with your MAOIs, was out here to leave me another of those stupid plates, which, incidentally, are the best clue we've got *because* that behavior is irrational and therefore a map to the real person. But you wouldn't understand that. Next you show up to tell me you're probably moving to Philadelphia and then spend hours talking about a drug. Why does it surprise you that I'm a little *stressed*?"

The last word, I realized, had been shrill, but I didn't care. Roxie just stood there as I found the keys under a half-empty bag of corn chips on the counter and grabbed a jacket from an arm of the couch.

"I'll be back," I said as I opened the Dutch door to gusting wind. "I don't want you to leave and I know you don't understand, but I just need some time."

Outside, I felt the characteristic ambivalence of these moments. My behavior was in one sense pointless melodrama. Where was I going to go this late at night? In another sense, however, my behavior was necessary, normal. And I didn't care where I was going. Although I knew where I was going.

Coyote Canyon. I could think there.

19

A Habitation of Termites

Borrego Springs was quiet as I drove through on my way to Coyote Canyon Road. People were staying at home, out of the wind. Nothing on the streets but tumbleweeds. I watched one of them bouncing along in my headlights, the globe-shaped skeleton of a plant called Russian thistle. The biggest ones are six feet across, but even the little ones make people start humming the theme from *Bonanza*. Tumbleweeds have become a symbol of the American West, but in reality there weren't any here until 1873 when the seeds of the first batch arrived mixed in with some flax seeds sent from Russia. Now they're everywhere, breaking off from their taproots in autumn and rolling for hundreds of miles in the wind. I wondered if they were trying to roll back to Russia. And I wondered where I was trying to roll, too.

Roxie would unquestionably take the project director job in Philadelphia, I told myself as the paved road ended and I felt my tires sink slightly in damp sand. The job would be a stepping-stone to more important things later. Rox had worked all her life for chances like this, chances to make a difference in the lives of the seriously mentally ill. My task would be to make it easy for her to go. Or at least not to make it impossible. I owed her that much simply because she was an honorable person.

"I'll do right by you, Roxie!" I yelled through tears as the truck lurched and banged down a wash and up the other side. Desert canyons are good for these moments of emotional wretchedness. You can scream your heart out, sob until you feel dry and empty as a shed snakeskin, and the rocks just loom anciently around you, absorbing it all. They aren't indifferent; it's just that after several million years they've refined patience to an art. *This will pass,* they croon as the wind sweeps over them. *Everything does.*

The message falls short of sweetness and light, but it works for me.

Rox and I had been honest with each other from the beginning. I knew her life was devoted to the practice of psychiatry before all else. She knew I was devoted to nothing except perhaps trying to figure out what, if anything, might be worth my devotion. So far nothing had seemed all that compelling, so I was devoting myself to making money. Call me old-fashioned, but I've got an aging father who exhausted his resources on lawyers while trying to keep my wayward twin brother from spending the rest of his life in prison. That same brother will probably get out of prison in a few months with no marketable job skills. David can't even rob a bank successfully. And his new wife is expecting their baby next year. Money is going to be needed.

"So, I can make money in Philadelphia," I said aloud, slowing as the dirt jeep track through Coyote Canyon narrowed to a rock-strewn path just wide enough for my truck.

But I didn't believe my words. What Roxie calls irrationality in me is to some extent just the long view social psychologists tend to take. It's a perspective born in statistical analyses, where predictions are based on vast numbers. But not everything can be analyzed or predicted. Social psychologists know that better than anyone else. So the perspective is one from which it becomes obvious that not everything can be understood. That many things are fragments of a larger pattern which remains forever out of view. Also obvious is that the only choice we have is to hang on for the ride or get off and hide.

I'd hang on, I knew. I might even go back East with Roxie for a while to get her settled, but I wouldn't stay. The pattern cast by that phone call from Philadelphia was hers, not mine. Part of a path chosen long ago by Rox and her grandma when there was nothing they could do to help an ill and terrified woman they wanted to love. Roxie's mother, lost to them in the shadows of an illness called schizophrenia. I might have no place on that path, but I could, and would, respect it. That is, I would as soon as I stopped crying.

Which apparently wasn't going to happen anytime soon. But the canyon walls were there to hold me, so I kept sobbing and driving. Deeper into granite rubble and resinous plants that filled the dark with scents. After a rain the desert smells like wet chalk and iron and sage. I rolled the driver's-side window all the way down and let the cool air blow across my face. It wasn't Roxie's beaded braids, I thought, but it was enough. It would have to be.

About then I realized what I was doing. In the rational sense, that is. I had hiked most of the way through Coyote Canyon in the past, but I'd never gone all the way to the end. And I'd never driven it. Now I was, and the result would be a smashed oil pan and differential housing, unaligned tires, scratched paint, and, with truly rotten luck, a broken axle. That is, if I didn't get stuck in the wet sand first, which I undoubtedly would if I tried to go all the way through.

Coyote Canyon splits at its northwestern end into Horse Canyon, which goes nowhere, and Nance Canyon, which comes out near the tiny town of Anza. Neither is really a canyon, but just a long wash. The climb up out of Nance is a nightmare even with four-wheel drive, which my truck doesn't have. The road's just a boulder-riddled sheep path that seems to go straight up. Now muddy and impassable. I'd turn around in relatively flat Figtree Valley at the base of Nance Canyon and go back, I decided. When I got there I stopped and breathed sage-scented

air for a while. But the journey seemed incomplete. And Nance
would be easy enough on foot, I thought. Imperative to finish
this, go all the way. Who knows why, but I had to do it.

So I locked the truck and stumbled up the rocky trail out of
canyon shadows to the desert surface, falling enough times to
get bruised and muddy, not caring. Something pulling at me.
Something I had to prove in the dark, alone. Okay, irrational,
but I did it. Panting and staggering at the top, I could see a
few lights from Anza four miles away, just yellow bubbles shim-
mering in the wind. Nearby were empty sheep and cattle pens,
a few darkened ranch houses. And something else beside me
just off the road to my right.

A ruin of some kind, half buried in creosote bushes and darkness. An old adobe line shack, I thought. Built long ago to
house the crews who set up poles and brought electricity to
Anza and the handful of other tiny communities out here. Communities of sheepherders and cattlemen who rode horses until
1956, when the first paved roads were laid and a way of life
died overnight. I squinted against the wind at the crumbling
adobe building. There was something oddly familiar about it.

Set at the top of Nance Canyon, it faced Coyote Road, which
at the lip of the canyon ceased being a road and became again
the rugged trail I'd just climbed on foot. The building also faced
a ridge that cast half its facade in impenetrable gloom. Curious,
I moved closer, wishing for a flashlight. I'd never climbed Nance
Canyon, never been there before, and yet I was sure I'd seen the
old shack, was familiar with it. But I couldn't place it, couldn't
pull up an identity for it. An adobe line shack, desolate and
abandoned.

Isolated places always harbor these structures—miners' shacks,
solitary chimneys rising from bare dirt, a fire ring of stones
where someone unaccountably tried to burn a wall clock and
one tennis shoe. Evidence that people have come and then vanished, both for unknowable reasons. Nothing unusual. I'd probably seen a hundred crumbling adobe buildings since moving
to California, I told myself. This one just looked like the others.

The building's door and three front windows had been covered with sheets of corrugated steel, rusted long ago. One kick from my foot and the flaking orange metal behind the doorframe fell inward, raising whirlpools of dust that immediately caught the wind and blew away. The sheet metal had at one time been nailed to the doorframe but now merely leaned there. Invading teenagers, I thought.

Beneath my boots the doorsill crunched softly and turned to wooden crumbs as I stepped inside. Termites had done their work and then left, like everybody else. The interior smelled of dry rot, animal scat, and a medicinal odor I associate with wasps. From the door a gray rectangle of moonlight struggled to illuminate the dark corners and failed. I could see the dim outline of an overturned table, some seatless chairs with rusty chrome legs, and a bar or counter against the far wall. The place had been a saloon or eating place at one time, I assumed. Maybe after the line crews left it had been used as a watering hole for local ranchers and the occasional prospector still combing nearby canyons for overlooked caches of gold.

In the interim it must have been a hangout for teenagers with a satanic bent, I assumed, since the walls had been decorated fairly recently with pictures torn from magazines. Most of them were obscured by darkness, but near the door I could make out several pictures of owls and one of a dragon I suspected was the logo for a popular teen rock group.

Even so, the place felt so empty it seemed to swallow light. I pulled the corrugated metal against the doorframe again and stepped back outside. On the ground beneath a clump of bur sage, half buried in sand, I saw a hand-painted sign fallen from above the door. DESSERT Something-or-Other, it had once announced in dark paint on a whitewashed board. Apparently someone had once provided desserts here, like the apple pies that now drew people to Julian. The second word had been obscured by time. When I picked it up the board was as light as balsa wood, just a fragile shell left by termites.

Time to go home, I told myself. Go home to Brontë, who would stay at my side until her death, and Roxie, who wouldn't.

And shouldn't, my Midwestern ethic insisted. Roxie should be helped along her path by me and then let go. It was true and it's the hardest thing in the world to do.

"Dammit, I *hate* this!" I yelled into a wind that blew my voice away like smoke.

At the top of the trail I turned to look back at the strange place which I would remember, I thought, as the scene of my personal despair that night. And I'd take the old sign with me, I decided. Take it home and patch it together and hang it over my door. A symbol for the passage of time which would eventually make of Roxie Bouchie just such a forgotten place in my heart.

It's how I operate, the deliberate imposition of images on my mind. It's how I don't forget what's happened to me, how I don't forget my life. Later I'd provide a sound track for the scene in my mind. Something unbearably sad. Paganini's *Variations on a Theme,* maybe. That haunting melancholy. I liked the mental composition I was creating. It meant I'd survive.

I felt valiant and wise as I tucked the old sign under my arm and loped toward the jeep trail and my truck below, turning to look back one last time. That's when I saw it. That's when I saw why the place had seemed familiar. From that angle it *was* familiar. There was a picture of it on my living room wall! A black-and-white photograph of the building as it once had looked at dusk. Half of it darkened by the shadow of the ridge behind me, the other half blasted by light from a setting sun. The same photograph in moonlight.

"Oh, my God," I said so softly the wind took my words before I heard them. I don't usually believe in coincidence, as I've said, although there are coincidences. They're meaningless. Running into your next-door neighbor at a movie theater three miles from your house is a coincidence. Noticing that the woman sitting in front of you at that movie is your high school English teacher from twenty years ago and fifteen hundred miles away isn't. What it is, is something for which there is no word. Even if the English teacher died in Ethiopia with the Peace Corps three years after you graduated and the woman in front of you is just a body-double, it's not a coincidence. The world is divided into people who understand this and people who don't.

I had lived for two years within a day's hike of the old line shack, but I had never seen it. Then I'd bought a grainy photograph of it taken in the past from an odd angle and brought the photograph home. There I had hung it where only my dog could see it without looking down.

"Okay, Grid," I whispered to nothing but a concept I'd made up, "what does this mean?"

There was no answer but the howling of a wind which was beginning to annoy me. Apparently I would have to figure it out for myself.

"All right," I thought defiantly, "then I will." Meanwhile, I would help complete the job Roxie and I had undertaken together. I'd do everything I could to determine who among the Rainer medical staff had killed patients with a timed-release antidepressant that exploded their brains when they ate liver pâté. I'd stay up for days and nights running statistical analyses until my computer crashed in curls of smoke and I'd narrowed the field to one. One person and only one who met the criteria, who had motive. One person who was waiting to be caught. And I'd do it for Roxie. I'd do it to close the path behind her and free her to leave.

On the bump-and-bang trip back through Coyote Canyon I felt brave and strong. I would do the Right Thing for Roxie because I loved her. Someone less prone to solitary, dramatic scenes involving dubious moral decisions might have paused to consider the operative term, "love." Someone other than I might have remembered how deadly Jerry Russell Jones's love for Ruby Emerald had become in the hours before he shot her with a .22 handgun. Or the cruelty Pieter Van Der Elst's love for his wife, Kate, had caused him to unleash at her weakest moment. The love between Wes and Annie Rathbone, too, might be drawn into the analysis before a decision was made. But I didn't consider any of those things. In my mind was a picture of my sorrow, complete with music. I would make sure I earned it, paid the admission price to a movie of my own life. That was all.

Roxie's car was still there when I got home, as I'd known it would be. Roxie is rational and therefore does not do dumb things like drive over mountains at night in fits of pique. In the long run this quality might rub off on me, I thought as I killed the engine and let the truck coast quietly to a stop. Except there wasn't going to be any long run.

Brontë, of course, heard the truck and came sleepily to the door, licked my hand, and then trotted back into the bedroom. I took the old sign into the kitchen and propped it in the sink. Indoors, it looked phony. Like a ghost-town prop from a "South-western" catalogue also offering plastic steer skull snack-servers and Kokopelli toilet tissue. So I kicked off my boots, grabbed the sign, and padded outside to the pool. There I lay the sign on a chaise lounge and looked at the water, which seemed gray and forbidding without the underwater lights which would make it blue and sparkling again. Except the lights might wake Roxie, I thought.

But then so would I if I tried to clean up in the bathroom.

"Oh, hell," I whispered, then pulled off my clothes and slipped into the warm water at the shallow end. No splashing. No sound at all. Just soft, thick water holding me in the dark. I was tired, I realized. Every muscle limp and aching from exhaustion. The motel pool was quiet and felt as big as a lake. I'd been drifting for a while when suddenly I wasn't sure I was awake. Wasn't sure I remembered where the edge was, or how to get out. *So tired,* I thought. *So tired I can't make myself move.*

And then an awareness of depth. I'd drifted to the deep end, floating on my back, more than half asleep. Gallons of gray water beneath me, fathoms of gray. I could see the splash gutter all around me, see the rectangular shape of the pool against the decking. But I couldn't move. And then I was sinking. Or I thought I was, and I still couldn't quite remember how to move, how to make the dead weight of my body cross a few feet of dark liquid to safety.

A chill, then. Coldness drifting in my arms and legs like oil in a lava lamp. I felt the water close over my head and kicked a little out of instinct, but I wasn't sure which way was up. And the feet kicking at the ends of my legs didn't feel like mine. Feeling them was more like watching them. Like watching puppet feet on a screen inside my head. And then a kernel of panic burst somewhere and I was choking and thrashing as something crushed my chest. Something pulling me, hurting my lungs, the skin over my ribs. Something holding me so tight I couldn't breath, and then something hard hitting my head.

The splash gutter. The splash gutter had hit my head, and the thing crushing my chest was an arm, dark against my pale skin.

"Roxie," I choked.

She was in the gray water, one arm around the kickboard, the other around me. I could feel her trembling, feel it in the big muscles of her arms and shoulders. Without a sound she pulled me along the edge to the shallow end and then pushed me up the pool's steps. On the decking a black animal moved in worried circles, then pushed its face against my neck and licked frantically.

"Roxie?" I said again when she returned with towels and began scouring me until my skin burned. I could feel the race of blood in a million vessels, the pulse of capillaries stretching in my fingertips.

"I'm okay, Roxie," I said. "I don't know what happened. I didn't want to wake you. I think I fell asleep in the pool."

Her eyes looked strange in the dark and I could still feel the trembling inside her, beneath her wet skin.

"You're cold," I said, standing shakily. "Let's go inside, get into some dry clothes, have some coffee. I have to tell you what happened, what I found, Roxie. The shack. The one in the photograph I bought at the Aphid Gallery. I saw it, Rox. It's at the end of Coyote Canyon where it comes out above Anza. It's real. It's really there."

I hung on her, wrapped in towels, as we moved inside. I could hear myself jabbering about an adobe shack, saying the same things over and over while deep inside I faced an awareness I didn't want to face. That if I couldn't *tell* Roxie Bouchie about my life, if she weren't there to hear, then whatever might happen in my life would be less real than it really was. Years spun out ahead of me in which my own experience could never be as intense and clear, as *defined* as it was when I simply told it to Roxie Bouchie. The awareness felt like drowning.

"Rox, say something," I begged after we'd gotten into dry T-shirts and I'd reassured Brontë with a liver treat that I was okay and she could go back to sleep. But Roxie just clenched her fists and walked into the darkened bedroom alone.

"Please," I whispered, following and crawling into bed next to her. "I'm sorry I took off and left you here, but I had to. When you told me about Philadelphia—"

"Blue, there's something I didn't tell you about the MAOIs," she said, pulling me fiercely to her. "You left before I had time. And I don't feel like telling you right now. Stop running, Blue. You're always running. And I'm asking you, just this once, to stop."

It occurred to me that drowning in the night-gray water of my pool felt preferable to her request. Running is what I do, who I am. Running, always observing and thinking and assessing everything, watching my own life like a movie seen through a moving car window. As long as I'm running, I'm safe. Whatever it is I fear can't catch me. But Roxie was asking for a kind of courage I'd never displayed. She deserved my best. And she would have it.

"I'm not running," I told her. "I'm right here."

After that we didn't talk but made love all night as if it were the first time, or the last. And I was there. I didn't run.

Eventually I must have slept because I woke up suddenly, a knot of fear in my gut. It was almost nine o'clock in the morning, somebody was pounding on the door, Brontë was barking, and Roxie was beside me in bed but fully dressed and watching me anxiously.

"Oh, Rox," I mumbled, "what's going on?"

"A lot. Hard to know where to begin. But first I have to know if you're still here, or if you've gone off in your head again like you do, running away."

"Rox, *I'm* not the one who's going away," I began. "And who in *hell* is that at the door? And why aren't you at work? What's going on, Roxie?"

"I took the day off," she said, not moving from my side. "Personal leave, and God knows, honey, this is personal, except now we don't have time for it. At the door we have the FBI. There are a few things I need to tell you, Blue."

"FBI? What's the FBI doing here?" I croaked, lurching toward the bathroom. I wanted to be alone with Roxie and have a hot shower and a huge breakfast with a lot of fresh coffee. In that order.

"That's one of the few things," she answered. "I'll just ask them to wait at their campsite for a few more minutes. But then we'll have to talk to them, Blue. We have a lot of work to do today."

"What campsite?" I yelled as she went to the door. There was a businesslike drone of conversation between Rox and two male voices, and Brontë stopped barking.

"The one fifty yards outside your door," Rox yelled into the bathroom as I wasted a lot of water in a full-blast shower. "They've been out there since seven, even have a chemical toilet."

Minutes later I looked out the little bathroom window that faces the back of my property. In a hollow partway up a wash I saw a tidy campsite outfitted with everything you'd need to scale Everest except the oxygen tanks. Seated on folding camp chairs were two men in khaki shorts and T-shirts. One was watching the desert through binoculars the size of a good dictionary. The other was talking on a cell phone. Both wore sidearms in holsters. Across the lap of the one with the binoculars lay a high-powered rifle equipped with a day scope. It seemed clear they weren't there to meditate.

"Roxie," I singsonged, hopping around my bedroom pulling on underwear, "it's time to tell me now. There are heavily armed Eagle Scouts in my yard. What did I miss last night?"

She sat on the edge of the bed.

"Remember when I was talking to Wes about Bettina Ashe

and all the foods you can't eat if you're taking MAOIs?" she asked.

"Yeah."

I'd grabbed a beige knit skirt from the closet and was trying to pull it over my hips. Already I knew it was going to be a skirt day. Already I knew I was going to be working. Hard.

"Remember when I told you everybody started yelling around him and he had to hang up?"

"Yeah, Rox, get to the point."

I found a bra, then a blousy white knit top with a cowl collar. Gold earrings. Professional look, I thought. Or at least it would be when I put on some shoes.

"Listen," she said, and I did. "Now, what happened at police headquarters last night was a phone call from the Secret Service advising the San Diego Police Department that the FBI would now be involved in the Sword of Heaven case. Wes called back right after you left. Sword is the FBI's prey now. Our tax dollars at work. He's briefed the agents already. They know about the connection between you and Sword, about the plates. They think he'll visit you again. They're waiting."

"But Roxie," I said, wanting to talk about nothing but last night and how was I supposed to let her go live in Philadelphia when she was inside my mind now, permanently, "why? The Rainer Clinic is virtually closed. Sword can't kill again, at least not immediately. The local police didn't request FBI backup before. Why now?"

"Because," she said, knitting her brow, "our woman vice presidential candidate is making an unscheduled campaign stop here tomorrow morning. It's in today's paper, but the news was on the Internet last night. Sword saw it. Go look at your e-mail."

Rox had already booted up my computer, so I clicked on the server's icon and waited. In seconds the list of mail was visible. One from dad, as usual. Two from book companies tracing out-of-print books for me. Five or six from discussion groups. One from "Godsword@bluebay.com." It had been copied to me from an original sent to the *San Diego Union-Tribune*, with copies to eighteen network and cable TV stations and the SDPD.

I brought it up on the screen and noticed its buttons. Three little blue willow plates now, not two.

The third time's the charm.

"Vice President is a man not a women," it said. "This women tyring to be a man is an abomination must dye. The Sword of Heaven is swift and will kill with guns this time."

The predictable typed signature was, "The Sword of Heaven."

20

Pirates, Diners, and Desert Rats

At least 'abomination' is spelled right," I told Roxie.

The word made me think about Old Testament vengeance and Lilith and wild places and the photograph of an adobe shack on my wall. I thought about a grid of universal intention whose purposes were apparently served at the moment by a woman running for the second highest office in the United States. And the killer who threatened to stop that. The killer who kept leaving me blue willow plates. No coincidence, none of it. And my only choice, I realized, was to hang on for the ride or . . . well, there was no other choice.

"Probably copied it out of the Bible," Rox answered, pouring coffee. "I have to leave soon, Blue. I'm meeting Jennings Rainer and Kate Van Der Elst at the Rainer Clinic at noon."

I'd been deep in thought, planning what to do. The plan felt right even though nobody else would see it that way.

"You're what?" I said. "What for? And it won't take you three hours to get down there, anyway."

"Not everybody drives twenty miles over the speed limit," she mentioned. "And the reason is that we're going to run a blood test on Kate, see if she's got an MAOI in her system. If she does, there's a pretty good chance my theory's correct even though we'll never really know unless Sword tells us. Rainer has the equipment to run the test at his clinic. I'll draw the blood, Rainer will run the analysis, and then I'll have the test replicated at another lab in case it's needed later as evidence. And there's something else—"

"How did Jennings Rainer get involved in this?" I interrupted over a bowl of cereal I was trying to eat before the bran flakes got soggy. "And where did Kate stay last night? Did she stay home or go to the hotel where Pieter is?"

"She went to a different hotel," Rox said approvingly. "It was good for her to take control that way, meet her need for security on her own. You gave her good advice, Blue. Same with Rainer. He called me yesterday afternoon, said you'd referred him to me. I can't see him because there'd be conflict over my working for the police on a case in which he's technically a suspect. He understood that. I referred him to another psychiatrist, someone I know, and then checked to be sure he'd made an appointment, which he had. I asked him to do the blood test on Kate today, Blue. I wanted him to feel that he'd done his part to help the police find the killer."

"But Rox, what if he *is* the killer? You're sending Kate right into his hands!"

"I don't think he is, and he won't be touching Kate in any event," she said. "The other thing I didn't tell you is about the list of medications BB saw in Isadora Grecchi's medicine cabinet."

"Yeah?"

"They're all antidepressants, Blue. And two of them, Parnate and Nardil, are MAOIs. Looks like Grecchi's got a serious problem with clinical depression and her physician's trying everything in the book. Nobody prescribes MAOIs now unless the client is unresponsive to everything else. But there it is. Grecchi's got the stuff. It doesn't look good for her."

"Oh, no, " I muttered. "Did you tell Rathbone?"

"I told him, but I also told him depressed people are usually only a danger to themselves. They commit suicide to escape the indescribable despair of depression, but generally they don't commit murder. I don't think he really understood, but he did understand that Grecchi's possession of MAOIs doesn't mean she's the perp. It only moves her up a slot in the list of suspects. Anyway, you and I are supposed to be in Rathbone's office by one o'clock for a briefing with the FBI guy who's in charge now, and—"

"Roxie, could you handle that alone?" I interrupted. "You'll have the results from Kate's test. If she's got this MAOI stuff in her blood, then you're the one to explain it to the FBI. I don't know anything about antidepressants and blood pressure. Neither do I know anything about psychiatric profiles of serial killers. There's something else I need to do, okay?"

The look I got was the same one my mother gave me when I was eight and told her I would be digging for buried pirate treasure in the backyard all day and therefore could not go to school. To her credit, my mother took the time to explain that as far as anyone knew, no pirates had sailed the sea of corn surrounding Waterloo, Illinois, ten miles from the Mississippi River, and so could not have buried treasure in our yard. Roxie merely fumed.

"Blue, Sword has killed three people already and now threatens to kill a vice presidential candidate within less than twenty-four hours! What can you possibly have to do that can't wait?"

I let Brontë lap the rest of the milk from my cereal and eyed Roxie sitting next to me at my kitchen counter on a barstool. In her black turtleneck she looked like an undercover agent. She also looked puzzled and harried. She glanced at her watch, cocked her head at me. Irritated. I'd expected this, but if Rox and I wanted to have anything resembling the serious relationship that kept shaping up between us, then I had to make something about myself crystal clear.

"I need to talk about last night," I began, facing her squarely. "Something hap—"

She grabbed both my hands in hers and looked even more harried. "Girl, I know," she whispered. "But not now. There's no time. We've got these bozos outside who want you to tell them about every damn snake trail in the desert, and then we've got to help Rathbone. We've got a *job* here, Blue. It's important."

"Rox, last night—"

"I know," she said, holding my hands so tight it hurt. "But we can't go there now, understand? There isn't *time*. We'll talk later. I know we have to talk. I'm not trying to duck the Philadelphia thing, Blue. It's tearing me apart. We'll work something out. I don't know what. But right now—"

"It's not about Philadelphia and you leaving or me staying, it's way beyond that. I learned to trust you last night," I went on determinedly. "Now I'm asking you to trust me."

She shook her head and her beads rattled with impatience. "I do, Blue, but—"

Taking a deep breath, I launched into the defense of a decision that hadn't existed three minutes earlier.

"I'm asking you to trust me, trust the way I am and think, even though it's not your way," I said. "I'm asking you to trust me out of the dark, out of bed, away from each other without this thing that pulls us together and blinds us to everything else. There are some things I need to do today and they aren't 'rational,' but I think they might have something to do with Sword. I don't even know why I think that, I just do. But I can't defend my thoughts in your terms, so I don't want to talk about them. I just want you to trust me. Will you?"

There was a long silence in which I could hear my stomach reducing bran flakes to chemical gruel.

"Okay, yes," she said somberly. "Girl, I *do* trust you."

I hadn't planned on getting married in my kitchen with two armed FBI agents in camp chairs outside the window, but that's what it felt like.

We decided that I'd brief the agents on the desert terrain from which Sword might reappear, since Roxie knew nothing about the area except that it was hot and short on buildings. The two men sat on my couch happily perusing maps of the Anza-Borrego Desert and asking questions about what they called the "plate drops." What time, where, and did I understand the significance of the plates, the blue willow pattern? The FBI is not without impressive resources, but I was still stunned when one of them unfolded a large diagram of a blue willow plate on my coffee table. Somebody, I knew, had been up all night drawing it on a computer.

"I don't know what the plates are about," I told them, "although I do know a lot about the plates. The design reflects an Asian story, but it was first used on plates in England. It is . . ." I said, pausing dramatically, "the most popular china pattern *in the world*." I was sure Hutton Pierce, the curator, would have been proud.

"It's real popular with us right now, too," one of the agents growled amiably, pointing to the three little figures on the bridge. "You're a psychologist, right? One of our guys at Quantico is guessing the perp has had some problem with authority figures, maybe an abusive mother since the victims are women, and feels trapped like the characters in the story."

"I'm a *social* psychologist," I replied, wondering how many more times I would have to explain this before I died. "I analyze tons of data and draw conclusions based on it. I can only talk about the likelihood that a certain proportion of a defined population will do or not do a particular thing. I can never talk about individuals. I have no idea what motivates the perpetrator of these crimes."

"So what proportion of a population defined as 'blue-willow-plate-nuts' is likely to kill women in positions formerly reserved for men?" the other one asked.

These guys weren't dumb, I realized. It was a good question. And I'd walked right into it. I could feel Roxie smiling beside me even though I didn't look at her.

"I talked to a woman in Phoenix who's something of an expert on these plates, and she said—"

"Name?" the first guy interrupted, grabbing a pen from the cargo pocket of his tan shorts. "We'll need her name and phone number."

"Um, Lauer. Jackie Lauer. I didn't keep her number, but you

can find her on the Internet. Look under either 'blue willow' or 'Crankshaft Car Club.' And what she told me is that blue willow collectors break down into two categories—people who want the plates for their potential monetary value and those who are attracted by the design. One's purely practical, the other is emotional. The second category is comprised primarily of women. I'd say Sword is attached to these plates emotionally rather than practically."

"So you think our guy's a girl?"

"I think the gender markers are inconsistent," I concluded, wishing I didn't sound like a pompous windbag.

"Yeah," they both said.

"So what are you going to do if the perp shows up out here with another plate?" Rox asked them.

"Capture him or kill him."

"What if it turns out to be a woman?"

"Capture her or kill her."

I'm always impressed by solid priorities, even though they often fail to provide for the unforeseen.

"Um, Sword isn't likely to come anywhere near here," I mentioned. "Your camp is sort of noticeable."

"Meant to be," the first one said. "Our expert agrees with Dr. Bouchie here. The guy expects to get caught. If he's out here he'll regard our presence as inevitable and come in for the showdown. And of course we won't be at the camp. It's only a lure. We'll be nearby, though. We'll get him."

With that they strode out the door and into dusty glare that was already hot.

After Roxie left I packed some jeans, a sweatshirt, and tennis shoes in a duffel and threw it on the floor of the truck cab. Wrapped in the sweatshirt was my little snub-nosed Smith and Wesson, now an illegal "concealed weapon." Then I called Brontë to take her seat on the passenger's side and slammed the door. It was going to be a long day, I thought. Already the FBI agents were invisible, holed up behind boulders somewhere with gallon jugs of water and binoculars, watching. They'd watch all day and all night, I realized. They knew what they were supposed to do.

I didn't, exactly. But at least I had a plan.

First I gassed up the truck in Borrego, then headed over the mountains to Julian, where I took State Road 79 to State Road 371. The route was the long way from my place to the little town of Anza, where 371 became the main street. There wasn't much there. Just a gas station, two roadside hamburger joints, and a convenience store that seemed to do most of its business in video rentals. Then I saw what I was looking for. A Realtor's office. I parked the truck under a sign reading PEACEFUL DESERT HIDEAWAYS—RENT OR BUY—EASY TERMS and pushed open the glass door.

"Hi," I said to a huge blond man with a curly beard and mischievous blue eyes. "I'm curious about that old adobe line shack on Coyote Road where Nance Canyon comes out. Do you know anything about it?"

"County declared it a hazardous structure and boarded it up years ago," he answered. "It'll collapse any day now. Even the teenagers don't sneak in there anymore. Why? If you're interested in some nice desert property with a view, I can show you—"

"No, I'm, uh, doing some research for an art exhibit. Photographs. You know, 'Desert Legacy, Places Time Forgot.' An old photo of that building was recently featured at a San Diego gallery, and it got me to thinking. There are so many stories out here. Prospectors, ranchers, mule trains, and the Pony Express. Do you know if anything interesting ever happened there?"

He grinned, showing white and charmingly crooked front teeth. "Well, some kids knocked one hell of a wasp's nest off the side of the chimney a few years back. Got stung so bad one of 'em had to be hospitalized. Miracle the chimney didn't fall on 'em while they were at it. But you're looking for history, right?"

"Yes," I agreed. "Is there any?"

"Let me call my mother," he answered. "This is her agency. I'm just here helping out. Got me a place in Warner Springs, little apple orchard. My wife loves it. But mom, she thinks the boom's going to be up here. People from L.A. and San Diego buying land to get away from the city. She's probably right. She's always right."

"Is your mother from here?" I asked as he dialed the phone.

"Nah. Kansas City. I grew up there, was stationed here with the Marines. Loved it, moved out here when I got married. So after my dad died mom just packed up and came out, too, eventually started the agency up here. She's already worth six big ones, but she says she wants to die rich and leave my kids enough money to support me."

This wasn't what I'd been fishing for.

"Mom," he said into the phone, "lady here wants to know about the old line shack on Coyote Road. History stuff. Anything ever happen there?"

I admired a changing display of color photographs on the agency's computer monitor as he said nothing, apparently listening. All the photographs were of bleached-out desert "hideaways" that might have been the same hideaway photographed from different angles. At least one tumbleweed appeared in each.

Then, "You think I should send her to Waddy? Jeez."

"Waddy?" I said when he'd hung up.

"Old guy, hangs out at the Hamburger Corral or else you can find him at home. I'll give you a map. But let me try the Corral first."

After another quick phone call he said, "Nope, he's at the Corral. You can go on over there. He'll talk to you, let me tell you. He'll talk your arm off. Waddy Babbick's lived here since dirt. Used to run some cattle in the old days, I guess. He and his wife raised six kids up here when there was just a one-room schoolhouse, back in the fifties. Had to build a school just for the Babbicks. Mom says she thinks Waddy said something about that line shack being used for a diner a long time ago, if that's any help."

Diner.

"Thanks," I said with feeling, and gunned the truck three stops up the road to a place called Hamburger Corral.

Waddy Babbick had the leathery skin of a desert rat and narrow gray eyes under his bifocals. He wore an old-fashioned
white dress shirt, starched and ironed to a shine, with mud-
caked jeans and cowboy boots.

"I'm eighty-seven years young and I know more about this
place than God," he informed me when I joined him at the Corral's Formica counter. "Lotta people don't know this whole valley was a big Indian city before the white man came. Winter
city. Summers, they'd go to the mountains, of course. They
moved around, the Indians did, left pots and arrowheads, flint
knives, bone fishhooks, all over. I've got a whole collection—"

"I hear you might know something about the old line shack
on Coyote Road," I interrupted. "Was it used as a diner at one
time?"

"That place? Yeah, it was a diner here about thirty years back.
The Desert Diner, it was called. Some woman ran it for a while.
Her and her daughter. My wife was still alive then, bless her
heart, so I never ate there. Heard all they served was cheese
sandwiches and the like, anyway. Ate right at home, I did, unless I was out runnin' the cows to pasture or bringin' 'em down
to the railhead at Temecula before the spur went in. But let me
tell you about these flint arrowheads. See, I've got about four
hundred in *museum* condition, and they tell a tale, they do."

"I'm afraid my current research involves only the line shack,"
I insisted. "What else do you know about it? And is there anybody else around here who might know anything about it?"

"There's nobody else around here who knows as much as I
do about *anything*," Waddy Babbick told me, chuckling. "I'm
the oldest s.o.b. in the valley! Now, Reed McCallister, me and
her used to fight for the title, you know? Reed's damn near as
old as I am. She and her husband Bill had a spread over by
Bucksnort, ran sheep. Hell, Bill died from a rattlesnake bite
twenty years ago, but Reed, she stayed on out at their place
until, let's see, five years ago? Fell and broke her hip, had to
have the replacement surgery. Now, her son Bill, Jr., he lives
in San Diego, came up here and took her down to some 'retirement village' down there in Carlsbad. Sagebrush Resort, it's

called. I go on down to see her couple times a year, Christmas and all. Now, Reed, she had an interest in Indians, too. Used to make these baskets like they did, and—"

"When did the diner close?" I interrupted, beginning to feel irrational, foolish.

"Like I said, close on thirty years ago. Something happened, the law was involved. I think that woman that ran it turned out to be some kind of criminal hiding out up here, and they come after her. The wife and I, we'd gone back East so she could help one of our daughters with a new baby, so we wasn't here when they come after that woman. People talked about it for a time, but I didn't pay no attention. Now, my wife, she coulda told you. You know how women are."

"Yes," I answered, and slid off my stool. "Thanks so much, Mr. Babbick."

"Just call me Waddy," he said, waving a leathery hand. "And come on back when you wanna see those arrowheads!"

It was only four more miles to the line shack, so I drove up there and let Brontë run while I stared at it. In the bright sunlight I could see bare spots where the adobe had crumbled away, exposing rotted boards beneath. No one had been there since I kicked the door in. Everything was as I'd left it. In the light it looked like nothing in particular, just a crumbling shack that could fall in on itself and vanish by tomorrow. It meant nothing, told me nothing, and I felt like an idiot for imagining that it would. Still, I thought, it had been a diner, and diners used blue willow plates . . . but no, it was far-fetched. I'd asked for Roxie's trust in the middle of a serious professional obligation involving both of us. It was time to earn it.

"Come on, Brontë," I called. "We've got real work to do."

21

Bones

From Anza the quickest route down into San Diego is I-15, which descends through broken granite foothills and fields of huge, pale boulders. I was in a hurry, so I took that route. Advertising is not permitted on interstate highways, but a sign announcing a large shopping mall in one of the suburban communities was nonetheless visible, perched on a hill. And a large shopping mall would have what I needed. Ten minutes later I stood in an electronics chain store overflowing with unidentifiable merchandise.

"I want to buy a cellular phone," I told a young woman with seven earrings in the cartilage of her left ear. She was reading *Moby Dick* and seemed delighted to put the book down and tell me about the differences between analog and digital.

"Just something cheap and serviceable," I told her as though I were buying shelf paper. "I don't expect to use it very much. In fact, I may never use it again after today."

"Oh, you'll use it," she said knowingly. "They're addictive."

Twenty minutes and a lot of paperwork later I showed Brontë

a tiny phone with a flip-down mouthpiece. I grew up watching *Star Trek*. I knew what I had.

"Beam me up, Scotty," I said to a Doberman, and then headed south toward Jeffrey Pond's low-rent apartment.

He wasn't there but his mother was, and she was asleep. Or had been until I woke her.

"I told those FBI men when they came in the hospital last night," she said through the three-inch gap allowed by the chain lock, "we don't know nothing about whatever it is happened at Jeffrey's clinic. Now my husband went in the hospital yesterday afternoon with a heart failure from pulman eneema, they said, and Jeffrey and me, we been there straight through since four o'clock. That's four o'clock yesterday. Jeffrey, he's still there, but I come on over here to get some sleep since I been up all night. We sure would appreciate it a lot if you people would just go on and leave us alone, you understand? We got our hands full here without all this trouble."

"I'm sorry," I said to the sleep-creased face regarding me with firmly controlled hostility. "Please tell Jeffrey that Dr. McCarron sends best wishes for his father's recovery. You go on back to sleep now. I won't bother you again."

I had lapsed smack into the heartland behavior that is my birthright. Nothing is dearer to the soul of a Midwesterner than saying something polite and then getting the hell out of other people's business. It occurred to me that as a model for human interaction it wasn't half bad.

It also occurred to me that Jeffrey Pond was one of those people who appear to be cursed. Disaster upon disaster. An ugly divorce, false accusations of rape that destroyed his right to be comfortable with his daughter. Financial ruin, suspicion of serial murder, the loss of his job with the closing of the Rainer Clinic. And now the additional burden of his father's serious illness. I hoped he had his Silly Putty with him at the hospital.

In the truck I made the first of twenty free cellular calls that came with my sign-up package. The call was to the Rainer Clinic, and Jennings Rainer answered.

"It's Dr. McCarron," I said. "Is Dr. Bouchie there?"

"She's right here," he answered, sounding a little better than he had when I last saw him. "I do appreciate your help in referring me to Dr. Bouchie," he added. "This situation is terrible, but somehow I don't feel as crushed by it as I did. I've already seen the psychiatrist she recommended, and just having someone to talk to has helped, although he did prescribe a medication for me, which I will take until my life is under control again. And I do feel that I'm helping the authorities now. I feet that I'm doing what I can to help right this horrible wrong."

"I was worried about you," I admitted unprofessionally. "This must be the worst thing that's ever happened to you."

"No," he answered thoughtfully, "that was losing my wife. This was just a business and I was about to retire in any event. What's terrible is that someone I know and worked with every day has taken *other* men's wives, other men who must now feel as lost and alone as I've felt. And I didn't even see it. Neither did Megan. We were responsible here. This was our clinic. Yet we saw nothing and now three women are dead and one of my employees has threatened to kill a vice presidential candidate. It's really more than I can comprehend. Oh, here's Dr. Bouchie."

"Rox, I've just been by Jeffrey Pond's apartment," I began. "Do you have any idea what a 'pulman eneema' might be?"

"At another time I might make rude references to lower g.i. practices performed aboard trains," she answered. "But not now. It sounds like somebody trying to remember 'pulmonary edema,' which basically means your lungs are a mess. Don't tell me Pond has it."

"No, his father does. The father's in the hospital and Jeffrey and his mother have been there with him since four yesterday afternoon. I'm sure the FBI already has this information and has checked it out. They tracked Pond to his father's hospital room last night. If what Mrs. Pond says is true, Jeffrey couldn't have orchestrated all that publicity about himself last night. E-mails were sent to the papers, TV stations, the police. And to me. Pond wasn't even near a computer. I'll check it out with Rathbone, but I'm afraid Pond's not Sword. So what about the blood test on Kate? And is Pieter there with her? Has he come around yet?"

"Apparently Pieter left a message on Kate's home answering

machine this morning," Rox said. "He told her he'll be leaving for Holland on Thursday and prefers not to speak with her between now and then. Meanwhile, Kate's blood is positive for trace amounts of an MAOI. It's almost gone now. The big surge would probably have been four or five days ago. She's shaky but she's taking it pretty well. I'm going to call Rathbone right now with the test results."

"Five days ago was Friday, the night of her fundraiser, Rox," I said. "And somebody sent a deli tray containing everything necessary to kill her."

"Yep, right down to the canned figs," Roxie agreed. "But she didn't eat any of it because she's on this diet, so she's fine. Sword may have been at that fundraiser, Blue. If our perp's a male, he might have been there to get a trophy of some sort. Might even have been taking photographs of the event. If it's one of the women then probably not, but who knows? Do you remember seeing any of the Rainer staff there that evening?"

"Rox, I'd never seen any of the Rainer staff at that point, and there were seventy-five people milling around an art gallery where all the lights are on the art, not the crowd. There was a photographer, but then there always is at these things. I think he ducked out right after the news about Dixie's death, probably to get the photos in to his paper. Everybody there except BB and Kate were strangers to me. It's not likely I'd remember if I *did* see somebody like Eldridge or Grecchi or Megan, although I might have remembered Pond. He'd have been the only muscle-bound bodybuilder in a sea of oxford cloth and trendy little suits. I don't remember seeing him, though, and he's out of the running since last night, anyway."

"Probably," she agreed. "I need to go, Blue. Have to be at Rathbone's office in a half hour. Do whatever it is you have to do, but there's no point in placing yourself in danger. The FBI and the police will handle it from here. Stay away from the rest of the Rainer staff, okay? Especially Grecchi. I don't like what's shaping up here and I don't want anything to do with it. The FBI and the cops will have to take it from here."

"Okay," I said. "I'll call you at home later."

I knew what Roxie meant. I'd mentioned it when we discussed taking this case. If Isadora Grecchi was the killer, then her depressive disorder would be seen as a cause of her criminal behavior. The publicity attendant upon Grecchi's capture would only reinforce the public's belief that everybody with a psychiatric diagnosis is a violent predator.

The media would have a field day, running sidebars about Jack the Ripper and interviews with colorful "mental health professionals" whose credentials could be traced to mail-order diploma mills in Texas. Some of these would hint broadly that demonic possession is more prevalent than we think. In short, Grecchi's history of depression would turn an already horrible situation into a debacle of escalating ruin. It would hurt thousands of people. I didn't want it to happen any more than Roxie did.

And maybe I could head it off, I thought. Maybe I could talk to Grecchi, not asking her to admit guilt but nonetheless orchestrating a tidy conclusion in which she'd be whisked to some secure facility with no fanfare. I'd be a negotiator, I decided. I'd seen this done in movies.

I didn't call first, merely drove to Isadora Grecchi's home in Mission Hills and parked in front. Then I let Brontë out on the passenger's side and we climbed the steps to Grecchi's porch. I didn't look behind me, didn't scrutinize a plumber's van across the street that might have been a plumber's van and might have been a stakeout. It seemed best to pretend I didn't know they were there. If they were.

"Dr. Grecchi?" I called through the screen door. "It's Blue McCarron. I need to talk to you. There's no one with me but my dog, Brontë."

There was no answer from inside. No smell of oil paint, either. No sound. I could see through the house to the deck over the canyon behind it. Three pigeons were walking around aimlessly on the redwood decking as though waiting for a phone call that would tell them what to do next. And yet the place didn't feel empty. What it felt like was *wrong.*

"Dr. Grecchi?"

Still no response but she had to be there. The house was open, doors and windows admitting the warm, dry breeze. The screen door latch turned in my hand, and I yelled one last time before going in.

"Dr. Grecchi!"

It was Brontë who found her, no doubt drawn by the scent of blood. I could smell it myself by the time I reached the bathroom door where Brontë was snuffling and whining at a puddle of dark red liquid filling the grout lines between the bright yellow tiles of the floor. A sweet, metallic scent like wet iron railings. Isadora Grecchi sat on the floor, her back against the side of a yellow bathtub. She was wearing jeans and a white T-shirt, and in her right hand was a knife fitted with a single-edge razor. Artists use these knives to cut canvas prior to stretching it on a frame. Her left wrist was slashed on its interior side so deeply I could see the white bones inside. Bones I'd learned in junior high school are called the radius and ulna.

We feel these bones in our own arms every day and know their Latin names. They aren't as unfamiliar as, say, the vomer, a flat bone lying vertically in the middle of our skulls. The top edge of the vomer forms part of the septum of the nose. Still, we expect to go through whole lifetimes never actually *seeing* a radius and ulna, ever. I hated myself for feeling sick.

"Oh my God!" I said, grabbing a thick white washcloth from a bar on the wall and clamping it over the wound and the naked bones with my hand.

Isadora Grecchi wasn't dead. Her eyes were open and moving as she watched me kneeling in the mess, telling her to hold her left arm up, finally compressing the wound by wrapping the washcloth in about a mile of dental floss I found in the medicine cabinet. Neither was she saying anything. The only sound for several seconds was Brontë's nervous whining.

"I'm going to leave you here and go call 911," I finally said. "I want you to give me the knife."

I saw her glance at the object still clutched in her right hand as though identifying it required effort. Then it clattered to the floor. Leaning across her, I grabbed the knife, wondering how long I would remember this strange moment of intimacy with one of the cultural icons of my time—a serial murderer.

Roxie had said this would happen. That Sword would probably become so tormented that suicide would be the only source of relief, and Grecchi's history of clinical depression made it a certainty. Sprinting to Grecchi's wall phone in the kitchen, I jabbed the three numbers before realizing the line was dead. The cord running into the wall had been cut, probably with the same instrument she'd used to reveal the bones of her arm. She wanted to make sure she couldn't change her mind and call for help at the last minute, I thought. Or else she hadn't wanted to hear the phone ringing as she slowly bled out alone on her bathroom floor.

Brontë had followed me into the kitchen, her nails clacking against hardwood. I could see her pawprints, dark red against the polished floor. Only then did I notice that I was about to vomit. The smell was everywhere. Blood. It was on my hands and Brontë's paws. It was dripping from the hem of my skirt where I'd knelt in a pool of red to bind a washcloth around Isadora Grecchi's wrist. I had to get outside, quickly.

On the porch I took deep breaths and told Brontë to *stay*. Then I started toward the plumber's van across the street until a chubby red-haired man in a blue uniform pulled a spool of plumber's snake from inside the van and took it into one of the houses. So it really was just a plumber's van complete with a real plumber. Where are the cops when you need them?

I remembered the cell phone and dashed to my truck to make the call. Yes, I would stay with the victim until the paramedics arrived. No, I didn't know the next of kin.

Isadora Grecchi probably didn't have any kin, I thought as I went back into her house, taking the cell phone and the little .38 with me. Isadora Grecchi would turn out to be a loner, a social isolate whose private thoughts and fantasies became real to her over time because there was no one around to curb those fantasies. I'd seen it a hundred times in books and movies. The weirdo who lives alone in the old house for years, tearing the wings off flies. And then one day the Avon lady mistakenly rings his rusty doorbell and is not seen again until a hardened police detective turns green at what is pulled from the well in the property's overgrown garden.

She was still sitting on the bathroom floor when I returned, still silent.

"The paramedics will be here within five minutes," I told her, feeling suddenly edgy.

She was too weak to move and seemed to be in a kind of trance, but I was afraid of her. Not because I believed she'd killed her own patients with an obscure chemical. I hadn't seen her do that; it was abstract. I was afraid of her because she'd laid open her own wrist. Because she'd brought light to something that is never supposed to be seen. Those bones. The sight of what lies beneath the skin, of the truth behind the facade, is taboo. The sight of those white bones made me sick with a fear I recognized as primitive and magical, but there was nothing I could do about it.

"I have a gun," I said, slapping the pistol held against my side by the elastic waistbands of my skirt and half-slip. "Don't try anything."

The words sounded stagey and laughable. Like bits of conversation overheard in restaurants. Hearing them, it was obvious how much we try to make sense of our experiences through the dialogues of fiction. Which are invariably not quite right.

When I glanced at Grecchi again there were tears spilling from her eyes. But she didn't move and then I heard the siren of an emergency vehicle. As the paramedics worked on her I called the Rainer Clinic again on the cell phone. Roxie might still be there. I needed to hear her voice, to hear her explain oh-so rationally what had just happened. Why I saw those bones. But it was Rainer who answered.

"No, Dr. Bouchie left just after speaking with you," he said. "I was about to leave as well. Perhaps you can reach her at the police station. She said she was going there."

"I'll call her there," I said, nervous about how the old fellow would react when I told him. He'd worked with Isadora Grecchi for years. But then he'd worked with all of them for years.

"Dr. Rainer, Isadora Grecchi has just tried to take her own life,"

I pronounced quietly. "She cut her left wrist with an artist's canvas knife. I'm at her house. I've called 911 and the paramedics are here now. She's alive and conscious, although she hasn't said anything. I think we've got our killer, Dr. Rainer. I think this thing is over."

The silence then was too long. Five seconds, six, seven.

"Dr. Rainer?"

"No." His voice was strangled.

"What?"

"No!" I couldn't tell whether he was angry or stricken with grief.

"I'm so sorry, Dr. Rainer," I bumbled on. "It's got to be a shock for you. But it would have been a shock no matter which one it was. Is there someone you can call? Someone who can be with you now? I'll phone Megan and tell her you—"

"Stop patronizing me, Dr. McCarron," he interrupted. His voice now had an edge, like a knife felt through cloth. "You don't understand this at all. Now please, tell me where they'll take Isadora. Which hospital?"

The paramedics were strapping Grecchi onto a wheeled gurney in the hall. Her eyes were still open, watching them. They looked like the eyes of refugees, that hollow, bereft look.

"Which hospital will you take her to?" I asked.

"University of California San Diego Medical Center," one of the paramedics answered. "She's gonna be fine."

"Did you hear that?" I asked Rainer. "UCSD."

"Yes. Tell her I'll be at the hospital immediately. I'm leaving now. Are they giving her blood? How much blood did she lose?"

"Her employer, a doctor, wants to know how much blood she's lost and if you're . . ."

"Tell him she'll be okay," was the flat answer. But my question brought a fresh spill of tears from Grecchi, who was trying to shake her head, trying to say, "No," to something.

"Dr. Rainer will be at the hospital soon," I told her. The statement caused an increased tossing of her head that the paramedics curbed with a head clamp designed to stabilize the neck in spinal injuries. Her right arm was already secured to the side of the gurney with a leather cuff, and webbed plastic bands crossed her chest and legs. I remembered that UCSD's medical center has a psychiatric unit. And I realized that's where they were taking Isadora Grecchi.

"She's very disoriented," I told Jennings Rainer. "Perhaps it would be best if you didn't come right away. I imagine the police and FBI will want to talk to her first, as soon as she's able."

"Dr. McCarron, your assumptions are in error," he said, angry now. "Isadora is not the perpetrator of these crimes. You must explain that to the authorities."

There was no point in arguing with him, I thought. He was in shock and irrational, unable to process the situation. That would take time.

"The paramedics are leaving now, Dr. Rainer," I said. "I need to phone Detective Rathbone."

"You must tell Detective Rathbone that Isadora could not have sent all those messages last night threatening to murder the vice presidential candidate because she was with *me* all night and I would have seen if she had."

With that he hung up. I watched Isadora Grecchi's face as they carried her out, trussed to the gurney so tightly she couldn't move. Terror in those dark brown eyes. Her face seemed gray and spittle was forming at the edges of her mouth as she thrashed against the restraints and tried to say, "No, no." Serial killer or not, I couldn't stand it.

"Look," I said, "I'll follow you to UCSD in my truck, okay? I'll be right behind you."

Without meaning to I reached down to touch her hand, which felt like a frozen glove.

"You won't be alone," I told her. "It's not far to the hospital and I'll be right behind you all the way."

Brontë was happy to leave her station on the porch and eyed me curiously as we scrambled into the truck.

"Don't even ask," I told her.

But I didn't feel sick anymore.

22

One for the Books

From the hospital emergency room I called Rathbone, who was with Roxie and the FBI field agent in charge of the investigation.

"Grecchi's tried to kill herself," I told him. "Cut her wrist. I found her, called 911, I'm at UCSD Med Center with her now, and Rainer's on the way. He says Grecchi was with him all night last night and so she can't be Sword."

"He's protecting her," Rathbone said after conveying the information to everyone else. "Stay there until we get there."

So I stayed with Isadora Grecchi as I'd promised, although they'd run a blood test and then sedated her within five minutes of our arrival. She now lay stuporous behind a curtain in one of the e.r.'s examining bays. There seemed to be no rush about sewing up her arm, which was no longer bleeding and was of interest to various medical personnel who drifted in and out muttering things about "flexors" and "the median nerve."

"Need a reconstruction consult," said a young man in scrubs, jotting notes on a chart. "Afraid she's gonna lose some mobility in that hand. Get a plastic surgeon down here *now,* please," he told a nurse.

"A surgeon is on the way," I announced from my post beside Grecchi's inert form. "Jennings Rainer. He'll be here shortly."

"Rainer?" the young doctor said. "I've heard of him. Hear he's good. Have to clear it, though. He's not on staff."

"I'm sure there won't be any problem," I said as though I knew what I was talking about.

Even sedated, Isadora Grecchi seemed tense. Her dark, unruly hair stood out from her head in clumps against the pillow, and her facial muscles moved randomly from time to time, pulling her mouth into eerie, childlike grins that vanished in seconds. She was shivering and her skin felt cold. Since no one was paying any attention to me I opened every closet and cabinet until I located some blankets and piled them on top of her.

"It's Blue McCarron. I'm still here. You're not alone," I told her repeatedly even though she couldn't hear me. "And Dr. Rainer should arrive any minute."

I wondered what would happen to her now. She'd be handcuffed to her bed under the eye of an armed guard in the hospital, probably. Then jail and a long, complicated trial. Then prison. Maybe a sentence of death, although it would never be carried out. The appeals would last longer than Isadora Grecchi, at fifty-one, would live. And why? Why had she chosen to kill women she herself had rendered unconscious and vulnerable, with a chemical she herself might have been prescribed? None of it made any sense.

I saw Jennings Rainer enter the e.r. examining area before he saw me. And if he'd been upset before, he wasn't now. Dressed impeccably in a black cashmere jacket over a white polo shirt and khakis, he looked as though he'd been summoned from a golf course.

"Where is Dr. Grecchi?" he inquired politely of a nurse.

"Right over here, Dr. Rainer. Dr. Chattin, our chief of staff, would like to see you after you've examined her. She'll be prepped for surgery shortly, and it has been suggested that you'd be willing to operate. You'll need to scrub in about forty-five minutes if Chattin okays it."

"Of course," Rainer answered.

To me he said, "I'm so grateful to you, Dr. McCarron. You may have saved her life. And you can have no idea what your presence here has meant to Isadora. But why did you come? Why did you extend yourself to a woman you believe to be a murderer?"

"She was frightened, Dr. Rainer, and despite what the paramedics said I wasn't sure she'd live. There was so much blood. It was awful. Do you have any idea why she'd kill these people? It's so strange. . . ."

"Isadora is incapable of harming anyone except herself," he said dispassionately, removing the bandage at her wrist. "I'd like to speak with you for a few minutes after I've completed my examination of the wound. Would you wait for me in the driveway outside the emergency room doors? What I have to say is confidential."

"Of course," I answered in the same tones he'd used with the nurse, and went outside.

The blood on my skirt had dried to a blackish brown crust, so I turned it backward and sat on the grass to wait. I didn't have to worry about grass stains, I thought. As soon as I could get my other clothes from the truck, the skirt would be thrown in a trash can. I never wanted to see it again. Or Isadora Grecchi, for that matter. Or the bones inside her left arm.

"There you are," Rainer said minutes later. "I may be able to save the mobility in her hand, but it's going to be difficult. Let me just thank you for your help and then tell you what you will find out in any event. After that I must speak with Dr. Chattin and prepare for the surgery. I'm sure it will be allowed. I've known Chattin for twenty years."

He was standing over me, apparently not in the mood to sit in the grass and chat, so I stood as well.

"Let's go over here in the shade," he suggested, moving some distance from the e.r. door to stand near an oleander at the edge of the hospital property. "You see, Isadora is more to me than just a colleague," he began. "I've known her since she was very young, a child. It was in Denver. I was doing my residency at a hospital there, and she was brought in. The injuries were, well, very serious. Isadora was only ten years old. She'd been raped, Dr. McCarron, and not for the first time. The rapist was her stepfather, a drunken bastard—and I make no apology for my language—who should have been put to death for what he did to her. I assisted with the surgery. We were able to repair the damage to her spleen and the large bowel, but not the uterus, which had to be removed. Isadora cannot bear children.

"He'd infected her with syphilis as well, and it was already at the latent stage, which meant she was infected at least a year prior to that hospitalization. The large doses of penicillin necessary to kill the syphilis spirochetes at that stage of infection can make an adult very sick. You can imagine what it did to a ten-year-old child already traumatized by near-fatal internal injuries."

I was feeling nauseous again. "Where was her mother?"

"Isadora's mother suffered very severe depressive episodes, often requiring hospitalization. There were no other family members to care for Isadora, so during her mother's hospitalizations she was left in the care of her brutish stepfather. After the rape in which he came very close to killing her, her mother committed suicide."

"God," I whispered. "The police did turn up the fact that she was made a ward of the court in Denver, but no other information because juvenile records are sealed. Rathbone said they'd subpoenaed the records, but it would take weeks."

"As I said, you were going to learn her history anyway," he went on. "Now that the FBI is involved, those records can be accessed immediately. The next part of what I have to tell you is quite painful to me, but I want you to know. It's necessary.

"Marlis and I had been married for four years at that time and had been unable to conceive a child. We were tested; there was nothing wrong, but it just didn't happen. Marlis wanted a child so badly. When I came home and told her about Isadora, she said she wanted to visit the child, cheer her up during her stay in the hospital. In those days doctors' wives often volunteered at the hospitals where we were on staff, so it was perfectly normal for Marlis to do that. Then when the time came for Isadora to be discharged there was some problem with the social services agency. No foster home was available in the area, and she was to be sent to another town. Mar asked me if we could take the girl in, become foster parents for her until a local placement could be arranged. Mar wanted to stay in contact with her, you see."

"So you're Grecchi's foster father?"

He stared at the oleander, then said, "No. We did take Isadora to live with us for a time, even considered adopting her, at first. She was a lively little thing, but so damaged by the abuse she'd endured. Temper tantrums, soiling the bed, lashing out at us physically, deliberately breaking things. And then Mar became pregnant."

"With Megan?" I asked, already knowing what had happened next.

"Yes. We were overjoyed, but fearful, too. Mar had a difficult pregnancy in the beginning. There was some bleeding. She was terribly ill and we were afraid she might lose the baby. After a month it became clear that she couldn't handle Isadora alone while pregnant, and I was always at work, of course. We were very young and there wasn't much information at that time about the difficulties presented by an abused child. We didn't know what we'd gotten into, only that we couldn't go on with it. We had to take Isadora back to the social services agency, allow her to be placed in a foster home out of town."

He took a deep breath, tugged a pink oleander blossom from the bush, and regarded it bleakly.

"I did it, I took her away," he went on. "Marlis was too upset to go along. I took Isadora to the agency offices with her clothes and all her little things, little toys and a brown corduroy teddy bear Marlis had made for her out of a jacket I wore in college. Mar used the cuff buttons for its eyes. Isadora loved that bear, wouldn't be parted from it. Until Mar's death two years ago, that was the worst day of my life."

I watched as he dropped the pink blossom to the grass at our feet, and didn't mention the brown corduroy bear on the mantel in Isadora Grecchi's living room.

"I don't know what to say, Dr. Rainer," I replied in a voice I'd heard Roxie use when talking to her patients on the phone. Quiet and calm. "It was obvious from Isadora's reaction to my bodyguard that she mistrusts men. I suspected that she might have been raped, but of course I didn't imagine anything of this magnitude. It's beyond imagining."

"Yes," he said, "but let me tell you the rest, and then I must go. Isadora needs me. Do you know, Dr. McCarron, that an obligation to a broken child, once undertaken, cannot end? Isadora is fifty-one years old now, and I am sixty-seven. Forty years have gone by, Marlis is dead, and Megan has established a life with her own husband and children, and Isadora still needs my care. Perhaps it would have been different if she hadn't inherited a genetic proclivity to depression from her mother, but she did. And given the intolerable stress in her young life, there was no way that proclivity could have remained inactive."

"What happened after she went into foster care in another town?" I pushed.

"It was in Colorado Springs, a well-meaning family but unfortunately of that 'Christian' fundamentalist type who manage to think the Bible is both historical fact and absolute law despite all reason. Stupid, pathetic people lost in punitive beliefs they then inflicted on the children in their care. Mar and I tried to visit Isadora every month or so, less often after Megan was born, of course, but we kept up the contact. We knew things weren't going well for Isadora there, but there was nothing we could do. Then one weekend I was in Colorado Springs for a medical conference and happened to have a few free hours in the afternoon. I went to this foster home unannounced to visit Isadora, who was then almost twelve, and walked in on a scene that shocked me."

"What? What happened?"

"The poor girl," he went on, clenching and unclenching his fists, "was being punished for something. Isadora was always doing something, was always in trouble both at home and in school. I don't mean to suggest that she wasn't a difficult child. But these people, these foster parents, had made her strip to her panties and stand in the middle of the living room while the father read aloud from the Bible."

Of course. The Sword of Heaven.

"That's what I walked in on—Isadora standing there, not crying but miserable, trying to cover her little breasts with her arms. There were other children in the home, Dr. McCarron, including three boys, one of them half grown and already shaving. They were allowed to watch Isadora's humiliation. Apparently the others were so accustomed to the spectacle they were bored with it by then, because one of them had made a bowl of popcorn and that seemed of more interest to them than Isadora. I threw my jacket over her and took her out of there that minute. The father recited something about the 'Whore of Babylon' as we left, but didn't attempt to stop me.

"I took her back to Denver and insisted that the agency find a better home for her. By then I was on staff at the hospital and had the community standing granted to doctors. I could throw some weight around, and I did. Isadora went to another placement, this time in Denver. Later there were two more foster homes, and then when the depressive symptoms began to manifest when she was about fourteen, she was sent to a facility for emotionally disturbed children. A sort of combination hospital and orphanage, where she could be monitored. There were a number of suicide attempts during those years, Dr. McCarron, one of them almost fatal."

I thought about the bones I'd seen, and a child of fourteen, and tasted bile in the back of my throat. I could not have survived one week of Isadora Grecchi's life, and I knew it.

"That facility was the best place for her," Rainer continued hurriedly. "The staff were trained and for the most part kind. There was an arts and crafts program taught by someone from a local community college. Isadora was encouraged to paint and found in that a way to release some of her rage and pain. Marlis and I continued to visit with her, occasionally brought her to the house for a weekend, although these events were exhausting."

"How did she get from there to becoming a doctor?" I asked. "It seems unlikely, given what you've told me."

Rainer glanced at his watch. "I only have a few more minutes," he said. "Isadora tried a number of things after she turned eighteen and was no longer under the jurisdiction of the court, some of them criminal but nothing serious. Drugs, petty thefts. I was always able to prevent her spending time in jail. Eventually she asked if I'd pay her tuition for college, and I agreed. There were starts and stops, but she's quite intelligent and found a way to build self-esteem by getting good grades. She was given a partial scholarship to medical school, and I funded the rest. Her choice to become a doctor was merely an attempt to please me, I'm afraid. Isadora merely regards it as a job. She has little or no real feeling for people, but neither is she hateful, which is my point in giving you her history. You must understand. I *know* Isadora."

"Yes, you do," I agreed as we walked back toward the emergency room doors. "Dr. Rainer, that blue willow plate on the wall of your surgical waiting room. Is that plate Isadora's?"

"Dr. Bouchie told me this murderer has some connection to those plates," he said, frowning. "No, Dr. McCarron, that plate belonged to my wife. Marlis decorated the waiting room. I had a professional do the rest of the office, but the waiting room was Mar's project. Years ago, after Megan went off to college, Mar developed an interest in antique china, joined a collector's club. The blue willow was the best piece in her collection and she felt it should be displayed. She created that wall of plates to complement the blue willow. Isadora had nothing to do with it and in fact probably couldn't name the pattern if asked."

"Why did Isadora choose to go into anesthesiology? If she were basing her career choices on yours, wouldn't she have chosen cosmetic surgery?"

Rainer sighed and then nodded. I had the feeling he'd thought about the answers to these questions for years.

"Marlis and I had hoped Isadora would marry, maybe adopt

children, have a life like ours," he said, shaking his head. "We still didn't understand how impossible that was. At one point we suspected the existence of a lesbian relationship with one of her professors in med school. I know I appear an old fuddy-duddy to you young people, Dr. McCarron," he said, smiling for the first time, "but let me tell you that was *fine* with us. We just wanted Isadora to have a deep connection, a love to make her life as complete as we knew it could be. But I'm afraid we were only imagining loves for Isadora. In truth, there were none, have never been.

"Anesthesiology is lucrative but requires very long hours," he explained. "Few women specialize in it for that reason. It's incompatible with family life. Isadora wanted a great deal of financial security, wanted to repay me for the costs of her education, and did. She knew she would never have a family. Anesthesiology seemed the right choice."

His hand was on the e.r. door now, and I could see Roxie, Rathbone, and a man with a cord running from his shirt collar to his right ear hurrying from the parking lot across the street.

"But here is what you must know in order to understand both Isadora's innocence of these crimes and the reason for what must seem an incriminating attempt to end her own life. Last night she came to me, came to my apartment, with an investment idea. I don't have time to explain it in detail, but it involved our jointly underwriting a breast-surgery clinic she would direct. She wanted me to be on staff for occasional reconstructive surgeries. We talked until very late, and then she stayed and slept on the couch. I know she didn't leave because the door can only be unlocked from either side with a key. It was locked, and I had the key. She could not have sent those messages last night, Dr. McCarron.

"Isadora is a difficult, troubled woman and always will be," he concluded. "She must live with a serious psychiatric disorder and the baggage from a brutal childhood, but she isn't a murderer. These facts do not make her a murderer. I hope you and the others"—he nodded toward the three approaching figures—"are able to draw that distinction."

"But did you agree to this investment idea, this clinic?" I yelled as he went inside.

"No," he called over his shoulder. "I've decided to move up north to be near Chris and Megan and my grandchildren."

A few things were beginning to make sense, I thought as the door closed behind him. Grecchi had needed to hold on to Rainer, her lifelong source of stability. With the closing of the Rainer Clinic she'd come up with a plan, a new clinic they'd fund jointly. She'd be the director and he'd be around to do surgeries when his skills were needed. Mostly, he'd be around. But he'd said no, plummeting her into panic and suicidal despair. I guessed it made sense.

Except why would she undermine her own security, represented by Rainer, by killing patients at his clinic? To get even with him for abandoning her to a Denver social services agency over forty years ago? The child Isadora, I imagined, would have been jealous of Megan Rainer, who had supplanted her in the Rainers' home. Had the adult Isadora transgressed an unthinkable ethical boundary and killed patients as a way of hurting Megan? But Megan wasn't going to take over the clinic, anyway. Its closing now only benefitted her, allowed her the fulfillment of her dream two years before she'd expected.

And the enigmatic blue willow plates. I remembered feeling that a child had been outside my place that night, that I'd been playing hide and seek with a child who'd left me a strange gift in the dark. Did that child live inside the mind of a fifty-one-year-old woman whose blood now dried on the hem of my skirt?

The train of thought was like a maze. It led nowhere, didn't work, made no sense. But then real people have never made much sense to me, only numbers. Charts and graphs and statistical estimations make sense. So does my notion of the universe, the grid, although the sense is beyond comprehension. Hard data and a slapstick universal irony are my realms. Forget everything in between.

"Girl," Roxie said with concern as she and Rathbone and the FBI field agent reached my side, "you're a mess."

"So it's Grecchi," Rathbone noted, unfazed by my bloody skirt and fingernails. "You and Berryman nailed it during the interviews. Has she confessed?"

"She hasn't said anything, Wes," I explained. "And she's sedated now. Rainer's going to try to repair her arm. The doctors were saying stuff about ligaments and nerve damage. She won't be able to work if she's lost the use of her hand."

The FBI agent looked a little like a balding Lyle Lovett, but his eyes lacked that lost-boy confusion. He seemed deeply focused.

"She's not going to be working anytime soon," he announced authoritatively. "Not where she's going."

"How bad was the cut?" Roxie asked.

"To the bones."

"Might be able to restore some mobility if they get to it soon," she said. "And it's not her working arm, anyway, is it? People usually cut both wrists. I imagine she instinctively saved the hand she uses professionally. What a sad story."

For a second I remembered Grecchi as she looked when BB and I had left her house, painting in the sunlit studio off her kitchen. Painting with her *left* hand, I remembered, as with her right she flipped us the bird.

"Rox, she's left-handed!" I whispered, not wanting Rathbone and the agent to hear, although I didn't know why.

"One for the books," the agent said, his voice resonating with victory. "One of the first female serials. Fits the 'organized' profile in every way except sex. White, a loner, professional job, every which way except she's not a he. Gonna rewrite the profile with this one. Crazy, too. I always thought the bureau ought to keep records on crazies, everybody the shrinks keep under control with medications. Be easy enough to do through the pharmacies. Make our job a lot easier."

I could see the muscles flexing in Roxie's jaw.

"You'd have nearly half the population of the United States on your list," she said softly, but he didn't hear her.

"One for the books," the agent said again. "They're almost

always white males, but not this time. This time it's a crazy woman and it's on my beat."

"I'm going to go home before I kill that man," Roxie said through clenched teeth as the two men pushed open the emergency room doors and vanished inside. "Then I could take out a couple more of them and become the first *black* female serial killer in history."

"*Really* one for the books," I replied, grinning. "But first let's get some coffee. There's something not right about what's happened here, this thing with Grecchi."

"I been noticing that," Rox said dismally. "Girl, I been noticing that."

23

Pieter, Pieter, Pumpkin Eater

I changed into my jeans in the truck and tossed the bloody skirt in a city trash receptacle as Rox and Brontë and I walked to a nearby Starbucks. We sat outside and I watched as Rox toyed with a cappuccino. At an adjoining table a couple in nearly identical business suits were discussing the presidential campaign.

"You're going to vote for the ticket just because the vice presidential candidate's a woman," the man said.

"And you're not going to vote for the ticket just because she's not a man," his companion answered. "You can't stand the idea of women in positions of power."

"No, I can't," he agreed. "A woman vice president would be like a whale conducting a symphony. Ludicrous. Call me a retro pig."

"I wouldn't dream of it," the woman said through a dazzling smile, standing to leave. "Pigs are intelligent."

Roxie and I applauded as she walked away, leaving him with the check.

"So what do we do now?" I asked after relating the story of

Grecchi's life as Jennings Rainer had told it to me. "Rainer says she was at his place all night last night and so couldn't have sent the spate of e-mails advertising Sword's latest threat, but everything else that's happened points to Grecchi as the killer. And yet something doesn't feel right about it. I'd cross the street to avoid Isadora Grecchi; she's rude and unpleasant. But when I saw her lying on the gurney, she looked so scared. I felt sorry for her, Rox. How could I feel sorry for a woman who—"

"She could have loaded the e-mails in a program that automatically sends at a preselected time," Rox interrupted. "You should know that, but Rainer wouldn't. He's computer-illiterate. Where Grecchi spent the night is irrelevant. What bothers me is the suicide attempt."

"But you said Sword might do that. She's done just what you said."

"I don't know what she's done," Roxie muttered, continuing to stir her cappuccino with a plastic straw. Her braids were adorned with bright yellow straw beads that day. They matched her silk blouse but made no sound as she moved her head. The absence of clacking made me feel deaf.

"What do you mean? She sliced open her wrist."

"Blue," Rox said, finally discarding the straw and sipping her coffee, "Grecchi is a doctor."

"So, many people are," I replied. "This one's a doctor with a childhood from hell and a depressive disorder who for some reason went 'off,' killed or attempted to kill prominent women in her care, and then tried to kill herself, just like you said. She's even got the crackpot religious history from a foster home in Colorado Springs. That's where she probably heard the Isaiah 34 stuff like my dad said, the Sword of Heaven. It's all there."

"Yes, but any first-year med student knows that cutting the ventral side of the wrist is one of the least effective ways to die," Rox went on. "There's only one very small and easily missed artery and the veins are also tiny. The normal clotting action of the blood will seal both in a matter of minutes after an initial and dramatic bleed. The only way to lose enough blood even to *faint* from a wrist cut is to keep the wound submerged in hot, preferably running water, which prevents clotting. Grecchi knew that, and yet you didn't say anything about hot water or any water. She was sitting on the bathroom floor next to the tub, but she wasn't holding her arm under the faucet to facilitate a bleed-out. This was no suicide attempt."

The news made me feel good, for some reason.

"What was it, then?" I asked. "People always say when this happens it's a cry for help. Was she crying for help?"

Rox finished her cappuccino and ordered another, eyes narrow with concentration.

"For the moment let's assume Grecchi is innocent of the Sword murders but is depressed. It's apparent from the several different antidepressants BB saw in her medicine chest that something wasn't working and her psychiatrist has been trying her on different combinations, different meds. Eventually one of them will work and she knows that intellectually, but the depression makes her *feel* there's no hope, so she wants to make that desperate gesture that signals a need for somebody to help her. She chooses the traditional wrist-cutting, but knows she isn't really going to die. Which means she knows she's going to be working again, using her dominant *left* hand. What are the odds she'd cut her *left* wrist, knowing as she does the risk of impaired mobility?"

"I don't know," I said. "Aren't people sort of irrational at that point? Not thinking clearly?"

"Sometimes, not always. And if she weren't thinking clearly and just acting out of despair, she'd automatically hold the knife in her dominant hand, cutting the nondominant wrist. More to the point, Grecchi's fifty-one. From what Rainer said, she's been dealing with clinical depression since she was fourteen. She's experienced. Plus, she holds down a professional job, does volunteer work on the side, enjoys art as an avocation, maintains, from what you say, an attractive home, keeps herself presentable personally. She's socially competent and successful. There's been no break in this pattern. Then all of a sudden she falls apart overnight? It doesn't work that way, Blue. It doesn't happen that fast. There's just something fishy about the way this happened."

"You don't think Grecchi is Sword, do you?" I asked, giving Brontë a piece of hazelnut biscotti.

"She could be. Everything points to that. I don't know, but if she isn't—"

"Then somebody else is going to try to kill a vice presidential candidate tomorrow morning," I finished the thought. "But who?"

"That problem must be handled by the FBI and the Secret Service," she said flatly. "I'm going back to the hospital, where I will explain my concerns about Grecchi to Rathbone and that FBI control freak my federal tax dollars are paying. Then I'm going home. This has been difficult for me, Blue. It's hard listening to a guy with a phone in his ear tell you your profession is a pansy-assed joke, which is what I was doing when you called about Grecchi. Even Rathbone winced when the jerk told me to 'stop using such big words.'"

She bent the plastic straw and then twisted it until it broke into two pieces.

"Wanna know what 'big word' scared him?" she went on. "'Chronic.' Two whole syllables, twenty million Americans hear it every day in TV aspirin commercials, but real men don't say 'chronic.' It's not guy-speak, so it's sissy-speak by default. And so, according to him, is the entire language of psychiatry.

"Blue, when the FBI takes over the world, there will be only them on one side, 'bad' people on the other, and between them an average vocabulary of eighteen one-syllable words, twelve of which will refer to bodily functions."

"As long as one of the words is 'dude,' they'll get along fine," I replied, remembering the communication between BB and Jeffrey Pond. "I've been thinking about researching a paper on the contemporary male's rejection of speech as a means of communication. It's curious."

"Posturing and chest-beating are so much more eloquent," she said with a laugh, pounding her chest. "Ouch."

"Always a problem." I giggled with her. "Don't worry, Rox,

the FBI hasn't even seized a major city yet. There's still time to talk, which reminds me—"

"I know, Philadelphia," she said. "But not now, Blue. And not tonight. I need some time to think. See, I just realized that while I'm trying to figure out why a few thousand guys rob and rape and kill every day, the real power's all in the hands of an identical set of guys who get off on chasing the first bunch. They don't care about why. All they care about is 'Go Directly to Jail.' That's the end of the game for them. They get to be heroes. Caring about why is girl stuff."

"Most people would agree with them, you know," I said.

"Yeah, and listen to those same people weep and wail when it happens again and again. Another mass murder in a public building, another serial killer with twenty-three graves in his backyard, another few hundred children raped and scarred for life, more and more prisons and no end in sight. That's what you get for not caring why."

"Do you want to be a hero, Rox?" I asked as we started back toward the hospital.

"Damn right," she said, leaning to pet Brontë fiercely. "But I want to do it by trying to understand things, not by eliminating understanding as an option."

"Stay out of law enforcement," I said.

"I work in corrections, Blue. What do you think that is?"

"Oh."

I could see where this was going and that I might have the FBI to thank if Roxie took the new job in Philadelphia. She wanted to figure things out, make a difference. She could do that directing a research project on head injuries and genetic psychiatric proclivities. She couldn't do that working for the man. The two systems were incompatible.

"I might call you later tonight," she said as Brontë and I got into my truck.

"Okay, here's my cell phone number in case I'm still out," I said, trying to be cool about leaving her alone. "I think I'll start carrying the phone when Brontë and I are out hiking in the desert. Might come in handy."

"Yeah." She was gone already.

I watched her leave the hospital parking lot, her bright blouse like a determined sun threading between the cars. She'd tell Rathbone and the FBI about her unease over assumptions of Grecchi's guilt and then go home to brood over the fate of psychiatry in a culture addicted to quick and simple answers. Brontë's quizzical expression reminded me that I had no idea what *I* was going to do.

"Kate Van Der Elst should be informed of what's happened," I told my dog. It sounded reasonable.

"Oh, Blue, I really appreciate your keeping me in the loop," Kate said when I called her at home. "I've been so upset, you know, about *everything*. This makes me feel a little better. I do think it's Grecchi, don't you? It even makes a little sense when you look at the history you just told me about. She worked on all these privileged women who seem never to have suffered anything more heartbreaking than cellulite buildup on their thighs. We must have appeared despicable to her, superficial and narcissistic. Yet we had everything she could not—husbands, families, in some cases important public careers like Mary Harriet Grossinger and Dixie. Her funeral was, well, it was very sad. I missed Pieter, Blue. I can't believe he didn't come, if only out of respect for the Ross family. We've been married for sixteen years and he's never . . . well, this isn't the time to talk about Pieter. Thank you so much for calling, Blue. I'll be at my campaign headquarters later. You will let me know if anything else happens."

It wasn't a question, but I said, "Of course," anyway and flipped my little phone shut. Then I drove downtown to the twin-towered Marriott overlooking San Diego Bay. No one said anything about dog exclusion as Brontë and I moved through the lobby crowd of tourists and multilingual participants in a convention that had something to do with international paint sales. A courtesy phone was visible on a table beside an arrangement of fresh flowers that wouldn't have fit in my truck. I picked up the phone, asked to be connected to the room of Pieter Van Der Elst, and was.

"It's Blue McCarron, I'm in the lobby, and I must speak with you," I told him.

"No, we don't think Kate is in any danger now, but she was, Pieter. She was one of those picked by Sword to die, but she was protected by her diet. It looks as though the anesthesiologist, Isadora Grecchi, is the perp. Please, let me come to your room and explain what's happened."

As I'd hoped, curiosity overcame his reluctance to lay eyes on me. Brontë seemed to share my sense of accomplishment, because her docked tail wagged happily as we rode an elevator to the fifteenth floor. Or else she was thrilled to be in surroundings opulent by comparison to my monkish digs in the desert. She likes opera. I should have known she'd have a taste for the finer things.

"Okay," I told her as we walked soundlessly along the carpeted fifteenth-floor hall, "I see your point. We *could* afford to live someplace with running water, at least. So here's the deal. If we wind up going to Philadelphia for a while, I promise you we'll stay someplace nice."

Conversations with dogs can be so useful when trying to identify your own intentions.

Pieter Van Der Elst had lost five pounds since I last saw him, all five from his face. His skin was sallow, the pale blue eyes as dim as dusty glass. And despite a crisp blue oxford-cloth shirt and immaculately pressed khakis, he seemed tarnished. And ashamed.

"Please come in," he said, gesturing to the living room of his suite. "And who is this?"

"My dog, Brontë," I explained. "There's an FBI stakeout at my place, or there was, and I couldn't leave her alone all day. She'd have done nothing but bark."

"Ah, Brontë," he said, toying with another arrangement of fresh flowers on the coffee table. "'Life is a passing sleep, / Its deeds a troubled dream . . .'"

"Charlotte or Emily?" I asked of the quotation, probably from a Brontë poem.

"Branwell," he answered. "The profligate, failed brother."

"'Shall Earth no more inspire thee, / Thou lonely dreamer now?'" I answered in kind, also meaning it as a question.

"Emily." He identified the author but didn't answer the question. "All of them so passionate, and yet—"

"Pieter, you seem ill," I interrupted, moving to the window to pull open the heavy drapes. The darkened space with its flowered maroon fabrics felt like the terrible "red room" scene from *Jane Eyre*. A focus on the doomed Brontës seemed unnecessarily morbid.

"I'm fine," he said unconvincingly. "Please, tell me about Kate." When I had finished, he merely said, "Ah."

"Pieter, I don't want to be intrusive, but I don't think you understand why Kate refused to drop out of the race," I said, feeling intrusive. "Maybe it's a cultural thing. American women aren't—"

"The Netherlands is one of the most egalitarian cultures on earth, Blue," he said, stopping me before I blundered further. "I didn't do what I did because I felt I had a right to control Kate. I simply couldn't bear the thought of harm to her. I couldn't bear the thought of her . . . death. I was out of my mind with fear, and I—"

"But Pieter, Kate must understand that," I went on. "And she needs you. She's tried to reach you, but you won't talk to her. Look, I know this is none of my business, but you can't just abandon her now because she didn't do what you wanted. It's not right."

The last remark, I knew, had come straight out of Waterloo, Illinois, where everybody knows *exactly* what it means. Which is that "doing right" is the magnetic axis around which everything spins and the only standard against which everything must be measured, sooner or later. You can run from it to the far corners of the earth, but it will pull you back as inexorably as if you were bound to it by huge rubber bands. All of Middle America from Canada to the Gulf of Mexico understands this perfectly. But I doubted that the worldly foreigner petting my dog in an expensive hotel room would quite grasp the homespun concept. And I was wrong.

He looked up from Brontë on the floor at his feet and regarded me somberly. "You don't know what I mean by 'what I did,'" he said. "And what I did was despicable. I tried to frighten Kate into quitting. I didn't care that it might have destroyed her to do so. I didn't care that only a hollow facsimile of Kate might be left, as long as that facsimile was alive."

"Pieter, what are you talking about?"

He drew a shuddering breath and squared his shoulders.

"I created the threatening letter, the one on green paper, Blue. I made it and said I'd found it slipped under the door of Kate's campaign office. I lied to Kate, as well as to you and the police. Now you've told me this poison was in Kate's body all the while, that I betrayed her trust pointlessly, that even if I'd been successful I couldn't have protected her. It's ironic, isn't it?"

His prematurely white hair shone like feathery metal in the sunlight from the window.

"Don't get me started on irony," I said, trying to lighten the mood. "Let's just say it was time for you to learn something, and you did. Flying off to Rio won't change that."

"Amsterdam," he corrected the awkward attempt at levity. "Kate can never trust me again. That's what I can't face. Leaving her seems the only thing to do."

I wished my father were sitting there instead of me. He's good at that sort of thing, but then, it's his job. I made gestures indicating an intent to go. Leaning forward, digging car keys from purse. The usual.

"I think trust is overrated," I said. "It assumes an impossibly identical reality shared by two distinctly different people. Ultimately, it can't work. What works is honesty, if you've got the guts for it. Only a coward would get on that plane tomorrow, Pieter. Only cowards run and hide."

He didn't say anything as Brontë and I left, merely closed the door firmly behind us.

In the silent hall I contemplated the fact that I'd been insufferably arrogant and insensitive as well as rude. It felt good. Then I realized that my pompous little lecture to Pieter Van Der Elst had even more relevance when applied to myself. That didn't feel good. It meant I had to face the fact that hiding out in the desert was just another way of running and hiding. And it would have to stop now. There was sufficient reason for it to stop. The path Roxie Bouchie had chosen for herself was not my path, but that didn't mean my own path couldn't run beside it.

"Okay, here's what I know about Pennsylvania," I said to Brontë in the elevator. "There are Amish quilts and hex signs painted on barns."

It wasn't much, but it would do. Maybe I could find a place with a shed and paint a hex sign on it. The thought was like an anchor and made me smile.

24

The Sagebrush Resort

The phone in my purse started ringing as we loped through the lobby, causing a basset-eyed French tourist to whisper "*Madame, a sonne?*" preparatory to inviting me and presumably my dog for a drink.

"No, I didn't ring," I told him, tapping my ear and shaking my head. "It must be *retard de jet*. Jet lag. They say drinking a lot of water helps."

It was Wes Rathbone on the cell phone.

"Got your number from Roxie," he told me. "Look, I need to stay at the hospital until we can get a statement from Grecchi, and that may take hours. She's in surgery. No telling how long. But both Thomas Eldridge and Megan Rainer's husband, Christopher Nugent, have called downtown demanding to know what's going on. Apparently Megan became upset when she couldn't reach her father on the phone, and Kara Eldridge got scared when she tried to call Grecchi and heard a tape saying the service was disconnected. Everybody's got the jitters. The desk sergeant told both of them somebody would be around shortly

to bring them up to date, except there isn't anybody to do it.
Would you mind? You're still on the payroll, you know."

"No problem, Wes," I agreed. "By the way, are the Power
Rangers still camped out at my place?"

"Nothing changes until we get a confession from Grecchi," he
said. "They won't move until we're sure she's our man."

I didn't point out the logical inconsistency of his remark.

"I'm on my way to the Eldridge place," I said. "Then I'll see
Megan Rainer and Chris Nugent on my way home."

"Good. I'll have somebody call them, tell them you're on the
way. We've already left a message on Pond's machine, asking
him to contact you for an update. He'll get the message when
he gets home. You don't have to go by there."

"Roger," I said briskly.

On the drive up I-5 to the Eldridges' home in Carlsbad I
thought about Isaiah 34, blue willow plates, and female serial
killers. If Isadora Grecchi was the perp, why had she chosen
the plates as an icon for whatever rationale had driven her to
murder? They didn't match her decor. And even if she'd heard,
in that long-ago foster home, the Old Testament tale of Edom's
grisly destruction at the hands of a violent deity, why would
she identify with the destroyer and call herself the Sword of
Heaven? The plate icon and the dramatic title were, I thought,
nothing but advertising. The attention-grabbing narcissism of
small children and some immature men, whose need for recog-
nition does not abate until late in life, if then. Even if that recog-
nition is for murder. The female murderer has no such need
and *never* advertises her crimes. It just doesn't happen.

"Maybe Isadora Grecchi is really a man," I told Brontë, fully
aware that I would need a degree in psychiatry to understand
what I'd just said. The tools of my own profession could only
reveal what most men and most women, regardless of any variable other than gender, actually do. On the subject of one woman
who advertises herself as a killer in order to get public attention, the field of social psychology is silent.

I was still pondering that silence as I pulled to a stop in front
of the Eldridge home. There was a small van in the driveway

with an auto-rental agency's sticker on the rear bumper. The side door was open and I could see that the back of the van was packed with a number of bulging trash bags. As I closed the truck, leaving Brontë inside, a blonde girl in jeans and sneakers tottered from the house under the weight of another bag.

"Namey, hold it from the bottom, so it doesn't tear," Kara Eldridge called from the door.

Or at least I thought it was Kara Eldridge. But she looked different. Her hair was shorter, attractively styled, and woven with platinum highlights. Gone were the unflattering culottes and in their place a trim pair of black slacks that made her look ten pounds thinner. On the front of her tan T-shirt was a black silkscreen of Stonehenge with the words GIVE ME THAT OLD TIME RELIGION. And she was wearing makeup.

It must be Kara's sister, I thought as I approached her. Maybe a twin.

"Oh, Dr. McCarron, the police called to say you'd come by," she said. "They wouldn't tell me anything, but I know something's happened because when I called Isadora her line was dead. I just got a tape saying, 'This number has been disconnected or is out of service.' We had planned to talk before . . . well, I knew something was wrong, so I called Jeff, but he wasn't home, and then I called Megan and she said she was worried about Dr. Rainer because she couldn't reach him, and you know, Isadora has some problems and we thought Dr. Rainer might be with her, but . . . well, please, just come in and tell me what's happened. Is Isadora all right?

"Namey," she said to the girl, "I want you to go out in the backyard and play with your brother while I talk to Dr. McCarron."

"But you said we were going soon," the girl sulked dramatically. "You said—"

"Naomi Ann, *go.*"

It was Kara Eldridge. But she no longer reminded me of the cement sculpture of a girl reading a book on the front of a library. She was anything but oblivious.

"You just missed T.J.," she said as we sat on the pink and

green plaid couch. "He dashed in for a bite to eat and then left for the Realtor's office. I'm afraid I didn't have time to make him much more than a snack, but I did manage that. A bowl of tomato soup and a baloney sandwich. And of course he's got his cheese and crackers with him, so he's all set. We're, well, in an upheaval here. See, I had a wonderful job offer in Los Angeles, writing computer programs for . . . Oh, that doesn't matter. But with the clinic closing and T.J. going to be out of work, it seemed wise for me to take the job and they want me to start immediately, so the kids and I are going on up and will stay with my cousin in Redondo Beach until he can sell the house and then join us. But tell me. What's happened to Isadora?"

She seemed overwhelmed by the sudden move and new job, but there was something else in her eyes as well. A somber determination she was making no attempt to hide. It was like an organ sonata in a minor key heard in a busy marketplace. Jarring.

"It appears that Dr. Grecchi may have, um, harmed herself," I said, not knowing how these things are put. "Her wrist. Ah, she cut her wrist, very deeply. She's going to be all right, though. Dr. Rainer is doing the reconstructive surgery now. Her phone line was cut. That's why you couldn't get through."

"That's what I thought," Kara said, the bleak determination in her hazel eyes deepening as she looked straight through me. "I was afraid something like that had happened."

It wasn't clear whether she was speaking to me or to herself. Nor was it clear what she was afraid had happened.

"Has Dr. Grecchi had these . . . these problems often since you've known her?" I asked.

Kara Eldridge seemed to remember suddenly that I was there.

"Oh, no," she said, "Isadora has never . . . I mean, we all knew about the depression, everybody at the clinic knew, and then she told me about it herself. We got to be friends after Marlis Rainer died. Isadora told me, well, a lot of things. She's the one who encouraged me to go to a community college and get myself some training so I could make a living if I needed to. She even helped me out with . . . with the money. She paid for it,

paid for me to go to school. T.J. would never have allowed . . .
But no, Isadora hasn't tried to, to kill herself."

"But you said you thought that's what had happened."

For a moment the earlier oblivion was back. The blank face
BB and I had seen on the day we interviewed T. J. Eldridge.
Dim, childlike.

"Well, you know," she said vaguely. "People who are depressed sometimes do that, don't they?"

"The officials think Grecchi is the killer," I told her.

"Yes, I suppose they do," she replied, that minor-chord aura
surfacing again and doing something to her face, tightening the
muscles until she looked like an expensive professional photograph of herself. The character lines visible. A competent adult
woman.

"Mo-om," a blond boy of about five whined from the kitchen
door, "if we don't go now maybe we won't have time to see
Disneyland tomorrow. You said we'd go soon. I wanna *go*."

"In a minute, Zeke," she told him, then addressed me urgently.

"Please tell Isadora I'll be in touch with her as soon as I can,"
she said. "Tell her I'll be back to see her as soon as I get the
kids settled in school and myself clear with this job. And tell
her I said thanks."

"But Isadora is going to be in jail, Kara—"

"Just tell her, Dr. McCarron. Now I'm afraid I do have to finish packing our things and get on the road."

"Of course," I said as the girl, Naomi, emerged from the garage
with a stack of framed photographs in her arms. The one on
top showed Kara Eldridge in an apron slicing cheese in their
kitchen. She looked like a mannequin.

"Should we take these?" the girl asked.

"No, we'll leave those for daddy to bring," Kara told her. "Remember? One of them got broken and he wants to fix it."

"Daddy broke it," Zeke insisted. "It didn't *get* broken. He threw
a sandwich in it. I want to ride Space Mountain. Can we go
now?"

"You said your husband was going to a Realtor's office?" I

said, standing. "Could you tell me where it is? Maybe I can catch him. I'd like to ask him a few things about Dr. Grecchi while I'm here."

The question seemed to startle her.

"Um, it's in the big shopping center just east of the Coast Highway," she stammered. "Century 21, I think. He was going to talk to several of them, but that's where he was going right now, or at least that's what I think he said. You don't need to get back on the freeway. Just take the main drag through town and turn right where you see that big retirement complex on the beach side. Sagebrush Resort, it's called. They've got a nice sign, looks western. You can't miss it."

Sagebrush Resort.

Wasn't that the place Waddy Babbick had mentioned? I thought as I said good-bye to Kara Eldridge and her children. He'd said his rival for the title of "oldest s.o.b. in the valley" had moved there from Anza after breaking her hip. A woman named Reed McCallister. Her husband Bill had died from a rattlesnake bite. And she might, the old desert rat told me, know something about the adobe line shack that had once been used as a diner.

A snapping, sizzling sensation made me dizzy for less than a second, but there was no ignoring it. My pal the grid, back again. I felt the way you do sometimes while reading and watching TV at the same time. When the two stories seem to overlap and you have to tell yourself, *No, the drug-addicted doctor who's about to operate on the child he doesn't know is his son is the TV story, and the secretive woman lawyer* isn't *the TV doctor's ex-wife, but the lover of the embittered veterinarian who rescues abused race horses in the novel.* That the sorting out is accomplished instantly is a tribute to the cognitive dexterity of our brains. Mine was dextrously pointing out to me that this was what I'd told Roxie I had to do. That I had to follow an irrational path paved erratically in glaring coincidences that blazed and vanished like mirages in my field of vision.

"We're going to see somebody in an old-folks home," I informed Brontë. "Somebody named Reed McCallister."

Old-folks homes had obviously changed since my brother,

David, and I dutifully went once a month with the Episcopal Youth Fellowship to take cookies to the institutionalized elderly of dad's church. I had expected to see a lot of spindly, sad old people playing gin in a sterile day room that hadn't been re-decorated since World War II. Instead, I seemed to have walked into a Las Vegas theme hotel, complete with a small casino.

"We find that a bit of gambling keeps some of our guests on their toes," the receptionist told me when I gestured quizzically toward the room full of flashing lights and intent octogenarians playing blackjack and slot machines. "They win scrip that local businesses match when they donate it to charity," she went on. "Or they can use it to buy things at the coffee bar and the gift shop here. Flowers are very popular. Our ladies love to get flowers, and our gentlemen love to gamble for the scrip to pay for them. But how can I help you?"

"I'd like to visit a guest named Reed McCallister. And is it all right if my dog comes along? She's had her shots."

"Oh, we encourage people to bring pets. They're wonderful for some of our older guests who are a little frail. Just petting a dog or cat helps them feel attached, you see. And let me check on McCallister. Ah! She's in our assisted living unit, has her own little apartment on the grounds but eats communally in the dining room with her 'village.' You're in luck. They were planning to attend the *Death of a Salesman* matinee at the Per-forming Arts Center in Escondido today, but the star is sick and they weren't interested in seeing the understudy. You'll proba-bly find Reed in the gym. It says here that's where she usually is when she's not at the pool. Just go through those double doors, across the courtyard, and into the activities center. The gym's on the left and there will be an attendant there to help you locate her."

The attendant pointed me to a wiry and deeply tanned woman with long white hair in gray sweatpants and a hot pink T-shirt, lifting five-pound free weights as she sat on a bench. Brontë wandered off to greet a man lying on his back on a table with a pile of little red sandbags on his chest.

"Well, hello!" the man wheezed, and scratched behind her ears, which she loves.

"Mrs. McCallister?" I began, sitting on the weight bench. "My name is Blue McCarron. Waddy Babbick told me you might know something about that old adobe line shack on Coyote Road outside Anza, about when it was used as a diner."

"Uhh-huhh!" she said, caramel-colored eyes behind thick tri-focals alert with interest. "I wondered when that thing would come around!"

"What thing? What do you mean?"

"Here. Could you put these weights back in the rack for me?" she asked. "Got a bum hip. Have to be careful about carrying weights. One of the reasons I prefer swimming. That and the fact that I always wanted a pool but Bill died before he got around to putting one in. God, it gets hot up there in the desert!

"But you came to hear about Lorene and her daughter Tommi, didn't you? I figured someday somebody would come asking. Even kept a few clippings from the newspapers, although I'm afraid they're in a trunk at my grandson's house. You know how you just *sense* some things, like they're written in the air and waiting all invisible, and then one day folks can see it, see what's written there?"

"Yeah," I answered, noticing how clean the gym smelled. Like fresh towels and lavender. "I do know about that."

Then I told her about everything that had happened, including my unintended visit to a crumbling shack I'd never seen except in a photograph on my own wall.

"So who are Lorene and Tommi?" I concluded.

"It's quite a story," Reed McCallister said, dabbing at her fore-head with a towel draped around her neck. "And I'm probably the last person alive who knows it, or at least knows it all."

The line shack, she told me, had been built on Bureau of Land Management land by a special permit granted to the util-ities company. When the line crew finished its work and left, the structure's complicated legal status prevented its being sold, so it just sat there empty for years. Her husband, Bill, and oth-ers had used it from time to time to store feed, but it was inconveniently far from the herds and eventually they all built ramadas for that purpose closer to the grazing areas. After that, transients wandering through camped out in the place, a practice frowned upon by Anza's residents. It was decided that a committee of townspeople would voluntarily manage the property until either the BLM or the utilities company decided what to do with it, which they never would, Reed explained, because it was too remotely situated for either agency to care about.

So the town fixed it up a bit and rented it out for Cattlemen's Association meetings and the like, school campouts and picnics, eventually a concession from October through June as more and more hikers found their way through Coyote Canyon after the Anza-Borrego Desert State Park was created.

"Of course, the wives had to do all the work," she went on, smiling. "Wives of the Cattlemen's Association, wives of the Sheepmen, wives of the Anza Development Commission. Somebody had to sit up there selling lemonade and cold sandwiches from a cooler all day as the locals and hikers and school groups came in and out. This was over thirty years ago and we all had families, you understand. I was raising a set of grandchildren at the time after one of my sons got into trouble with drugs, got divorced, what a mess. Anyway, after a while nobody wanted to do it. Nobody had time to sit up there all day."

"So what about this Lorene and Tommi?" I asked, watching as Brontë left the man with the red sandbags on his chest and went to be petted by a heavyset woman in tights and a leotard who was doing something with a CD player.

"It's almost time for wheelchair aerobics," Reed explained. "And I'm about to tell you about Lorene and her daughter."

Around that time, she said, a woman and a girl of eight or nine had turned up in Anza. The woman, Lorene Smith, said her husband had gotten a job as a ranch hand somewhere south of there and sent for her and the girl to come out from Kansas. Except the husband got killed in a brawl while the wife and daughter were making the long bus trip, and now they were stranded and didn't have any money. Somebody had told Lorene there was a family up in Anza looking for a housekeeper and cook, so she got some bus money from Travelers Aid down in Los Angeles and came to apply for the job.

"Now, *nobody,*" Reed said, "ever had a housekeeper in Anza or ever said they wanted one. Not only that, there wasn't any bus through Anza that morning Lorene said she and the girl had got there on the bus. What I'm saying is, it looked like they'd *walked* there from someplace. Both of 'em like skinned rabbits, pale as ghosts. It was Waddy Babbick's wife, Dot, took 'em home for a meal, let 'em stay for a while. See, in those days, even into the 1970s, little places like Anza were still sort of the Wild West. People didn't ask too many questions, just lent a helping hand if they could."

A lot of elderly people in wheelchairs were rolling themselves or being pushed by attendants into the gym. The woman in tights had made the musical selection for the aerobics class. Kenny Rogers. Loud. Most of the class was robustly singing along with "Reuben James" as they began their warm-up exercises.

"We're going to have to get out of here," Reed noted, unfolding an aluminum walker as she stood. "They tend to get rowdy. Let's grab a latte at the coffee bar and then sit out by the pool. I think you're going to be very interested in what I have to tell you next."

25

The Dessert (sic) Diner

I was beginning to question my impulsive decision to visit Reed McCallister by the time we were settled at poolside with our lattes. She was definitely a character and loved to talk, but then, I thought, don't older folks always love to talk about the past? Her detailed history of the shack in my photograph was taking forever and would lead nowhere. And I had no idea where I expected it to lead in the first place.

"I'm afraid I'll have to go shortly," I told her. "You're very kind to talk with me, but—"

"But you're starting to wonder if I'm a crazy old coot who'll never shut up," she finished the thought. The caramel eyes watched me with amusement from behind three different lenses. "You young people are always in a hurry. Remember, this story has waited almost your entire lifetime to be told."

"I'm sorry," I said. "It's just that I follow these wild goose chases nobody sees but me while everybody else does the real things, the important things. My partner says I'm irrational."

"Of course you are, dear," she replied, smiling. "What has being rational ever gotten you?"

"But this is serious," I argued. "It's not about me. Four prominent women are dead, a suspect has attempted suicide, the *FBI*
is involved, for crying out loud, and I'm chasing a story about
a shack."

"You've come to the right place, then," she said. "Now, what
happened was that Dot Babbick came up with the idea that
Lorene and Tommi could live up there in the old line shack,
and Lorene could run the concession. Lorene was grateful for
the roof over their heads and agreed to do it. She got to keep
twenty percent of the concession proceeds to save up for their
bus fare back to Kansas. Only thing is, they never did go back.
They stayed for two years."

The mother and daughter settled in, Reed explained, like they
were born to the place. Lorene sold lemonade and cold sandwiches as usual, but then she ordered a big coffeepot through
mail order, a couple of electric grills for hot sandwiches, and
some dishes. Bill McCallister found an old restaurant counter
somebody had dumped in a wash, and the men hauled it out
with a couple of pickup trucks, painted it and put on a new
Formica top, and installed it in the line shack for Lorene. The
place became a local hangout, and the little girl, Tommi, made
a sign she hung over the door.

"Dessert Diner, she called it," Reed went on, spelling out the
words. "Blue letters on white. Real pretty sign even though she
spelled 'desert' wrong. See, Lorene kept Tommi at home, didn't
let her go to school with the Babbick kids and mine and the
others, so she didn't spell too well. Tommi just ran wild, roam-
ing the canyons when she wasn't helping her mother. She'd
been a timid, sickly little thing when they got there, but after
a while everybody could see the child was thriving. That's why
nobody pushed Lorene about putting Tommi in school. Sometimes it's best to let people manage their own affairs even
though we all knew the girl was in danger, running around in
the desert all alone."

The other mothers had tried to protect the girl, Reed explained, by sewing jackets and dresses for her out of bright

fabrics so she'd be easy to see if she got lost or something happened to her and there was a search.

"Probably would've saved Bill, he'd been wearing a bright red shirt or something when the rattler got him," she noted. "But Waddy and the others out looking went right past him within thirty yards and didn't even see him. By the time somebody brought dogs, it was too late. Anyway, Tommi spent all her time out in the canyons, kept bringing injured birds and lizards and what have you back to the diner, where she'd nurse them and Lorene would help her. Tommi never said much, but she had a big smile for anybody and we all tried to look after her. The kid was happy. Of course, she eventually got in trouble out there by herself. We all knew it had to happen."

Dot Babbick had taken Lorene down to San Diego for a doctor's appointment, Reed said, and Tommi was supposed to manage the diner while her mother was gone. Except when the first rancher showed up that morning for his coffee, there was nobody there.

"Coffee all brewed and ready, but the place was empty."

After an hour a small search party was organized and the girl was quickly found, her bright orange jacket a beacon among the dun-colored rocks. She'd turned an ankle, fallen, and apparently hit her head while hurrying back toward the diner from a little cave she'd fixed up, where she'd taped pictures from magazines all over the walls.

"Pictures of pretty houses," Reed said thoughtfully, "pictures of food, ads for appliances like where a woman's standing in a kitchen smiling at a toaster oven, pictures of dishes and pots and pans. Bill was there. He said it was the strangest thing he ever saw, all those magazine pictures taped to the rocks and rustling in the wind. Said it was like a kind of shrine."

Tommi was brought to the McCallister place so Reed could care for her until Lorene and Dot Babbick got back from San Diego, Reed concluded, slurping the last of her latte. She'd wrapped the sprained ankle and kept the girl awake long enough to make sure she didn't have a concussion, then given her an aspirin and let her sleep.

"Washed that orange jacket and red dress she had on, too," Reed said as if this information had great significance. "Just told her to give me her dirty clothes and go lie on our bed in her panties. I put a nice warm afghan over her, but she kept kicking it off in her sleep. You know how fidgety kids are when they're hurt."

"Um, no, I don't have any children," I said with a growing desperation to escape. Reed McCallister wanted to tell me the story of her kindness to a hurt child thirty years ago, I thought. It was very nice, but it didn't have a damn thing to do with anything. I felt like a fool for getting myself into the bind I was in.

"Well, after that all hell broke loose," Reed went on, picking up the pace as if she knew I was going to leave the second I could get a word in. "About a week later some folks saw the sheriff's car drive through town and go up to the diner. Two deputies in it and a man in the backseat."

Her eyes narrowed and she watched me closely as she continued.

"Next thing we knew, Lorene's in the back of the sheriff's car. They came and took her away. To prison. She died there a year later. Nobody ever saw Lorene again after that day."

"Why? What happened?" I asked in spite of myself.

"The man was Tommi's father, Lorene's husband. Seems Lorene had tried to kill him over in Riverside, tried to stab him in his sleep two years back, a couple of months before she showed up in Anza. She was on the run, you see. She and the little girl. Guess they'd been all over Southern California before they showed up there. Guess they were just about at the end of their rope. And then I guess Lorene was too tired to move on when she had the chance. Or else she was just waiting for the day they'd come for her."

"What happened to the little girl, to Tommi?" I asked.

"Well, like I said, in those days people minded their own business. Now, Bill said for sure he saw that man walk back toward town with Tommi wearing that same red dress I'd washed, and somebody told Dot Babbick later that they must have hitched a ride out because they sure didn't stay in town. But it wasn't two months later Waddy was running one of his herds up in a mountain about thirty miles from Anza, and said he saw the man, Lorene's husband, up there hunting with an old bolt-action rifle. Said he was sure it was the same man, and Waddy always had a good eye from searching out all that Indian stuff he collected. Didn't see the girl, though, just the man."

"So you don't know what happened to Tommi?" I said as the phone in my purse rang. "Excuse me."

"Blue, where are you?" Wes Rathbone asked urgently.

"I'm in Carlsbad."

"You're still at Eldridge's? Okay. We've got a mess here. Grecchi's out of surgery but still in post-op. Nobody's allowed in with her except Rainer. He says she's not coherent, but she is talking. What she's saying, according to Rainer, is stuff about Megan. Like, 'He'll get Megan next. He'll kill Megan.'"

"He?" I said.

"Who knows? Rainer may be making this up as a cover for Grecchi, but he also may not be. There's more bad news."

"Oh, God. What?"

"The FBI put the thumbscrews on Jeffrey Pond's ex-wife, Gwen, and her friend Jeri. You know, the one who claimed he raped her? Well guess what? Both women admitted under heavy questioning from the FBI that Pond had paid them to drop the rape charges. Jeri's saying now he did rape her. Gwen, the ex-wife, says she doesn't believe it was rape because she knew her husband was having an affair with Jeri for at least six months before their divorce. She'd hired a snoop, had pictures to prove it. So when Jeri cried rape, Gwen knew Jeri's husband must have caught on and this was Jeri's way of covering up. But Gwen had the pictures, right?

"So what the FBI thinks happened," he went on, "is that Gwen saw Jeffrey going to jail on this trumped-up rape charge, and there goes the alimony and child support. Pond's in prison, she gets nothing. So Gwen goes to Jeri with the pictures, tells her to drop the rape charges or she'll show them to Jeri's husband. But Jeri's no fool, sees the dollar signs in Gwen's eyes, and decides to grab something for herself. Her marriage is in the toilet, anyway, and she's going to need money. In the end, both women go to Pond and tell him the rape charges will be dropped *and* the evidence of adultery not introduced into the divorce proceedings if he pays them a little blackmail. It's possible he's still paying and will be for a long time. It's possible this guy has learned to *really* hate women."

There was a certain sleazy justice in the story I'd just heard, but I didn't mention it.

"But Pond was at the hospital all night last night," I said instead.

"His mother says he was," Rathbone went on, "which isn't very reliable, and even if he was, he could have sent those e-mails by picking up a phone and calling his own computer if he'd programmed it that way. What's even more troubling is that Pond left the hospital shortly after his mother did this morning. That gives him plenty of time to get to Grecchi's, cut her phone cord and her wrist, set it up to look like a suicide, and then, if Grecchi's story is credible, drive up to Julian and take out Megan Rainer before he does himself in. We've just talked to Rox. She says it makes some sense. I always knew this perp was a man, Blue. It's always a man."

"But what about the blue willow plates? And why would Jeffrey Pond be hanging around my place leaving them for me?"

"Who knows? Right now we've got San Diego County sheriff's deputies and FBI all over Megan Rainer up in Julian and at your place. If Pond shows up, he's hamburger. I'm just calling to tell you to stay away from Julian and don't go home. Go to Roxie's. Don't go home until this is over."

"Yeah," I said as he hung up.

"What's happening, dear?" Reed McCallister asked, looking strangely like Jennings Rainer's schnauzer with her wiry hair and bright eyes. A schnauzer in trifocals.

"I have to go," I told her. "Something's come up. Thank you so much for talking to me. You've been very helpful."

I'd go by the Eldridge place, inform Kara of the developments, I thought. I might be able to catch her if I hurried.

"I haven't been helpful yet," Reed said, grabbing her walker and following me. "I haven't told you the really interesting part."

I am incapable of turning my back and walking away from an elderly woman in a walker who is trying to keep up with me. Reed McCallister knew it and played it masterfully, stumbling a little, wincing in pain. Brontë trotted beside her and gave me recriminating looks.

"There really is something I must do," I tried, and was ignored.

"Over the years Bill and Waddy and the others saw Lorene's husband up in the mountains, usually with a teenage boy after that first time. See, they were living wild up there, living off the land. Never said much to the herders, just a tip of the hat. And then they kidnapped that young woman."

"What young woman?" I had to ask, stopping in the hall outside the casino.

"She was a student with a college group doing field research. They had a base camp and were searching for Indian artifacts. Should've asked Waddy, saved themselves a lot of time. Anyway, the girl was scouting in a canyon alone when Lorene's husband showed up out of nowhere aiming that old bolt-action rifle at her. He told her his son was old enough for a wife, and she was going to be it!"

"What?" I said.

"Yep. It was in all the papers back then, all over the country. He forced her at gunpoint back to their camp hidden way up inside a wash where nobody would ever see it. He told her he was 'bringing' her for his son. When they got to the camp he tied her hands and feet, and then he and the boy just waited for her to calm down and accept her fate. She told the authorities later that the old man read aloud to her from the Bible constantly. She said he actually believed that women were placed on earth to serve the needs of men, particularly the sexual needs which the teenage boy was experiencing. Said it was in the Bible and any woman who refused was 'an abomination to the Lord.' The old man told her he assumed she was a 'virgin' and so he would 'break her in' for the boy. When he tried to rape her, she shot him with his own gun. Right through the heart. Dropped him like a bird."

"But you said she was tied up," I pointed out.

Reed McCallister sighed with satisfaction.

"The boy had untied her hands," she said. "And the boy had left the gun where she could reach it."

I was almost to the door of the Sagebrush Resort.

"Wow, that's quite a story," I said, looking at my watch. "But what happened to the boy? And I still don't know what happened to the old guy's daughter, Tommi."

"The boy was barely fourteen and was placed in foster care in Riverside," she said, watching me closely. "After that I have no idea."

"And the little girl?"

Her caramel-colored eyes sparkled as she shook her head.

"Haven't figured that out yet, huh?"

"Figured what out?"

"The little girl sleeping on my bed in her panties was no little girl," Reed told me. "I was a married woman with a daughter, two sons, three grandsons, and four granddaughters by then, but it doesn't take that much experience to tell the difference between boys and girls when you see 'em in their underwear. Lorene Smith's little girl, Tommi, was really her little boy, Tommy. She'd been dressing the kid as a girl so the old man couldn't find 'em."

I felt as though I were swimming up through dark water, just about to break the surface.

"Reed, what was the old man's name?" I asked. "Do you remember his name?"

"Think it began with an E," she answered, nodding thoughtfully. "Etheridge? Something like that. I've still got the newspaper clippings, but like I said, they're in a trunk at my son's house. I can have him bring them over sometime if you'd like to see them."

"Was it Eldridge?" I said. "Try to think back."

"It could be. It sounded like that. It could be Eldridge."

It was all falling into place. Everything.

"Is there a Bible handy anyplace?" I asked.

Reed led me into a parlor adjacent to the casino.

"Honey," she said, "we've got more Bibles here than sense. Every church group in San Diego is convinced the elderly wear out at least ten Bibles a week, preparing for the inevitable, so they bring us more."

She opened a rough-hewn cabinet, revealing shelves of Bibles.

"You want the Douay, King James, Jerusalem, Good News, Revised Standard, or one of these new ones written in street slang? We also have large type, Spanish, French, Portuguese, German, Chinese, Japanese, Vietnamese, and Tagalog editions and a set of twenty of the Torah in both English and Hebrew. Now, down here are some unusual translations and a nice one with illustrations by the Old Masters, as well as—"

"Anything in English," I said, laughing. "I just want to check something in Isaiah before I go."

Owls, dragons, bitterns, mountains of rotting corpses, streams of hot tar, and a mythological woman called Lilith. It was all there. I grabbed the cell phone again.

"Do you remember the plates that Lorene got to use in the diner?" I asked Reed. "Remember? You said Lorene got a coffeepot and fry grills and dishes from a mail-order catalogue."

"Oh, yes," she said brightly. "They were those old blue willow plates the diners all used to have. Weren't too popular by then, though. Most places had started using that pale green Melmac. Lorene probably got those plates for a song."

"She probably did," I agreed, giving her hand a squeeze before I headed out the door. "Reed, I think you've just saved the life of a woman vice presidential candidate. Have your grandson bring those clippings to you and get ready for a lot of company. You're going to be famous."

"Then I'd probably better do something with my hair," she said, grinning as Brontë and I dashed out.

In the parking lot I called Rathbone at the hospital.

"It's Eldridge!" I yelled. "Tell the FBI to forget Jeffrey Pond and find Thomas Joseph Eldridge. I don't know where he is, but his wife said—"

The phone was making a crackling noise.

"Hello?" Wes Rathbone said again. "I can't hear you."

The battery, I realized, was dead.

26

Edom Revisited

I found a pay phone next to Ralph's Grocery in the shopping center across the street from the Sagebrush Resort.

"Wes, my cell phone is dead," I said after phoning the hospital, depositing ninety cents, and waiting for the hospital switchboard to contact the nurses' station on Grecchi's floor and then for somebody to go get Rathbone from the surgical waiting area. In a half a day I'd learned exactly why people love cell phones.

"You have to recharge the battery," he mentioned before telling me the latest. "Listen. Pond's flown the coop. He never showed up at Megan's place in Julian. We think he's—"

"Wes, it's not Pond, it's Eldridge!" I broke in. "Let me tell you what I just found out. See, Eldridge lived up in Anza for about two years when he was a kid around nine or ten. He was with his mother, Lorene, who called herself Smith but her real surname was Eldridge. She'd tried to kill her husband in Riverside and was on the run. She dressed T.J. as a *girl*, Wes, so if the husband or the police came around asking about a woman and a little boy, everybody would say they hadn't seen a woman and a boy. But then the police and the husband caught up with them, and Lorene died in prison. T.J. went with the father, who was some kind of Bible-thumping survivalist, lived in the wild up there for years until—"

"Blue, we're sure it's Pond," Rathbone interrupted. "He fits the profile better than anyone else, he worked as a technician in a psychiatric hospital during a time when MAOIs were still widely in use, so he had experience with the drug and knew what it could do. He has motivation, and he ducked out of his father's hospital room the minute his mother left and just vanished. The FBI went through his place and found several small containers of an unusual pink plastic substance they think may be symbolic trophies for his kills. The stuff is like a soft, stretchy glob. The theory is these things represent wombs to him. They're all covered with his fingerprints. Looks like he sits around squashing them in his hands. Sick, huh?"

I felt as if I were in Sri Lanka trying to define "Missouri" in English to a peasant. That certainty that you're not going to be heard.

"That stuff is *Silly Putty*!" I told Rathbone. "He's into body-building and he squeezes wads of it to build the muscles in his forearms. Wes, the killer is *not* Jeffrey Pond. It's T. J. Eldridge. He was a medical corpsman in the service. He could have learned about MAOIs there or from Grecchi. But get this—he and his mother ran a diner up in Anza. Just a little place, mostly hikers and locals coming through, and they used blue willow plates!"

"Blue, every diner in the country used blue willow plates at one time. And Pond's mother has a kitchen clock made out of a blue willow plate. She told the FBI her husband made it for her years ago from the last of a set that had belonged to *her* mother. Those damn plates are everywhere. Hell, I think Annie has a blue willow cup and saucer her sister got her in Singapore."

"Wes, Thomas Eldridge's father was some kind of religious fanatic who raised him alone up in the mountains after Lorene was arrested. The father *kidnapped* a female student from a college anthropology campout to be used by T.J. as a 'wife.' The father was going to rape the girl to 'break her in' for a fourteen-year-old boy, but T.J. had untied her hands and left the father's old bolt-action rifle near her. She shot and killed T.J.'s father. Apparently the story was in papers all over the country thirty years ago. The woman who told me still has clippings. I mean, this can be *proved*."

"Okay," he said, "if Pond turns up clean, then it's Eldridge. I'll put the word out, put this story out about Eldridge. Blue, are you sure this really happened, the father kidnapping the girl and the shooting? Who's your informant? Where'd you hear this?"

"A woman from Anza named Reed McCallister. She lives in a retirement center in Carlsbad now. The Sagebrush Resort."

"And how old is this McCallister?"

"I don't know, Wes, late eighties. But she was *there*."

"Late eighties. Great," he said. "Blue, go to Roxie's. I'll call you there as soon as we get a statement from Grecchi. If she didn't cut her own wrist, if Pond or Eldridge did it, she'll tell us. There really isn't anything else to do right now. Just relax."

The phone felt hot and slick in my hand as I hung it up. I was sweating, I realized. Because nobody was listening to me. I hate it when people don't listen, when they don't hear. It reminds me of the twelve thousand times I tried to tell my twin brother crime doesn't pay. Probably he hears that in prison now, too.

Next I called Roxie, who didn't want to talk.

"Blue, the authorities are handling things now," she said. "Our part is over. And I meant it when I said I need some time alone to think."

So I didn't tell her about Reed McCallister and the story of Thomas Eldridge. I just hung up and noticed darkness falling indifferently around me. The feeling was strange. I imagined it was like what the first tiny sliver of consciousness must have been for the first protohuman who experienced it. Long-armed and heavy-browed, she would have thought, *I am,* for only a split second and then, seeing no answering spark in the black, simian eyes of her companions, known that she was alone.

In the phone booth I curled my fingers, apelike, over the

palm of my hand and thumped my breastbone. This was what it would be like, then, I realized. This was what it would be like not telling my life to Roxie Bouchie. A primordial loneliness so intense it rocked me back on my heels for a second, made me gasp. But it didn't really change anything. I still knew. And I had things to do.

I went in the grocery and got some chocolate milk and enough tuna-vegetable medley from the salad bar for both me and Brontë. After we'd eaten in the truck I drove by the Eldridge house, which was dark and silent at five-thirty as neighbors came home from work, their automatic garage doors whirring in the dusk. I let the truck idle in the driveway for a few minutes, then killed the engine, got out, and knocked on the door. There was no one there and no sense that anyone would ever be there again. The posing couple BB and I had seen on these steps was gone. They wouldn't be back, ever.

Through partially open picture window blinds I could see the pink and green couch, the pale rectangles of paint where photographs of Kara Eldridge had once hung over a fireplace. Photographs of Kara cooking, caring for children, wearing a corsage. Behaviors acceptable for a woman. Except the little boy Zeke had said daddy threw a sandwich and broke one of the pictures. What had happened? I wondered. What had shattered that glass and a statue's oblivion, and released the woman imprisoned within? And where was Kara now, and where was Thomas, who had spent two happy years as a girl thirty years in the past and now was killing women in the name of his father? The Sword of Heaven.

I didn't know what to make of Kara Eldridge. Had she known what her husband was? Had she even suspected that the man beside her in bed had changed from whatever he'd been when she married him and become monstrous? When did he change? And why? And if Kara knew, when did she learn? And if she knew, why didn't she tell somebody?

"Because nobody would have believed her," I said aloud in the warm, dry gloom of an October evening in Southern

California. The farthest edge of the continent. From where there's no place left to run.

Nobody believed me, either.

From Carlsbad it was easy to take a connecting county road to I-15 and head up into the mountains that way. It was dark by the time I reached the village of Julian and the Rainer/Nugent house on the side of a hill. No lights were on, and the tattered structure looked forbidding in the gathering shadows. Remembering the Boston terrier, Elsa, I left Brontë in the truck as I approached the door. When something hit me in the chest with a painful sting, I thought it was a bat, although bats' radar prevents their running into anything and I knew it. My knit blouse was wet where the thing hit me.

"Don't take another step!" Chris Nugent's voice boomed from the porch.

"Chris, it's Blue McCarron," I yelled. "What's going on?"

"Oh, Dr. McCarron, I'm sorry," a woman's voice answered as the porch light was turned on and I could see Chris and Megan standing there, Megan holding what looked like an assault rifle in firing position. The damn paint gun. The fluid soaking my blouse was red.

"I don't believe this," I said. "Where are the sheriff's deputies and the FBI?"

"They were here, but he showed up and they went after him," Megan said. "Except I was afraid he'd doubled back. I mean, I thought you—"

"Turn that light off," I said. "Who showed up? What happened?"

"It was Pond," Chris Nugent said.

"I shot him," Megan Rainer added. "Or at least I think I did. The deputy said it will help them identify him if he's gone into Julian and he's covered with red paint."

"You shot Jeffrey Pond with a paint gun?" I said, incredulous. "Did you see him? Are you sure it was Pond?"

"No, but everybody said it was," Nugent answered. "We were watching from a window upstairs, saw somebody come out of the woods on the side of the house. Too shadowy to see him clearly. Megan had brought the paint gun upstairs and was ready," he said proudly, wrapping a big arm over his wife's shoulders.

"I don't believe this," I said again. "Where are the children?"

"They're inside," Megan answered. "We were about to leave, take the kids and stay in a hotel down the hill, when this happened."

I felt momentarily useful as I ran back to the truck and got the Smith and Wesson.

"This is a real gun," I told them when I'd joined them on the porch. "I want you to tape a large note to the door telling the authorities that you've taken the children to a safe place and will contact Wes Rathbone with the location and phone number of that place when you get there. Do it now. I'll cover you as you get the children into your car. Everyone but the driver should lie on the floor until you're out of this area. I don't believe you shot a serial killer with a paint gun!"

"Mom was really cool," Joshua Nugent yelled from behind the screen door. "Can we take Elsa? We *have* to take Elsa."

"Absolutely," I answered.

The family of four and a Boston terrier dashed to their car as I ran beside them, aiming the little .38 at every shadow moving at the edge of the woods surrounding the house.

"Did the man you shot have a gun?" I yelled as Chris gunned the engine.

"I think so," he answered. "He was carrying something that could have been a rifle."

"It was T. J. Eldridge," I said, but they were too far away to hear me. And the shadows were suddenly too dense. Time to go. But go where?

I couldn't go home. The place was crawling with armed people waiting to capture or kill another armed person. I would only be in the way. Roxie's place was out of the question. I wasn't really wanted there, and so even though Rox would welcome me if she knew what was going on, I'd freeze to death standing on a drifting ice floe before I'd go anywhere near her, not that there are a lot of drifting ice floes in the mountains above San Diego. The First Law of the Heartland involves a cast iron and often disastrous pride. Probably handed down from Scots-Irish ancestors, it's ludicrous, but if it's in your head you have to obey it. And it's definitely in my head. I'd go to a motel, then, I decided. A big one off the freeway where I could sneak Brontë in a side door after I'd registered. But first I had to do one more thing. I had to prove I wasn't a fool, if only to myself.

It was dark by the time I slowed to drive through Anza's little main drag. Colored pools of neon light spilled across the pavement from the diner, the gas station, and the convenience store. A few people were about, but Anza was as peaceful and quiet as its chamber of commerce promised. Nothing much ever happened in Anza, I thought, unless you knew where to look.

There was a late-model car parked a quarter of a mile up the road, but the old line shack seemed deserted when I stopped the truck outside and let Brontë run for a while in moon shadows. The air had the musky smell of the desert verbena growing in patches on the ground around the shack, and I assumed Brontë was responsible. She'd bruised the leaves with her paws while dashing around, causing the release of scent. A lot of people don't like the resinous odor of desert verbena, which is like a mixture of sweet milk and tobacco, claiming something about the scent makes them nervous. The verbena seemed to be making Brontë nervous, because she kept sniffing the ground and running in circles, her growl a soft murmur. Maybe a rabbit had just scuttled past, I thought. Or her favorite lizard, the reclusive chuckwalla that blows up one side of its body in order to flatten the other side into a crevice. My last guess, as it turned out, was close enough.

"Come on, girl," I called after she'd run around for ten minutes or so. "Up in the truck. There's broken glass on the floor in there and I don't want you stepping on it. You wait here. Brontë, *stay*."

The .38 was lying on my sweatshirt on the floor of the truck cab, and I stuffed it in the waist of my jeans before pulling the sweatshirt and tennis shoes on. Then I grabbed the penlight I keep in the glove compartment. It would provide enough light to see what I wanted to see.

The corrugated steel panel left smears of rust on my hands as I moved it away from the door, stepped inside, and clicked on the penlight. The torn magazine pages were still there, taped to the walls like pictures in a gallery. In the stillness I walked to my left, aiming the narrow beam of light on the images one by one. The two owls I'd seen before, torn from a child's nature magazine called *Ranger Rick*. A pen-and-ink drawing of a dragon with the log line from a Goth magazine popular with teenagers who wear black. Pictures of corpses stacked in a woods outside Dachau in 1943. A stunning illustration from an edition of *Sleeping Beauty* depicting a murderous wall of thorns in which were imprisoned the skeletons of the princes who'd tried to rescue the sleeping princess and failed. A unicorn from a medieval tapestry, more owls, a heron, the raven illustration from a book of Poe. A photograph of a steaming, sulfurous creek from a travel promo for New Zealand, the water inked in black. Another dragon. I knew what I was looking at. I was looking at a vanished biblical nation called Edom.

"'And it shall be an habitation for dragons . . .'" I whispered, quoting from my old King James Bible.

"'. . . And a court for owls,'" another voice answered as frost raced in sudden sheets down my neck and arms and back.

Oh, shit!

Instinct wrapped my right hand around the grip of the snub-nose at my waist and I felt my thumb push the safety off as I turned toward the voice, gun in firing position. He was hunched behind the old counter at the far end of the structure. In the gloom I could see concave half circles behind his head where round rocks had fallen from a fireplace chimney. I could also see that he held a bolt-action rifle in both hands, braced on the counter and aimed at me. The counter protected most of his body. Nothing protected mine.

"Drop the gun," he said evenly. "I don't want to kill you."

"If that rifle is your father's, it's so old it may not fire," I answered, fighting to keep the panic out of my voice. "I'll take my chances."

My right hand was hot and sweating around the gun's grip, but it wasn't shaking.

"My father's rifle was taken as evidence by the Riverside County Sheriff's Department at the time of his death over a quarter century ago and was never returned," Thomas Eldridge told me, a note of approval in his voice. "The weapon in my hands is similar but new. Drop your pistol or you'll force me to kill you."

The logic was unassailable. And nobody would hear the shots. I dropped the .38, which clattered on the cement floor.

"Now what?" I said.

"I'll tie you up, then ease your truck over the lip of Nance Canyon back there. Nobody will find it until tomorrow, and I'll be gone by then. I'll be in San Diego at a pep rally for a woman who thinks she's a man. I've already told them. There's no secret about where I'll be tomorrow. I'm going to kill her."

He wasn't raving, wasn't wild-eyed, or even agitated. If anything, he seemed tired. A sense of exhaustion was audible in his voice, the set of his shoulders. Coming out from behind the counter, he kept the rifle trained on me until he reached my gun, then leaned over and picked it up without taking his eyes from me.

"Do you understand why I've had to do this?" he asked, holding me in the sights of my own gun now and stashing the rifle under the counter. He was wearing jeans, a green polo shirt, and a dark nylon windbreaker, which he was carefully removing. And he was splattered with red from head to toe. I could see the glint of moonlight on the military watch at his wrist. We might have been chatting somewhere. Casual acquaintances at a chance meeting just before which one of us happened to have lost a companion to a grisly accident involving a land mine. The red paint made him look like a ghoul.

"No," I answered as he walked behind me and pushed me toward the counter, the snub of my gun at the base of my neck. "And right now I don't care. My dog, Brontë, is in my truck. I hope you'll release her before you push the truck into the canyon. If you don't, she'll be injured or killed. You once," I said, turning to look him in the eyes as he shoved me against the counter, "took care of injured animals, nursed them. I'm asking you not to injure an animal. That's all."

"I will free your dog," he agreed, slamming my head down on the dusty, cracked Formica as he bent to tie one of my ankles to the counter's rust-pocked chrome footrail with the nylon jacket. The knots were so tight I knew they could never be untied, but I could find a way to rip the fabric between my leg and the rail if I had a chance, I thought.

There was nothing on the counter I could hit him with, no point in trying to fight in the few seconds it took him to secure my leg to the rail. If I did, he'd kill me.

"Thank you for promising not to kill my dog," I said.

"You're like my mother," he mentioned seconds later. "That's why I liked you. She took care of animals and things. You're like her, living out here all alone. I guess you have your reasons, just like she did."

"I have my reasons," I said inscrutably, trying to get a fix on what he was saying. It was fine with me if he thought I lived in the desert because I'd attempted to murder a husband. Just fine. As long as it kept me alive.

"He beat her," T. J. Eldridge said, again behind the counter as he unzipped a backpack he'd pulled from the floor. "My father beat my mother so hard her ears bled and once her eye popped out and hung down her face on its cord. He raped her, too. He did it in front of me once when I was six. He said in the Bible six is the age of reason and I was old enough to learn what women are for. He beat her unconscious and then propped her on her stomach over a chair. I hated him. I was glad when my mother stabbed him. We thought he was dead when we left. But then my mother saw in the newspapers that he didn't die. She read it to me. She said he'd try to find us and so I had to wear dresses and pretend to be a girl so he couldn't."

His voice was flat, emotionless. The sentences clear but simple, like a child's. I couldn't see his eyes.

"I'm sorry about your mother," I said as if I were standing near a casket at a funeral parlor back in Illinois. *She looks so nice,* is the next line in the heartland script for these occasions, but it wouldn't do here.

"You should be sorry about my father, too," he replied. "Another woman killed him. He was going to rape her so she'd be ready to be my wife, but I untied her hands and she shot him."

He was looking at my hands on the counter as he spoke. We both wore laced athletic shoes. He could have tied my hands with shoelaces the way his father had tied the girl's, but he didn't.

"T.J., why did you kill those women that way?" I asked. "Why did you hide little MAOI time bombs in their surgical incisions so days or weeks later they'd eat some salami or a handful of fava beans and die?"

"Because I could," he answered in that flat, tired voice as he took a plate and a large plastic Baggie from the backpack. "I took the pills from Isadora's purse a long time ago, when I found out what Kara had done. Somebody has to do something, and yet nobody does. My father was a cruel and stupid man, but that doesn't make the Bible wrong, Dr. McCarron. My father taught me the Bible. It's all in there. It says the man must rule over the woman and the woman must be subservient to the man. It says any woman who refuses to be subservient, any woman who tries to have power like a man, is an abomination to the Lord. Women have forgotten their place and that's what's destroying this country. You do agree with that, don't you, Dr. McCarron?"

I could feel my heart pounding, the blood singing in the elegant road map of my circulatory system. I could *taste* oxygen molecules from that blood feeding my brain. In my brain the molecules tasted, I thought, the way ginger smells. The molecules tasted like being alive. I was determined to stay that way.

"Of course I agree with that," I lied, casting about for something to say in support of it. "I mean, look at what happened to Edom."

He was arranging chunks of cheddar cheese on the plate. Beneath the heavily scented orange cubes I could see three little figures fleeing over a bridge, a pagoda, a willow tree, two birds in the air.

"'There shall the night hag alight,'" he quoted from what I thought was the Revised Standard Version of the Isaiah 34 text. "The night hag is Lilith, you know. The night hag is any woman who won't obey the law of God. Would you like some cheese? It's extra-extra sharp, pretty good. My mother always made cheese sandwiches here, you know. Have some. We're going to be here all night. Eat something. You'll get hungry."

"Take, eat . . ." I remembered the words from the sacrament of Holy Communion I'd heard every Sunday of my life as a child. Women's words in the mouth of a man. So who had stolen the power from whom? I thought as a man named Thomas Joseph Eldridge wolfed down at least a pound of cheddar cheese in the gloom of a rotting adobe shack. Courteously, I nibbled at one of the squares.

"How nice of Kara to make you a snack," I mentioned, taking a risk. It was impossible to know what might set him off.

"Kara is a disciple of Lilith now," he said somberly. "She has been for two years, but I didn't know. She lied to me. Before, when Mrs. Rainer was alive to show her the way, Kara was perfect. I thought Mrs. Rainer was like a mother-in-law to Kara, like Naomi in the Bible. That's why I named my daughter Naomi. But Isadora lured Kara away from the right path and so my daughter couldn't be called Naomi anymore and I had to call her by her middle name, Ann. It was Isadora who talked Kara into sneaking around behind my back and going to school, even gave her the money. Before that Kara was a natural woman and obeyed me. But then she sneaked off and went to school and even *graduated*. If she hadn't done that, maybe she could have been all right. Of course, I killed Isadora. I have to be the Sword of Heaven. *Somebody* has to be."

He seemed overwhelmed by the task but determined to carry it out.

"Of course," I said, dipping my head as we do in high Episcopal churches when the crucifix is carried past in procession. It seemed to work even though I remembered Eldridge was a Methodist.

"I've got a bottle of water down here," he said, leaning beneath the counter. "Cheese is salty."

My gun lay on top of the counter, his left hand loosely over it but not holding it. My one chance and I took it, grabbed the base of the grip softly between my thumb and third finger and then ripped it from beneath his hand and into mine. Then I held the barrel hard against his neck where the carotid artery pulsed as he leaned over, both index fingers on the trigger as I began the careful, sure pull. There was no other option. I was going to have to kill him.

27

The Dance

But I didn't. Something happened. Everything slowed to a stop as I squeezed the trigger, or thought I did, and nothing happened. It was like trying to move inside clean, solid ice. Everything visible but frozen in place. Several conversations were taking place inside my head simultaneously as no time passed. Not a single second, not a heartbeat.

"Thou shalt not kill," a male voice boomed.

"Okay, nice rule for large social control, but does it apply to this situation? No. Kill him before he has a chance to grab the gun and kill you, you idiot!"

I guessed that voice was mine.

Then another. "You can't shoot someone who's feeding you."

Dog-brain, I thought. We must be closer to dogs on the evolutionary tree than we thought.

"Shoot, shoot, he's a murderer and he's going to murder *you*!"

Me again. The survival thing.

"But he could have killed you already and he hasn't. He *likes* you."

Female brain, I realized. We always think that. Probably a chemical effect of estrogen.

They were all me, I knew.

Then time resumed and Eldridge moved his arms. Not toward me and the gun, but to his head. He seemed not to know I was there as he stood, heels of both hands pushing against his temples, his eyes bulging. Even in the dark I could see his face grow purple as his mouth made an open O. Then he fell.

I stood on the footrail of the counter and leaned over it, the .38 trained on the body-shaped shadow below.

"Don't move!" I yelled, teeth chattering. "Don't move or I'll shoot."

But T. J. Eldridge didn't move. Nor did I. I clenched my teeth to stop the racket and heard gurgling sounds from the form on the floor but no breathing. Still I held the gun and waited. A minute. Two minutes. Three. Nothing. Then an odor as his bowels evacuated. It happens shortly after death. I knew Thomas Joseph Eldridge was dead.

I fired the Smith and Wesson once, into the sturdy fabric of the jacket tying me to the counter. The bullet hole in the jacket's back gave me a weak spot from which to tear the nylon and free my leg. Brontë had begun to bark frantically at the sound of the shot, and I could hear her, although she sounded like a fake dog. She sounded like a cartoon. My foot seemed fake, too, dragging its tightly knotted nylon sleeve.

A little psychological shock, I told myself. It would wear off. Meanwhile, I rounded the end of the counter where a woman who called herself Lorene had once served coffee and sandwiches to sunburned ranchers while a boy in a dress played outside. I hoped she wasn't able to see what lay on the floor behind her counter now. This couldn't have been what she had in mind for her only child.

I felt his wrist and neck. There was no pulse. Then I walked out, leaving the rusted corrugated-metal sheet where I'd pushed it away from the door. Behind me a dragon moved slightly in the air disturbed by my passage, and then was still.

The smell of death on me made Brontë frantic, so I had to

drive back into Anza with the sound of howling. It seemed appropriate. From a pay phone at the diner where I'd talked with Waddy Babbick I called Wes Rathbone at the hospital.

"Blue!" he erupted, "Damn your cell phone! Where are you? Nobody could reach you. Grecchi's coherent now. It took longer than it should have because Eldridge had sedated her before he cut her wrist, and it didn't show up on the blood test they gave her when she was brought in, so she was sedated again, and—"

"Wes," I interrupted, "Eldridge is dead. His body is in an old adobe line shack where Coyote Canyon ends four miles east of Anza. I didn't kill him, he just died. I'm not going to stay with the body. I'm going home. Don't ask me what happened. I don't know."

"Blue . . . ?"

"Not now, Wes. Just let me go home. I'll talk to you later."

Before he could say anything else I hung up the phone and went into the ladies' room to wash the smell of death and cordite from my hands. In the car Brontë continued to whine, but we made it home without further howling. There were more people in khaki shorts and FBI windbreakers outside my motel now. All of them had cell phones. In the distance over Coyote Canyon I could hear a helicopter.

"The body of Thomas Eldridge has been secured," a young agent informed me as I climbed out of my truck. "We'll need to take a statement from you."

"Not now," I said. "And I'm not the person who knows the whole story, anyway. In an hour or so I'll talk to you, give you the name of an informant who has the whole history, including newspaper clippings. Right now I insist on the right to a stiff drink and a hot bath."

"Roger," the boy said efficiently. "And oh, yeah, your friend is inside."

I wasn't sure how I felt about seeing Roxie right then. I didn't want to have to explain what couldn't be explained. That everything is part of a pattern that some of us see occasionally, and some of us never do. I was too tired to try, and she'd never get it, anyway.

But it wasn't Roxie sitting on the floor of my living room under a photograph I would later learn T. J. Eldridge had taken of the line shack with a child's box camera thirty years ago. It was BB.

"Been worried," he said. "Nobody tell me what's goin' on, so I had Matt bring me out here. Figured I'd just wait. Oh, your brother called. I accepted the call, talked to the dude for a while, tol' him what I knew 'bout all this. He say you *always* up to you ass in some mess. I say, 'Dude, who talkin'?'"

I had to laugh at that, which felt good. Laughing broke the skin of whatever state I'd been in since not pulling a trigger and killing a man. I realized I wasn't sure I was really still alive until BB made me laugh. I think I suspected T. J. Eldridge had in reality jerked up, roaring, grabbed my gun from my hand and shot me through the head. That I was really lying on the floor of the shack with my brains on the wall, and this was just the last little fantasy those shattered neural cells could patch together before an absence of oxygen cloaked them in perfect, permanent darkness.

"Oh, BB," I said, slumping to the floor next to him. "Am I really here?"

"Look like it," he said, draping an arm over my shoulders while I sobbed with relief.

Above our heads a photograph of an old adobe building was blasted with light and lost in shadow at the same time.

The following week's edition of *Time* had Reed McCallister on the cover and an open letter from the vice presidential candidate thanking the police, the sheriff's department, the FBI, and everyone in Southern California for the speedy closure of this tragic and lethal case. Kate Van Der Elst got a boost from the mention of her name all over the country as a targeted victim of the "Tummy-Tuck Killer," as the media named Eldridge, and handily won her seat on the city council, from which she announced her intention to "make San Diego safe for women and children," whatever that means. She and Pieter reconciled before the election, but they're still circling each other like boxers in a ring as they negotiate for a forgiveness both want and neither is quite ready to give.

At Kate's victory celebration Pieter brought me a glass of generic champagne and said, "She wants to run for state assembly next. If you hadn't pointed out to me that my behavior was cowardly, I would have left her and wouldn't be facing an eternity of cheap white wine and soggy crackers. Thanks, Blue." He was laughing, but not entirely.

Isadora Grecchi lost almost no mobility in her left hand and continued to be nearly as unpleasant after her ordeal as she had been before. She was, however, planning to take an intensive art course in Italy during the spring semester and was furiously learning Italian within twenty-four hours of leaving the hospital. She would fly to Florence the day after Christmas, and Jennings Rainer planned to visit her with his grandchildren over their spring school break. She and I skirted each other warily on the one occasion we were all together for a catered celebration at Rainer's condo. We didn't want to talk to each other, and we both knew why.

Chris and Megan planned to relocate to Northern California on the same day Isadora left for Italy, having discovered that moving two children and a houseful of books and furniture cannot be accomplished in two weeks. Megan gave up paint ball and in fact won't even talk about it. She will talk about her new plan to raise alpacas for their wool. I have been promised enough homespun alpaca wool for a sweater, if I can find anybody to knit it. Courtesy precluded my pointing out that it's never cold enough for a wool sweater here, and besides, I might be able to use one in Philadelphia.

Jennings Rainer would keep his condo in San Diego but had contracted for the construction of a cottage on Chris and Megan's two-hundred-acre property up north.

"It's my grampy flat," he told everybody proudly. "Snuffy and I will fly back and forth, as I'll still do the occasional surgery here."

Jeffrey Pond turned up at a Holiday Inn in Fresno the same

night Eldridge died. The authorities easily found him because he'd charged his motel room to his credit card and then made several phone calls to his mother both at her home and at the hospital where his father seemed to be recovering nicely. He said he'd looked at his father on the hospital bed and seen himself in the future, except at least his father had a wife to care for him and medical insurance. He said he'd just cracked under the awareness that his life was a mess and had run, but that once on the road he realized he had no idea where to run *to* and was planning to come home the next day, anyway.

Roxie and I didn't have a chance to talk until the night after Eldridge's death. We met in town, at Auntie Buck's, where we sat at a table and stared at each other as Garth Brooks sang from the jukebox that missing the pain involves missing the dance, too.

"Why didn't you call me?" she asked, tears welling up in her brown eyes. "Why didn't you come to my place to stay instead of running up there alone?"

"I did call you," I said, tears welling up in my goldish hazel ones. "You told me to leave you alone."

"But I didn't know what you'd found out from McCallister. I didn't know what you were going to do. If I'd known, I wouldn't have said that. I would have told you to come on over, or I would have gone with you, or something."

"How could I tell you something you'd just made it clear you didn't want to hear?" I insisted. "You can't have it both ways, Rox. You're either there for me or you aren't. Yes or no, always, not just when it's convenient."

"Girl, there's nothing *convenient* about you," she replied, rattling the beads in her hair angrily. Wooden beads now, carved in African designs. "You can't live in town like other people live, no, you've got to be out there with your rocks and your damn Pergo floor. And you don't *think* like other people think, and—"

"And I don't want to," I finished the litany. "Not even for you, Roxie."

Her hand clamped over my wrist then, hard.

"I want to dance with you," she whispered, and I said okay, and we did. Roxie leading, the whole dance floor to ourselves, Garth telling the truth from a jukebox. Not a step missed, not a turn two degrees short, no failure to anticipate each move exactly, and the next, and the next. Sometimes words only snarl like thread. We went home to her place after that, saying nothing. She walked Brontë and came back, and we didn't talk, the dance still in us, all night.

In the morning she only said, "There's got to be some way to make this work, Blue," and left for her job.

I watched her drive away and said, "There is."

She's in Philadelphia now for her interview. When she comes back, if she's decided to take the job, I'll tell her I'm going, too. I'm not going with her, I'm just going. Then we'll see what happens. I've already picked the hex sign I'm going to paint on my shed.

Kara Eldridge was located at Disneyland with both children the day after her husband's death. They were staying at a nearby motel and there was no mention of either a cousin or a job when Rathbone filled me in, and I didn't mention them to him, either. Kara declined to make arrangements for her husband's funeral, so those arrangements were made by the County of San Diego and he was buried quietly in a pauper's field with only a handful of strangers, Wes and Annie Rathbone, and me, in attendance. Wes had brought me the blue willow plate from the shack, one of the early English ones, a real collector's item, and I laid it atop Thomas Eldridge's coffin before the winch creaked and he was lowered into the ground.

"That's from your mother, Tommy," I said, and then we left before they began to backhoe the dirt in.

Annie Rathbone had decided on the new floor over breast surgery and was planning a big party for as soon as Wes finished the job.

T. J. Eldridge's body was autopsied the night of his death, and a significant amount of MAOI was found in his stomach along with partially digested tomato soup, baloney, and several ounces of aged cheddar cheese on which the digestive processes had failed. The kind labeled "extra-extra sharp."

Representatives of both the FBI and the San Diego County Medical Examiner's office determined that the death was a suicide despite the absence of a suicide note, and complex analyses of T. J. Eldridge's motives up to the moment of his death were generated, published, and discussed on talk shows all over the country. The official cause of death determinations and the analyses which followed were largely dependent on my comments during interrogation late in the night after Eldridge's death.

"Yes, his behavior suggested that he knew he would die and intended to kill himself when he ate the cheese," I confirmed their theory over and over.

"Yes, it does seem that he returned to the line shack, the scene of the only happiness he'd known as a child, to commit suicide amid bizarre magazine pictures of owls and dragons and mountains of rotting corpses that represented his twisted, murderous psychology."

Certainly these pictures could be regarded as "trophies" consistent with the FBI's profiling of serial killers, although, of course, I was a social rather than a clinical psychologist and so these things were beyond my expertise. But I did have an interesting photograph taken by Eldridge as a child. A fluke, really, I'd picked it up at the very same gallery where Dixie Ross was going when she died. But it did suggest, didn't it, that Thomas Eldridge had handpicked all his victims, including himself?

The signature, I said, "Greave." See how the letters are the initials of all the intended victims? Grossinger, Ross, Emerald, Ashe, Van Der Elst, and at the end, Eldridge. The media had a field day with that, especially after the FBI discovered that Eldridge had consigned his collection of photographs to the exhibit organizers a month before the first death, when all the target surgeries were scheduled but had not yet been performed. It seemed clear that Eldridge had both selected his victims and planned to kill himself when he signed his photos with an anagram of initials of the intended dead.

Actually, it was BB who noticed the coincidence as we sat

on the floor that night beneath the picture with its spidery signature. And of course there are no coincidences, only jokes told
by a universe of which we are only dimly aware. I didn't tell
the authorities that Thomas Eldridge couldn't possibly have
known the names of his victims and woven their initials into
that signature. I didn't mention that I thought the signature was
merely a message. A message to a world over which he finally
lost control when his wife got a community college degree in
computer programming. A world in ruin because women are
destroying the natural order by failing to obey men. "Grieve!"
he was probably urging poetically. But T. J. Eldridge was a lousy
speller.

I also didn't mention that Kara Eldridge had prepared the
tomato soup and baloney sandwich that contained the lethal
quantity of MAOI found in Eldridge's stomach and bloodstream,
as well as the aged cheese which naturally contained more than
enough tyramine to, when it hit his stomach and could not be
oxidized, elevate his blood pressure until an artery burst in his
brain. I didn't mention that Isadora Grecchi had helped Kara Eldridge get the education that would end her dependency on
her husband. Nor the fact that Grecchi, a physician with a long
history of clinical depression, had earlier in her possession two
different types of MAOI medications, one of which she had
given to Kara Eldridge for the purpose of killing T. J. Eldridge
in the same way he had killed his victims. I failed to mention,
finally, that Kara had been in contact with Isadora just before
Eldridge ate his tomato soup and baloney sandwich. Kara had
agreed to call one last time before leaving town in a rented van
with her children.

"It's done," I imagined Kara would have said to Isadora in
that phone call. "He's dead."

There didn't seem to be any point in mentioning any of it to
anybody.

Acknowledgments

The Last Blue Plate Special is a work of fiction and any similarity between its characters, settings, and events and anything occurring in real life is purely coincidental.

Several real people did graciously offer advice and expertise, however. I would like to thank them. Any mistakes herein are mine, not theirs.

First, huge thanks to psychology professor Horace Marchant, Ph.D., for the weird idea, tons of arcane references, and his heroic willingness to vet an entire book in e-mails.

Thanks also to Dr. John Alexander for technical advice on cosmetic surgery; to Steve Davis, M.D., and Alan Abrams, M.D., J.D., F.C.L.M., for technical advice on both general and forensic psychiatry; and to Gaylynn Speas, M.D., for technical advice on anesthesiology.

The expertise of Gene Riehl, FBI-retired, law professor Marilyn Ireland, and editor Sara Ann Freed is deeply appreciated as well.

Abigail Padgett
San Diego